Search

A Memoir

with Recipes

by

Dana Louise Potowski

A Novel

Michelle Huneven

Penguin Press · *New York* · 2022

PENGUIN PRESS
An imprint of Penguin Random House LLC
penguinrandomhouse.com

LIBRARY OF CONGRESS CATALOGING-IN-PUBLICATION DATA
Names: Huneven, Michelle, 1953– author.
Title: Search : a novel / Michelle Huneven.
Description: First edition. | New York : Penguin Press, 2022.
Identifiers: LCCN 2021021041 (print) | LCCN 2021021042 (ebook) |
ISBN 9780593300053 (hardcover) | ISBN 9780593300060 (ebook)
Subjects: LCGFT: Autobiographical fiction.
Classification: LCC PS3558.U4662 S43 2022 (print) | LCC PS3558.U4662
(ebook) | DDC 813/.54—dc23
LC record available at https://lccn.loc.gov/2021021041
LC ebook record available at https://lccn.loc.gov/2021021042

Printed in the United States of America
1   3   5   7   9   10   8   6   4   2

Designed by Cassandra Garruzzo

For Jim Potter

Preface to the Second Edition

I never thought I'd be writing this preface. Who knew that a comic memoir (with recipes!) about a church search committee could ever go into a second printing? Nor did I expect the talk-show attention, the op-eds, and the late-night parodies. Or the sales! But this, my fourth book, seems to have struck a chord not only with many churches and academics but also with the religiously unaffiliated, who found in the seemingly tame subject of a church's search for a new minister a surprisingly dramatic, cutthroat adventure.

To answer a few of the many questions readers have asked: Yes, this is a memoir of a real experience. It is not fiction. I was on a search committee for a senior minister and this is my story of that search. Others might tell it differently. That said, names and certain details have been altered to protect identities. Several of the living have recognized themselves, although sometimes in the wrong character.

Libel law offers clear guidelines for making a person unidentifiable in print—change three characteristics, for example—and I followed them. The talk of lawsuits has subsided.

Some readers—and many who haven't read the book—argue that I have talked too much out of school, and by exposing the behind-the-scenes machinations of a church and its search committee, I have disclosed too many secrets, certainly more than the average credulous churchgoer cares to know. I believe that the more the average credulous churchgoer knows, the more responsible their decisions will be when choosing a leader. The health and future of their institution depend on it.

A church is a human structure. We build it and inhabit it, and immediately stories and secrets abound within. It is my hope that the stories and secrets related in these pages continue to entertain and, with luck, enlighten.

Dana Potowski, June 20, ——

1

⌁

A Visit

I hadn't been to church for close to three months when Charlotte Beck called at eight o'clock on a Monday night and asked if she and Belinda Bauer could stop by.

"Of course," I said cautiously. These were two of the most prominent members of the congregation. "What's up?"

"There's something we want to ask you," Charlotte said. "Something we'd like you to do. We'll be there in a few."

Charlotte had just been the church president and was now the ex officio; and Belinda, at eighty-three, was a former president and a member for more than fifty years.

What could such a delegation want with me? Except to drag me back to the pews. Not that we had pews. We had comfortable upholstered teak chairs.

I thumped the pillows on the kitchen sofa and put the kettle on for tea. The pledge dinner, which kicked off the annual fundraising drive, had come and gone, so they wouldn't want me to organize that. The Cooking for Cash dinners—where people paid to eat at one another's homes, all proceeds to the church—were over. Might this be about the Juneteenth barbecue? Really, I had no idea.

My husband, Jack, was reading lawyerly documents on his desktop computer while a rock video played on his laptop. "Two big-deal women from church are stopping by," I said. "Like, half the executive committee."

"At this hour? What do they want?"

"Maybe to scold me for missing so much church?"

"More likely to recruit you," he said. "For the board. Or church president, I bet."

"I doubt that's it," I said. Our presidents tended to be administrative types like Belinda, a long-retired high school principal, or corporate types like Charlotte, a recently retired contracts lawyer. I'd been on the church board twice, but I wasn't presidential material. Twenty-two years ago, thinking I might be a minister, I had attended two years of seminary, but my church activities since then were always more metaphysical—and culinary—than managerial. While Charlotte led pledge drives and capital campaigns, I'd taught Writing as a Spiritual Activity and holiday cooking classes and led some of the small monthly discussion groups we call Soul Circles.

I didn't want to be church president or serve another term on the board—I wasn't sure I still wanted to go to church. Almost everything in the Sunday worship had begun to annoy me. Announcements. The drippy stories read to the kids. Responsive readings. Most hymns. I'd come to hate both the handbell choir and this thing the minister did after the benediction, when he had us turn to each other and repeat a phrase from his sermon, like *Open wide your big Universalist heart* or *We shall overcome* or (this on Easter) *Happity hoppity Easter.*

My church was the Arroyo Unitarian Universalist Community Church, which everyone called "the AUUCC" (pronounced *awk*). I'd been a member for twenty-four years.

Once you skip a couple of Sundays, I'd found, it's easy to keep skipping.

I stuck the cozy on the teapot and Bunchie, our terrier, started leaping and barking. I led Charlotte and Belinda into our newly built kitchen.

"Look at your beautiful high ceiling," said Charlotte. "Those beams!"

"Good counter," said Belinda, touching the dark, white-veined soapstone.

I poured out cups of ginger tea. We settled in at the kitchen table.

"Thanks for letting us barge in on you," said Charlotte. Even retired, in her pale pink twinset and preternaturally smooth pageboy, she was the brisk, capable attorney.

"It's so good to see you two," I said. Seeing them did stir a deep current: Charlotte and I had been in the same new-member orientation class twenty-four years ago, and we often sat together at church, as her wife, Sheila, attended rarely, and my Jewish husband never. I'd come to know Belinda through my cooking classes.

"We miss seeing you at church," said Belinda.

When I first came to the AUUCC, Belinda had already retired and was filling in as the church secretary, a supposedly temporary arrangement that ended up lasting twelve years. She was small, five foot one, and had enormous eyes. An old-timer told me that she'd once been the most beautiful woman at the church, but in the AUUCC's office she'd been brusque and impatient, and treated us all like wayward tenth graders. You had to go through her for the key to the copying machine or an appointment with the minister; she was the dragon guarding the pearl and she terrified me until we found common ground at the stove. She was a serious, adventurous cook.

"I figured you must be on a book tour," Charlotte said.

My most recent memoir, *Yard to Table: A Suburban Farmer Cooks*, had just come out, and on one of the Sundays I'd missed, I was up north promoting it.

"This one's my new favorite," said Charlotte.

"I still like your second book best, maybe because I knew your mom," said Belinda. That book, *Our Best Year*, was about my senior year in high school when I took over cooking dinner from my working mother, thus inadvertently and radically improving our relationship, if only for a year. "But I'm only halfway through the new one," she added. "I do enjoy how you write about gardening."

One great thing about church friends: they buy and read your books.

"Thanks, you guys," I said. "It means a lot that you're such loyal readers."

"Our pleasure," said Charlotte. "And now, Dana, we could really use your help. It concerns Tom."

"Tom? Tom Fox?" The senior minister. "What about him?"

"The executive committee thinks his heart's not in it anymore," Charlotte said.

"He's tired," said Belinda.

Tom Fox was sixty-four. When he came to the AUUCC eight years ago, everyone knew he wouldn't stay that long, certainly not as long as his predecessor, the Reverend Dr. Sparlo Plessant, who served for twenty-eight years.

Charlotte had never liked Tom Fox's sermons. I knew this because she and I avidly took them apart every Sunday after worship. She still missed Sparlo Plessant's intellectually rigorous, witty sermons, which were undeniably spellbinding. Having tackled sermon writing in seminary, I thought Tom Fox's efforts excellent in their own way: they were deceptively relaxed and in fact were quite a nimble blend of ideas, anecdotes, and poetry. Charlotte didn't appreciate how skillfully he made complex ideas so accessible. "You've never liked Tom's preaching, Charlotte," I said.

"And it's gone from bad to worse," she said.

Tom duly emailed me his sermons every time I ditched church. Just that morning I'd received his most recent offering, along with a message that said *Missed you today. Lunch this week?* I hadn't answered yet because, if I went to lunch, I was afraid he'd ask about my ongoing truancy and I didn't know what to say.

"I like Tom's sermons a lot more than you do," I said. "What I can't stand is that thing he does at the end, where we have to say those dumb things to each other."

"I don't mind that," said Charlotte. "In fact, I like it. But Sheila hates it so much, she won't come to church anymore. I told Tom he was alienating people, but he insists that repeating silly things sets a warmer, friendlier tone."

"Not for introverts like me," I said.

"More worrisome," said Belinda, "is what I'm hearing from the staff. Tom's not getting the order of service in on time, he's missed appointments, and he's only ever in the office on Wednesdays for staff meetings." She set down her teacup. "We need to find out if and when he plans to retire."

"Why not ask him?" I said. "Though I suppose it's a delicate question."

"It *is* delicate." Belinda turned her enormous brown eyes to me. "Which is why we thought you should ask him."

"Me?" I said. "Why me?"

"Because you're good friends with him," said Charlotte.

"I suppose," I said.

"Don't you two go out to lunch all the time?"

Was once a month all the time? And I thought of our lunches in more practical terms: I was a restaurant critic and Tom Fox was game to go with me on review meals—and it's not so easy to find people free midday in the middle of the workweek to drive to Venice or Covina for lunch. That's not to say I didn't enjoy Tom's company and conversation. I did, often enough, and eight years of monthly lunches had made us close. "I'll probably have lunch with him this week," I said.

"Perfect," said Charlotte. "So you'll ask?"

"If I can. But what good will it do to know if he is retiring?"

"It's information," said Belinda. "If he's planning on five more years—"

"God help us," said Charlotte.

"—then he needs a fire lit under him. If he's leaving soon, well, then we have to start planning for an interim and budgeting for a search."

"Something has to change," said Charlotte. "There's been a real drop in attendance. You yourself have been pretty scarce . . ."

Here I thought I was having a midlife spiritual drift; come to find out, I was part of a general trend. "Worship has seemed tedious. I thought it was just me."

"It's not just you," said Belinda.

I saw them out. "And I thought you were going to ask me to be church president."

"You'd be president?" Charlotte turned to Belinda with a bright look. "Perfect! We'll put you in the chute! Oh, Dana! You've just solved our other conundrum!"

"No, no," I said. "I was joking. Please! Don't put me in the chute!"

The church presidency was a six-year commitment: you spent two years as vice president, two years as president, and two years as president ex officio.

As they trundled down the porch steps, I called after them, "Seriously, don't put me in the chute!"

But I was thrilled to be asked.

2

We Lunch

The AUUCC's 290-plus members are a raffish mix of the highly educated left: Caltech and NASA scientists, schoolteachers, entertainment types and hospital workers, college professors, political activists, artists, and local soreheads. We're not as integrated as we'd like to be—especially considering that our west Altadena neighborhood is about forty percent nonwhite—but we're working on it. The church is famous for its preaching, its social activism, and its enchanting if derelict three-acre gardens.

Tom Fox was the AUUCC's fifth minister and the first not to hail from New England. A lean, broad-shouldered Texan, he stood six foot four, with pelt-like white curls. The two of us had been going out to lunch since he first came to the AUUCC. Sparlo Plessant, his predecessor, had told him that I was a restaurant critic and knew all the good places to eat; also that I'd been to seminary. So a month into his first year, Tom invited me to lunch and, over Shanghai-style hand-torn noodles in San Gabriel, he asked me to be on his ministerial relations committee.

But before I decided, he said, I should know that he didn't believe in ministerial relations committees: they encouraged malcontents to bellyache to committee members rather than approach the minister directly. But since the AUUCC's bylaws mandated that he should have such a committee, his would meet for a friendly lunch. My joining would be a favor to him, he said, and a way for us to get to know each other.

Flattered that the new minister wanted to get to know me, I perhaps didn't quite absorb the distinction between friendly lunch and functioning committee.

The committee consisted of me, Norma Fernandes, a quiet hospital administrator who kept our lunches to a strict one hour (thank god!), and Sam Rourke-Jolley, a retired finance guy who played golf with Tom. At our inaugural meeting, Tom reiterated that he would not countenance any complaints relayed from the congregation.

Sam Rourke-Jolley either ignored or forgot Tom's edict because every month he reported a complaint: some people didn't like it that Tom didn't wear a robe; that the choir, too, was now robeless; and worse, that clapping went unchecked during worship.

"Those aren't real issues," Tom said, "but attempts to split the congregation. And I will not respond to any grumblers too cowardly to face me."

I once asked Tom why he'd put Sam on the committee.

"We have a good time on the golf course," he said. "And I needed a Rourke."

The Rourkes were founding members of the AUUCC and, three generations on, still our greatest benefactors. Sam had married into the clan; his mother-in-law, the ancient Faithalma Rourke, was known to make the largest pledge every year—by a lot—and Sam's wife, Emma Rourke-Jolley, twenty years his junior and head of an HMO, was the only person ever to serve two terms as the AUUCC's president. "Emma," Tom added, "is too much of a powerhouse for such a low-impact committee."

I—so not a powerhouse—spent two years on that do-nothing committee. We met at a ladies' lunch spot in Pasadena where Tom Fox, in his lovely Texas accent, described movies he'd seen and articles he'd read; he told stories we'd heard in sermons or would hear shortly. I like to think we helped perfect his delivery. We paid for our own lunches, too, a cost I deducted from my taxes.

Shortly after I rotated off the ministerial relations committee, Tom Fox convinced the board to amend the bylaws and eliminate it. He and I kept going to lunch, though, which, as I've said, was useful to me. One-on-one Tom could be an excellent conversationalist; he was well read, thoughtful, and capable of the depth I usually reached with close female friends. I was hungry, too, for the conversation I'd loved in seminary, intense discussions of spiritual issues, theological trends, and ministry itself; subjects that my husband and my a-religious friends were not inclined to explore: faith, surrender, Baptist polity, the flames all mystics see—that sort of thing. Some days, though, I couldn't get a word in edgewise with Tom. The man could talk."

I was still hesitant to go to lunch with Tom because I knew he'd ask why I'd been ditching church. And what would I say? That his liturgy annoyed me?

Somehow, having a mission—to find out if and when he planned to retire—emboldened me. Plus, a favorite Vietnamese place had opened a second location that I needed to review. *Yes to lunch*, I wrote to Tom. *Thursday?*

At the new Golden Deli 2, we scored a booth—yes!—and ordered bun and the house specialty, cha gio, fried eggrolls.

The bright new storefront restaurant had the same menu as the original, but not the scuffed, broken-in charm or—thankfully—the knot of people waiting to get in.

The eggrolls arrived first. Blistered and dangerously hot from the deep fryer, filled with wood ear mushrooms, glass noodles, and ground pork, they came with a heap of lettuce leaves, bean sprouts, sliced cucumber, and herbs. To eat one, you flatten a lettuce leaf; set an eggroll on it; scatter mint, basil, cilantro, and shiso leaves over it; add sprouts, cucumber, and pickled carrot; then roll it up. A messy business! We each wrapped a roll as snugly as we could—not very—and dunked them in a clear, cold, salty-sweet sauce. The first bite is a jolt of simultaneity: hot and cold, meat and herbs, sweet and salty, deep-fried crunch and fresh lettuce crunch. . . .

We devoured our first rolls in reverential silence.

Tom Fox wrapped his second roll and shook its frilled green end at me. "Congrats on the new book," he said. "The reviews I've read have been great."

"Thanks. Except now my agent's all anxious to sell the next one, strike while the iron's hot. But I have nothing for her. Not a single idea. I'm not sure I have another book in me. In fact, I'm pretty sure I don't."

"You said that after the last book." Tom took a big bite, chewed until he could talk again. "Maybe you should come back to church. Lots of ideas there."

"I know," I said. "Sorry I've been scarce."

"Anything the matter? Anything you want to talk about?"

"I'm just taking a little breather," I said.

"What I'd like to know"—Tom set down his eggroll and drew himself up—"is why every time I make a friend in the congregation, they stop coming to church?"

The anguish in his voice surprised me. "That is weird," I said. Apparently, I was caught in yet another pattern larger than myself. "It's just that Sunday mornings at home, especially in our new kitchen, are so . . ."

"I like Sunday mornings at home, too." Tom dipped a napkin in his ice water and began wiping his fingers. "Reading the *Times*. Eating waffles. Not fussing with a sermon. I like Sunday mornings so much, I've made a decision, and I'll tell you what it is, but you have to promise not to tell anyone before I go public."

I like secrets, they're rare glimpses into a person's interior, and I'm good at keeping them. I promised.

"My alma mater in San Antonio has offered me an endowed chair in religion and philosophy—one graduate seminar a year, no committee work. I'd be on tap for the occasional sermon, convocation, or prayer breakfast. I'd start a year from June. I'd go today, but Pat"—his wife, who worked for the county—"has a year left on her contract."

"You'll leave ministry?"

"I would've retired two years ago except I needed more in my 401(k). I'll announce to the congregation in two weeks and stay through the next church year. I'll recommend that the search for a new minister be held concurrently. The AUUCC's in good enough shape, there's no need for an interim minister. I'm sure the board will agree since the last interim was so unpopular . . ."

"Wow," I said, recalling the grief when Sparlo left. "This is heavy."

"The church will be fine," said Tom. "The church is fine."

"Sparlo always said, 'Ministers come and go but the church endures.'"

"I loved Sparlo, as you know," said Tom. "But following him has not been the easiest thing I've ever done. No matter what, I will forever fall short to his champions."

Guilty as charged. Tom was a fine, masterful preacher, but Sparlo had been brilliant, exceptional by anyone's standards. He never preached from a manuscript; his sermons showcased a beautiful, disciplined mind at work. He read up on a topic all week, packed in the ideas, and then—as they tell you to do in seminary—he "preached from the overflow," tossing out stories, facts, and poems until it seemed impossible for him to connect them all—and it was thrilling when he did. I have to admit that in the way people have the one dog of their life, Sparlo was *the* minister of my life. "But you have a lot of your own champions," I said to Tom. Which was true.

Had I first come to the AUUCC when Tom was the senior minister, I might have cathected with him as profoundly as I had with Sparlo—and there were many people at the AUUCC who had; they adored Tom and came to church to hear him, and might never attach as ardently to any other minister. Like baby ducks, we were imprinted by the one we knew first.

"I was thinking," Tom said, "that you should be on the search committee."

"Me?" I said, honored. "That's looking ahead. I don't know. Maybe."

"You'd have to apply like everyone else. I'll only be unofficially consulted. But you're respected and beloved, so you'll probably get on. And I'll feel better about leaving if people like you do the search."

My interest was definitely piqued. "I'll have to think about it."

"Think hard, though. If you're feeling disconnected from the church—if that's why you haven't been coming—a search committee is no way to reconnect. They're an enormous amount of work and often so contentious, they can strain even the strongest bonds. Search committees have the same attrition rate as church presidents. Did you know that half of all church presidents leave a church after their terms are up?"

I did not. "Burned out?"

"And disillusioned. Not everyone survives prolonged exposure to all the behind-the-scenes and inner workings of an institution."

I sipped my cold, strong, headache-sweet iced coffee. I hadn't enjoyed church lately, but was I actually *disconnecting*? If I was, why was the idea of picking the next minister so compelling?

"If you do intend to put your name forward," Tom said, "you should keep a high profile till the committee is chosen."

"You mean come back to church on a regular basis!"

"Wouldn't hurt."

I laughed. "You're so obvious."

"I'm serious. You should be on the search committee. And come back to church."

I thought of saying, "I will if you stop doing that silly, repeat-after-me bit after the benediction." Instead, I laughed again and said I'd think it over.

3

My Brief Brush with Ministry

This seems like a good a time to tell how I almost became a minister.

Twenty-two years ago, in my early thirties, I had been trying to get started as a food journalist. I had a twice-monthly gig at a little local weekly, the *Madre Mountain News*, reviewing local restaurants for eighty-five dollars a column. Really, I was just showcasing the restaurants, not critiquing them; negative criticism, the editor said, could discourage potential advertisers. I also taught English part-time at a private high school. Two years of this, and I'd become desperate to do something other than gush about chain pizza joints and teach Elizabeth Bishop's "In the Waiting Room" to another crop of resistant teens. Sparlo Plessant was still going strong then, and one Sunday it struck me that I'd like to do what he did, which was to study a spiritual topic all week and then report back on what he'd found in that particularly lovely, versatile literary form, the sermon.

Sparlo was erudite, humorous, widely read, and metaphysically profound. I aspired to those qualities. I'd never have a mind like Sparlo's, or even close, but a small church somewhere might find me adequate and afford me an interesting, meaningful life's work. For more than a year, I told nobody that I was thinking of becoming a minister lest the idea fade away as had other once-consuming notions—like getting the tattoo of a whippet on my ankle or having a crush on a man I'd never spoken to. Did persistent ministerial ideation constitute a call to the ministry? For more literal religious people, a call was God tapping your shoulder, or saying your name in the wind, or ordering you around in dreams the way Yahweh harassed the prophets. In our progressive, rational, scientifically minded denomination, a call isn't—or shouldn't be—so supernatural. A friend might say, "Have you ever considered being a minister?" and strike a deep chord. Or a call could be the sense of a deep desire stirring, or perhaps, as in my case, an idea that won't go away. I kept my new ambition secret even from close friends. All the while, I studied Sparlo and how the church worked.

Sparlo Plessant was a fourth-generation Unitarian minister; he was the first family hyphenate (Unitarian-Universalist) because it was very early in his career, 1967, that the two denominations merged. I could go into some detail about the theological and class differences between the two groups but suffice it to say that Ralph Waldo Emerson was a Unitarian and P. T. Barnum a Universalist.

During the months that I privately pondered the ministry, I attended many church events—the Labor Day picnic, the rummage sale, the book sale, the Christmas service, the egg hunt, the Memorial Day picnic, the mid-week service, and the pledge drive dinner. I made zucchini bread for bake sales; I participated in the "secret friend" Christmas and Valentine programs for the kids; I took religious education training and taught four unruly sessions of Sunday school at the junior-high level. When one of the coffee servers had a stroke, I volunteered to serve coffee on the patio after church. I raised my profile to such a degree, I was asked to join the church board.

There were twenty-four people on the board then: lawyers and schoolteachers, two Caltech professors, one accountant, a medical doctor, a stay-at-home mom, various retired people, a TV actor, and me. Being on that board was like being a part of a well-functioning brain. I admired the way decisions were made, with people first objecting to a new idea—a new sofa for the rec room, say, or raises for the ministers, or repainting the parking lot—and then systematically dispatching their own objections. Yes! The lines in the parking lot would be repainted. Yes! The ministers would get raises. Usually the most generous decision was reached. The AUUCC had a culture of yes.

When eighteen months had passed and I hadn't stopped considering the ministry, I called the church and left a message on Sparlo's extension. I was thinking of applying to seminary, I said, and would like to discuss it with him.

The church secretary—the then-terrifying Belinda Bauer—called and set up an appointment in two days' time. I worried about what to wear. Although my girlfriends said that I was "fashion forward," my mother, who was of Sparlo's generation, had called me a little brown bird. My smarmy editor at the *Madre Mountain News* (also in Mom's and Sparlo's age group) said that I dressed like a communist, which of course referred not only to my preference for solid colors, basic shapes, and natural fabrics, but also to so few overt signifiers of sexual availability.

I hadn't a clue what female ministers wore. At that point, twenty-plus years ago, I'd seen only two or three, all guest ministers who'd preached in robes. For this very preliminary interview concerning my possible ministerial future, I didn't want to make too bold a fashion statement, but I also didn't want to come off as a little brown bird or a communist. I decided to wear a hand-me-down from a wealthy friend, a pretty off-white rayon dress made in France that had small navy-blue polka dots, mother-of-pearl buttons, and a soft, full skirt. I wore it with a black cardigan and, to balance the strong feminine elements, my black lug-soled Mary Janes. I pulled my fine, fly-away dark brown hair into a black scrunchie and put on small gold hoop earrings. I looked like a capable thirty-three-year-old French housewife—not a bad look, I thought, for a thirty-three-year-old disappointed writer aspiring to a second career as a minister.

I had never been alone with Sparlo before. I'd seen him up close in board meetings, and I'd shaken his hand after Sunday worship and said how much I liked the sermon, and that was as close as I'd come to a one-on-one. His office was upstairs in Arroyo House, the Italianate mansion on church property. Downstairs, in the main office, I clutched my elbows and waited for Belinda to finish a call. She was in her sixties then, her skin still luminous and smooth, her brown eyes keen, her self-possession intimidating. She ended her call, glanced at me, and punched a button. "Your three-thirty's here," she said. "Dana. Yes. Dana Po-tow-ski."

"You can go up," she said to me.

As I ascended the mansion's ridiculous marble staircase, I was acutely aware that I was doing this entirely by myself, for myself. Nobody had suggested ministry to me; not even my close friends knew I was meeting with my minister to discuss a career change. My breath was shallow, my heart thumped. I clutched a manila folder containing half a dozen clips (reviews and food articles), my CV, and the short essay I'd written in the new member orientation class about how I'd come to the AUUCC.

I tapped on the open door and was called inside. Sparlo stood behind an enormous wooden desk. Slim and just under six feet tall, he had a narrow, handsome face and well-barbered, thinning brown hair. "Ah, Dana, yes, of course," he said, clearly recognizing me from the board and coming around the desk to shake my hand. He motioned to the two sofas facing each other. He sat on one and as I sat opposite him, my skirt ballooned with a big air bubble that, embarrassed, I subdued by patting it frantically with my manila folder.

A glass-topped coffee table stacked with books and newsmagazines stretched between us. "And what has brought you here today?" he said.

"I've been thinking of going to seminary," I said. "To become a minister."

"Ah, yes," he said. "So tell me: What brought this on?"

"Well," I said, "right now I make a living as a freelance writer and part-time English teacher. I never wanted to teach school. I want to write, but my journalism career hasn't gone anywhere. I can't seem to get beyond writing puff restaurant reviews for what's basically an advertising circular, and I'm desperate to do something more meaningful, and interesting, and challenging with my life."

"Ministry is certainly all that," he said. "But why ministry in particular?"

Hearing him preach, I said, had given me the idea. I was drawn to how he immersed himself deeply in a spiritual concept, then reported back to us what he'd learned. Also, I had developed an intense interest in the church—how it functioned and what it gave to its members.

"And what does a church give to its members?"

I hadn't prepared an answer to this. "I can really only speak for myself,"

I said. "Church is the one place I know that privileges the soul, that focuses on spiritual values and bases a community on them." I heard a whinge in my voice that comes when I'm trying too hard to please. I took a moment to reset. "Church gives me more capacious and compassionate ways to think about my life—and the world. And it provides opportunities to be of service to others."

"To be of service how?" said Sparlo.

I'd been thinking of my coffee commitment—"Caf or decaf, Mrs. Greene?"—but that seemed too paltry for this conversation. "Serving on the board," I said. Then, afraid that being on the board was more an honor than a generosity on my part, I added, "And, you know, social action."

"Ah, social action? You're a follower of Rauschenbusch and his Social Gospel movement?"

I had no idea what he was talking about. "Um."

Sparlo clasped one knee and pulled on it. "A vocal minority here dearly wants us to take on more social activism," he said. "Are you one of them?"

"Not really," I said, sensing that this was the right response.

"Nor am I," said Sparlo. "Our members all have their own liberal causes. I'm very involved with the ACLU, and Belinda downstairs is the regional president of the League of Women Voters. And it's not as if we don't have an awful lot of good programs already—after-school tutoring, the Healthy Youth program, the partnership with a women's shelter, our sandwich-making for the homeless. The Quilters for Justice. But one faction still lobbies to let the homeless pitch tents on our lawn and another faction wants to sell off the gardens and give the money to Central American refugees." He released his knee and leaned forward. "This is the kind of thing you'll face as a minister. Factions! I enjoy steering a ship through competing demands. If this sort of thing appeals, then ministry will be a good fit for you."

This alarming aspect of ministry hadn't occurred to me, but I nodded vigorously. "Yes, yes, it does," I said, unsure that I could steer any ship anywhere.

"Good," said Sparlo. "Now tell me a little about yourself."

I told him how I'd grown up in Altadena, gone to public schools. At

UCLA I'd majored in journalism and philosophy. During and after grad school—UC Berkeley, School of Journalism—I'd worked in restaurants to support myself. I'd been a waitress, a general manager of a small restaurant, and then I'd managed quite a large catering operation. I had enough management experience, I said, to know it was impossible to make everyone happy all the time."

"That gives you a big head start with ministry right there," he said.

After I moved back to Altadena, I went on, I went from working in restaurants to writing about them. I'd been a small-potatoes restaurant critic for three years now, and to make ends meet, I also taught English. Since I'd never wanted to teach high school or write puff journalism as my life's work, I was eager to apply my abilities, such as they were, in a more meaningful capacity.

"Ministry does involve a lot of writing," said Sparlo.

"And I love the sermon," I blurted.

I knew, I went on, that there was much more to church than preaching. The more involved I'd been over the past two years, the greater my interest in church administration, governance, and polity. I didn't know if this interest constituted a call, I said, but I'd been having ministerial ideation for well over a year.

"Ministerial ideation," he said. "That's a good one. And you know, Dana, ministry is not an improvident choice. UU ministers are among the highest-paid clergy in America. Settle in a good church and you'll make a comfortable living—between your housing allowance and salary, yes, yes, quite comfortable."

Such bald practicality startled me. I hadn't given a thought to money. I'd assumed that ministers made an adult living, which to me was any amount where you didn't have to shop at Goodwill and juggle bills at the end of every month.

"Will you have to go into debt to attend seminary?" said Sparlo.

"Not really." I'd been surprised at how affordable the degree program was. "I have some savings, but if I need to, I can take out student loans."

"And your husband or partner, are they supportive?"

"I'm single," I said.

"Okay then." The cadence of closure rang in his voice.

I stood. "Well. Thanks for talking to me."

He followed me to the door. "If you can afford it, why not go?" he said. "Seminary can't hurt you. At the least it will enrich your life. And if you don't go, you'll always wonder what might have happened if you had."

He'd turned away when I realized I still held the manila folder, "Oh, Reverend Plessant," I said. "I might need to ask you for a reference. Is that all right? I brought you a CV and some of my writing so you'd have something to go by."

"Of course. That's thinking ahead," he said, and took the folder.

Going down the stairs, I checked my watch. We'd talked for eleven minutes.

Like a silly fool, I waved at the dragon Belinda Bauer in her office—she did not return the wave—and hauled open Arroyo House's heavy oak door.

That night, I went out to eat (professionally) and came home to find a message on my answering machine. "Sparlo here. I read through your folder. And, Dana, you are a very frank and funny and fearless writer. I admire your audaciousness. You've inspired me to be more audacious myself."

Tears filled my eyes.

"I hope you do go into ministry," he went on. "We'd be lucky to have you in our ranks. Please keep me in the loop. I'll be very interested in your progress."

I spent two years at a progressive Methodist seminary thirty miles to the east. I stopped teaching, kept writing restaurant reviews, and lived meagerly on two small scholarships (one from the school, one from the UUs), and a two percent student loan.

As progressive as the Methodists were—God at their seminary was gender neutral, which meant that the grade on your paper would be lowered a full point if you referred to God as *He*—theirs was still a Christian seminary, and while some professors described themselves as post-Christian, others and most of my classmates had unabashedly Jesus-centric theologies.

We UU students stuck together. I made one close good friend in particular who shared my wry, slightly askance view of life among the believers; she and I studied together and laughed at the sappy prayers and bad sermons in the student-run chapel, and the futile attempts of the evangelicals to evangelize us. We'd read each other's papers, crammed each other for exams, and otherwise encouraged each other through two years of classes and for some time afterward until, sadly, I lost touch with her.

I'd loved the arcana of church history and the mental convolutions of theology, although to me Christianity was a melting ice floe that the very best minds had abandoned. I would look around me and think, How can so many seemingly intelligent, intellectual people still believe in the virgin birth, the miracles, or the resurrection? Some didn't. My New Testament professor, a well-known scholar and author, announced that there were only three things known for certain about the historical Jesus, i.e., things corroborated by texts contemporary to Jesus's time: he was born, he ate some meals with people, and he died, *possibly* by crucifixion. In his class, we read the New Testament as a collection of texts belonging to—and reflecting the values of—various distinct communities.

I did my first-year fieldwork at the AUUCC: every Sunday morning I taught a class called Writing as a Spiritual Activity. We met for an hour before church and wrote short personal essays based on a topic I determined. There was a core group of about ten of us, but some days we swelled to fifteen or shrank to five or six.

I met with Sparlo every month; I was a willing repository for his stories and instruction. Pragmatic and clever, he was quite Machiavellian in his approach: "It is better to be feared than loved," he'd say. "Hide your vulnerabilities . . ." "Pick your own time and place for confrontations . . ." "Be truthful but not offensive."

Since I'd moved so decisively toward ministry, it seemed a prank of fate when my journalism career took off six months after I started God school. The *Times* offered me a position in the food section. (My comic send-up of the racetrack canteen in the *Madre Mountain News* had caught the editor's attention.) I was to review restaurants and write food articles. Before I finished my first year in grad school, an editor at a good publishing house asked for a collection of my articles. *The Pecking Order,* my first book, was written in ten months, even as I wrote my weekly columns and term papers and studied for finals. I knew I'd have to choose one career eventually, and discussed it endlessly with the other UUs, my secular friends, my colleagues, and Sparlo.

In this blizzard of work, I completed four semesters in seminary. Ah, the energy and ambition of encroaching middle age! But then came the internships required to graduate. I simply didn't have the time: a chaplaincy was full time for ten weeks, a church internship was half time (but more in practice, often much more) for six months. I had to make a decision.

Sparlo said that good ministers were rare, but excellent journalists were even more so—and they reached a larger audience. I never regretted a minute or a cent spent at seminary, but I chose my first vocation.

I never lost my interest in the church or ministry. Sparlo and I continued to meet, even during the first two years of his retirement, when he was required to stay away from the AUUCC to let the search committee do its work and the new minister settle in. Sparlo and I kept meeting until his death three years ago. Thanks to him, I became friends with his successors, first the interim, then Tom Fox.

I often wondered what kind of a minister I would have been and what a life in the church would have made of me. In fact, since finishing *Yard to Table,* and having no ideas for another book, I'd been haunted by a now-familiar regret—that I'd chosen the wrong path.

4

Search Committee Ideation

After church the next Sunday (yes, I went to worship, and yes, it was annoying), Belinda, Charlotte, and I walked up to Arroyo House and climbed the marble staircase to the library, with its high floor-to-ceiling shelves and massive oak table. "Adrian will be here in a minute," Charlotte said softly, closing the door. "He'll be the one to talk to Tom, if that has to happen."

A soft-spoken therapist in his forties, Adrian Jones was the AUUCC's current vice president/president-in-waiting. He and his wife, Jill, joined the church twelve years ago and had since founded the People of Color Social Club, the POC (now BIPOC) Film Society, and the Beloved Conversation forum.

"What would Adrian say to him?" I said.

"He'd urge Tom to up his game," said Charlotte.

Smart. Tom liked and respected Adrian, who had helped him do what most UU ministers hadn't been able to, which was to diversify an older, all-white congregation.

"And here he is," said Charlotte.

"Hey, everyone. Dana P! Great to see you."

I knew Adrian from one of my Soul Circle groups where, at the first meeting he'd cheerfully declared, "I am not here to be anyone's shrink or expert on race. I've come to feed my hungry little soul, just like the rest of you puppies." Tall, with short-cropped hair and a friendly, handsome, wide-open face, he was ever-ready to be amused, and had a full-throated laugh so gratifying that I'd spent far too much of our group's time trying to elicit it. We'd had some long, post-meeting conversations in the parking lot that I thought were the start of a friendship (in particular, one intense discussion about various religious temperaments), but once the group ended, we'd only greeted each other at church.

"So, Dana, what did you find out?" said Charlotte.

"I can't say," I said.

"What can't you say?" Belinda asked.

"Whether Tom's retiring or whatever," I said. "He swore me to secrecy."

"What *can* you say?" said Belinda.

I considered this. "That you'll find out all you want to know in two weeks."

"What else?" said Belinda.

I wanted to give them something if only because we'd bothered to come up to this dim, muffled, book-lined room. "Charlotte will be pleased—" Seeing Charlotte's face brighten, I quickly added, "But her gratification will be delayed."

Charlotte said, "She giveth with one hand and taketh away with the other."

"What kind of a delay are we talking about?" said Belinda.

"I've probably said too much already," I said.

"In your opinion, should Adrian go ahead and talk to Tom?"

"My advice is, wait two weeks and you'll know what to do."

Belinda harrumphed softly. Charlotte was tight-lipped, clearly displeased.

Adrian smiled at me. "No problem, Dana. It's not a conversation I'm dying to have."

"But you are the person to do it. Tom would listen to you." To the others, I added, "Sorry I'm not more helpful."

"I respect your discretion," said Belinda.

"It makes me crazy," said Charlotte.

"And I'm glad to be off the hook!" Adrian said. "For now, at least."

.   ఈ   .

After that eggroll lunch with Tom, I began having search committee fantasies: I imagined myself among focused, intelligent adults engaged in heady theological discussion, my seminary education finally being put to use. Those two years were the deepest lived of my life intellectually and spiritually. I'd fallen in love with church history, the mystics, William James, and Lacan. I still yearned for the immersion in spiritual thought and values, the ongoing conversation with school friends that moved from classroom to cafeteria to phone calls, and I never missed that intense engagement with ideas more than when I was dashing off puff pieces for the food section and not doing any of my own writing, as I was now. Presently, in anticipation of summer fruits, I was testing pie pans. Which was better: glass, metal, ceramic, or enameled cast iron? (My vote? Glass—the best preventer of soggy bottoms.)

The search committee, start to finish, was a one-year commitment. One night, when I was sleepless in the wee hours, it came to me that a year was book-length. There had been a recent flurry of books about intensive twelve-month undertakings: a year of reading only the Bible; a year of having sex every day; a year of not generating any trash, of not buying anything. The search committees I knew about—the one for Tom Fox and the one for Amira Turner, our assistant minister—met over potluck dinners.

I had despaired of ever finding a subject for my next book and here it was: *The Search Committee Cookbook.*

I did attend church more regularly. Or I tried. One Sunday when the dreadful bell choir was scheduled, I made it only as far as a courtyard in the gardens where I sat in the moist, cool, gray-May air and watched the mist burn off the mountains while mourning doves *hoo-hoo*ed and wild parrots squawked in the deodars. The AUUCC's historic, once elegant three-acre park was overgrown and shaggy, its hardscape crumbling in places and all the lovelier for it. My soul was fed as richly on that bench as in any hour in the sanctuary. Nor was I the first Sunday garden truant. Old Nadine Fremont, RIP, was so infuriated when Sparlo refused the book on vegetarianism she tried to give him, she never attended another one of his services; instead, every Sunday morning, she'd arrange the altar flowers then dig in the flowerbeds until church let out, when she'd join her friends for coffee on the patio.

For future bell-plagued Sundays, perhaps gloves and a trowel were in order.

Tom Fox's announcement came as a shock, even to congregants who complained about him. The most grief-stricken and rattled were those members who had come to the AUUCC during his reign and stayed because of *him*. Some of them loved Tom as some of us loved Sparlo, ardently and unconditionally.

"It's good news hiding bad," muttered Charlotte as we shuffled toward the exit. "He's leaving, but we still have another whole year of him."

The board accepted Tom's recommendation not to call an interim minister and promptly convened an inelegantly named three-person committee: the Committee to Select the Search Committee, whose chair was the ancient, retired Caltech physicist and (yet another) former church president, Arne Greene.

A notice went out through every church channel—snail mail, email, newsletter, order of service, kiosk flyer, and pulpit announcement: Anyone interested in being on the search committee should apply by letter.

I took Tom's point that if I was pulling away from church life, if my connection had truly frayed, a search committee was not the way back in. Of course, everyone faded in and out of church activities over time; some faded clear away, others reentered church life with renewed vigor.

It came time to raise the subject with Jack. "What if I got on the search committee for the AUUCC's new minister?"

He and I were eating a review dinner in a busy ramen hall in Rosemead.

"How big a time commitment is it?"

"A few hundred hours over a year."

He squirted sriracha into his broth. He could hardly object. He'd just come off his synagogue's board, a two-year commitment he'd presented to me as "a once-a-month meeting" that, in fact, had frequently required his presence two or three times a week.

"I thought you weren't so interested in church anymore. You hardly go."

"I'd go if it was different," I said. "Tom's been running on fumes. Which is why I'd like a say in who replaces him. Get someone with a new vision and more energy."

I could practically see the objections forming in Jack's broad forehead. "Will you have the time?" he said. "What if you want to write another book? You complained all during the last one that you didn't have enough time to do your own work."

"But you see . . ."—I leaned closer—"I was thinking this would be my next book: *The Search*, or how five or six intelligent, well-meaning people select their new leader. A study of democracy in miniature. A fractal of the national process. Plus recipes."

"Hah!" He stayed impressed for about two seconds. "And the other committee members, will they know what you're up to?"

"God, no."

"They might not like being in a book," he said.

Since the publication of *Yard to Table*, in which I profiled Jack as my "suburban farmhand," he'd been the brunt of friendly teasing in his office and had since forbidden me to put him in any more books. (Apparently one lawyer had called down the hall, "Why, it's the man who kisses chickens!")

(For the record, Jack does pet and kiss our chickens.)

"I'll change everybody's names and stuff," I said.

We ate a few more feet of noodles. Then Jack said, "Do you really think it's fair to the church to join such an important committee just to get a book out of it?

"It wouldn't be just to get a book out of it," I said, irritated. "It wouldn't be a good book if I wasn't deeply invested in the matter."

"True," Jack said, poking around in his bowl for some meaty bit. "But remember—keep me out of this one."

(So I did. But when he read the first draft of this, he wanted back in.)

Jack and I—his given name is Jacob—had married late, after a two-year courtship. I was forty-six and he was forty-two at the wedding, which was co-officiated by his rabbi and Tom Fox. Along with our shared love of pets, gardens, and food, we considered our degree of religious commitment—his to Judaism, mine to Unitarian Universalism—a common value. While dating, we'd sporadically attended each other's worship services; perhaps we both nursed secret hopes of enticing the other over to our side. My parents were Jewish, but nonpracticing, and I had never been to synagogue before dating Jack. He had been bar mitzvahed and sent to Jewish summer camp as a boy, so he found a continuity and joy I couldn't in the Hebrew songs and prayers at his temple. While I tried to be open-minded, I was bored and resentful in those mostly Hebrew services: I have never understood the allure of worshipping in a language one doesn't understand. Jack, in turn, found the AUUCC's Sunday services both too secular and too much like church for his taste. Not long after we married, we reached a religious détente and have since worshipped separately, he on Friday nights, I on Sunday mornings. We do have an agreement: If and when one of us needs the other at a religious occasion—for a big fundraising dinner, say, or a wedding—the other will cheerfully show up.

I took to heart Jack's concerns about my being on the search committee. Would I be serving the church or my own ends? (Both, I decided. Two to four hundred hours of work was not a negligible contribution, and if I got material for a book as well, who could say I hadn't earned it?) And honestly, I wanted to be on that committee: I wanted a say in who the next minister would be. I wanted an inside seat to the process. I wanted to help shape the AUUCC into a church that would engage me. And, in my writer's shameless soul, I wanted the scoop. The book. My application letter went, in part, like this:

> My parents were members at the AUUCC when I was away at college, but I never went to church with them then. A dozen years later, six months after my mother died, I was driving past the AUUCC with a friend, who said, "I hear the minister at that church is amazing." I slipped in that Sunday—it seemed a good way to honor my mother's memory.
>
> As soon as I sat in the sanctuary, I began to weep. These were not tears of grief (I knew too well what those were) but tears of profound relief, as if my soul had been waiting all my life to come here. The woman beside me passed me a tissue. Then another tissue.
>
> The AUUCC has been my spiritual home ever since. . . .
>
> Please see the attached sheet listing my church involvements over the years.
>
> I'd bring twenty-four years of engaged membership, a seminary education, and writing skills to the committee.

My work at the *Times* was hectic just then, with the seasonal changes on restaurant menus to address and a long profile of a peach farmer I was trying to finish. I managed if not to forget about my pending application at least not to obsess over it.

At dinnertime on a weeknight in mid-June, the ancient voice of Arne Greene quavered through my landline. "I have some splendid news for you," he said. "You have been selected for the search committee to find the AUUCC's next senior minister. Of course, the congregation still has to vote on our roster, but I anticipate no problems."

"Oh," I said. "Wow. That's amazing! Thank you."

"You do realize it's going to take up hundreds of hours in the next year and a great deal of hard work with colleagues with whom you won't always agree?"

A pang of pure dread hit. I let it pass. "I understand."

"Do you need some time to think about it?"

"Not really," I said.

"So you will accept this enormous and important responsibility, Dana? I would be so pleased if you would."

Arne's warm, old-world formality was itself irresistible. "I will."

"Well, that's just splendid. Assuming the congregation votes you in this Sunday—and they will—we'll meet Monday night at seven in the minister's office."

Only after we hung up did it occur to me that I should have asked who else was on the committee. I was about to call Arne back when the phone rang.

"What did Arne do?" said Charlotte. "Pull names from the fishbowl at the last church raffle?"

"Are you in, I hope?"

"And Belinda."

"So far so good." I jotted our names on a pad by my landline.

"Yes, but then there's Sam Rourke-Jolley."

The doofus-head who'd been on the ministerial relations committee with me! "Oy," I said. "If they needed a Rourke, why the dullest one of all?"

"Dull! You're too kind! He's dumb as a mud fence!" said Charlotte. "But he's probably the only Rourke who hasn't been on a search committee. Now Belinda really likes this kid. Riley Kincaid?"

"Noooo," I howled.

"What's wrong with him?"

"He conducts the bell choir!"

"What's wrong with the bell choir?"

"The suspense is excruciating! Can they hit their notes? Can they keep time? With that kid's wild baton work, you'd think he was conducting a symphony orchestra. And . . . you can go to sleep and wake up and it's still the same song!"

"All true," said Charlotte. "My concern is that he's only been here two years. Belinda insists that he's smart and dear and philosophically one of us. Let's hope, because we've got Jennie Kanematsu-Ross to deal with."

"I didn't know she was back in town." The last time I'd seen Jennie, Sparlo was in the pulpit and she was a goth teen hawking lemon bars to send the youth group to church camp, so at least eleven years ago. Then, I'd heard, she'd gone east to college.

"She came back last summer with a husband and a baby. They live in that apartment above Vergie and Ed's garage. You haven't seen her because she's always in the nursery. She's covered in tattoos—I wonder what Vergie thinks of that? Though a grandchild makes up for a lot. Did you ever have Jennie in RE? Very bright, but so willful. She attracted a little band of kids who'd do anything she told them to."

"I just remember that clash with Sparlo during her coming-of-age ceremony. What did she call him? A patriarchal oppressor?"

"Racist homophobe was in there somewhere."

I looked down at my notes and counted the names. "That's six," I said.

"Oh. Curtis Acevedo."

"Never heard of him."

"Mark Danton's husband? An adorable, sweet guy, but he just started coming to church three months ago. Three months! I'm not sure he's even a member. What was Arne thinking? A search committee is no place for a rank newcomer."

Nor, probably—guilt pang—a drifting old-timer.

"Except for you and Belinda," Charlotte said, "it's not the crew I would have chosen. Oh! But Adrian's on."

"He's fantastic."

"Yes. And if Belinda's right about Riley, and we count Sam—Emma will keep him in line—we might have enough like-minded people to get the job done."

This was not quite the group of brilliant, wise deliberators of my fantasies.

I had another pang then, a literary one: Was this committee, this cast of characters, sufficiently compelling for a book?

5

We Meet

The search committee gathered for the first time on a cool evening in June in the minister's office—the very room where twenty-two years before I had come to consult Sparlo Plessant about entering the ministry. Tom Fox had long since replaced Sparlo's leather Chesterfield sofas and bosky landscape paintings with his own beige slipcovered furniture, Georgia O'Keeffe posters, and faux Navajo rugs. Soon these, too, would be gone, and what would replace them?

At the door stood spindly, ancient Arne Greene, chair of the Committee to Select the Search Committee, and a woman he introduced as "our ministerial search representative."

"And here is Dana, our famous author," he said to her.

I winced. "Hardly."

The rep held out her hand. "Trish Morningstar." All business.

I sat between Charlotte and Belinda and waved to Adrian on the opposite sofa.

"Dana P!" he said. "Excellent. Now we'll have some fun!"

Pleased, I ducked shyly, and Belinda added, "Yes, so glad you're here, Dana."

Sam Rourke-Jolley sat beside Adrian. "Charlotte, Belinda," he said, then looked at me expectantly, as if waiting to be introduced.

"Hi, Sam," I said.

"Nice to see you, uh, is it Brenda?" he said.

"Dana. Dana Potowski. We were on Tom's ministerial relations committee."

"Yes, yes," he said without conviction.

A large young woman in cutoffs, her black hair pulled into a messy topknot, came in talking loudly to the small, elfin-looking director of the bell choir. "Over there by me, Ri," she said, pointing out two armchairs. This could only be Jennie Kanematsu-Ross in a heftier, grown-up version of her teenage self. Beside her, Riley Kincaid seemed even dinkier than usual, dressed in what looked to be a bigger boy's baggy cargo shorts and sport shirt.

"Is this the search committee?" A beautiful man peered in at the doorway. Tall, dark-skinned, with shiny black hair, he had flashing eyes and bright white teeth. I'd never seen him before. I would've remembered.

"Curtis, here!" Jennie Kanematsu-Ross patted the sofa arm on her other side.

So we were eight. Four women, four men. Five of us were white; Jennie was mixed race (mother Japanese American, father white); Curtis was Filipino American; Adrian, Black. We had at least one person per adult decade: Jennie, for the twenties; Riley, early thirties; Curtis, late thirties/early forties; Adrian, late forties; me, fifties; Charlotte, sixties; Sam, late seventies; Belinda, eighties.

Trish Morningstar passed out an agenda and Arne opened the meeting by lighting a votive in the stemmed Anasazi pottery bowl Tom Fox used as a chalice.

"The search for a new minister," Arne began in his slow, raspy quaver, "is a sacred task to be undertaken with reverence and humility. You are as pilgrims embarking on a long journey to find your new leader. As with most spiritual undertakings, there will be hills to climb, dark valleys to cross, with doubts, missteps, and bugaboos along the way. I was on the search committee for Tom Fox, and I can tell you, surprises hide around every corner. You'll encounter jolts, joys, disappointments, and many wondrous moments. A holy search is the experience of a lifetime. You'll come to know your companions well, and become marvelously close."

We gave one another nervous glances, except for Sam, the obligatory Rourke, who was studying the agenda and pulling a long white eyebrow to an impossible-seeming length then letting it spring back. Was closeness possible with a man who didn't recognize a person he'd eaten lunch with every month for two years?

"Forty-seven people applied to be on this committee," said Arne. "Together, you represent as many aspects of church life as we could assemble in one group." Arne's voice rose with emotion. "Together, you form a church in miniature and, as such, you'll choose the next minister for us all. Also, every one of you wrote the same thing in your letters. Before we leave tonight, let's see if you can figure out what it was."

"Time to burn?" said Belinda.

"Out of our minds?" said Adrian.

Trish Morningstar, slim, fiftyish, gender fluid in jeans and a flannel shirt, her short hair shaved up the back, handed out two Xeroxed booklets, the thick *Settlement Handbook* and the slimmer *Resources*. These, she said, contained all the hard-won wisdom from forty years of searches. "Read them thoroughly," she said, "religiously."

A soft snort from Adrian echoed my own.

These guides, Trish said, and her own experience would save us from many mistakes. "I'm your on-call search expert. Any question, any concern, call me." We'd be her tenth search committee. She'd seen brilliant successes— and one disastrous, demoralizing failure: a whole year's work lost because that committee *had ignored the guidelines* in the handbooks and *had not called her* when problems arose. A failed search, she declared, is a tragic defeat for all concerned, and should be avoided at all costs.

"Finding your minister," she said, "takes nine months—a full gestation. By the time they're vetted and voted in, it's a whole year."

In the summer we'd get to know one another, starting with a retreat. "I cannot overemphasize the retreat's importance. It sets the tone for all that follows." One search committee that had a successful, hardworking retreat, she said, still met socially five years later. Another committee, which had forgone a retreat, had stopped speaking to one another even before they picked a candidate. Our retreat should take place in the next few weeks and run from Friday evening to Sunday noon.

Fall was for getting the congregation involved. There'd be a survey, discussion meetings called "cottage groups," anti-oppression training. We'd also compile a "packet," the church's online profile that introduced us to prospective ministers.

"But not everyone has to do everything, right?" said Jennie Kanematsu-Ross.

"We'll get to role assignments shortly," Trish said.

In winter, we'd meet applicants, first by mail, then by Skype. We'd choose three or four "pre-candidates" and fly them out one by one for intensive get-acquainted weekends.

This was beginning to sound like a lot.

In the spring, we'd select our "candidate," who'd come for a "candidating week" at the church. If ninety percent or more of the members voted to call the candidate, we'd have a new minister.

"I believe the cutoff is officially eighty-five percent," said Belinda.

"Many ministers won't accept a call without at least ninety-five percent support," said Trish.

We'd meet weekly, ideally in one another's homes. We'd eat together. Drink wine.

"A lot of wine!" chirped Arne from behind our sofa, and everybody gave a nervous laugh including Charlotte, who'd been sober for more than thirty years.

We then went around the room and introduced ourselves. "And just for fun," Trish said, "tell us something that makes you happy."

"Jennie Kanematsu-Ross here, and my first memory in life," she said, "is me in the sandbox by the old RE building. I had this little shovel . . ." She squinted, as if trying to see it. "I went through every module of RE here, plus sex ed and the coming-of-age group. Twice, I was youth representative at General Assembly."

As a teenager, Jennie had ratted her hair into a goth monument, a far cry from tonight's sloppy topknot. Her thin baby-blue T-shirt allowed for a shadowy glimpse of something winged inked on her chest: bird, insect, or angel. "After college," she went on, "I interned at UU headquarters in Boston and met tons of ministers, so I know all the big up-and-coming stars. And seeing I'm the youngest here, I'll rep the young." Jennie reached up with both arms and tightened her topknot. A line of black words marched up the milky inside of one forearm, but I couldn't make them out. She sat back, then bounced forward. "What makes me happy? Getting a full night's sleep, or even four hours at a stretch! And I'm happy to be on this committee. I was afraid I'd be too busy with Jaz, and Eric working nights, but Mom said she'd babysit if I got picked."

"Thank you, Jennie," said Trish. "Yes, Curtis?" The beautiful man, his dark eyes flashing, had raised his hand. "Did you want to go next?"

"I will, but first I have a question. What is this RE thing that Jennie mentioned?"

"Religious Education," we rang out in unison.

"Sunday school," Jennie added.

"Got it, thanks," said Curtis. "So . . . do you want me to go? I'll go."

Curtis Acevedo. He lived with his husband, Mark Danton, and their two-year-old son, Max. (I knew Mark. He'd been in my last Soul Circle group. Sweet guy. Kindergarten teacher.) While Mark had been an AUUCC member for years, Curtis attended First Calvary until this past March, when their second surrogate pregnancy ended in a miscarriage at six months. "I couldn't stop crying," Curtis said. "Rev Alario at First Cal was so mean—he said it happened because the pregnancy was against God's plan. He got me so scared and upset, Mark had Rev Tom come talk to me . . ."

Charlotte's arm pushed mine. *Rev Tom!* Nobody called him that! Nobody dared!

". . . and he was so nice to us. So I started coming here to church, and that's made me happy. Mark said I was crazy to try to be on the search committee since I was so new. But I thought picking the next guy sounded cool, so why not try? I read that the committee needed someone to do surveys and statistics, and I can do all that."

"Thank you, Curtis," said Trish. "I'm very sorry about the miscarriage. But I have to ask about something you said—that picking the new guy seemed cool? Do you assume the next minister will be male?"

"Well, Rev Tom was. Is. So yeah, probably . . ."

"Could you imagine the next minister being a woman?" said Trish.

"I don't know. I haven't thought about it. But if you think so, sure. Why not?"

"Good," said Trish. "I want us all to be aware of any unconscious preconceptions we might have. If you're set on a man or a woman, a straight, gay, or trans person, a person of color, or if you think only someone able-bodied will do, you could overlook the best minister for this church." She gravely checked with each of us. "So let's keep our minds open. Okay?"

A dutiful murmur signaled assent.

Adrian said, "Jill and I moved here from DC for her work. She's an actress. Our minister at All Souls sent us to the AUUCC; we caught Sparlo's last year—now there was a preacher! Only problem was, you didn't look like us. My first day in church, I counted four other people of color in the sanctuary. Last Sunday, I counted twenty-one. Getting there! Seeing the color in this room makes me happy." He nodded to Jennie and Curtis, then turned to Trish. "But don't you worry, Miss Morningstar. When it comes to our next minister, my mind is wi-i-i-de open."

"Charlotte Beck. Twenty-six years ago, my oldest daughter came home from high school one day and said, 'Mom, I think I'm gay,' and I said, 'Me too.' I was thirty-nine and five years sober, but in the next two years, I came out, divorced my husband, and got together with Sheila. I'd been raised by secular Jews and Sheila was an atheist, so we looked for a spiritual community that was at least as open-minded as the Twelve Steps. We both liked Sparlo's preaching and landed here. And for those of you who don't know, my daughter is married to a terrific man and has two beautiful girls. Those little girls make me very happy.

"And I've never been a pet person, but someone left the tiniest biscuit-colored kitten in our recycle bin and I'm in love. The four-year-old named him Witty. I hesitate to say this in adult company, but that's short for Wittle Witty Wat."

The problem with a church committee, I thought, is that nobody's very wicked. This group in particular might be altogether too wholesome, too politically correct, too bland for a book.

I gave my usual pitch: how in college I'd seen the AUUCC newsletters stacked on our kitchen table but hadn't gone to church until after my mom died. I mentioned seminary, my abiding interest in the ministry. "I can help with any writing we might need."

"The happy part?" Adrian murmured.

Right. "My husband, Jack, and I live on a big piece of property about five blocks from here. We have a terrier, two cats, a parrot, and six chickens; and now we're fostering two mini donkeys, Caspar and Ralph. Nothing makes me happier than hearing the donkeys bray as I'm pulling into the driveway," I said. "Sometimes I hear them at the stop sign at the end of our block. They do not have mini brays."

"I wonder if that makes your neighbors so happy," said Belinda.

"Nobody has complained," I said. "They were already used to our roosters."

Adrian said, "My grandfather had a donkey named Calvin. Once Calvin brayed right by his ear. My grandfather had a ringing headache for a week and suffered permanent hearing loss."

"I've had that ringing headache already," I said.

"It's funny that you mention the newsletters, Dana," said Belinda. "Our stack was two feet high at one point."

"Ours, too," said Sam. "At *least* two feet."

"I miss those newsletters," said Charlotte. "They were iconic. The online version just isn't the same."

"Yeah! In that nobody reads it," said Belinda.

"I hated the color of the paper they used." said Jennie. "Dog-puke yellow."

"People!" Trish called sharply. "Unless you have all night, maybe limit the cross talk? Sam? Can we hear from you?"

Sam told how he and Emma Rourke met at the AUUCC thirty-six years ago; she was twenty-two, he forty-two; theirs was the first wedding Sparlo performed there. "In marrying a Rourke girl, I pretty much married this church," he said.

He'd been chair of the old finance committee and often board treasurer. "I can be your money guy," he said. "And being involved with people makes me happy. I was on a jury last fall, a long murder trial, and just enjoyed the heck out of it."

"Fifty-two years ago," Belinda said, "long before Sparlo, Monty and I wanted our boys to have some religious education. A lot of young parents were here then, and the kids all came up together in one big church family. I've served on the board and as president. In the seventies, I helped rewrite the bylaws and starting in the eighties, I was Sparlo's secretary for twelve years. And now I'm the unofficial church historian—I'll be your living data bank.

"What makes me happy? Digging through the archives at the Huntington Library. Also gardening and cooking and my French conversation group."

Riley Kincaid's flat, triangular face ended in a sharp little chin that gave him his impish, sprite-like aspect. He grew up, he said, near Santa Barbara, in "a rural hippie macrobiotic UU family." (His small size and sallow skin did suggest an early protein deficiency.) "At Cal, I started playing the bells at the Berkeley church," he said, "which inspired me to minor in music composition and conducting. In grad school, I led the bells at the Palo Alto church. Coming here for my postdoc, I looked for a UU church with a bell choir and found the AUUCC right after the last conductor left. Bells make me happy. I have computer skills, and I'm into mixology—I'll help with intoxication."

We laughed, even sober Charlotte, and for the first time I regarded Riley with interest. Perhaps my book could have a cocktails component.

"Is that everyone?" Trish checked her watch. "Excellent! Right on schedule. Let's take a short break. Cookies and hot drinks are in the kitchen. When we come back, we'll elect officers."

6

We Elect Officers

rroyo House's swooping marble staircase had an intricate iron railing. All descents seemed grand, even those of a church committee clambering down for a snack. "Dana!"

Jennie Kanematsu-Ross caught up to me on the landing. "Remember me?" she said.

"Of course. Though I miss your magnificent beehive."

She touched her hair. "Oh that! God. So much hairspray! And the backcombing! Who has the time anymore? Not when you have an eighteen-month-old." On her shoulder, a horse head's mane flew back in a scattering of tiny violets. "I'm so excited you're on the committee. My mom just loaned me a copy of your book."

"The new one?"

"Um. I haven't read it yet," she said. "But I need some advice. I've kept a parenting blog since I was two months pregnant and everyone says I should make it into a book. So maybe you can read some and tell me what to do."

"Not sure I'd know," I said. "But I'll take a look."

At fifty-four and childless, I wasn't keen to read anyone's parenting blog, but Jennie and I faced a year in close proximity, so why not start on a generous note? We'd reached the checkerboard marble foyer. She touched my arm. "Remind me, and I'll text you the website," she said, then called out to Riley. "Ri, wait for me!"

Belinda came up beside me. "Buckle your seat belt," she said. "This could be a bumpy ride."

Back upstairs, Trish said we needed a chair and a cochair, a salary negotiator, and a recording secretary right away. The other "roles"—like the
survey and reference coordinators—could wait.

Riley nominated Belinda to be chair and Sam nominated Charlotte. I sat
between the nominees. Charlotte, being younger and our ex officio president, was more front and center in the church. But Belinda knew all there
was to know about the AUUCC. We shut our eyes for the vote. I discreetly
raised an index finger for Belinda.

Charlotte won. And I was glad.

We somehow agreed without discussion that the cochair should be one
of the younger members. Belinda nominated Riley; Curtis nominated Jennie. Despite his bell ringing, Riley struck me as the more adult. He won.

"Really?" Jennie glared at each of us in turn.

Sam, uncontested, became the negotiator and just as swiftly I found
myself the recording secretary.

"Guess I need this." I pulled a yellow legal pad from my purse. Of course,
I'd already secretly jotted notes at the break.

"You'll face difficult decisions," Trish said. "Passions and tempers will
flare. To create a safe environment where everyone can speak candidly, you
need ground rules. That's what a covenant provides, so get that done right
away."

"Belinda and Dana?" Charlotte said. "Will you draft the covenant?"

Next, we needed a date for the retreat and a weekly meeting time.

We couldn't pin down the retreat before spouses were consulted.

For our weekly meetings, Tuesday was the only day the majority agreed
on—only Jennie couldn't do it. "Actually," she said, "Thursday's the *only*
night I can meet."

"Then I'm not sure you have the time for this committee," said Trish.
"Weekly meetings are just the start of what you'll do. With a toddler, this
might be too much to take on. There's no shame in withdrawing, Jennie,
and now, early on, is the best time."

"We have alternates!" Arne called out cheerfully, giving us all a little
start; we'd forgotten he was there.

How many alternates? I wondered, thinking that I, too, should probably quit.

"Thursday's the night my mom said she'd babysit," Jennie said in a smaller voice. "But I'll check." Furious texting ensued. "Okay. Tuesday—but not next week."

"Good." Trish stood to close the meeting.

"Arne?" Adrian called out. "What was it we all said in our letters?"

I'd forgotten about Arne's challenge.

Arne stood. "You each used the word *home* to say what the AUUCC meant to you. For everyone here, the AUUCC is their spiritual home."

"Ahhh," we murmured to our laps.

Trish had us join hands and sing one verse of the hymn printed in the agenda.

Although she had picked one of Sparlo's favorites, I tend to be flat, so I hate singing in a small group without accompaniment. Luckily, Adrian, Sam, and Riley were strong, unabashed singers. "'Come share a rose with me,'" the rest of us mumble-sang along, "'that I might know your mind,'" and Trish blew out the chalice.

Trish Morningstar?" Tom Fox said dully. "She's okay." We were at a catering café in Eagle Rock sharing cold cucumber soup and an enormous grilled vegetable sandwich. "She's got her agenda: her last three searches have hired lesbians. Coincidence?"

"They've hired a lot of lesbians at the newspaper, too," I said. "My editor says lesbians are the new white males."

Tom pushed the pale pureed soup toward me. "I'm glad you're on, but the committee is not well conceived. Too large, for one. That Curtis is a sweet, sweet guy, but he's an Evangelical Christian and knows less than nothing about the church, the denomination, our history, our governance, or progressive religion. And you can't repeat this"—Tom gave a quick glance behind him to see who might be in earshot and then leaned in—"the only reason Jennie Kanematsu-Ross got on is that her parents gave the church twenty thousand dollars and made it clear they wanted her chosen."

I was genuinely shocked. "That could actually happen?"

"Don't be naive! Why do you think Sam's on? Emma called it in."

"At least he'll do all the financial stuff."

"Anyone could do it—you could do it. It's not that complicated."

"At least Charlotte's chair. She'll run a tight ship," I said.

"Charlotte." Tom grew glum. "We used to be close, but about a month ago she really let me have it, regaled me with a laundry list of my short-comings. My sermons are thin, her wife hates being told to say things to people. I'm not in the office enough—as if Sparlo was ever at Arroyo House, and nobody complained about that."

"Sure they did," I said. "All the time."

"I explained to Charlotte that saying stuff to each other at the end of worship breaks the ice, makes us seem more approachable to newcomers. She seemed to get it; I thought we'd parted on good terms. But I've asked her to lunch twice and both times she wrote 'Thanks, no.' Did she think I'd change my liturgy just for her?" Opening the sandwich, he frowned at a dark, oily slice of eggplant.

"That must hurt," I said. "I'm sorry."

"Charlotte's real issue is, I'm not Sparlo. I loved the man, too, but I'd bet my right hand his sermons were nowhere near as electrifying as they've become in the AUUCC's collective memory. And you're right." Tom closed his sandwich. "Charlotte will be a good chair. You and she and Belinda are all deep church and know what to look for; it's the others I worry about."

"Adrian's good," I said.

"One of the best. But he's also heading into the presidency and has taken on too much to be effective everywhere. Who else?"

"Sam Rourke-Jolley's deep church, too."

"I'd never call him deep anything. But Emma will see to him."

"And Belinda likes that Riley guy," I said.

"Riley Kincaid? Belinda likes him because he drives her to church and chats her up. But what does he know about the AUUCC beyond the bell choir? He's already too busy at his lab, he says, to attend worship planning sessions."

"Maybe he'll quit the bell choir," I said.

"We can only hope."

"I thought you liked the bell choir."

"That eighteen-minute performance last fall was six minutes longer than my sermon! I've since given him a three-minute limit, but he's never kept to it."

"Can you schedule the bells less often? Like once or twice a year?"

"I might, now that I'm leaving. But they do serve a purpose."

I knew what that purpose was. Our music director had insisted on auditioning singers for the choir; to assuage and occupy the musically rejected, a former congregant named Hildy Ashfelt had started a bell choir. Her six or seven players performed with endearing imprecision at two services a year and the pancake breakfast. When Hildy defected to St. Joe's, the large activist Episcopal church in town, we had some blissfully bells-free months until Riley Kincaid revived the bell choir and, doubling its size, convinced Tom to let them perform monthly.

The performances were hokey and harrowing. Riley's baton ticked, jabbed, and swooped. He crouched, he reared up, he crept forward and back. Despite these mighty efforts to keep the tune aloft, hesitation was rampant, as were thunks in lieu of clear, ringing tones. Every variation was played, every repeat taken. Last fall, a new ringer, an elderly woman, struggled through one verse, then froze, bells in hands. Riley pushed on, with gaps when the woman didn't ring. Her neighbor reached to take over her bells, but the old gal held on, her expression glazed, as if she was far away, perhaps revisiting some long-buried, parallel humiliation in childhood.

"The bells have their fans," said Tom. "Between them and the players, limiting performances might disgruntle too many people."

I shrugged. So what? People were disgruntled now—for example, me.

We were still eating our enormous half-sandwiches when the waiter set down a great slab of carrot cake. Tom promptly conveyed a fingerful of the ivory-colored frosting to his mouth. Did I know about "the rule of seventeen"? he asked.

I did not.

Seventeen, he said, is how many people it takes to instigate a coup in a church. Once seventeen people have banded together, he said, they can start a civil war in a congregation; they can remove a choir director or a minister, they can pull down a sanctuary—they could sell the AUUCC's garden acreage to developers! Seventeen is the critical number for revolt. If he eliminated the bell choir or even cut back performances, Tom said, it could inspire enough malcontents to mass up and wreak havoc. As minister, he said, he had a lot of power, but the congregation had the most power—always!—and no minister should ever forget that.

"But you're leaving!" I said. "You could dump the bells on your way out."

"Yes! My parting shot!"

"I was thinking more, your final act of mercy. Like a presidential pardon."

The waiter refilled our iced mint teas. "I prefer to leave without controversy. Let my replacement do what he or she wants to with the bells."

"Do you have any thoughts about who your replacement should be?"

"Anyone who makes me look good!" Tom barked. He helped himself to another fingerful of frosting. "Seriously, I want the same minister you all do: a bang-up preacher who'll keep the church in robust financial and spiritual health. I imagine this one will be a woman—it's time, and there are great ones out there. For twenty years now, often half of our seminarians have been female, and some are now in their prime. What kind of a minister do you want, Dana?"

"I'd like a woman, but I'm open to anyone so long as they can preach like a son of a bitch. And are a dead-eye shot."

Tom caught my reference, which was to the unforgettable three-minute "charge" that Sparlo Plessant delivered nine years ago at Tom's installation.

The installation happened at the end of Tom's first year. His friends and colleagues came from all over to honor and exhort him before his new church. Tom's best friend preached, his old mentor led the opening prayer, and the AUUCC's own minister emeritus—Sparlo Plessant—delivered the "charge," a brief, eloquent instruction to the new minister. This was Sparlo's first post-retirement appearance at the AUUCC after the traditional two-year banishment. Although Tom's best friend preached for a full twenty minutes, I can't remember a thing he said. Sparlo, on the other hand, spoke for under three minutes and nobody has forgotten a word. He said that having given much thought to ministry over the years, he had reached a single conclusion: "A minister's sole sacred duty is to stand watch—and shoot predators on sight."

That's what I was referring to when I told Tom Fox that I wanted a minister who was a dead-eye shot.

Tom's face softened: he had loved that charge—and tried to obey it. "It's good you're on the committee, Dana. This church is in your bones."

That night, Jack came home late, around eight. "It's probably good you have your search," he said, dumping his knapsack onto the sofa.

He'd been given a big case, he said, suing an oil refinery near Bakersfield. Owned by a quarrelsome, infighting family of Orthodox Jews, the facility was obsolete; twice, hydrogen fluoride had escaped, forming toxic clouds that bumped over the ground toward nearby neighborhoods. "So Ima be crazy busy for the next six to eight months, maybe a year," he said. "And no, you can't put any of it in your book."

We'd see about that.

7

﹡

We Covenant

C hurch was out for the year in June—that is, the ministers were off duty, leaving the pulpit to seminary students and those congregants eager to try preaching. I always took the summers off. One Sunday, though, I met Belinda after worship to draft the covenant. We walked up to Arroyo House and set up in the library. Adrian, who was manning the BIPOC table on the patio, would join us once the crowd thinned.

I opened my computer on the dark oak table. "So what do you think of our committee so far?" I asked Belinda.

"Not the group I would've chosen," Belinda said. "But we'll do our best."

"And who would you have chosen instead?"

"The bylaws stipulate five to seven long-standing, involved members who have a thorough understanding of church polity and governance."

"Not sure I'd have made the cut," I said.

"You're ideally qualified." She landed a playful pat on my wrist. "And you add a dash of glamour."

"Hardly." Was she referring to my rustling poplin skirt or my (everglorified) job as a restaurant critic? Either way, it was alarming how much Belinda's opinion meant to me. "I wanted you for chair," I said, "but Charlotte will be good."

"Oh, I voted for Charlotte," said Belinda. "I want to be the arranger. Let Charlotte herd the cats. This won't be an easy group."

I was dying to get her take on everyone but didn't want to seem like the avid gossip hound I am. "A year from now, it'll be over. And we'll have a new minister."

"Let's hope."

"Why, do you think we'll botch it?"

"We'd better not. Searches are expensive and time-consuming. And too much is at stake: a failed search can demoralize and destabilize a congregation for years afterward." Belinda pointed to my computer. "Let's see what you've got."

I had drafted a sample covenant by cobbling together statements from examples in the handbook. As Belinda read, Adrian slipped in and stood behind us.

> We, the members of the AUUCC search committee, joyfully undertake
> the search for a new senior minister. We acknowledge the substantial
> commitment required and agree to give our time and energy willingly,
> with humility and mutual respect.

"I like the 'joyfully,'" said Adrian. "Especially since Arne says we're headed for some dark and thorny woods."

We then agreed on a series of statements that essentially behooved us to do our work and behave like adults. We would "covenant" to:

> Attend all meetings and meet all deadlines;
> Listen deeply and respond thoughtfully;
> Refrain from dominating the discussion and draw out those with
>   quieter, less forceful voices;
> Stay at the table when the process becomes challenging;
> Present a unified front;
> Honor the confidentiality of those being evaluated.

"It's so preemptive," I said. "You can tell the past incidents that inspired each statement. Someone left a meeting in a snit; someone blabbed too much out of school . . ."

"Someone never shut up," said Adrian.

Belinda, paging through the bylaws, said, "We need something in writing about what can get you kicked off the committee. How's this?" She slid the page to us.

Failure to attend meetings or perform assigned tasks; violating confidentiality; and other distressing, impeding, or disruptive behavior can result in dismissal.

"That should quail a fractious heart," said Belinda.
Quailed mine.

Walking home in the sunshine, I fretted: Was I already breaking the covenant's confidentiality clause by secretly gathering material for a book? Of course, I'd change everyone's names and identifying details. And I wouldn't even start on the book until the search was over. The writing would take one or two years; another year or two would pass before the manuscript was sold, edited, and published—assuming any publisher would buy it. By then, who'd mind a well-disguised, largely fictionalized account of this search?

At home, I told Jack how our covenant read like a chronicle of past problems and the (no doubt futile) attempt to circumvent them this time around.

"People say the exact same thing about the Torah," he said.

A magnificent umbrella pine leaned out from Belinda's yard over the sidewalk. Her big blowsy hybrid tea roses were aglow in the falling dusk. Early because I was bringing the appetizers, I banged the knocker, a heavy brass lion's paw.

Belinda answered in the kind of zipper-front rayon floral housedress my grandmothers used to wear. Was it vintage? Or was there a secret source whose address magically appeared in your contact list on your eightieth birthday?

She led me through the dark, teak-lined living and dining rooms to a large bright kitchen. I hadn't been in Belinda's home since the awful time after her husband, Monty, and younger son, Stan, died within six weeks of each other. For two months, I'd brought soup or stew and fresh garden lettuce to the Craftsman and never once found Belinda alone. Women from church—mostly widows—bustled in the house and yard. Was this another gift of churchgoing—to be eased into widowhood by those who'd come before? (I was four years older than Jack, though, so I had some chance of predeceasing him.)

In the kitchen, Belinda handed me a serrated knife for my baguettes and pretty wood bowls for the almonds and olives. She opened the oven to check on a large copper roasting pan of chicken fiesta, a chicken and rice dish ubiquitous at AUUCC potlucks. The recipe was from the *Times*, but decades before I came to the food section. I'd first encountered chicken fiesta twenty-some years ago, at my first Pledge Drive dinner. Funds were short that year, so in lieu of caterers, volunteers signed up to cook an agreed-upon menu. I was helping in the kitchen the afternoon that twenty pans of chicken fiesta arrived. It was hard to believe they all sprang from the same recipe. There were chicken fiestas in Pyrex, in cheap oven-darkened metal pans, in painted Italian ceramic, in cast iron, stainless steel, copper. A few cooks used only breasts, some a whole cut-up bird, one sent only drumsticks. The rice ranged from fragrant basmati and plain white to undercooked brown and mushy, beige MJB. Several versions suffered from obvious economies (those drumsticks! And green bell peppers where the recipe called for red). Belinda's version, then as now, was definitive: plump jasmine rice, well-browned thighs and breasts, the eponymous "fiesta"—a sauté of corn, red peppers, and purple onions—scattered over the top with fresh cilantro.

Charlotte arrived with bags of baby lettuce and a store-bought vinaigrette. Riley, on her heels, lugged in ingredients for a cocktail he'd dubbed The Loquatious, a pale orange drink made with homemade loquat syrup, golden rum, lime juice, and soda water. He made a virgin Loquatious soda for Charlotte.

We filled our plates in the kitchen. In the dining room Charlotte lit a chalice and read Mary Oliver's "Wild Geese" poem: "You do not have to walk on your knees . . .". We checked in as we ate. I took the minutes on my lap.

For her turn, Belinda passed around an old postcard she'd found from the 1911 Rose Parade: a donkey cart festooned with flowers had a placard that read ARROYO UNITARIAN CONGREGATION.

"Maybe Dana and her donkeys can re-create this for the Altadena Days Parade," said Adrian.

Coming from him, this sounded like a good idea. For a moment.

Curtis, checking in, said his parents were visiting, and his mom's cooking made the whole house smell like fish.

Jennie complained of infant bed-hogging. "Dana," she called across to me. "Are you taking notes?"

"Minutes!" I said.

"Why so secret—under the table like that?"

"I'm used to taking notes on my lap when I review restaurants."

"Ahh. Sneaky!" Jennie's frown released. "Hey, could you ever take us on a review?"

"Maybe not everyone at once," I said. "But I always need eating partners."

Everyone agreed that it would be a great adventure to go on a review. I didn't say how unglamorous it usually was, how hit-or-miss, like trying any old random restaurant.

For my check-in, I told everyone about hiking with the donks to Inspiration Point, ten miles round trip. "Some tugging was involved. Much pleading. And waving of sticks."

"Sounds like life with my mother-in-law," said Sam. "The less mind she has, the more stubborn she gets."

Sam and Emma had moved from their house by the golf course to care for Mary's ninety-five-year-old mother in her historic mansion on the street known as Millionaire's Row. The wealthiest, and for years the AUUCC's most powerful member, Faithalma Rourke was determined to die at home. "Guys, don't ever let me get like her," Sam said to us. "The trick is to take the pills before you forget where you hid them."

Once check-in was over, conversation petered out. Forks tinked on plates. Belinda brought the chicken around again, and Charlotte admired the copper pan, which reminded her, she said, of copper pans in the scullery of a British TV show about servants and aristocrats in a big house. Every-one then talked about that show, the characters they liked or hated, which plots rang true or false. With Häagen-Dazs and the Milanos, they listed other shows that were as good or better. Adrian knew all of them and his wife had acted—bit parts, mostly—in a few. I, on the other hand, watched very little TV and could contribute nothing. I kept busy by jotting down the names of the shows mentioned, twenty-three in all.

If this was what passed for conversation in this group, I thought, I had some serious catching up to do, which meant cajoling Jack to watch more than one episode at a time. Any more than that he deemed bingeing.

With the table cleared, our first order of business was to schedule the retreat. Nobody was available for the same two nights all summer. Jennie wasn't available for two nights ever. We settled on a Saturday morning through Sunday noon in late July, more than a month away.

"Didn't Trish What's-her-name say we should do it as soon as possible?" I said.

"This *is* as soon as possible," Belinda said.

The last roles were assigned: Belinda became the arranger, which meant she'd handle the logistics for the visiting job applicants. Curtis took on the survey. As for the packet—the AUUCC's online profile—Adrian was in charge of the content and Riley the web design. (Before the internet, "pack-ets" were three-ring binders with laminated pages of photos and docu-ments. Churches and ministers "swapped packets" to learn about one another, and it was up to the packet person to drive the ministers' packets from one committee member to the next so that everyone could read them; the sheer mechanics of this limited the number of packets exchanged to three or four at the most. Now, since everything was online, a search committee could easily review packets from a dozen ministers.)

By default, Jennie became the reference coordinator: she'd assign and keep track of references consulted in the vetting process. "So I have nothing to do till we have pre-candidates—in, like, January?" she said. "So, Riley, since you get to do the website, why don't I be cochair now? And when I have to do the references, we can switch back."

"Um." Riley swiveled from Jennie to Charlotte.

"Jennie," Charlotte said mildly, "there's plenty to keep you busy till Jan—"

"I'm talking to Riley, not you," Jennie cut in.

Hands reached for the wine bottles on the table.

Riley, quietly: "I should probably stay cochair, Jen."

"I'm feeling so not listened to here," said Jennie.

Into the silence came the swish of a passing car. Charlotte said, "We can start interviewing the staff now."

"Staff?" said Curtis. "What staff?"

"The staff that runs the church," said Charlotte. "How do you think it operates?"

"I never really thought about it," said Curtis.

"Let's see," Charlotte said. "There's Amira, the associate minister; Shelly, the church administrator; Georgia, the music director; Loren, the director of religious ed; Evelyn, our social justice coordinator; Maureen, the rental-and-events coordinator; Hanjo, the accountant; Robbie and Alain, the janitors. Have I missed anyone?"

"Secretary!" Belinda called out. "Vera!"

Curtis: "So many!"

"Some work only a few hours a week. But we need to talk to all of them since we're hiring their next boss."

"Wow," said Curtis.

Curtis, I wrote, *learns the existence of staff.*

Amira, the associate minister, had to be interviewed right away, Charlotte said. "Because if she throws her hat in the ring, that obviates the whole search process."

Jennie waved her hand. "What do you mean, *obviates* the search process?"

"Cancels it," Charlotte said. "Makes an outside search irrelevant."

"How does that work?" Jennie asked.

Amira, at thirty-five, had come to us four years ago, hired straight from seminary as an assistant minister. When her three-year contract ended, we'd voted to "call" her to the more permanent position of associate minister. If she now aspired to become our senior minister, Charlotte explained, we wouldn't conduct a full search. As an internal applicant, Amira would automatically become *the* candidate, and no one else could apply. She'd get a "candidating week" to sell herself to the congregation, then submit to a vote. If ninety percent of the congregation voted in her favor, she'd be our new senior minister.

"Eighty-five percent is the real cutoff," Belinda said. "But like Trish said, most ministers insist on ninety to ninety-five percent support to take the job. Nobody wants to start off with detractors."

"So if Amira's interested," Charlotte said, "we need to know right away."

"Why can't she just be one of our finalists?" said Riley. "I mean, shouldn't we at least consider her along with some others?"

"If an internal candidate throws their hat in the ring, it means they're confident they have the congregation's support. It's not fair to have other ministers go through all the travel and interviews when the job's already sewn up."

"Does anybody here think Amira has that kind of support?" asked Adrian.

"Oh god yes. Amira's fantastic," said Jennie. "I'd vote for her in a heartbeat."

"Yeah. She's super-cool," said Curtis.

"She's not half the preacher Tom Fox is," said Sam. "Much as I like her."

"Are you kidding?" said Jennie. "Her sermons are so-oh-oh much better than Tom's dry old me-me-me boring white guy shtick."

I checked Charlotte: the faintest smile, instantly suppressed.

"Won't the congregation want to choose from a slate of candidates?" said Riley.

"The congregation never sees a *slate* of candidates," Charlotte said. "We alone choose three or four pre-candidates, meet them, then choose *the* candidate, whom the congregation accepts or not. This is all in the handbook, Riley."

Riley went pink along the rims of his ears. "Busy couple of weeks," he muttered.

"About Amira," I said. "If we don't support her, can she still be the candidate?"

"I believe it's a courtesy to give her a candidacy if she wants one," said Charlotte.

"Oh my god, she'd be so great," said Jennie.

"She's been okay in a secondary position," Sam said, "but the AUUCC really needs an older, more experienced senior minister."

"You mean a man?" said Jennie.

"I didn't say that," said Sam. "Please don't put words in my mouth, Jennie."

"But everyone knows what you meant," Jennie said.

Again hands reached for the wine bottles.

"But I didn't mean that," said Sam. "Tanya, you know that's not what I meant."

He seemed to be looking my way. "If you mean me, it's Dana," I said.

Adrian cut in with his low, reasonable, persistent therapist's voice. "Let's say Amira does want to be considered and we give her a candidating week, but she doesn't get the votes. Do we then conduct a full-scale search?"

"Her defeat would be considered a failed search," said Belinda. "This committee would be disbanded and a new one formed. There'd likely be a second search, too, for a new assistant minister, since Amira probably wouldn't stay on after a losing vote."

Riley said, "So Amira could hijack our whole search?"

"I doubt she will," said Charlotte, "or we would've heard something by now. Still, we have to ask what her intentions are. Dana? Would you mind talking to her?"

"Me?" I stopped scribbling. Talking to Amira seemed a huge responsibility.

"I'll talk to her," Jennie said. "I probably know her the best . . ."

"Jennie, I need you to talk to the RE director and the social justice staffer," Charlotte said.

"Yeah, but I don't mind talking to Amira, too."

Charlotte looked steadily at me. "Dana?"

"I'll do it."

"And Sam," said Charlotte. "Will you talk to the accountant and the janitors?"

"We interview the janitors?" said Sam. "They don't even come to church."

Adrian said, "They come to BIPOC meetings."

"Excuse me," said Curtis. "I'm so sorry. But what are these BIPOC meetings?"

"Meetings for all Arroyo's Black, Indigenous, and People of Color members," said Jennie. "You should come check us out."

"And Sam," Belinda said, "janitors spend more time on church property than anyone else. Only they know where the fuse boxes, hoses, and light-bulbs are. The new minister has to work with them, and not everyone can, as we saw with the interim."

"If you say so," said Sam.

By the time we got around to discussing the covenant, everyone was tired and the draft Belinda, Adrian, and I had cobbled together was approved with no discussion.

I helped Belinda clean up. As I dried the copper pan, she came very close. "You know, Dana, you might take Jennie Ross in hand," she said. "She clearly looks up to you and wants your approval. You could be a real socializing influence."

"Not sure how I'd go about that."

"Take an interest in her. She's always checking to see how you take her antics. If you took her along on a restaurant review, she'd follow you anywhere."

"Not sure anyone could have that much of an effect on her."

"Just a thought. She could use a sane adult role model." Belinda squeezed my wrist. "Someone kind, calm, and rational, who models self-restraint."

Walking home on wide, dark streets, I wondered if such had been Belinda's strategy with Riley—and me! Were we taken in hand and craftily molded? As I'd entered church life, a number of women my mother's age had taken an interest. They'd welcomed me onto their committees and seemed thrilled by whatever I wrote, even in the throwaway *Madre Mountain News*. When I started seminary, an older woman I barely knew offered to help with my tuition; I didn't take her up on it, but even now, long after her death, the offer still moves me. When I chose journalism over ministry, the AUUCC women still filled my cooking demos and paid a hundred bucks apiece to eat my Cooking for Cash dinners; they tried my recipes in the *Times*; they bought and read my books. I was invited to Thanksgiving, introduced to single sons, offered furniture. (The eight-foot French farmhouse table May Vardot gave me when she moved to a senior residence is the centerpiece of my new kitchen.) Helen Froelich, whose daughter was a Scientologist, told me how much she wished her girl was more like me—clearly, some of these church mothers had been as disappointed by their own daughters as my mother was by me. But the AUUCC encouraged a remedial, openhearted love, one uncontaminated by familial stickiness. I think this served us all well. I'd been a grieving thirty-year-old woman on an uncertain path when the AUUCC gathered me up, provided the last bits of parenting I needed—the bits my parents couldn't or didn't supply—and nudged me gently into an adult life. Was this what Belinda hoped I'd do for Jennie?

I got home well before nine o'clock.

Here's something else a churchwoman taught me: before joining the AUUCC, I left a lot to the last minute—getting dressed, chores, writing assignments—despite the tug of anxiety this added to my days. After Charlotte and I took the AUUCC's new member orientation class, we were asked to co-lead the next session. We met to plan it and parted with lists of new members to contact. Half an hour after I got home, Charlotte phoned to report on her calls. Until then, it had never occurred to me to do a task as soon as possible. While I still procrastinate, especially with writing, I am now diligent about dispatching little jobs that can grow irksome when put off.

Thus, while Bunchie the terrier still wriggled with joy at my return, I phoned the associate minister and made a date to visit her the next night. Then I made myself a cup of ginger tea, googled Jennie, and found her blog, MammaTat.com. I read "The Dirty Diaper Business" and "Best Ever Breastfeeding."

> Allow me to recommend the shawl! Yes, that old-fashioned fringy thing Grandma hugs round her shoulders in front of the fire. For breastfeeding moms, shawls are the bomb. They give you portable privacy and—when you learn to tie them à la the Mexican rebozo— they're the perfect sling for baby.

Enough! In Jack's office, I caught him listening to the Grateful Dead and reading the newspaper online. "Come watch TV with me," I said. "There are so many shows we haven't seen, we've become culturally deficient!"

8

Amira

That night, after the meeting at Belinda's, I woke after 3:00 a.m., which was not unusual for me. This is when the day's problems loom largest and when I think about death (when it will come, how I'll face it, and what *it* is). Many women I know, even Charlotte, have said that they, too, are awake then and similarly ruminating. I find it comforting, less lonely, that our minds are roaming the same dark, miry wilds.

Tonight, fears about the search assailed. What busywork had I signed up for? How to face hundreds of hours with Riley the bell ringer? Sam the dud?

Such a random, poorly conceived, TV-mad group.

Just one coconspirator could make a difference. If I ever end up in a depressing county-run old-age home or (unimaginably) in prison and I have just one close friend, one good, laughing interlocutor, I'll get by. One reason I'd loved seminary was because I'd had such a great friend there, a smart, sly, laughter-loving confidante. On the search, Charlotte with her sharp, dry wit was the most likely choice, but her precision grooming and crisp, corporate coolness still made me feel like a messy, pesky child. Adrian, the best laugher, would be the coziest and most fun; I'd thought we'd gotten close in our Soul Circle, but once that ended—nothing. Twice, I'd asked him on a review meal, once with spouses, once without, and both times he demurred. I left it with "Any time you want the *Times* to buy you dinner, let me know." He never had.

I loved and revered Belinda—her recent fond pats had been as unexpected as a bear's lick—but I couldn't imagine her gossiping gleefully or cackling over idiocies.

I could resign. There were alternates! Anyway, who'd want to read a book about a church committee? Potowski, I told myself. Get out while you can.

Jack slept on beside me, with an occasional soft snore. If he would be working twelve to sixteen hours a day on his refinery, I'd need something to occupy myself. Was a search committee the right immersion? Why not an art or poetry class? Or a night class at the seminary? Though none of those would give me a book.

I worried again that I should have been a minister instead of a food journalist. I was only fifty-four. I'd had classmates that age in seminary. I could quit the *Times*, do my internships—and any new requirements—to get ordained, then serve a small church till the end of my working years. Surely that could be a book.

And so went my busy, chattering mind until sleep rose up and shut it down.

I was blearily slicing one of the year's first peaches onto yogurt when Charlotte phoned. "I had the worst night," she said. "Terrible commitment anxiety. What have we gotten ourselves into?"

"Me too!" With the sun burning off the morning fog and pink peach juice on my fingers, my fears had faded—a little. Hadn't I similarly dreaded every church group I'd ever joined, every class I'd taken or taught? Each new matriculation brought an urge to cut and run. And then the group members began to talk, personalities unfolded, friends were made, flowers bloomed. "But you seemed so calm and in control last night."

"I didn't feel so calm with Curtis so dense and Jennie challenging me at every turn. If I wasn't so worried about who Arne would replace me with, I'd quit."

"Me too!" I said. "Exactly!"

"Don't you dare quit, Dana Potowski. Promise. I couldn't bear it without you and Belinda."

"The whole enterprise is terrifying," I said. "A year with everybody."

Amira lived in a small fifties-era apartment building on the steep part of Lake Avenue near the mountains. Hers was the ground-floor unit with an enormous double stroller parked outside.

She had come to the AUUCC fresh from seminary, where she'd started as a Presbyterian; a crisis of faith in her first year led her to forsake Christianity for our creedless denomination. Of Irish American and Pakistani descent, Amira was short, plump, and friendly, with a childish lilt in her voice. She preached five or six times a year, not enough to become proficient—yet. She was listened to politely and encouraged; the AUUCC has always been a nourishing soil for young ministers.

If preaching wasn't Amira's strength, she worked tirelessly in those parts of ministry Tom Fox had no interest in: community relations and social justice. Amira flew to Sacramento to lobby for gun control and clean water initiatives; she represented us at interfaith prayer breakfasts, and every week discussed religion and politics on a progressive FM talk show. Her pet project was an ongoing exchange with a local mosque; she and the imam swapped pulpits, held joint movie nights and get-acquainted potlucks.

In her four years at the AUUCC, she'd had three children, a boy now three, and twin girls, six months. Her internist husband was a hands-on dad, and how they balanced parenthood with two demanding professions was a wonder to all. ("Daycare, seven a.m. to six p.m." was Amira's stock reply.) AUUCC members were universally fond of Amira, but since so much of her work was done out of sight, and since self-promotion never occurred to her, few knew the full range of her accomplishments.

Amira met me at the door with a twin on her shoulder. "We ate a little late, so now we've got to have a little burp," she said and, thumping the baby's back, led me to the kitchen nook. "Tea?" With the baby still clapped on, she set out a teapot and small glasses etched with gold lace. An arm-thick braid hung to her waist. Filling the kettle, she spoke sideways, over the infant's head. "You want to know if I'm throwing my hat in the ring."

"That's one of my questions. Are you?"

"Anthony!" she called. Her husband appeared in a T-shirt, scrub pants, and sleep-smashed curly brown hair. "If you get them bathed and in bed, I'll get them to sleep," she said, and neatly swung the baby girl into his hands.

"We have maybe twenty minutes," she said to me, and rinsed a hank of fresh mint before cramming it into the pot. We sat in the nook while the water boiled and Anthony called for the three-year-old boy to brush his teeth. A wail went up. Amira said, "You can tell your committee that I won't be their candidate."

"Oh! May I ask why not?"

"No support!" Amira cried out. "Not one person has suggested I put my name forward. Except Jennie Kanematsu-Ross when she called last night." She got up, poured the boiling water into the pot. "Even Tom Fox said it's not the right time, with where I am in ministry and the kids so small."

"And what do you think about that?"

Amira stirred and poured the tea, adding a sprig of fresh mint to each glass. "I wasn't planning a big career move so soon. I need to build up my preaching and management skills before I have a church on my own, let alone one as large and staffed up as the AUUCC. So you can tell everyone I won't co-opt their search."

"Not quite how I'll put it," I said.

"Put it any way you like!" she burst out, sounding like a petulant teenager.

Baby clothes dried on a rack by the table. Bottles filled the dish drainer. A vapor of milk and steam and drying laundry thickened the air. "On another topic," I said, "given our current transition, how do you think the AUUCC's doing?"

"The AUUCC is fine. But I'm not. I can't stand that Tom's leaving. He's been a kind, patient mentor, more like a father than a boss. I'm so afraid I won't make it through his going-away party without breaking down."

"You won't be the only one crying," I said, recalling how the whole church had snuffled during Sparlo's last worship service. I was sitting with his wife, Lois, and somehow neither of us had thought to bring tissues, so I went to the bathroom and brought back a roll of toilet paper; when Lois saw it, she burst out laughing. She still laughs about it. "You brought me toilet paper!"

"The AUUCC is almost weirdly healthy," Amira said. "No crises, no rifts, no simmering discontent—because Tom Fox addresses problems before they fully form!"

"Like what?" I asked. "Just out of curiosity."

Last fall, she said, Tom noticed that the midweek service, led by a student intern, had attracted a core of people who then weren't showing up on Sundays. "You can't have two congregations, no matter how small one is," said Amira. "It sets up a potential schism. So Tom cut the midweeks back to once a month."

"Ah, so that's what happened." I'd assumed the midweeks were limited for lack of interest; I hadn't been to one in years, finding them too hokey and amateur hour, with too much drumming and bowing to the four directions and rattling of rain sticks.

"And what traits would you like in a new boss?" I said.

"Someone more interested in my ministry—social justice, political activism." She poured more, stronger tea. "What really worries me is, Tom makes twice what I do, but he has thirty years' more experience. What if the new minister is a hot young star about my age? A big pay gap won't be so fair then."

"Good point. I'll alert the negotiating team." The moist milky air and hot tea conspired with last night's sleeplessness. I yawned. "Anything else you'd like?"

"Two X chromosomes," Amira said. "There are some great women ministers out there. I gave Jennie a few names."

"Not sure that's kosher," I said.

"Well, Jennie was saying all the big up-and-coming stars she knew about."

The sarcasm with which Amira drawled "stars" made it clear that she was hurt and resentful not to be considered one. "Amira, you could so easily be a star, too," I said. "You just have to toot your own horn, so people know all the great things you do."

Fresh wails issued from the far end of the apartment. "That's my signal," I said.

Amira walked me to the door and, opening it, said: "Nobody takes me seriously because I'm short and fat."

"Amira, you're adorable," I said.

"Exactly—but that's not the same as commanding or impressive or charismatic!"

"You have a lot of charisma," I said. "And many devoted fans."

"Not enough of them, obviously!" she said with a shrill laugh.

I touched her shoulder and hummed in a way I hoped was consoling.

At home, I typed a short report for the committee and in it alerted the negotiator (i.e., Sam) to keep in mind salary parity between the senior and junior ministers.

I slept through the night without interruption.

9

We Retreat

The retreat center, a former monastery, sat perched on a hill in residential Sherman Oaks like a tiny Italian hill town. I drove there early on a Saturday morning in late July, stopping at a bakery I knew in Studio City for a dozen small pastries, each with a jewel-like fruit center of rhubarb, fig, or greengage plum. I checked in at the center's office, then took my tote to my room, a narrow cell with a cot-like bed and a portrait of Jesus in his crown of thorns. I found my group—only the women so far—in the dining hall.

"Hello, hello!" I grabbed a plate for the pastries, arranged them, then stuck my nose into a lavish bouquet of Belinda's roses. "Gorgeous!" And to Jennie: "Nice sunflowers," referring to the profuse Van Gogh–ish blossoms inked on her right thigh.

A tall, slightly hunched woman in a pink T-shirt and a long, pale green skirt came toward us. "Ah, our facilitator," Charlotte said. "Everyone, this is Helen."

I knew her. Helen Harland was my long-lost friend from seminary. One of the five other UUs in my class, she'd been my confidante there, my study partner, my ally. I hadn't seen her in sixteen years. Unlike me, she'd finished her degree and been ordained. She'd then taken a job at a small church with an ingrown, hidebound congregation—no seasoned minister would have touched it! The two years she spent there were so difficult that when she left, she left ministry. For a while, she worked at a retreat center near Santa Barbara, and she planned to go to grad school again, this time to become a therapist. She called me the night before she left for a month-long silent meditation retreat. That was sixteen years ago and the last I ever heard from her.

Yet here she was—and back among the Unitarians! Her face had softened and creased; her curly brown hair was streaked with white. Always self-conscious about her height, her chronic hunch was morphing into a dowager's hump. "Dana!" she called.

We hugged warmly, even as I shunted aside old hurt feelings from the calls and letters she'd ignored. She squeezed my hand. "Let's find a time to catch up."

Riley entered, rumpled and texting, followed by Adrian calling, "Mornin', comrades!" Curtis arrived with Sam, whose right hand was wrapped in gauze. Helen led us to a thick-walled conference room with a garden view. Adrian sat next to me.

"I'm your facilitator—or, as I prefer, your *felicitator*," Helen said. "I'm a part-time consultant in ministerial transitions and a full-time psychotherapist."

So she had become a therapist!

We'd all been sent personality tests, which Helen now asked us to hand in. Riley and Sam furiously began filling out theirs.

"Today you'll write your check-ins," Helen said, "while I collate your tests."

Charlotte passed out wide-ruled journals with different colored covers and good gel pens.

Helen opened a large newsprint pad on an easel to reveal a prompt:

IMAGINE YOUR LIFE AS A MOVIE THAT YOU'VE STEPPED OUT OF TO BE HERE TODAY. WHAT'S THE TITLE? THE SETTING? THE PLOT?

We hunched over our journals. I wrote:

My movie's a YouTube video called "Yard Life with Restaurants." You'll see me feed the chickens and our two mini donks. Next, I'll pick tomatoes, beans, and cucumbers and gather eggs. Then I'll drag my husband to the first of the weekend's four restaurant meals. . . .

Adrian was the first to read. His handwriting, I saw, was large and full of loops.

My movie is a sports comedy—my wife, Jill, just got a new series about a women's Olympic track team, so she's in marathon training, and reluctantly so am I. The title is *The Laziness of the Long Distance Runner*. . . .

Belinda read:

My movie is very low-key, a low-budget art film called *A Simple Life* . . . Just an old widow lady going through her day. She tends her garden. She calls her son, Peter. She fries a small lamb chop for dinner. She resists the urge to call Peter again. Now she's at her kitchen table reading *Fleurs de Mal* for her French conversation group. . . .

"Are we supposed to give feedback?" asked Jennie.

"Perhaps it's best just to listen," said Helen.

Sam held up his bandaged hand. "I was finishing my personality test, so I'll just say what I would've written.

"As most of you know, Emma and I live with Emma's mom, Faithalma Rourke, in her six-bedroom white elephant. The old gal's ninety-five with dementia and round-the-clock care, but her will's as strong as it's always been.

"At five this morning, Faithalma got outside, and there, in her nightie on the front lawn, she starts baying for help." Sam's switched to a falsetto: "'Help! Help me! They're holding me prisoner!'"

Charlotte and I widened our eyes at each other.

"Emma and I and the night nurse ran outside," Sam went on. "The nurse reached her first, and Faithalma swung 'round and slugged her on the jaw. I went to restrain her and she bit me." He held up his bandaged hand. "Old gal has quite the clamp. Drew blood. Emma finally calmed her down, lured back inside with the promise of food. Old thing lives to eat. So five minutes later, she's packing in the oatmeal with no memory of what just happened. Everyone else is a wreck! The medication nurse came and bandaged my hand. Any red streaks, she said, I'll have to go to urgent care."

Helen said, "Let's keep an eye on that bite, Sam. And everyone, let's stick to reading what we've written. Things will move faster then, and we've got lots to do."

Curtis's movie, he said, was *The Two-Year-Old King.*

A king named Max rules our house. At six this morning, he summoned his dad Mark, then his dad Curtis; then his grandma Lola, then Hugo the cat . . .

Jennie had brought a plate of large thick cookies embedded with shards of dark chocolate. I took one for pure anxiety eating. The chocolate was high quality and the cookie itself so wonderfully gritty, buttery, and salty-sweet, I barely heard Jennie's movie: "a domestic comedy of diapers, toys, and high chairs, all of it sticky."

"Jennie," I said, "these are the best chocolate chip cookies I've ever eaten. So addictively gritty. And such good chocolate."

"They're one hundred percent whole wheat!" she called out. "With Valrhona seventy-four percent!"

Everyone reached for a cookie then. Even skinny Charlotte broke off a piece.

Helen sent us to refill our coffees while she finished tabulating our personality tests. As we left the room, Charlotte pulled on my arm. "Did you notice? The women all brought stuff—flowers, cookies, pastries, stationery—but the men brought nothing!"

Helen had chosen this particular "personality compass" for us, she said, because it was based on the Indigenous American medicine wheel and the four directions. *Norths* were warriors, who organized and led people, and our warriors were Charlotte and Jennie. *Souths* were healers, who loved and nurtured: Sam and Curtis. *Easts* were visionaries and artists, who saw the world in new ways: Riley and me. *Wests* were sages and teachers, who trained and enriched our minds: Adrian and Belinda.

"But, Helen . . ."—Jennie waved her hand—"in young leadership groups, I'm always an *East*! I'm totally an *East*! Dana or Riley should switch with me. I'm so not a *North*!"

"Everyone's a bit of everything," said Helen. "This exercise is designed to demonstrate some of the different ways people think and make decisions. So maybe you can be a *North* for us just for today." She squinted at her hand-book, then looked up. "But Jennie, you're a total *North*: decisive, independent, a fast worker, a leader!"

"Fine." Jennie's glance cut sideways, to see if we'd registered these virtues.

A person could probably be flattered into any category.

I suspected that Helen, rather than using actual guidelines, had strategically matched us to our nemeses: Charlotte, the true leader with her young challenger; Belinda, who knew everything about the AUUCC, with Curtis, who knew nothing; and Riley, the lover of handbell choirs, with me, loather of same.

Helen sent us off with a list of questions to ask each other. (How well did we fit our sign? What could our sign do for the group? What do other people say about us?) Riley and I chose a table in the pergola. "Not sure I'm so creative," he said. "When I compose, I just systematically try different combinations till I find something I like."

"Sounds like creating to me," I said.

His glasses were opaque with fingerprints. His knee jumped up and down. I stifled an urge to still and smooth him, clothes, hair, and tic. Younger, I might have been drawn to his lack of self-care: the man needed *tending*.

I fit the sign, I said, because as a writer, I was used to generating something from nothing. But I was hardly a visionary, though I had predicted this year's savory porridge craze. (Congee and savory oatmeal were every-where!)

As we raced through the questions, Riley kept hold of his phone.

I said, "Some people say that I'm critical and judgmental—and I am! I'm a critic. But people also say I can be a lot of fun . . ."

Ding!

"Sorry," Riley said, and started texting.

Had he paid attention to anything I'd said? I decided to test him. "Hey," I said. "Will you do our report to the group?"

"Sure," he said, and recommenced typing.

Around the courtyard, the other signs were deep in conversation. "Tell me," I said when his thumbs paused. "What got you interested in mixology?"

"I had this amazing cocktail and wanted to make it at home." He peeked at his phone before turning it over. "At first I used store-bought juice and it tasted like flat cherry Coke. So then I tried making my own juices." A quick check of his phone. "I liked doing that, so I moved into syrups, and then started fermenting stuff like liqueurs and brandies."

"And how did you get into handbells?" I said.

"I had bad OCD in college—" A winsome smile, and my first hint of the waiflike sweetness that must have beguiled Belinda. "And my therapist said I needed something to calm and focus me. I always loved the sound of bells . . ."

As if on cue, bell tones rang out. "Sorry again," he said and, turning aside, took the call. He was still whisper-hissing into the phone when Helen summoned us back inside.

Jennie presented for the *Norths*. As warriors, she said, she and Charlotte were pragmatic, direct, and fast. So fast, they'd answered all the questions in a minute, long before the rest of us. "We'll probably get impatient with all you slowpokes!

"Joking!" she added.

Belinda said that she and Adrian, as sages, would no doubt drive the *Norths* nuts. "My husband always claimed I ask too many questions and

want too much information. 'Just this once, Belly,' he'd say, 'make an educated guess!'"

Belly! Charlotte and I exchanged a bright glance.

Curtis, handsome and resort-ready in shorts and a drapey white linen
T-shirt, reported that people often said that he and Sam were "nice guys."
"And we're a little like healers because we like to calm other people—and
that's how we calm ourselves."

Riley said, "I'm not creative like Dana—she's the real deal. People say
she can be critical—but hey, she's a food critic—and they also say that she's
lots of fun . . ."

He'd listened!

After lunch, we had half an hour free. I left a message for Jack. "Still
alive," I said, then lay down on my narrow nun bed and slept ferociously for
twenty minutes.

As we reconvened, Helen gave us half an hour to write about our most
satisfying experience at church. Outside, I wrote under a wisteria arbor:

> I loved going to church on Christmas Eve for Sparlo's ten-thirty "mid-
> night" service. At the door, we were given a new candle, unlit, with a little
> paper skirt to catch future drips. As the service began, the sanctuary
> doors were closed and all the lights turned off—and I mean *all* the lights.
> We sat in a dense, velvety blackness for what seemed like an age, but was
> probably two minutes. We couldn't even see one another's faces. Yet
> that darkness was alive. Breathing. Full of expectation. I wept from the
> moment the lights went out—many did—so here we were, weeping si-
> lently in the darkest time of the year. Then the rear doors opened, and
> we stood. The choir, holding lit candles, came in singing "O Come All Ye
> Faithful." They lit the candles of the people sitting at the end of each row,
> and the light was passed person to person until we were in a candlelit

hall, the ceiling and corners all lost in an ancient, glowing darkness, like the dark background of Rembrandt paintings. Into the absolute darkness, so dense and full of human longing, the light had come.

After Sparlo left, the interim minister moved the Christmas service an hour earlier, and then Tom Fox moved it to 8:00 p.m. Both ministers turned off only some lights, so the barely dimmed room never inspired the ancient awe that Sparlo had so skillfully stage-managed. I'd stopped attending years ago.

Belinda's most satisfying experience at church was her son's memorial service. Adrian's was last year's Juneteenth picnic, with the blues trio, the visiting Muslim congregation, the halal barbecue, and everyone dancing on the grass. Predictably, Riley's most satisfying moment was when the bell choir performed his arrangement of "Ode to Joy," the very halting, excruciating, and endless performance that inspired my bell choir boycott. Sam read:

> When Justin Ramsay was hit on his bike and in a wheelchair for a year, he couldn't go to school without a companion who could lift him. I volunteered on his hired companion's day off. Justin wasn't happy having this old guy around, and could get pretty mouthy, but in the end we grew very close. He's in med school in San Diego now, so when we go to see our son and grandkids there, we always have a meal with Justin, too.

Even I was moved.

In the next few hours we wrote a mission statement and did a series of dumb group-building exercises like constructing a "cathedral" from stuff you'd normally use to make a kite. We called out what we loved about the

AUUCC (the community, the gardens, its sturdy staff and finances) and what we wanted to change (the ugly sanctuary, the older white demographic, "a sometimes ponderous traditionalism").

"I'd like to see a high school student on the board," said Jennie.

"I'd like more ways to meet people," said Riley.

Curtis said, "And don't you think there could be more, I don't know, religion?"

We all stared at him.

"What?" he said "It is a church, and Rev Tom is a great guy. But I keep waiting to hear, you know, about God and Jesus and what we're supposed to believe in."

"But Curtis, that's exactly what you'll never hear at the AUUCC," Charlotte said. "We don't push any dogma, doctrine, or creed. It's even fine that you're a Trinitarian."

"I'm a what?"

"A Trinitarian. You believe in the Trinity, the father, son, and holy spirit."

"And you guys don't?"

"We're *Uni*tarians. That means that we believe in one god."

He looked around a little wildly. "So you *do* believe in God?"

He had us there.

Jennie said, "Not me. But nobody's stopping you."

Charlotte said, "At any rate, nobody will ever tell you what to believe."

"Really?" said Curtis. "Huh. Okay, then. Never? What if I'd like to be told? I mean, isn't that why you go to church? To be told what to believe?"

Next, we called out what we liked about Tom Fox (good preacher, worked hard for people of color, didn't try to be a big star, good sense of humor); then what we'd like the next minister to be (female, a great preacher, inspired in social justice work).

"Sermons with more spiritual depth and intellectual content," said Charlotte.

"Someone with an efficient, organized management style," said Belinda.

"Maybe we need novelty," I said. "Novelty in the theological sense—something altogether new, sui generis, that we can't even imagine yet."

"Perhaps we should be careful what we wish for," Belinda said.

The more specific we were about what we wanted, Helen said, the better chance we'd find a good fit. "And beware," she said, "of ministers looking to pre-retire at a smaller church in sunny SoCal. With only a few working years left, they won't care so much if the fit's not great."

At five, Helen gave us an assignment due in the morning. "Write about what brought you to church and what has kept you there over time. Dig deep on this one."

Before we left the room, Sam made an announcement. "We fellows are hosting a cocktail hour at six-thirty in the library, if you ladies care to join."

The men had brought something after all: liquor.

In my austere little cell, propped up in bed by one flat pillow, I wrote:

My mother died suddenly when I was thirty-one and within a month my seventy-year-old father was dating. Within four months, he'd sold the tree farm he and my mom had bought to retire to and moved to Phoenix to live with a chilly, jealous woman named Joanne. I phoned, but rarely heard from him. My brother had married and settled in Georgetown. That left me in Altadena grieving, without family. During this time, I wandered into the AUUCC. Sorrow brought me, but Sparlo's preaching and the acceptance and affection of other members—and the gardens!—kept me coming back.

The gardens take me into a quieter, dustier, older California. I walk the dog and donkeys there, where I sit in the courtyard with the wide round fountain and watch the sky reflected in the water as the donks weed between the stepping-stones and Bunchie keeps the squirrels in the trees. Vera (the church secretary) keeps a bag of carrots in the Arroyo House's fridge for the donks, so now they run up to her. Bunchie, never to be out-done, has also developed a taste for carrots.

When I'm stymied, troubled, or sad, I go to that sun-warmed stone bench where my soul—subdued by deadlines, to-do lists, by my inces-sant inner chatter—unfurls and stretches like a cat. Should I never enter the sanctuary again, I'd always find succor in our leaf-littered paths and courtyards. The old deodars and oaks are like calm, noble parents. I al-ways leave feeling new. Just driving by the property, my soul stirs.

I met Belinda coming out of her room and together we walked across the courtyard to the library. "They put us in there for our cocktail hour because the other group on retreat is from Alcoholics Anonymous," Belinda said. "Makes one feel rather naughty."

Riley had set up a bar: corked laboratory beakers of syrups, liqueurs, and bitters; a plastic bucket of supersize ice cubes; and a printed menu:

The Michael Servetus: habanero-steeped tequila, lime, Seville orange liqueur, and smoked salt

The Trinitarian: pomegranate, huckleberry, and plum brandies with soda and fresh fruits

The Mary Oliver: white wine spritzer with fennel ferns and ginger bitters

The Carrie Nation (NA): huckleberry and plum syrups, cream, soda water, and fresh fruits

I looked around for Helen, but she had gone home, so I claimed a deep armchair with bald armrests, my legal pad on my lap. A Trinitarian went down like soda pop, with slices of cold plum at the bottom.

"I can't believe you're still taking minutes, Dana," said Jennie.

"Riley's drinks are too clever not to mention in my next newsletter post."

Someone sat on my chair arm. Adrian. He leaned over to read my legal pad and pressed against my shoulder. "It says here 'Jennie Ross is a beautiful, badass aro ace.'"

"It does not," said Jennie. "Let me see! Dana doesn't even know what that means. Does she? Really?"

I smiled slyly and slid the notepad into my big leather purse.

Charlotte asked Sam how his hand was.

"Hot. I'm a little afraid to look at it."

"Let's have a peek," she said. Unwrapped, you could see the teeth marks, black-red crescents, but no streaks. "Nobody's going to urgent care before dinner," Charlotte said.

"In that case, I'll try a Trinitarian, please!" said Sam.

Belinda, queenly in another armchair, held up her glowing orange Michael Servetus, named for the brilliant sixteenth-century father of Unitarianism whom John Calvin burned at the stake. "Riley, this is delicious and downright scorching!"

"'Scorching'—that's the perfect word," said Jennie. "Put that in the minutes, Dana. Say that Riley's Michael Servetus cocktail is 'scorching.'"

We joined the buffet line behind the AAers, a women's group from Glendale. Charlotte knew some of them from meetings and lively, laughing greetings were exchanged while the rest of us deliberated between wan chicken breasts and tilapia fillets. We carried our plates to the seminar room—as we had wine, we were again exiled from the AAers, whose frequent bursts of raucous laughter carried across the patio. "Makes you wonder what they were like when they were drinking!" said Belinda.

"I like your friend Helen," Adrian said quietly, taking the chair beside me.

"Except I haven't heard from her for, like, sixteen years." The bitterness in my tone surprised even me. "She dumped me and a lot of other people after she quit ministry."

"I remember in Soul Circle, you used to say losing a friend 'is one of the great, under-reported tragedies of adult life.' So true."

"It is," I said. "In every small church group I've ever led, someone talks about a friendship that ended and how blindsided and grief-stricken they were, and then everyone chimes in with their stories. It's as if they were all waiting for the chance to talk it out. But you must get that in your work."

"A little," Adrian said. "Were you glad to see Helen anyway?"

"Oddly, I *was* glad," I said. "But with a big bass note of caution."

"So maybe you'll be friends again."

"It could never be as full-blown as it was," I said. "Or as innocent. We were incredibly, intensely close for four years."

"Hard to maintain any relationship at such a pitch," Adrian said.

I regarded a forkful of balsamic-stained lettuce. "True." I'd long understood that the more intensely a friendship burned, the more likely it was to end. My later-in-life friendships—especially my friendships when married—were never as close and intense as those I'd had when younger and single. Jack was so companionable, so cozy, the sharp hunger for more than a few close friends had dulled, mostly. I did hanker for a lively coconspirator on the search. I eyed Adrian: him?

Seeing one another in sleepwear, I suppose, was to heighten familiarity. So after dinner we duly changed and met again in the library for what Helen's agenda dubbed "Pajamarama and a Movie."

Enough! I thought. Enough with these engineered intimacies!

I wore an Indian block-print "nightie," sufficiently dress-like to wear in public. Making a paper cup of instant cocoa, refusing a dollop of brandy, I sat for a few minutes of *The Philadelphia Story*. Adrian, in a purple velour tracksuit, again perched on my chair arm as Jimmy Stewart and Katharine Hepburn bantered manically. "Witty, amusing conversation is a lost art," Adrian said. "I wish people still talked like that."

"They never did," I said.

"If this is what y'all consider witty, then yawn!" Jennie—still in her cut-offs and tank top—stood, dropped her cup in the trash, and left the room.

"I'll try not to take that personally." Adrian said.

The cocktails and the wine at dinner had made me muzzy; I was the next to fold. I phoned Jack to say good night and then, between intermittent bursts of laughter from the AA women, and men, somewhere, singing old standbys—"Goodnight Irene," "Danny Boy"—in raggedy barbershop harmony, I found my way to sleep.

Jennie was not at breakfast. Nor was her red Fit in the parking lot. In the seminar room, Helen had lit the chalice and given a short speech about not focusing on one kind of minister—a man, a woman, a person of color, or someone within a certain age range—when the person who most needed to hear this slipped in.

Her bright turquoise shift dress barely skimmed the tops of her sunflowered thighs. We older females exchanged looks of wonder that a plump young woman would wear so little in public, let alone to a church retreat. (Still, having spent most of my young adulthood believing myself unlovable for the extra five pounds I carried, I found her in-your-face-weight refreshing, liberating, even sexy.)

"Sorry, sorry," Jennie said, dumping her large straw bag on the table. "Eric couldn't get Jaz down last night, so I had to dash home."

"You might have told someone," Charlotte said. "We were getting concerned."

"But I brought supplies." Out came a sack of those chocolate chip cookies.

Helen laid out our fall agenda: we'd conduct a survey, we'd lead "cottage groups" with church members about the search. We'd receive anti-oppression training and create a "packet." As recording secretary, I'd write newsletter squibs to keep the congregation informed of our progress.

Clearly, my vision of the search committee as a series of intense theological discussions was a chimera! We wouldn't even meet our first applicant till mid-January!

"Before we check out," Helen said, "who'll read their journaling assignment?"

"I didn't know we had to share it," said Riley.

"You were assigned to write it," said Helen. "Reading it is optional only because we're a little pressed for time. Are you volunteering?"

"Can't," Riley said. "I forgot to do it."

"He sang all his cares away," said Sam.

"I forgot too," said Jennie. "After I got called home."

"That was you guys singing last night?" I said to the men. "You're not bad."

"Between you men and the rowdy sober drunks, it's a wonder anyone got any sleep," said Charlotte.

Helen waited for us to quiet down. "Anybody want to read?"

Silence. I didn't want to be the only one and kept quiet.

Curtis picked up his journal. "I'll go."

My family is Evangelical Christian.

I used to go to First Calvary in Glendale because my aunties go there. First Cal's small, but very loud and friendly, even if they don't like how you live your life. My family all know I'm gay and support me though they think I would be happier straight. When Mark and I got married, I asked Rev Alario to do the wedding with Rev Tom, but he doesn't believe in gay marriage. Some of the ladies pooled together anyway and gave us Tupperware and a big rice cooker for wedding presents.

When we had Max, my aunties held a baby shower. The ladies from First Cal came and gave us baby presents. When we lost our second baby, I was so sad, Rev Alario called for a healing prayer circle for me after church. Everyone made a circle around me and put their hands on me. They went around, praying for the baby's soul to go to God. They went around again, telling me how with Jesus's help I could stop choosing the path of sin. Then it was how God was punishing me for breaking His laws and if I married a woman, I could have many beautiful children. They shouted, "Satan, let him go!" and "God forgive him, take back your prodigal son." I am ashamed now that I didn't say anything. I let them go on and on, though it hurt so much. I even thanked them for their prayers. I kept telling myself, They know not what they do.

When I got home, I couldn't stop crying, so Mark asked Rev Tom to come over. Rev Tom said that losing our child was not a punishment and miscarriages happen for medical reasons. He was so kind and nonjudgy, I decided to come to your church and left First Cal. I have felt so accepted, especially here, on this committee, which is such an honor to be on. I am so thankful for all of you.

When he finished, nobody else offered to read. Outside, the heat shimmered off the patio. Inside, Curtis's story hung in the air like a banner.

Adrian said, "Oh man. So glad you found us." And we all echoed, "Yes, so glad."

Checkout was quick.

"Sorry I had to go home," said Jennie.

"Great time," said Curtis. "I love all you guys."

Sam said, "Thanks for keeping an eye on my bite."

"Loved singing with you all," said Adrian.

"A good start," said Charlotte. "And we love you, too, Curtis."

"Me too, Curtis," I said. "So fun to see everyone's pajamas."

"You've done beautiful work this weekend," Helen said. "Good luck with your search." And out went the chalice.

10

꙳

A Love Match

I'd packed up and was leaving my little cell when Helen came to the
door. "Are you in a rush? Shall we take a short walk? The grounds
here are so pretty."

In a long, sleeveless, full-skirted white dress, she looked like a tall, old-
fashioned girl. "Sure," I said.

She waited in the courtyard while I put my tote in the car and texted
Jack.

"How're you feeling about the search?" she asked as I joined her.

"This morning I had the mad hope that Jennie had left us for good," I
said.

"I knew she'd be back," Helen said. "She's in with both feet. You'd quit
long before she ever would."

This stopped me. "What makes you say that?"

"Jennie has an agenda. You're still equivocating. I watched you observing, taking notes. Hugging the sidelines. Not sure if this is your milieu—
just like you were in seminary: never sure if you should be a minister or a
writer, so not committing to either."

"I still wonder if I made the right choice," I said. "But am I really that
obvious?"

"I see it," Helen said, "because I have my own ambivalence."

"I have to say, I was pretty surprised to see you back in with the UUs."

"I know, right? I can't believe it myself."

We walked through a parterre herb garden and into an oak glen where we turned down a fire road shaded by dark, thick branches. Helen had been the most idealistic, energetic new minister, but her small, toxic first congregation beat the starch out of her. I knew every detail of her struggle because she'd called me nightly—we were both single back then—to hash out her problems with the board and one malcontent member after another.

"I never gave up my UU affiliation," she said. "I knew better than to burn all my bridges. Even after I started my psychotherapy practice, I stayed on call at the Santa Barbara retreat center, moonlighting there when they needed me. Around four years ago, they asked if I'd run a district meeting of UU ministers. I knew a lot of the attendees, of course, and on the last day a group of them staged an intervention of sorts, insisting there must be something I could do in the denomination. And there was: to process my failed ministry, I'd written my MSW thesis on how different religions settle their clergy, so I knew a lot about ministerial settlement. Someone hooked me up with the UU Transitions office and I've been a search consultant ever since—and for other denominations, too. In my therapy practice, I sit for thirty hours a week; this consulting work gets me out of that damn chair! I just finished a yearlong contract with the Methodists."

"I thought Methodist bishops just decided which minister went where."

"There's a process. First, the churches and ministers each have to figure out if they want a change or not, then they let their district supervisors know. Once a year, the bishop and supervisors get together and work out who should go where; it's like a giant puzzle, or a mass arranged marriage. I was hired to help the churches discern their needs and work more effectively with their supervisors." She pointed to a bench with a view of the San Fernando Valley grid. "Shall we?"

We sat. "If the Methodists have arranged marriages," I said, "what would you say the UUs have—love matches?"

"Love matches based on a very brief courtship."

"And which method do you think is more effective?"

"Honestly? When professionals decide, it's cleaner. Search committees are amateurs, and apt to be dazzled by personality and lose track of what their church needs. Or they compromise on a third choice because the top two have polarized them: I want Minnie, you want Jim, so we'll settle for Harriet, whom nobody much likes."

"Neither way seems foolproof."

"Oh, occasionally a Methodist minister lands an odd appointment for a few years, but the bishop and supervisors genuinely want their clergy to be happy. Hey!" Helen bopped my arm. "You'll never guess who was at that district ministers' retreat and helped intervene me. Bert Share! Remember him?"

"Old BS? Of course!" I said. "How could I forget?"

Bert Share was one of the six UU students at our seminary twenty-two years ago. He was the only man and a very good-looking one. Deeply tanned, with crinkling eyes, coffee-brown hair, and a beard just alluringly shaggy, Bert was a year ahead of Helen and me, and he'd already served a small fellowship in Mendocino. (UUs can call anyone they want as a minister, ordained or not, UU or not; but clergy from outside the association doesn't get institutional support.) Eager to be official and serve an established (and more remunerative) church, Bert was getting his master of divinity degree. We five women thought him conceited and liked to torture-tease him, calling him BS and making endless stupid jokes about his name: *Would you like to Share?*, *Thank you for Sharing*, *Too much Sharing*, *Too much BS*, etc. He acted as if we were all in love with him and, like a bad boyfriend, he alternated between turning on the charm and being elusive. He'd grace our study group intermittently and always leave early as if we'd devour him if he lingered. (We might have.) My lasting image of Bert is of him backing out of a room—as if he dared not turn his back to us. How we'd laughed—but we could do so only because, despite his stuck-up, approach-avoidant behavior, he was a gifted, intelligent preacher and clearly going places.

"Same old Bert. Handsome, confident, flying high," said Helen. "He's at that big church in Philly now, head of his district ministers association, obviously aiming for the association presidency—though it's not such a clear shot for straight white guys these days. And . . ."—Helen lowered her voice—"one night on that retreat, when I was closing up the building, I saw him in the commons room with one of the seminary students. Female, of course. They were deep in conversation and awfully close. Nobody else was around. It was after midnight. They didn't see me, they were all wrapped up in talking. Maybe it was nothing. I never said anything to anyone. But you do hear things."

I said, stupidly, "I thought he was married."

"He was then. And is again, now." Helen pointed to my left hand. "You're married yourself."

"Eight years," I said.

"Congratulations! A love match, I hope?"

"Yes. But Jack's a smart, handsome Jewish lawyer," I said, "so I sometimes think my mom arranged it from the grave."

"Someone should have arranged my marriages," Helen said. "Not my parents, though, or I'd be an Orange County matron married to a yacht salesman."

"Have you married again?" I only knew about the one short marriage in her twenties to a jazz musician. Their breakup was what sent her to church, and from there to seminary.

"Married and divorced," she said. "I'll tell you the whole sad tale sometime. But you know me. There's always someone. Gus and I live a block apart in Oxnard by the water. He's a therapist, too. A Jungian. Maybe you and Jack will come spend a day at the beach with us."

"I'd like that," I said with some confusion. Were we really going to resume a friendship without acknowledging the sixteen-year gap?

The grid of streets below quavered in the hot air, with the Burbank airport to the east, the green Sepulveda wildlife preserve to the west, a ribbon of freeway connecting them.

"You know," Helen said, "I've read all your books. You don't mention church in any of them. I assumed you'd left it. So I was surprised to see you on this committee."

"I never stopped going to church. Though I'm a little sick of it lately. But I'm a little sick of everything—food writing, book promotion, restaurants.

I was stoked to be on the search committee, but so far it's not as compelling as I'd hoped."

"It will get more compelling. Trust me. Shall we?" She rose and we started walking back. "Every search committee I've worked with has been full of surprises. And you've got such an odd group. I love that Black therapist—what's his story?"

"Adrian?" A proprietary pang hit. Helen, as a therapist and spirited extrovert, was sure to interest him more than I ever could. "He's our president-in-waiting. Married to quite a successful actress—she's in that show, *Pandora's Hoax*?"

Helen shrugged; she'd never heard of it. "He's just darling," she said.

And when we got back to the center's courtyard, there he was, unlacing his running shoes at one of the concrete picnic tables. "Ladies!" he called. "I thought everyone had gone. I took a run in the neighborhood before it got too hot." He shoved his runners in a gym bag and slipped on blue canvas loafers. "So what does Madame Felicitator make," he said, looking up at Helen, "of our little committee?"

"It's not little enough," Helen said, sitting across from him. "Five or six people would be far more manageable. But Charlotte's super-sane and if anyone can hold your group together, she can. Belinda's a stable presence. And you two." She paused, thinking. "Riley seems sweet. What's his story—gay, right?"

Adrian, shrugging, turned to me.

"No idea," I said, and sat beside Helen.

Adrian said, "Would you consider it a successful retreat?"

"Time will tell," Helen said. "Eight's a tough number; too small to break into smaller groups, too unwieldy to unify in such a short time."

I said, "The kind of social engineering you do—the craft stuff and games, going around and around the room, getting people to talk or write—what's it supposed to accomplish?"

"I know how you hate that kind of thing, Dana," she said. "When I saw you were in the group, I almost revised my agenda on the spot. But some people reveal more about themselves in directed exercises than in years of casual conversation. You and I know how to talk; we even require intense conversation on a daily basis. Adrian, I assume you talk in depth for your work. But many—actually, most—people find our intensity of interest and focus and disclosure way too potent."

"Actually, I'm CBT," said Adrian. Seeing my confusion, he added, "Cognitive behavioral therapy. Can't say I hit the depths that much—no more than necessary!"

"You don't do long-term talk therapy?" I said.

"Not if I can help it! Give me an issue I can solve in ten weeks, preferably less. Far less! And I'd say some good information came from Helen's exercises."

"Maybe too much," said Helen.

"Like what?" I said.

"Like you have one official leader and one shadow leader," Helen said. "Charlotte will have to develop a strategy because Robert's Rules and a covenant won't contain that Jennie. She likes disruption. Adrian, what did you see?"

"I found it interesting that Charlotte cut a door into her cathedral wall, so people could get inside, and I made transparent windows, but Jennie and Curtis used big sheets of paper for their walls, no windows, no doors. And, Dana . . ." Adrian turned to me. "The look on your face when the whole thing popped apart . . . You were devastated!"

I'd helped to construct the flimsy frame. "Silly," I said, embarrassed.

"No! You cared! You were really invested. I was touched," he said.

Helen was laughing. "It's true, Dana, you did look horrified." She checked her watch. "Gosh, I actually have to get going."

We walked to the parking lot together. Helen promised—and made me promise—to keep in touch.

Once on the freeway, I thought what a relief it was to see Helen, as if a long-standing, needling splinter had been removed: she'd gone away and now she was back. And how easily we'd fallen into our old way of talking.

Could it be that easy? My mother used to say that with old friends "you just pick up where you left off."

I wished that my mother and I could pick up where we had left off. I understood her and her anxiety so much more now than I did when she was living. I like to think that, had she lived, we would've found our way to friendship.

She'd been a ballet dancer in her teens and danced professionally with the ABT until an injury at twenty ended that career. Sent to West Coast relatives for a change of scene, she lived in guest bedrooms and taught the odd class in small dance studios around town. A cousin brought her to a socialist meeting here in Altadena—on Charlotte's block of modernist homes, in fact—and there she met my father. They married six months later.

Once my brother and I were both in school, Mom finally went to college and became a notoriously strict high school French teacher. A hard grader. A rule enforcer.

She was strict and exacting at home, too. I was too sensitive and timid, she said, and too unkempt; my fine hair never took a curl, and even when chopped short as a boy's, it never stayed where combed. Worse yet, I was clumsy; I should be more aware of where my body was in space, she said. And I liked food too much. Far too much. I looked soft.

She herself ate meagerly; her chin and cheekbones, her shoulders and elbows were sharp angles, all.

Beginning when I was five or six we had terrible stand-offs in clothing stores. She was willing to buy me good clothes if and when we could agree on them. Her pastels and prints and frills seemed too bright, too obvious to me; and she disapproved of dark colors and solids on children. "I just want to pep you up!" she'd cry, and call me "a little brown bird." We compromised with stripes and mid-range solids. (To this day, my go-to uniform is a striped agnès b. T-shirt with the rustling poplin skirts I buy from a small designer in Paris whenever I'm there. Mom would not approve, though the fact that I have any fashion sense—however opposite to hers—must come from her.)

She was generous, though her generosity was always targeted. When I was in college, she'd slip me twenty or forty dollars with the command to replace a beloved vintage Toastmaster toaster or a prized, hand-pieced velvet quilt I'd found at a yard sale. She liked everything new. Antiques, she said, were "depressing." Often the cash came with the cry, "Do something with your hair!" Whenever I went home, she urged me to see Derek, her stylist; although he had never laid eyes on me, he had an idea what to do with my lank brown locks.

I made it a point never to lay eyes on him.

Mom found fault with my female friends—"Why doesn't she wear makeup?" . . . "So ill-mannered." . . . "What's with those gunnysack dresses?"—but she actively disliked my boyfriends. A painter was: "Not smart enough . . . He cuts meat with his fork! Doesn't he know how to use a knife?" Of a fellow journalism student: "His personality is like nothing, nothing . . ." A well-known, separated-not-yet-divorced ceramic artist I dated was "another one of your wounded birds . . ."

My majoring in journalism she endured as an undergraduate lark; she was proud of my early articles in the college paper, although my dark humor kept her from sharing them with her friends. But J school? Why not law school or a doctoral program that would make me a *professional*?

As you can see, I came by my own critical nature naturally.

And yet. I was connected to her as by a fine, live silver wire. I flinched when my father or brother snapped at her and worried when she reported upsets with friends. (She could dish it out, but she really couldn't take it.) When she and my dad retired and bought a tree farm near Escondido, I was afraid for her. *A tree farm?* So far from friends? What would she do all day? I wanted her somehow happier.

Once, as my twenties ended and I'd found neither a husband nor a staff journalism job, she took matters in hand. For my thirtieth birthday, she gave me a trip to New York with the caveat that I represent the family at a cousin's wedding in Newark; this was a male cousin my age, a chemical engineer, whom I hadn't seen since he and I were teens. Dropping me off at the airport, Mom said, "Wear your hair up. And use lots of spray so you don't get tendrils."

Tendrils—the bane of her bun-dos.

Apparently, she'd enlisted her sister, my aunt, who'd found a nice Jewish professional for me: one of the groomsmen, in fact, an anesthesiologist; he and I were seated together at the rehearsal dinner and again at the reception. A blond, aging frat boy in a tight gray suit, the anesthesiologist took in my vintage bronze silk sheath—so devoid of the lavish slits, tropical colors, and generous cleavage otherwise on display in the room—then offered me my choice from a palmful of pills (red capsules, green and white capsules, white tablets). When I demurred, he tossed all of them into his mouth and washed them down with prosecco. Joking loudly with his friends, he filled both my wine and water glasses to their brims with the pale wine and ate both our tasteless dinners. By dessert, he was in slow motion. He still managed to down three Courvoisiers and walk out of the place at a steady, magisterial pace. I expected to see him the worse for wear the next day, but this was a man who knew how to self-medicate; he was energetic and cheerful throughout the wedding ceremony and photos. As we sat down to dinner, he studied my silver qipao dress—so high-necked and modest in that crowd—tapped his nose, and invited me to the restroom. Again, I demurred. Off he went and never came back.

That night, I called from my hotel room to report on the wedding and right away my mother asked if I'd met the anesthesiologist and was there a spark.

Her death, less than a year later, at sixty from a long-undetected cancer, came fast, just weeks after the diagnosis. Concussed by the shock of it, I lost concentration for a year. In that time, I read exactly one book, *The Portrait of a Lady* by Henry James, and I started attending her church. As the months passed, a long-standing pressure began to ebb; my life grew roomier, easier, more open-ended. Some of that roominess came from the AUUCC, from Sparlo's sermons and the women there who drew me in.

11

A Very Busy Time

J ack and I went to Oaxaca for two weeks in August. We travel well together although he's a sightseer and can't pass up a museum or a temple, and I'm more interested in how people live, so I like to wander streets and markets, sit in parks and plazas, and chase down local food. With Jack I see more sights than I normally would; and with me Jack rambles more and eats more interesting things. In Oaxaca we climbed pyramids and ate clayudas, barbacoa, moles, and masa in many forms; we saw pre-Columbian art, read novels on park benches, and sampled smoky mescals—and I didn't have to write about any of it! Our one skirmish arose over some pottery I wanted. I couldn't get enough of its haunting acidic, algae-to-moss-green glaze. Jack, ever the environmental lawyer, had to google it. "Don't buy anything," he said. "It's full of lead."

"I don't care," I said. "We're old. It won't have time to kill us."

Jack, in fact, was looking quite young in his T-shirt and baseball cap. "You have a lot of mental acuity," he said. "I guess you could afford to lose some IQ points."

We compromised on flower vases.

I wish I'd bought the dishes anyway.

On the plane home, I looked up from my copy of *500 Spanish Verbs*. "I hope joining the search committee wasn't a big mistake," I said.

Jack looked up from his *New Yorker*. "Afraid it will take too much of your time?"

"More that it will be cheerless and lonely. If only there was one person I really clicked with . . . I love Charlotte. She can be sharp and funny. But she's not, I don't know, *chummy*. Adrian's possible, but he might be that person who's always so warm and charming but never actually becomes a friend."

"What about that woman you knew in seminary?"

"Helen? I wish. But she won't be at our regular meetings. We might talk some, though." I hoped this was true, but I was wary.

Jack and I read some more. He put a hand on my knee. "The search has already brought one old friend back to you," he said. "Who knows what else lies in store?"

Church started up after Labor Day. I was obliged to attend and wear a special blue name tag so that people would know that they could ask me about the search.

The bell choir played that first Sunday. Now that I knew that Tom Fox wasn't crazy about the bells, I amused myself by staring at him as they performed. From my seat, I could see around the pulpit to where he sat mansplayed and fidgety in an ornately carved throne chair. I stared, willing him to look at me. He lifted one eyebrow: a *Yes, I know they're tedious* look. I laughed. He glowered and set his jaw: his *You're annoying me* look, then smiled at his knees, trying not to laugh.

Because we'd let the summer slide by, the search committee had a lot to do. We agreed to meet alternately at Belinda's and Charlotte's houses— Belinda lived alone, so there was no one to inconvenience, and Charlotte's wife, Sheila, was "happy to be banished to the TV room." Adrian and I agreed to be backup hosts.

Our first task was to help Curtis with the survey. The boilerplate in the handbooks was way too long, so we edited, eliminating such questions as "On a scale of one to five, please rate the importance of the following to your spiritual life: Moses, Jesus, Buddha, Mohammed, Shiva" and "What best describes your view of immortality? Heaven, Ghosts, Angels, Reincarnation, Dust, None of the above."

I took the minutes. This, for example, is from our fourth meeting:

9/28 Belinda made roast cauliflower and mushroom lasagna. Adrian picked out mushrooms, sd: They are just weird. Fungus, you know? Riley sd he'd joined the search committee for Belinda's cooking. Me: How'd he know she'd be on search committee? Riley: Belinda's Ur-AUUCC, of course she'd be on.

Ch called meeting to order, lit chalice.

J read poem by Angelou. Week 3 minutes approved.

B demo-ed how to fold surveys (in 1/4ths for order of service, 1/3rds for mailings).

Discussed while folding: how people could fill out >1 survey.

B: Why would anyone want to?

J: To slant things a certain way?

Me: Like which way?

Sam: For a minister who wears robes.

Ch: Or the usual, to sell off the garden.

S: Good idea.

Me: WORST idea.

J: I'd do 20 surveys so we'd get a woman, except filling out even one is too boring.

B: That's why we'll be lucky to get even a 60% response.

When done folding, Ch produced mailing labels—to near rebellion—but it only took 15 minutes.

Checkout:

A: Another great night on the search committee.

6: Agreed.

J: Groan.

Jennie at the next meeting: "Did I really groan?"

"We have to be careful around Dana and her yellow legal pad," Adrian said. "Don't say anything you don't want in the public record."

Charlotte said, "Don't worry. The minutes are strictly confidential."

Guilt pang.

Afterward, Charlotte walked outside with me. "Of course the minutes can be subpoenaed in court," she said.

"Funny," I said. "Jack said that, too."

Riley's job was to set up the website for our packet. For content, committee members had to write short descriptions of themselves and seek out ephemera (photos, letters, clippings, memorial programs) that showcased the AUUCC in winning ways. Belinda sent in her best newsletter columns. I contributed two articles I'd published in the *Times*: one was about my writing group's bouillabaisse. (One person made the fish stock—the *bouilla*—and everyone else brought a pound of seafood—the *baisse*. Since we were UUs, no two people brought the same thing, making it "a delicious union of diversity.") The other article was about cooking with Amira and her Pakistani grandmother and included a recipe for the grandmother's lamb nihari that had been passed from mother to daughter for generations without ever being written down.

We set dates for four cottage meetings with two of us to lead each one. Charlotte nabbed Adrian as her co-facilitator and I got stuck with Riley again. To plan our meeting, I invited him to dinner on a restaurant review.

Minutes before I left to pick him up, he phoned and asked if his friend Eva could join us.

Fine, I said, if Eva didn't mind sitting in on our planning session.

Riley's apartment was across the street from the Altadena Sheriff Station and the celebrated one-hundred-and-fifty-year-old bay fig tree that now shaded the parking lot full of cruisers. The old tree's exposed roots looked like dozens of long, skeletal fingers clutching the earth.

I texted him and shortly Riley appeared with Eva, a tiny woman with short, curly blond hair. I recognized her from the bell choir. In a gray T-shirt, a flowered skirt, and clodhopper ankle boots that made her legs look impossibly thin, she clung to Riley as they crossed the street—if he was gay, I guess he didn't know it yet.

"Thanks for letting me tag along," she said, climbing into the back seat.

I'd chosen a new high-end Mexican place in Highland Park because their cocktails based on classic aguas frescas might interest Riley. I'd made the reservation in his name, for the sake of my anonymity. As we waited for the hostess to find him on her iPad, Eva cried out, "I was so jealous that Ri got to go on a *restaurant review*!" Hearing herself—or seeing the horror on my face—she clapped a hand over her mouth. The hostess, thank god, paid no attention.

Right away, we ordered the spiked aguas frescas. Riley approved. "Good ratcheting up of flavors," he said, singling out the nutmeg in Eva's bourbon-spiked horchata and the triple sec in his watermelon limeade tequila punch. My piña colada slush, laced with 180-proof rum, went down easily, and I began asking Eva questions I'd never ask Riley: how'd they met, how long they'd been together.

"Ri and Sal and I all played bells at the Palo Alto church," she said. "Sal and I were already together and we both fell madly in love with him, so we invited him in."

After graduating, they'd moved south together. Riley had his postdoc at Caltech, Eva was studying product design at ArtCenter, and Sal was at UCLA law school.

Riley was fidgeting—lifting and dropping and spinning his silverware.

"Have I met Sal?" I said.

"She's in the bell choir?" said Eva. "Chinese American? Long black hair?"

Yes—she'd been the expert player wanting to wrest the bells from the older woman who'd frozen during a performance. "Sal's our other," said Eva. "We're polys."

"Ahh," I said. "Polys?"

"Polyamorists!" she said.

Riley, burning pink along the rims of his ears and across his cheeks, met my eyes, gave a shy shrug, and smiled. The dawg.

I was interested, of course, and thrilled; I always need good hooks for my reviews, and instantly I started generating first lines: *The other night, at Casimiro, with two polyamorist friends . . . I was having dinner with the polyamorists when . . .* The word *polyamorist*, with all its frisson, was like a bright jewel plopped in my lap.

I said, "I've read that polyamory takes a lot of intense relationship talk."

"Oh god. We talk constantly! Everything goes right on the table." Eva gave our wood tabletop a hearty smack. Drinks jumped. "We discuss everything."

The constant texting and phone calls now made more sense.

The waiter came to take our order. We hadn't opened our menus.

"Order anything you want and as much as you want," I said, giving my usual instruction to first-time dining companions. "But no two of the same thing."

Riley frowned at the menu and jiggled. Eva said she didn't know what half the items were: chicken achiote, gorditas, huaraches. "Why don't you just order for me, Dana—I'll eat whatever you need me to."

"Me too," said Riley.

Had polyamory attracted or created such a willingness to go along with another's desires? I ordered appetizer-size tamales and taquitos; one watermelon and one cactus salad; chicken achiote, swordfish with black mole, and camarones habaneros.

"Oh my god—appetizers! Who gets to order appetizers? This is so much fun," said Eva. "It's like a dream—to order everything!"

A polyamorist's dream, indeed. "Do you all live together?" I asked.

"For three years now," said Eva. They shared two apartments. "Riley's made the upstairs one into his mad-scientist man cave, so we mostly hang out downstairs."

"I see," I said lamely. I'd also read that in polyamory there were finely differentiated types of sex—jealousy sex, makeup sex, reunion sex—and I was sure Eva would have cheerfully expounded on these and other aspects of multiple partner life, but Riley looked so uncomfortable—the whole table was a-jiggle—I checked myself. "And you're obviously open about being poly."

"Militantly so," said Eva. "Polyamory will be the next big battle for marriage equality. Poly families are actually more stable and healthy because more loving adults raise the kids. Why shouldn't we have equal status and protection under the law?"

"I can't think of a reason," I said. Having gulped my highly alcoholic slush, I now had a brain freeze. I was grateful when the miniature tamales and taquitos appeared.

"They look like doll food!" Eva cried.

Note taken.

Between bites of black mole and searing habanero-infused shrimp, Riley and I planned our cottage group: we'd hand out short ad-like "character profiles" of fictional ministers for attendees to vote on. After the first vote, we'd add complications to each profile. (A brilliant preacher, for example, might not be so interested in political activism, say, or have no social graces . . .) We'd each write two of these profiles. I'd write about 1) a brilliant Black preacher (who, it would turn out, was not gifted in office management); and 2) a sturdy experienced woman preacher devoted to social justice (who was more Christian and conservative than the AUUCC might tolerate).

Riley would profile a writer of exceptional sermons (who, it would be revealed, preached in a deadly monotone) and an exceptionally talented and charismatic young minister (who had been let go by his last church for anger issues, for which he'd refused to get help).

Later, dropping off the young couple, I watched them clutch each other as they walked to their door. Making a life with one other person, I thought, was both gratifying and complex enough for me; even the thought of adding someone else to our domestic arrangement made me anxious.

Jack, predictably, was at his desk staring at a screen of legal writing—I now recognized the format. "I just had dinner with two polyamorists—they live with a third. You have to be young and barely formed and not so set in your ways to do that. I mean, like, who of all the people we know would be *remotely* imaginable as our third?"

Jack swiveled in his chair to look at me. He has warm brown eyes, curly black hair wired in white, and lovely lips. "There is no good answer to that question," he said. When I opened my mouth to speak again, he added, "Or to any subsequent question in that line of inquiry."

My restaurant review, when published a few weeks later, concluded with: *With so many dishes here to love, Casimiro makes polyamorist eaters of us all.*

Sam and Belinda held the first cottage meeting fifteen minutes after church got out; thirty-four people attended. (As recording secretary, it was my job to count.) They handed out blank index cards for attendees to write questions for the prospective ministers. These cards were collected and read aloud. Afterward, I cadged them from Charlotte ("for the record"). Here's a selection:

- What if a registered sex offender asked to attend your church?
- Should the church install charging-station spaces for plug-in cars? Should we absorb the cost to encourage others to buy low-emission vehicles?
- The pastoral care team visits sick and homebound members, but when big donors get sick, the minister visits them. Should money really reap special treatment and access to the minister?
- Dog or God—Which is your copilot?

I was walking out when Adrian caught up with me. "Some of those questions made me crazy," he said. "That electric car one!"

"I didn't mind that," I said. But then Jack drove a plug-in.

Adrian stopped where the path split. "Dana, can I pick your brain sometime? I have a writing project and I could use some tips—like how to get started!" He laughed his rich laugh and bumped my shoulder. "Can I take you out for coffee sometime?"

Along with the pleasure of his attention arose a familiar irritation: how is it that so many people think, because you're a writer, you're on tap to assist in their amateur efforts? At the same time, an image bloomed of Café de Leche's patio at the foot of our steep, violet-colored mountains—and the two of us at a bistro table, heads almost touching, chattering away. "Anytime!" I said.

Charlotte and Adrian's cottage group took place on a Tuesday afternoon, attracting retirees and other homebodies. I'd had to finish a restaurant review, so I dashed in just as the attendees broke into small groups to compose want ads for a new minister. I got my hands on those index cards, too.

A group of three older men wrote:

> **WANTED:** A minister of unimpeachable character and superior intellect to join a long line of illustrious predecessors known for superb preaching and sound church management . . .

Together, two older retired women and a stay-at-home mom wrote:

> Healthy, midsized congregation in beautiful Altadena ISO a riveting, inspiring preacher who is also an approachable, loving, and wise spiritual adviser. You are warm, collaborative, present, and committed to lifelong religious education. . . .

Eighty-eight-year-old Marilyn Esterby wrote her own ad:

> **WANTED:** A minister who can laugh, preach like the devil, and choose hymns people can actually sing. At memorial services, this minister knows how to shut people up when they go on too long telling boring stories supposedly about the deceased but really all about themselves. This minister will kiss an old lady on the lips when she turns 90, and every year after that.

Riley called the night before our cottage meeting to say that he hadn't gotten around to writing his ads yet. "We're in a crisis over here."

"Is everyone all right?"

"We're negotiating new ground rules and some issues have come up."

I resisted prying. "I hope you guys work it out."

"Me too."

Our cottage meeting was Thursday at 7:00 p.m. in the Rourke Chapel. Twenty-one people showed up, but not Riley. Luckily, Charlotte, Adrian, and Sam were on hand; one more time, we explained how the search process worked, then I passed out Xeroxed profiles of my fictional ministers.

> Warm, second-career male minister (first-career nurse), 11 years' experience, a "destination" preacher with a deep commitment to diversity, social action, and spiritual growth. The AUUCC has long been my dream church due to its vigor and stability, the beauty of its grounds, and integrated Altadena. I am Black, married for 38 years with 3 grown children, in no hurry to retire. Hobbies: gardening, painting, conversation.

> Female senior minister; 17 years' experience. Present church thriving: my work there feels done. Preaching is a dialogue and I'm ready for a new interlocutor. Together let's grow our souls

and fight the good fight against poverty, racism, homophobia, transphobia, and other injustice. Warm and direct, I work (and play) well with others. Friends say I have a "delicious" sense of humor and a "rich, calm voice." White, divorced, with one grown daughter, two dogs, and a cockatoo, I enjoy Pilates, hiking, decorating cakes.

In a quick, first-impressions vote, fourteen voted for the man, seven for the capable female social activist. "Anyone want to explain their vote?" I said.

"The guy's it. Great preaching all the way."

"Love that he loves the AUUCC in particular."

"He sounds so down-to-earth, easygoing. Approachable."

"More likable, even just from the little description you gave us."

"But most of you just said you wanted a woman," I said. "So why not this one?"

"She seems sort of desperate—looking for a new life after her divorce."

"What exactly is an interlocutor? Why use such a strange word?"

"She comes off as, I don't know, self-aggrandizing."

Charlotte, I saw, was pale with anger.

I then revealed the "second tier" about these ministers—information that we would have received through their packets, references, and visits.

The Black male minister was sixty-two, only three years younger than Tom Fox! He had no experience serving a church our size—and his staff reported that he was disorganized (one of his references said, "A great, great guy without an organizational bone in his body") and chronically late, even on Sunday mornings.

"We've also been told," I said, "to watch out for ministers who want to pre-retire in California. They might not be as concerned about a good fit since they're only going to be around for a few years. As it happens, one of the reasons this minister knows about the AUUCC is that his son and grandkids live here in Altadena."

Assuming that she would be the favorite, I'd originally planned to reveal that the capable female minister was a theist who believed in a Christian God, which would have made her problematic for our more secular congregation. Instead, thinking on my feet, I tried to make her irresistible:

"This minister doubled the size of her last congregation," I said. "If we want to grow, she will make it happen. She's only fifty, she's deep into social action, focusing on homelessness and racial justice. This year, she's marched for immigrant rights in Washington, joined protests at the Dakota Access pipeline. Internationally, she's literally stood shoulder to shoulder marching for peace with Nelson Mandela and the Dalai Lama . . ."

A second vote yielded twelve votes for the man, nine for the woman.

Even five women didn't vote for the woman! "Just out of curiosity," I said, "why didn't most of you women vote for the woman, who's both younger and frankly, more accomplished, experienced, and organized than the man who mostly wants to hang out with his grandkids here in Altadena?"

"She doesn't sound stable—divorced, running all over the world."

"He just sounds, I don't know, more fun."

"Of course he'd want to live near his grandkids—what's wrong with that?"

"I'm sure he'd draw more people of color from the neighborhood."

"Actually," Adrian said, "the race of the minister has been shown to have little if any effect on the demographics of their congregation . . ."

"She just sounds too dry."

Adrian helped straighten up when it was over. "That was a little tough," he said.

"I don't quite know what to make of it," I said, carrying folding chairs to the closet. "They say they want a woman and more social justice, and I give them someone who's almost too good to be true—I only threw in the divorce to make her human—and they prefer some fiery old grandpa who can't find today's mail on his messy desk."

"You did come down pretty hard on that poor old Black guy." Adrian grinned.

"I made him up! He's an invention. And it's clear I wasn't hard enough!"

I shut the closet doors. "It's the deep misogyny in the women I find so alarming. They hold women to a much higher standard."

"An impossible standard," said Adrian.

"So who would you vote for?"

"Me? Well, you know me. As much as I admire your organized, globe-trotting divorcée, I'd have to cast my lot with Grandpa."

I skipped Curtis and Jennie's cottage meeting with the RE folks where they asked for letters to the new minister. One letter, written by a young girl, would go in our packet.

Dear Next Minister,

I am 10 years old and starting fifth grade. I have come to the AUUCC every Sunday of my life. I have learned the 7 UU principles, and now the world religions.

I am sad our minister Tom is leaving. My favorite thing he did was at the spring carnival. He put on flowery pants and got the rest of his body painted with flowers and made his white hair green. He looked like a wild jungle man and he danced all around for the kids. Everyone died laughing.

I hope you like being painted with flowers.

Our big garden is full of secret hiding places. If you want, I can show you some.

Yours,
Sandi Katzenbach

12

Beyond Categorical Thinking

AUUCCers! Get those surveys IN!! So far, only 81 surveys have
come in, a 44% response. Let's push for 100%!

UU headquarters required search committees to undergo anti-oppression
training "to promote inclusivity and discourage undue discrimination in
the search process." This meant a Saturday morning workshop. The whole
church was invited.

"I took that training during the search for Tom Fox," said Sam. "Since
then, we've hired, you know, what's her name? The associate minister? Isn't
she Muslim or at least Arab? And the RE director is lesbian, right? And the
events person, too? Charlotte here was president—and the one before Charlotte, Jennie's mom, was Japanese! And Adrian's coming up. We have half a
dozen committees dealing with race stuff. And all those potlucks with that
mosque? What more does headquarters want?"

"Apparently, ministers in search check to see if a church has done this
training," Charlotte said. "It tells them that we're open to self-examination
and can talk frankly about our biases. Also, Sam," she went on, "pointing
out that we've already hired and elected Blacks, people of color, and gay
people makes it sound like we've satisfied some quota and don't need to look
at other diversity candidates."

"Who said anything about a quota?" said Sam. "I'm just saying that we're obviously already open to diversity."

"Then let's impress the workshop facilitator and all the prospective ministers with our openness," said Charlotte.

"And my mom's Japanese American," Jennie said. "She's as American as you."

"I never said she wasn't."

"You said she was Japanese. She's an American citizen. By birth."

"Oh for god's sake. I've known your mom since before you were born."

"At any rate," Charlotte said, "we've got to do this training and who knows, we might learn something."

"I hope so," said Sam. "Because I obviously have no idea how to talk about these things. Every time I open my mouth, I get in trouble."

"I feel the same way," said Adrian.

On a Saturday morning in late September, the search committee duly clustered in the first two rows in the small Rourke Chapel, with thirty-odd congregants joining us. Our facilitator, Lecia Castillo-McClean, was a tall, young, stylish woman who introduced herself as "second-gen Dominican American." She wore lettuce-green cat-eye glasses and the tips of her shoulder-length brown hair were dyed hot pink.

We filled out questionnaires that asked if we had any concerns about hiring gay or disabled people, people of a certain age or class or gender identity, or people of different ethnicities and races—basically anyone who wasn't white, straight, able-bodied, and between forty and sixty years old.

"Excuse me!" Jennie said, waving her hand. "I have concerns about hiring yet another white male minister. Why isn't there a box I can check for that?"

Lecia, collecting the questionnaires, said they'd be compared with the results collected ten years ago during the search for Tom Fox. "Congregations and search committees often have subtle, even unconscious biases that can keep them from hiring the best possible minister," she said. "I'm here to make those biases conscious, so they won't mess with your search."

For example, she went on, one search committee was determined to hire a person of color and called a Black minister whose beliefs were very much in sync with their church. That minister, however, chose another church. So the search committee offered the job to their second choice, an Asian American woman—never mind that she was quiet, shy, and theologically more conservative than the congregation. Her ministry didn't last a year. The committee's third choice, an extroverted, straight white woman who shared the congregation's secular theology, would have been a better match.

"If you're too focused on a specific category, you could overlook the best hire for your needs. Our goal is to get beyond thinking in categories to see the whole person."

We broke into small groups, each representing a different category of the oppressed and marginalized, and were told to imagine how life might be different if we were one of them. "Use your own life experiences," said Lecia.

After five fast minutes, she called us back together and asked the gender group, "How would your lives have been different if you were the other sex?" The women said that as men, they'd be more ambitious, less focused on relationships, and wear more comfortable shoes. The men said that they'd have a richer emotional life as women and better relations with their kids. Curtis said that he would be happier as a woman because he'd always wanted to carry a beautiful purse. "A Birkin bag!"

Some people laughed—not meanly. "I'm not kidding!" he cried.

From our race and ethnicity group, a woman named Andrea said, "If I was a different color, I might have struggled to get a decent education."

Sam said, "If Black or Brown, I probably would've gone to prison."

Lecia took a deep breath. "Again, we have to make sure we're not unconsciously harboring stereotypes in selecting a minister. Do we assume a minister of color would have had a poorer education or a criminal record? Would these preconceptions, rather than a person's actual history, taint our preferences?"

"Excuse me." Sam waved his hand. "I wasn't saying all Black and Brown people go to prison—although a disproportionate number are incarcerated," he said. "I was speaking from my own experience, like you asked us to. I was busted for pot in college, but my folks made one phone call and got me released. If I'd been Brown or Black, it probably wouldn't have been so easy."

"Thank you, Sam," Lecia said. "You have taken a stereotype and shown how it arises directly from white privilege and the white supremacist justice system."

"I have?" Sam said.

Andrea now waved her hand. "Excuse me," she called. "I'd also like to clarify my response! When I was in high school, my best friend was Mexican American and couldn't get into AP classes. . . ."

Lecia cut her off. "These exercises bring up a lot of feelings, and I hope they will start many fruitful discussions to come," she said. "But given how little time we have, we must press on. Before we talk about how our life would be different if we were other-abled, I should say that there are no deaf or blind ministers, no para- or quadriplegics among our ministers. So we're talking about less extreme disabilities, like wearing a hearing aid, or being in recovery from an addiction, or having a chronic condition like diabetes, Crohn's disease, migraines, or depression. Many ministers with these conditions have experienced difficulty being hired."

"So even at thirty-two years sober, I'm disabled?" Charlotte whispered to me.

"Who isn't differently abled to some degree?" said Belinda. "You might as well add age to the disability list since everyone over fifty-five has at least one chronic condition. And everyone over sixty has five or more."

Charlotte, in my ear: "Just shoot me."

"There is a bias against ministers over sixty," said Lecia, "and under forty. And there's fear that a recovering alcoholic might drink again or a minister treated for depression might have a recurrence. But you could reject a minister who admits to decades of sobriety in favor of one who quietly drinks a bottle of wine every night."

Sparlo had drunk a bottle of wine at dinner—and that wine came after cocktails (plural!) and before postprandial brandies. Nobody ever called Sparlo an alcoholic—or disabled. Or impaired. They said, "Sparlo enjoys good wine." Sparlo himself said—in jest, or so I hoped—that addiction isn't a problem so long as you have a reliable supply of the necessary substance.

By noon, we were tired and restless—and hungry.

Lecia ended the workshop with interviewing tips that would prevent us from offending our applicants. She said, "LGBTQI, other-abled, and BIPOC ministers report that they're often asked if they'll preach a lot about their identity. Other-abled people are asked if such a demanding job won't fatigue them. Gay ministers are asked if they'll focus on gay rights. Yet who ever asks a white, straight, able-bodied minister if they're only going to talk about white, straight, able-bodied issues?"

Asking such identity-related questions, Lecia went on, was a dead give-away that we hadn't done this anti-oppression work—which might cause our ideal minister to lose interest in our church. Better, she said, to frame questions so they could be asked of anyone. *Most ministers have an overriding theme in their preaching: what's yours? How does your identity inform your ministry? How do you take care of yourself and set limits?*

Ministers in search would not only check to see if we'd done this workshop, Lecia said, but also how many members participated and if the session went well.

Adrian, in his sly, humorous voice, said, "How're we racking up, Leesh?"

"Not bad," said Lecia. "According to the questionnaires, you're where you were ten years ago: some issues persist around hiring trans people and the other-abled."

Jennie raised her hand. "To be clear, are you saying that after one hundred and twenty-six years of straight white male ministry we can't specifically seek out a woman or a person of color?"

"Don't limit yourselves to one facet of any candidate. That mixed-race woman who *looks* perfect for the job"—Lecia gave a little curtsy—"might not have the management chops or the pastoral gifts you want. Insist on the skills and qualities you need and not *just* the category of a person."

· ᥣᐣ ·

Ｔhat was *somewhat* clarifying," Charlotte said as she, Belinda, and I walked out into the early afternoon. "I've probably allowed too much talk about hiring a woman when we should be focusing on the skill set we need."

"I like her interviewing tips," said Belinda. "We should go over them again so there won't be any big gaffes when we start talking to ministers."

"We can go over them ad nauseam," Charlotte said. "But given our crew, I'll be surprised if we don't send more than one poor minister screaming into the night."

Ｏn Monday afternoon, I was transplanting lettuce starts in a raised bed when my phone lit up with Helen Harland's name. "A patient just canceled," she said, "so I have a free hour. I've been thinking about you and thought I'd call."

"Uh-oh," I said. "What were you thinking?"

"I was thinking about twenty years ago, and how badly we both wanted to do something meaningful with our lives, and how we both thought ministry was the way. And now neither one of us serves a church, but we've cobbled together these idiosyncratic, very meaningful lives."

Mine wasn't feeling so meaningful at the moment.

"I was thinking about you, too," I said. "We had anti-oppression training and the leader reminded us of how every minister has a theme in preaching. I was thinking how yours was *Include everybody!* and Lucy Strong's was *A better way to think about this.*"

"Yes! And Bert Share's was *How to be intelligently religious.* And yours . . . Yours was *How do we live in this world?* And it's still there, in all your books, again and again, using food and gardening as a lens: how can we feel at home in the world, how do we live fully in our own skins?" Helen's voice rose. "I never forgot, Dana, how you used to say, 'You're as spiritual as you are comfortable being alive.' And in *Yard to Table* you write about life with your garden and animals with such reverence, care, and humor!"

Is that what my books were about? In the writing, I struggled so much down among the sentences, I never stepped back for the grand overview.

"Well, I don't feel so at home in my life right now," I muttered.

"What's going on? Things okay with Jack?"

"They're fine. Great, in fact. But as Freud says, it's love *and* work that give meaning to life, and it's the *work part* that's bugging me. I'm just sick of writing about what I put in my mouth! And all the stupid roundups and listicles I have to do. I get this way after every book—postpartum-ish—when I'm thrown back on my day job. Itchy. Dissatisfied. And remorseful that I actually have spent my life writing puff journalism. This time's worse than usual. When I'm not writing my own books, the food writing seems so . . . inconsequential."

"Not to your readers," said Helen. "How's your meditation practice?"

"What meditation practice?"

"Any prayer? Any volunteer work? Charlotte says you were very active."

"I was. Now I take my garden produce to the soup kitchen. And there's the search." In fact, I had let a lot of things go—facilitating Soul Circles, all my writing and cooking classes, mentoring interns at the *Times*. "Some of it's being married," I went on. "I don't busy myself as strenuously as when I was single. I'm too happy staying at home, watching Ernst Lubitsch movies with Jack. Or reading with pets in our laps. And then writing this last book was so time-consuming on top of my job, I couldn't volunteer for stuff. But now that it's done, I feel empty and adrift."

"Any ideas for your next book?"

Helen might be a friend, but she was also our official search consultant, sent from headquarters; no way I'd confess to cannibalizing the search for a book. "Not really."

"So you're really betwixt and between," she said. "I sympathize. After my second marriage failed, I was uncomfortable and irritable for a year. Then I started this consulting work, and met Gus, and life filled up and got interesting again."

"That's hopeful." Glad to steer the subject away from myself, I said. "So what did happen with your second marriage, if you don't mind my asking?"

"Oh, gosh, no. I met Frank at a professional training session maybe nine years ago. He was the trainer. A brilliant, big guy, full of love and joy. We moved in together after six months and a year later we married. On our honeymoon in Costa Rica, he jumped too early off a zip line and herniated two disks. For the next three years, it was all doctor appointments and pain. Epidurals, a failed laminectomy, acupuncture, massage—nothing gave him relief—except meds, which he ate like M&M's. This was a guy who might have had half a glass of wine with dinner, and that only on weekends, and before my eyes, he went from this brilliant, loving psychotherapist to a self-obsessed, verbally abusive drug addict. If you recall, my first husband was a junkie, but high he was a sweet, blathering love bug. Frank turned mean.

"He went to rehab, but when he got out, he faced years of pain management. He couldn't do it. The fentanyl won. My concern oppressed him, he said. He wanted to medicate himself without a witness. By the time we split, I was relieved. But I worry: both my husbands wound up addicts. Do I drive men to drugs?" Helen gave a short laugh. "I'm always surprised by the patterns that surface in our lives."

"We're so old now," I said, "that we can actually see the patterns. It's a little terrifying."

"And isn't it all so interesting?"

With a sharpness that was almost a pain, I recalled how, in phone call after late-night phone call so many years ago, as Helen's first ministry failed and I struggled to write a second book, we'd reminded each other that life, in fact, was interesting, endlessly so; an adventure to be observed and intricately discussed. In this way, we encouraged each other—gave each other the courage—to keep going.

But then she went off on a meditation retreat never to be heard from until now.

I returned to transplanting lettuce: an oakleaf named Oscarde, a romaine named Dragoon, a butterhead named Nancy. I pressed soft black soil around the roots of the tender, four-inch seedlings. How easy and natural talking to Helen was, but were we really going to act as if nothing had happened, as if I hadn't been bewildered and bereft when she stopped returning my calls and letters? I'd bored my therapist on the subject. I'd read essays and books about broken friendships: dumpers who were relieved to be free from worn-out relationships; dumpees who exuded pain and bafflement at the cut; and everyone justifying themselves. Could Helen and I resume a friendship without acknowledging a sixteen-year hiatus—or how hurt I'd been?

Her preaching theme, indeed, her modus operandi, might have been *Include all!*—she was always dragging some person she'd just met to our lunches and meetings and events—but how abruptly and thoroughly she'd excluded me.

I've never lacked friends, but Helen was my only close friend from seminary, my one dependable, cackling companion through those months of classes and difficult decisions, and for a few years afterward. I understood that she associated me with her painful ministry, but I'd still felt abandoned and bewildered and missed her.

The air was warm, but the breeze carried an autumnal chill. The glossy all-black male cat watched me from a few feet away. Bunchie snorted under some bushes after lizards. I now had bright rows of fragile, lacy lettuce starts. From the barn area came the soft chuckle of the hens in their yard, the occasional hoof stamp of a donk in the corral. How do we live in this world where friends disappear for years and years and reappear as if nothing has happened?

Bunchie ran to the house. I heard a door open. Jack, home early for a change. I stood, brushed the dirt from my knees, and went, gratefully, to greet him.

13

༓

A Plot

Your search committee has been hard at work.

    We recently completed anti-oppression training, and now we're compiling data for our Congregational Record (think of it is as our initial "dating profile") and for our packet (the more in-depth self-portrait) that we'll swap with job applicants. If you have any marvelous photographs or intriguing documents of AUUCC life, please send them to adrianj@––.com.

Since we'd begun meeting in the first week of September, Jennie had attended only half the meetings. Her husband, a nurse, was pulling night shifts, and her mother, Vergie, who had promised to watch Jasmine, had become unavailable. Whenever Jennie missed a meeting, she'd call me the moment I got home and demand the minutes even before I'd typed them into my computer. "And don't forget, you promised to take me on a restaurant review!"

We spent several meetings collating the survey results. We ended up with a sixty-six percent response and no surprises: AUUCC members prioritized preaching, strong leadership and management, professional-level music, and social justice programming.

Belinda announced that she had secured four pulpits for Sundays in February and March where our "pre-candidates" would preach; if we only selected three pre-candidates, we'd have to find a speaker for the fourth. "Perhaps you'd like to dust off your preaching skills, Dana," she said.

Though pleased, I said, "Oh dear god, let there be four pre-candidates."

In early October, the days were still hot. I'd walked in a warm twilight to Belinda's. After the meeting, Adrian offered me a lift home.

"It's only four blocks," I said, climbing into his silver Volvo.

"That was good and short," he said about the meeting.

"Yeah, because our disrupter was absent."

"Jennie? That's just the brashness of youth. You've got to love her."

"No I don't. Turn here," I said at the corner. "And then there was Sam and his salary sheet. Did he have to go over every line? I wanted to yell 'Sam, we can read!'"

"I appreciated his breakdown. Who wants to get excited about a minister, then find out we can't afford them?"

"I guess." We'd reached the foot of my driveway. "This is good. I'll walk up."

Adrian pulled to the curb. "But—quickly, Dana. Do you have a minute? I bought your book and was wondering if you'd sign it."

Be still my heart. "Of course."

He reached under the seat and produced a copy of *Yard to Table* sheathed in a stiff plastic bag. He handed me a rollerball pen.

For Adrian,
A boon companion on The Search
Laughter will see us through!
Your Friend, Dana P.

"I can't imagine how you do it." He slid the book back into its casing. "I've got this pilot I'm trying to write for Jill. But just seeing the computer, I freeze up."

I told him what I tell students, when I have them: Set a timer and write for twenty minutes a day. "You'd be surprised what you can get done in twenty minutes."

"That's what I tell my depressed patients. Set a timer for as long as you can bear it—two minutes, six minutes—and clean the kitchen till the buzzer goes off."

"Same principle," I said. "What's the pilot about, can you say?"

"Sorry. We've got to keep a lid on it so no one beats us to the networks. But I'd love to pick your brain about process; let's have that coffee soon."

"Anytime," I said.

I dawdled up the driveway, pleased that he'd bought my book, amused and a little miffed that he kept his pilot a secret. Whose idea is so precious?

Secrets work on me like splinters. I like them *out*.

Jack was in his office at his computer watching a technical-looking video. I sat in his reading chair. Bunchie leapt onto my lap. Jack paused the video. "You all right?"

"I'm never going to have the trash-talking pal I need on this committee," I said.

"Not even what's-his-name—Adrian?"

"He's nice," I said. "But I can't get anywhere with him. What's that?" I pointed to his screen, a cartoon of chutes and cowlings and incomprehensible machinery.

"A video about a refinery explosion. Want to see?"

The animated simulation showed how first one valve, then another one didn't shut, so that a trickle of incoming fuel ran unimpeded to an ignition area and blew the place up. Windows blew out for one square mile.

"Wow," I said as Jack shut it off. "They should have run more tests to make sure their valves were working."

"They ran constant checks. But the whole system was too complicated. Too many things could go wrong at the same time. And they did."

This seemed like a metaphor for a lot of things, and as I lay in bed trying to sleep, I thought of how I'd work it into a sermon—just in case Belinda was serious and I'd be called to fill an empty pulpit.

❧

Around noon that Sunday, I sent Jennie a text inviting her to dinner at a new Greek place I was reviewing in Alhambra. By five, I still hadn't heard from her, so I sent an email invitation to the whole committee saying I'd take the first two respondents. Charlotte and Belinda replied instantaneously.

Jennie texted as we were driving to the restaurant. Her phone had fallen into Jaz's bath and she'd had it in rice all day, so she hadn't gotten my message. **Promise you'll take me next!**

Ikaria was a small mom-and-pop place in a new mini-mall near the car dealerships. Black-and-white photographs of Greek ruins and coastlines hung on the walls. The wooden chairs and wobbly Formica-topped tables were such as you see stacked to the rafters in the used-equipment section of restaurant-supply stores. The place was almost empty.

"I haven't had Greek food since I was a student," Charlotte said, "unless you count a gyro off a cart by the courthouse."

As a young wife, Belinda had spent summers in a house on Patmos, she said, and certain dishes—moussaka, Greek salads, and eggs scrambled with tomatoes, oregano, and garlic—were mainstays in her repertoire. "Not that I ever make them for myself."

A gawky teenage boy with big black curls handed us menus then backed away from the table. On offer were the usual Greek café dishes. I positioned my notebook on my lap and gave my standard instructions: whatever you want, but no duplications . . .

"So here we are," said Charlotte as we put our menus aside. "The backbone."

"I'm flattered you include me," I said, "since you two are the power-houses."

"Actually, Dana," said Charlotte, "I was thinking about you and the presidency. Your name came up a few years ago. Tom Fox was supposed to sound you out then about putting you in the chute."

I couldn't remember Tom saying anything about the chute. "I vaguely recall he once asked if I was interested in church government. It never occurred to me—till now—that he might've been feeling me out for the presidency. He was so offhand."

Charlotte said, "Tom, effective as usual."

"You're young," said Belinda. "You could be president whenever you want."

I guess to an eighty-four-year-old, fifty-four is young.

Over and above how flattered I felt, came an internal flash: *Don't even think about it!* "Let's see how this ding dang search goes first," I said.

The teenager approached again and set his pen to a pale green pad. So far, he had not spoken one word to us. For the table, I ordered saganaki, flaming cheese, three individual spanakopita, and an order of tiny lamb meatballs with tzatziki. When he went to the cook's window, we heard him say, "Mama, they want the fire cheese . . ."

"What unites the three of us," Belinda said, "is that we're Sparlo's vintage. We know what it's like to have a truly exceptional minister."

"Yes," I said. "And we've never really forgiven Tom for not being him."

"Tom's done a very good job," said Belinda.

"Adequate," said Charlotte. "Barely."

"We just happen to know what a truly inspired ministry looks like," Belinda said. "Most people never see it. In that sense, Sparlo spoiled us."

"It's impressive that you're still a fan after being his secretary for so long," I said.

"Sparlo and I understood each other. We both did our work and allowed other people to do theirs. Sparlo set the tone; he made us know that we could be a generous, healthy, well-run institution regardless of who was minister. Tom's both more and less controlling than that. He's a little lazy, so he likes that the church can mostly run itself, but he also likes and needs to be top dog."

"Yes, and he has a real fear of factions forming against him," said Charlotte. "And maybe he should, because he does make enemies."

"Sparlo had his detractors," said Belinda. "Someone was always furious with him. But he was gleeful about it. He loved adversaries. They energized him. He took his job seriously, but he had much more of a sporting approach to it than Tom does."

"Tom isn't as clever," Charlotte said. "Like when he fired Carol Granger as RE director? God knows, it was long overdue; she ran off teachers as fast as we recruited them."

"I was never exactly sure what happened there," I said.

"Everyone agreed Carol had to go. Tom's idea was to make the director-ship a paid staff position for a minister with a DRE degree and replace Carol that way."

"Smart," I said.

"Except Tom assumed that once the position was professionalized, Carol would bow out gracefully," said Charlotte. "Instead, she hit the roof and began to rally people to her side. It could have become a real problem except that her replacement was so superior, the outrage died away. But Carol never got over it; she and Tim cut their pledge by two-thirds and these days they only show up at memorial services."

"Now, Sparlo," said Belinda, "Sparlo would have found Carol another job—put her on some denominational task force or curriculum develop-ment team, and made it seem like an honor. He'd have lured her into the new position before replacing her—he loved playing a long game. Tom's mistake was not giving Carol something else to do."

The teenager brought us a small white plate with a square slab of white cheese doused in a clear liquor. He used a lighter and after several tries flames leapt up, surely singeing the hair on his fingers, then died down to a cool, stovetop blue before going out, leaving the cheese prettily browned and crisp. I wrote, *Saganaki—scary but fun.*

"Oh!" I said. "I forgot about the booze, Charlotte. That was insensitive of me."

"It's all burned off," she said. "Besides, if I'm going to blow thirty-two years of sobriety and get drunk, it won't be on flaming Greek cheese!"

We scooped it onto warm, puffy pita bread. "If I closed my eyes, I could be in Patmos right now," said Belinda.

A bowl of cunning little meatballs appeared with its snow-white yogurt and fish-egg dip. Another plate held three plump, golden triangular spinach pies.

Belinda watched me take a note on my lap. "I've been meaning to tell you, Dana," she said, "your minutes are the most entertaining I've ever read."

"Hey thanks," I said, moved as ever by her praise.

"I hope you're saving them. They'll be an important historical document."

"Yeah," said Charlotte. "You could call it *The True Life Adventures of a Misbegotten Search Committee.*"

"Good title," I said. Then the imp in me added, "Maybe I'll make them a book."

"I'd read that book," said Belinda.

"Hardly a bestseller," Charlotte said. "A committee of eight church people meet once a week for a year. Two are problematic—"

"Just two?" I said.

"So far. Jennie's out of hand. And Curtis! He's a darling and he tries, but he knows nothing about the AUUCC."

"He's getting quite the crash course," I said.

"A search committee is not the place to learn about a church," said Belinda. "And not much gets through to him."

"Except what Jennie says," Charlotte said. "They both have to go. We'll have a much more effective team once they're off."

I became still. "Off? You mean, like, off the committee?"

"Off the committee."

"Off the committee?" I said again, marveling. "Are you serious?"

"Don't look so shocked." Charlotte spun a meatball on its toothpick. "Jennie's absent half the time and when she's there, she confronts me at every step. It's okay to miss two meetings out of five, but she's missed four out of the last six—not counting the night she left the retreat. Her absences, her authority issues, and her disruptiveness, and Curtis's ignorance are all liabilities."

"Isn't it an ordeal to kick someone off?" I asked.

"The chair, the church president, and the executive committee need to authorize it," Belinda said. "That shouldn't be hard."

"Still." I dunked a meatball into the white tzatziki. "It seems like such a public punishment. Like putting someone in the stocks."

"We'd let her say she resigned because she couldn't make the meetings. New motherhood and all."

"Vergie won't be happy," I said, "after all the money she and Ed paid to get Jennie chosen."

Charlotte and Belinda exchanged a look. "Don't know how you heard about that," Charlotte said. "The money might have helped put Jennie on the committee, but it hasn't helped her to show up. Or behave."

Belinda said, "The bylaws are perfectly clear: she needs to go."

"You guys are tough," I said.

"Welcome to the pragmatic side of church," Belinda said. "Pragmatism was Sparlo's specialty. He knew you had to shoot predators on sight."

"Would you really class Curtis or Jennie as a predator?" I said. "I have as many issues with Riley, who's never done a single thing he said he would."

"He's just busy," Belinda said. "But he's an adult, and he understands how a church runs. We've had long talks about it."

"Really?" I said. "Long talks?"

"He drives me to church and sometimes, afterward, we'll talk in front of my house for an hour—or till I offer him lunch."

"Do you know about his two partners?"

"I know about his roommates."

Charlotte and I exchanged a look.

"Anyway," Charlotte said, "Jennie and Curtis should never have been chosen. Arne was bribed by Vergie, then swayed by Curtis being Brown and gay and lovable."

"He is all that," I said.

"Curtis spent the last decade at an Evangelical church with no idea of how *that* place was run!" said Belinda. "A church has staff? Gosh, what a surprise! He's probably the least qualified member of a search committee in the whole denomination."

"He did a good job on the survey," I said weakly.

"With our help, he put out an adequate boilerplate," Charlotte said. "But his idea for our next minister is a thundering Bible thumper."

I didn't blame Curtis for coming to what was nominally a Protestant church and expecting to hear about the Bible. I'd also had to adjust to the AUUCC's staunch secularism. Having been drawn there to grieve my mother, I would have loved some divine reassurance, but during my very first visit Sparlo said, "There are no answers, only the eternal questions," and I remember thinking, Damn, one more time, nobody's offering any certainty. (Not that I would've believed it if they had.)

"According to Riley," said Belinda, "Jennie already has some hot young minister she's determined to push on us."

I bit into a little spinach pie, shattering the crust and sending pastry flakes all over my lap and notepad.

"None of the young people knows how to be part of a committee," Charlotte said. "They're basically unchurched. I'm most afraid of a failed search—so much time and money and effort wasted."

"I'm sure," I said, "there'll be one minister we all like. Excellence has a way of surfacing." I was thinking how when the city's restaurant critics are all reviewing the same new restaurant, we often single out the same dish. "I like to believe there's an objective measure."

"I'd like to believe that, too," said Belinda.

The teenager cleared our appetizer plates with terrified care, then as cautiously delivered our entrees one by one: moussaka for me, a lamb kebab on pilaf sprinkled with fresh mint and crumbled feta cheese for Belinda, a small, whole striped bass, pan-fried to a golden brown, on fresh spinach for Charlotte. *Rustic, alluring presentation,* I wrote on my lap, *on thick white china.*

We were silent, focused, eating. *Flavors vivid and sturdy, like the best home cooking.*

"Sorry," I said after a few minutes, and nudged my plate toward Charlotte on my right, "but we have to rotate now." Belinda's lamb came to me.

I did think that the search committee would be better off without Jennie and Curtis, but I didn't want blood on my hands. "I'd hate to see Curtis or Jennie publicly humiliated," I said, "and I don't see a way around that."

"Jennie will squawk," said Belinda. "But Curtis will be fine. Technically, he's on by mistake. He's not a member. He's pledged, but he hasn't officially joined. The bylaws state that only members in good standing can serve on a search committee."

Charlotte gazed with dismay at the green oil seeping out of the moussaka then preemptively pushed it to Belinda and took the lamb from me, tidying up the rice and meat chunks before tasting them. "We'll tell Curtis a mistake was made and we're very sorry, but the bylaws are clear and objections have come in."

"Have there been objections?"

"As we speak." Belinda tasted the moussaka. "Very authentic."

"Curtis loves this church," I said. "It's been a real refuge for him."

"He's still welcome. He just doesn't get a privilege historically awarded to long-term, deeply involved members," said Belinda.

"I'd still feel bad for them," I said.

"We're not murdering them, for god's sake," said Belinda. "Though then you could make your book a murder mystery. *The Case of the Church Search Committee.*"

Yes, I thought for a mad moment, a murder! And all of us credible suspects!

But then, I realized, my book—this book—was already a mystery and not even its author knew the outcome.

"Of course, Vergie could make a big stink," said Charlotte.

"Again, we have the bylaws on our side," Belinda said. "And Vergie can't really complain after promising to babysit, then not."

"We'll wait till late December to make our move," Charlotte said, "so we won't get stuck with any of Arne's alternates. A committee of six is far more manageable."

Helen Harland had said the same thing.

The teenager nervously cleared our plates, the silverware clattering. *Service charmingly inept*, I wrote.

He brought out cups of gritty sweet coffee, three diamonds of baklava, and shots of arak—none of which we'd ordered. Belinda and I raised our shot classes, Charlotte her coffee. "To the committee!"

I felt like an equivocal Stalinist on the eve of a purge.

14

❧

Our Dating Profile

In Belinda's dark Craftsman, we drank Riley's cocktails, then ate Belinda's impeccable entrées: roast vegetable lasagna, chicken piccata, shrimp and grits, roast pork with prunes.

"This pork is amazing," said Jennie, present for the first time in weeks. "But I move that from now on, we don't have red meat or pork—not because I'm vegetarian but because those farming practices are so bad for the environment."

In fact, I didn't cook pork or red meat at home (except for brisket at Passover) for precisely Jennie's reason. As a restaurant critic, I ate—or at least tasted—everything. And as a guest, I'd taken the no-asshole pledge and ate whatever my hosts put on the table, though I drew the line at eel. (Some things are too ugly to eat.)

Murmured protests came from the meat-and-potato contingent (Charlotte, Belinda, Sam, and Adrian), but even they agreed that we could stick to chicken and fish.

"And only fish on the safe lists—low-mercury, sustainably farmed," said Jennie.

Adrian said, "Best quit while you're ahead, Jen."

Week after week, we checked in. Witty, Charlotte's kitten, now a feisty adolescent, caught his first lizard. Belinda's French group had moved to *In Search of Lost Time*, five pages a week: "Proust'll see me out," she said. Riley was adapting a Beethoven sonata for the bells. Adrian ran to Echo

Mountain every morning, shaving seconds off his time. Sam recounted life with his demented mother-in-law: "It's like living with a banshee." And I dreaded the holidays and all that extra food coverage.

Curtis's parents were still visiting, his house was full of aunties and food, which was stressful: "I am gaining!" His mother sent us her version of a buko pie—the sweet custard dense with coconut cream—and we understood his predicament.

I walked to the meetings and Adrian drove me home. I walked, in part, so that he could drive me home. We'd talk for a few minutes at the end of my driveway, sometimes about the search, although he would not gossip and did not find Jennie and Curtis as ridiculous as I did. I teased him, "How's the secret pilot?" to which he'd moan with the pain of not yet getting down a word.

"I saw your friend Helen at a Jung Institute lecture," he said one night. "Not the kind of thing I normally go in for, but a colleague invited me. Helen said that you two are talking again. I was glad to hear it."

I was touched that he cared about our tattered old friendship. "It's weird how easily she and I picked up again," I said. "Though we haven't talked about *it*."

The sixteen years of silence.

"You will when the time's right. You two have a special connection."

I wondered if he and I had a special connection.

Charlotte asked me to write the ministerial profile—a description of our ideal minister—for the Congregational Record, which the transitions director at headquarters would use to steer "good fits" our way. Despite spending a whole day on it, my end result read like every boilerplate in the handbook. What church didn't want a superb preacher with a lively intellect and a contagious sense of humor? Who didn't want a warm presence with a progressive social conscience, the management skills of a corporate CEO, and the work-life boundaries of a New Age life coach?

. ❧ .

Later that week, I had lunch with Tom Fox at a boreg bakery in Glendale. The cheese-filled pastry squares—a close relative to the Greek spinach pie—had come molten hot from the oven and we were waiting for them to cool.

"Word's out that I'm leaving," Tom said, "so I'm getting calls from my possible replacements."

"Anybody good?"

"Sure. And some not so good. Some who just want to move to California, at least till they find out how little the hefty-looking housing allowance actually buys around here."

I expected Tom to ask more about the search—I was dying to know more about those calls and if he'd caught rumors of a search committee shake-up—but he and Pat had just been to San Antonio to check out neighborhoods and find a real estate agent and that's what he wanted to talk about. "Private acreage or country club is our first decision," he said and, between bites of the now-edible boregs, he showed me listings on his phone of massive new homes.

The boregs' golden, flaky, house-made layered pastry was thicker than commercial phyllo dough, and more taut, so that each bite entailed a slight resistance before the burst of soft, salty sheep's milk cheese.

At some point, Tom lamented that none of his sons were coming home until Christmas and on impulse I invited him and Pat to Thanksgiving dinner at our house.

"I'd love it," he said. "Let me check with her and get back to you."

When I confessed to Jack that I'd invited them—Jack and I normally consulted on holiday guest lists—he said, "That's fine. Want to ask anybody else? Maybe someone from your search committee?"

I mentally ran down the list: Riley had his two young women; the others had their partners; I thought of asking Belinda, then remembered her son in Santa Monica. "Just Tom and Pat," I said.

"Okay. So I'll invite Lidia and Trixie." Jack's rabbi and her wife.

Thus was our religious détente preserved. Never mind that we'd now be cooking for twenty.

The time came for the search committee's online packet to take shape; it was due at headquarters for vetting by the first week of December. For weeks, Riley had been saying that the website was "ready to go live." Adrian had a date with him to add content and asked if I'd come along to write captions and proofread text.

"Maybe you two will be search committee pals after all," said Jack.

"He lacks an essential snark," I said. "But maybe."

I arrived early outside the polyamorists' apartment, so I sat in my car admiring the old bay fig tree and how in the deepening dusk its exposed roots looked like a deeply pleated skirt. Adrian's silver station wagon pulled in front of me. His white shirt glowed in the streetlight. "Dana P!" he called.

Crossing the street, I muttered, "I don't expect Riley's done much."

"Or anything," said Adrian.

The apartment block was prettily situated down a series of steps in a grove of oak and eucalyptus trees. Adrian pressed the buzzer. "Ready, pardner?" He nudged my arm. "We're goin' in."

Riley opened the door and, leading us inside, he gathered stray socks, tees, and sweatshirts. "Eva said she'd pick up today, but she got stuck at school."

The decor was basic bachelor squalor—webbed lawn chairs, cinder block and plywood coffee table, sheet-covered sofa—except for a computer setup fit for a spaceship. On a boomerang-shaped desk, amid a clutter of laptops and hard drives, an Xbox, a scanner, a printer, an electronic keyboard, speakers, and other (to me, unidentifiable) hardware, the largest screen shimmered with a rain of code. Jack, I thought, would love the profusion of tech.

"I had a bad crash." Seated in his supersize brown leather desk chair, Riley looked small, a baseball in a catcher's mitt. "I can't find the site.

I've been trying all afternoon to get it back. Or I'll have to start from scratch."

"We don't have time for that," Adrian said. "The program I use for my work website is easy. We can set it up in no time."

"Those preset programs are too limited for what we need." Riley stared at cascading code. "I can't believe I lost the site. I had the whole thing in one folder and now the folder is just gone." His right leg hopped uncontrollably.

"Come on, Ri," said Adrian. "My program won't be as elegant as yours, but we'll get it up tonight and be done."

Riley said, "I had it on a thumb drive. Oh! Maybe it's in my car. Be right back."

The door closed and Adrian waved at all the stray paper, clothes, abandoned cereal bowls, and overall dishevelment. "The man needs a civilizing influence."

"He's got two girlfriends right downstairs," I said. "They're polyamorists."

"That so?" Adrian burst out with his great, deep, gratifying laugh. "Polys! No wonder the poor kid can't get anything done."

Voices came through the floor—male and female, the main tone: earnestness.

"I'm buying my program." Adrian slid into the giant chair. "Because you know and I know there is no website and never has been. I'll pay. Sam will reimburse me."

Adrian was entering his credit card number when Riley returned, Eva in tow.

"I heard you were here, Dana," she said. "I came up to get you guys some drinks."

After weak protests—"Not Square Space!"—Riley took back his chair and began choosing templates and adding links. The build-your-own-website program was child's play to him, and before long we had a home page with photographs that changed every five seconds, starting with a full sanctuary that looked very racially diverse (taken the day we'd invited a nearby Baptist church to our worship service); followed by Amira officiating at a lesbian wedding; then a pan-racial group of laughing kids eating cupcakes (same Baptist church visiting day); a shot of Arroyo House foregrounded by orange trees, with the snow-covered San Gabriel Mountains behind; and last, a yoga class in the new chapel, ten human triangles in a downward facing dog.

Not yet needed, I wandered into the kitchen where Eva was shoving boxes of sugary kids' cereal into a cupboard. "Sorry for the mess. Sal and Riley are big slobs."

"We don't care." On the counter, a spill of cantaloupe seeds seeped off a cutting board onto a stack of sheet music. "We just want to get the website up."

"I guess Riley blew that."

"We've figured something out," I said, then lowered my voice. "Is Riley just overworked? He didn't show up for our cottage meeting, either."

She ran water. "He promises lots of things, then forgets to follow through."

"That must be annoying to live with," I said.

"I've learned to work around it. I'm all 'I'll believe it when I see it, Ri.'"

In my twenties and early thirties, I'd worked around worse: boyfriends who were alcoholic, chronic liars, married. "You guys all doing okay?"

Eva stepped closer and whispered, "Sal wants to bring in this fantastic new guy and Riley's freaking. He likes being the only man, and he's not bi, so he's jealous."

"Who can blame him?"

"Jealousy's just fear of loss," Eva said airily. "And Riley's not losing anything—he's gaining another person to love, who already loves him."

"Not sure I could be that enlightened," I said. "But I'm an old fuddy-dud."

"Oh god, Dana, you're the most open, nonjudgy old person I've ever met."

"Thanks," I said, then weakly, "I'm not *that* old."

"Sal and I are Riley's first-ever girlfriends, so these feelings are new and hitting him hard," Eva whispered. "He's so brilliant—getting his PhD at twenty-five, and now this second big postdoc at Caltech. But he's kind of retarded emotionally."

"Hard to believe he's so accomplished if he can't keep his promises."

"He's got a super-developed sense of what he can get away with." Eva wiped her hands on a rumpled tea towel, then began to dry the glasses she'd washed. "Right now, he's got a lot going on at work. And here at home."

"Which makes you wonder why he took on the search committee."

"He wants to make sure the next minister likes bells. He wants to perform more and put on whole concerts. Bells are his passion. And mixing drinks."

"And you, I hope."

A sweet smile brought a dark flash to her eyes. She arranged the four highball glasses on a tray and pulled out a Mason jar of purple juice from the fridge. "He's been making Bloodhounds—blood orange juice and lemon-vanilla-steeped vodka."

"Make mine a virgin," I said. "We have a lot of work to do."

"Make mine a triple!" Adrian came into the kitchen. "Joking!" he added with perfect Jennie intonation. *Joh—king!* "I need some captions, Dana," he said and, touching my shoulder, murmured, "It's going to be a long night."

I promptly texted that to Jack.

Riley kept trying to tweak the DIY program to make it do more than it was designed to do. Adrian quietly pushed him onward. "Come on, Ri, let's not complicate things." Eva tidied up around us, refreshed our drinks; after eleven, Adrian and I let her dunk in a little vodka. Twice, Riley read a text on his phone, then went downstairs to talk to Sal. We didn't mind; we got more done when he was absent. I worked from a lawn chair, my head level with Adrian's elbow, where I smelled his sandalwood soap and fabric softener. By 1:00 a.m., Adrian said he could do the rest at home.

Outside, Adrian staggered comically into the street. "I'm beat to hell," he said. "That poor kid. A few times, I thought he'd jiggle his way through the roof. ADHD, OCD, and some lover's quarrel with those girls. I'm amazed he gets anything done."

"You were so good at keeping him focused," I said. "So patient."

"I didn't feel very patient." Adrian looked down the broad, empty, well-lit street, as if deciding how much to say to me. "I did tell him to come talk to me. Pro bono. I'd like to give him some tools to deal with that anxiety. Maybe send him for meds."

"That was nice of you," I said.

"We'll see if anything comes of it."

We exchanged an amused, rueful look.

"Good night, my friend," Adrian said, coming so close I had the mad thought that he was going to kiss me. A long moment passed, my mind a white blank, until I realized I was blocking his car door. "Oh. Sorry." Hot with embarrassment, I stepped away.

In the cab of my little pickup, I had to settle down. Was it embarrassment or the fear of a kiss that had me trembling? I consulted the great fig tree, its dark crown surging and ebbing in the cool gusts of a desert wind. Rolling down my window, I took a few deep breaths of that dry, bracing air, then hurried home to my sleeping husband.

Dana? You went to seminary, right?" This was Jennie, calling one morning.

"Twenty-odd years ago."

"Did you like it?"

"Loved every minute. One of the best things I've ever done."

"So how come you never became a minister?"

"I went to seminary because after years of trying I couldn't make a living by writing. Then, almost as soon as classes started, I was offered a job at the *Times*. Eventually, I decided to go with the thing I'd spent so many years trying to do."

"You would've been a great minister."

"I don't know," I said. "I'm not very politic or tolerant. People bug me."

"Really? You're so nice. Everybody likes you."

"Hardly. But thanks," I said. "Why, are you thinking of ministry?"

"When Jaz starts kindergarten, I plan to go back to school. It's either seminary or becoming a shrink."

I didn't know what to say. I envisioned going into my therapist's office and finding Jennie in her chair. Hair-raising.

"Dana? Did we get cut off?"

I said, "Have you talked to Adrian about being a therapist?"

"And you know what he said? He said that first I should go to one. And I told him, I've already had therapy."

Me, weakly, "You have?"

"In college. Student health gave it for free. But I'm leaning toward seminary anyway, because a minister gets to do counseling, too."

Again, I had to locate my voice. "You have some time to decide."

"I like to have a goal," said Jennie, "and get it done."

15

I Take on Jennie

Happy Halloween from your search committee! It has been a jam-packed fall and now the survey is done and we've had four lively cottage groups. We are presently preparing our packet, which is the website seen by those interested in becoming our next senior minister. Don't forget, if you have a favorite photograph or newsletter column or other revelatory AUUCC document you'd like us to include, send it in to adrianj@—-.com.

Can you believe that Jennie wants to be a therapist?" I said as Adrian pulled up to the foot of my driveway.

"Why shouldn't she?"

"Oh my god. Don't you think she's too immature and neurotic?"

"No more so than most students in your average MSW program."

The man would not gossip! And I twanged with shame for wanting him to.

He turned off the Volvo. "But guess what, Dana? Big news! I'm writing! I use a timer, like you said to, and I've written every day for a week."

"So the secret pilot has taken wing!"

He gazed at me solemnly. "I'll tell you what it's about because I desperately need guidance. But you have to swear not to tell a soul. Will you swear?"

I swore.

The pilot, he said, was based on a real-life resourceful Black madam who, in the wild cow town of 1870s Los Angeles, became a land baron. His wife, Jill, would star.

In fact, I'd read a recent article about this madam—in the *Times*, no less, which meant that every other aspiring screenwriter in LA was probably writing the same pilot. "Adrian," I said gently, "if you got that idea from the article in the paper, you won't be the only person developing it."

"Jill said that, too," he said. "But the storylines are all mine." The madam, he went on to explain—at length—along with her secret army of gorgeous, cunning sex workers, would fight corrupt politicians and gangsters to buy land. White land barons would try to divert water from the madam's land to theirs. And there'd be a romance between a reporter and a young sex worker.

"Sounds good," I said. But what did I know? I hardly watched television.

We were parked in front of a faux cemetery the neighbors had set up in their front yard for Halloween. While Adrian described the land grabs and brothel life in subsequent episodes, I made encouraging noises and let my mind wander amid the fake gravestones and skeletons crawling out of the ground.

"And you, Dana P?" he boomed, startling me back to the present. "You started a new book yet?"

"Not really," I said. "Still in the research stage."

Your meetings are running so late," Jack said as I climbed into bed.

"Not as late as you usually work." I had to dislodge Bunchie, who'd warmed my spot. "Actually, Adrian and I were chatting in the car."

"Was that nice?"

"He told me the whole plot of the TV script he's working on. In great detail."

Jack took my hand. "I had no idea he did that sort of thing. So he's a writer?"

"Um. Well. No."

Happy Thanksgiving from your search committee!

We are so excited to enter the next stage of our search and go live with our dating profile—I mean, our Congregational Record. (Want to read it? Pick up a copy in the Arroyo House office.) It's our first salvo to the ministers who might be interested in serving as our next senior minister. Those who like what they see will click on a link, which gives us access to their profile (or Ministerial Record). If and when the attraction is mutual, we'll swap packets to learn more about each other.

In the meantime: Cooks: brine your turkeys, roast—don't boil—your brussels sprouts. And please don't end a beautiful meal with a pale or soggy piecrust. Bakers, bake those pies till they're good and done!

Jack was coming home at seven, eating dinner, then working till midnight, and the swing into the holidays was crazy busy in the food section—though I mostly worked from home. I wrote a feature (with recipes) called "A Dozen Pies" as well as a long, reported piece about two heirloom turkey farmers. (Nobody wants to read the grim details of mass-production turkey farming the week before Thanksgiving.)

On the day itself, Jack and I abandoned our desks and together we cooked for twenty-one people.

I got my pies in first thing. Mincemeat (homemade, no meat) and pumpkin (yes, I use canned pumpkin). Then we sat down with our coffees and tore up two loaves of Jack's day-old pain au levain for the stuffing.

The two of us in our big new kitchen, working together, was like coming up for air. We talked about who in the family was coming for dinner (one of his sisters, two of his cousins, their families) and who was not (our brothers, both of whom lived on the opposite coast; our parents, all dead). The rest of our guest list was made up of old friends, like the neighbor I'd known since high school and the couple who introduced us, plus various work colleagues, my yoga teacher, his running partner. Our clergy.

"At least my mother won't be making popovers," I said. "As if getting dinner on the table wasn't stressful enough, she always had to add the last-minute suspense of whether or not her popovers would pop."

"And did they?" said Jack.

"Sometimes. And sometimes they were eggy little plugs of disappointment."

Jack's sister was bringing their family's Thanksgiving essential: jellied cranberry sauce, glubbed from the can, ridges intact.

The pies came out and in went my 23-pound dry-brined organic turkey.

My next-door neighbor whom I'd known since high school brought over her chunky cranberry relish and a gorgeous apple pie. She sat down and together the three of us singed our fingers peeling hot chestnuts for the stuffing. When Jack got up to make the dinner rolls, we friends trimmed close to a hundred brussels sprouts.

I loved seeing Jack in his long apron and his wild, sticking-out hair as he formed dough into short ropes, then tied the ropes into knots for his dinner rolls. "Not to add any stress to the day," he said over his shoulder, "but I really hope these rise."

The parrot somehow sensed when we were handling the food she loved—nuts, celery, carrots—and screeched until we gave her some.

I have social anxiety when people from such different parts of my life gather in the same room—I worried, for example, that the anti-religionists would try to bait the clergy—but Jack relishes social experiments.

He asked his rabbi to say a blessing for the meal and I asked Tom to lead a moment of remembrance before dessert for those who couldn't be with us. The a-religious, I decided, would just have to cope—and they did: several of them let me know that they'd found the prayers moving and "surprisingly meaningful."

. ᎒᠍᠍Ꮧ .

On Sunday Jennie announced after church that she could go on a restaurant review that evening, if I drove. "Eric's home, but our car's in the shop."

Jack was glad to stay home, eat leftover turkey, and get in a few more hours of work. And I, who'd felt remiss for not pursuing Belinda's suggestion that I "take Jennie in hand," welcomed the chance to attempt it.

Jennie and her tall, quiet husband lived in the converted garage apartment behind her parents' house. When I arrived, Eric was feeding two-year-old Jasmine. His chest-long beard was trimmed to a near perfect rectangle—it was the kind of beard so many young men (and baseball players) grew that year, which made them look like nineteenth-century woodsmen and (one imagined) Old Testament prophets. Jasmine waved a pink plastic baby spoon at me as Jennie went to find her purse. "Thanks so much, Dana," Eric whispered. "She's super-stoked to be going on a review."

I'd chosen a small new Cal-French bistro in Highland Park; I'd been there once and eaten fresh, plump moules and a classic fish soup with some lovely, not expensive sparkling wine. As the young chef-owner's first restaurant, it was a modest production; so far, his wife was the only server. As she seated us, I ordered a bottle of rosé.

The walls and tablecloths were a warm gray, the banquettes, seat cushions, and napkins crimson. "These colors!" Jennie said. "They remind me of a bleeding mouse." She laughed, pleased with herself, then whispered, "You can use that in your write-up: say 'the color scheme is bleeding mouse.'" She glanced around. "And that chandelier is el cheapo from IKEA with extra stuff hung on it."

"It's expensive to open a restaurant," I said. "People have to make do. And there's a whole design cult of IKEA hacks."

"I could show them a few myself." She checked the back side of her silverware. "IKEA, too." She shrugged. "Maybe the food will be good."

"It was the last time I was here."

Jennie twisted in her seat to locate the server, who was talking to a table of four, the only other customers. "They should hire another waiter. That one spends too much time talking to her friends." Jennie leaned over to me. "You should put that in, too: the waiter talked to her friends while we waited for our wine."

Of the minerally rosé when it came, she said, "Definitely not two-buck Chuck!"

"Definitely not," I said, and we clinked glasses.

"So tell me, Dana, how much trouble am I in for missing all those meetings?"

"Are you in trouble?" I knew she was, of course, but I didn't want to get in the middle of anything.

"Charlotte snubbed me at church today. Blew right past me, not even a hi."

"Sounds like she was on her way somewhere."

"The thing is"—Jennie leaned in again—"my mom's not taking Jaz like she said she would because she's mad at me. And she's mad because I won't tell her what goes on in our meetings. She says if it wasn't for her, I wouldn't be on the committee, so I should tell her all the inside poop. When I don't narc, she stiffs me with the babysitting."

"What does your mom want to know that you can't tell her?"

"You know. What Charlotte says, what Belinda and you say. She wants to know if Adrian's pushing for a Black minister or if Curtis wants a queer one. I say general stuff, like maybe not a white male this time, but she keeps digging. She thinks Charlotte and Belinda make all the decisions. I keep telling her, 'Mom, they're just some postdated olds with one vote each, so chill, don't be so obsessed.' She doesn't like that."

"You know, Jennie, I'm just a few years younger than Charlotte."

"Oh, but, Dana. You're not like her. You're a writer. You're famous. And so fashion forward. Every week, I can't wait to see what you'll wear with that big beautiful red purse of yours. I mean, have you ever met anyone wound as tight as Charlotte? Those little polo shirts and creased slacks? And Belinda's borderline senile, with her huge dog eyes watching and judging everyone. Bylaws this, board approval that. Their idea of change is Tom Fox in a dress."

The waitress came to take our order. Jennie went first and picked the cassoulet.

"You know that has pork in it," I said.

"I know, but aren't we required to taste everything?"

I ordered the rouget and a green salad to split beforehand.

"Couldn't you tell your mom the stuff I put in the newsletter?" I said.

"I do, but she thinks there's more."

"There's not much more."

"I know, but we covenanted to keep it all confidential, even boring stuff, and not to gossip. My mom's always chomping for the gory details. And she has a big mouth. If it gets out that I've blabbed something I shouldn't of, I could be kicked off the search. I'm already on thin eggshells being absent so much. I want to help pick the next minister. I don't care if the olds hate me. My folks thought I'd be *their* tool, too, but I have my own ideas. Are you going to eat this last piece of bread? Can we get more? Anyway, I'm going to make up my own mind."

"Good for you," I said, impressed and even a little abashed; she was more discreet than I'd been. Or I intended to be.

The salad arrived, an artful stack of baby romaine leaves dressed in a lemony, mustard-spiked vinaigrette. *Bright-tasting, perfect,* I noted. *Juicy.*

Jennie poked at the lettuce. "This is just the Little Gem assortment from Trader Joe's," she said. "I buy it all the time. Don't you think that if you're going out to dinner, you'd want ingredients sourced from someplace better than the discount gourmet market everyone goes to? What's the point of ordering a twelve-dollar salad when you could make it yourself at home for a couple bucks?"

"Not having to make it at home," I said, "is the point."

Jennie frowned and kept eating.

"So what kind of minister do your folks want?" I asked.

"Who cares? They're olds, too. They want someone who will like them more than Tom Fox does. But I think we need someone younger and not some old-school lady minister going on and on with the Mary Oliver and the Annie Dillard."

I liked both writers and said so.

"They're okay, but why not read someone current like that smart Reza Aslan? Have you ever seen him in person? Cute, right? Also, how come everyone in this church is so dumpy? Nobody has any style, present company excluded."

"I agree," I said. "But, Jennie, Belinda and Charlotte aren't looking for another Tom Fox. And whoever comes will probably . . ."

"Do their funerals," Jennie cut in. "I know. They can want who they want, but for as long as I've been alive, it's been old white guys at the AUUCC. Then people wonder why it's all old people at church on Sundays. What's great about Amira is, she has a young family, like me and my friends; she knows what we're going through. Maybe she's not as great a preacher, but I'm sure we could get someone young who is."

"And who has the chops to run a staffed-up church like ours."

"You guys overprivilege experience. Every place is different, so there's always a learning curve no matter what experience you have."

"Hey," I said. "Are you still thinking of seminary?"

"Not for two or three years. I might have another baby first."

The waitress brought Jennie's cassoulet and my fish and again we grew quiet, eating. "This is delicious," said Jennie. "Although the sausage was cooked for so long, all its flavor has gone into the beans." She tapped her fork on the rim of my bread plate. "You can use that in your review, too. 'All the sausage flavor was sucked out by the beans.'"

Charlotte canceled the last meeting before our three-week Christmas break. On a walk in the Arroyo Seco, she'd slipped off a log crossing a stream and had to be carried out on a stretcher. She'd hurt her back and hip; scans revealed hairline pelvic fractures.

I made corn chowder and took it to her house. She was in bed, a walker parked nearby. The pain, she said, was intense. "When I went down," she said, "all I could think was that Riley can't possibly handle the committee—not at this juncture."

"Belinda and Adrian and I will help," I said. "And it's fine to miss this week. Then, after Christmas, it'll all be easier, with Jennie and Curtis gone."

"One hopes." Charlotte gave an exhausted sigh. "We can't make our move till after Christmas or Arne will give us alternates."

16

We Swap Records

In between Christmas and New Year's, Jack, Bunchie, and I took a day trip to Santa Barbara. We were in Oxnard by eight for breakfast with Helen and Gus. First, Helen said, we should take Bunchie to the beach. "They don't start policing until nine, so now is when she can run off-leash."

It was clear and cool, in the high forties. Bundled up, we walked a block to the sand, where I set Bunchie free. She had never been to the ocean and ran to and then away from the water in joyous, twisting leaps.

Gus was a large soft-spoken man, tall and slightly stooped—a true physical match with Helen. He and Jack immediately found their subject— home computer networks—and walked on ahead talking eagerly. "He seems sweet," I said to Helen.

"Right? He wants to get married, but I like things as they are. Two houses. His is full of clutter, he's a near hoarder, and I need near-empty rooms just to think. But we eat and sleep together, and that suits me fine."

"I get it," I said. "Jack and I were so old when we married, we were both trained to solitude. So it's good we have a large property and our own offices."

The wind made our clothes flap and flutter, the sand made our going slow. I heard myself say, "I guess if we're going to be friends again, Helen, we should talk about why you didn't speak or write to me for sixteen years."

She looked at me, then out at the surf. "I know," she said. "I've been wondering what to say to you because I really have no excuse. The last time I saw you, you'd come up to Santa Barbara to say goodbye to me and I had no idea that was it."

"I thought something had happened at that ashram." She'd gone on a month-long retreat in upstate New York.

"No, but from there I went to France and did a six-month silent retreat. We could only talk for fifteen minutes a night, and we couldn't write anything other than notes to our teacher. After that, it was easy to stay out of touch, and not just with you. Then the longer you and I didn't talk, the harder it was to reach out. I've read your columns and books, and wanted to call or write, but I was chicken, afraid you'd lost patience with me. Then when you were so open and warm at the retreat, I realized how stupid that was. I do hope we can be friends again."

"Being ghosted was very painful," I said. "I didn't know what I'd done or even if you were alive. So now, as happy as I am to see you again, I'm leery."

"Of course. I'm sorry I ghosted you. I like to think I've done enough work on myself that I wouldn't behave that way again. In fact, I can promise you that."

"Meaning the next time you drop me, you'll tell me you're doing it?"

Her face froze as if I'd hit her. Then she laughed, and I did too and somehow, we were over a hump.

"I say we just keep going and see what happens," Helen said.

And so we walked on into the cold stiff wind, hands in pockets, leaning forward. Bunchie ran up to me then away again to bark at the waves.

At a ruined pier, we turned around and headed back toward the house, the wind now pushing us along. "On a different note," Helen said, "I've been getting calls from ministers who want to talk about the AUUCC job. And a few have said it's not clear what exactly you're looking for."

"We want what everyone wants: great preaching, a good manager. We're hoping for a woman—but we can't say that explicitly. An infusion of new energy."

"That's all pretty vague."

"Are other churches more specific in what they want?"

"Oh god, yes. They'll say they want someone to help them work through their entrenched white privilege or someone to invigorate their social action programs. Or they want someone psychologically skilled and pastoral because their congregation's recovering from a trauma. Or they want a development type to take them through a big capital campaign to enlarge their campus."

"I'd say we mostly want a change in tone," I said. "Something less male and paternal. I adored Sparlo, but he was really the aloof, distant-yet-beloved patriarch. Tom is more like the easygoing dad next door. But still so male. We all pretty much agree that it's time for a powerful woman. I'd like someone as theologically sophisticated and adventurous as Sparlo was, but more metaphysical and visionary and, again, female. We've had such a long spell of dry, ultra-rational secularism."

"You should have written the minister profile for the Congregational Record."

I had written it, but I didn't admit this to Helen.

"Speaking of writing," Helen said, "I had an idea for your next book." She gave me a sly, sidelong look. "Maybe you should write about the search."

"Really?" I snorted to hide my surprise. "And bore everyone to death?"

"Things will pick up when you start meeting applicants. You'll have to interview and research them, do background checks, run down leads like a detective. You'll discover stuff you didn't suspect, good and bad. Of course you'd have to make it a novel and change everyone's names and hair color . . ."

"You've really thought this through."

"And then there's Adrian."

"Adrian? What about him?"

"He could be your love interest."

"The last thing I need at this stage in my life," I said, "is a new love interest."

"I mean, in your book."

"Oh. Right. The book."

. ❧ .

When Jack and I were back in the car, I said, "Did you tell Helen that I was writing a book about the search?"

"Why would I do that?"

"It's just that she suggested it. Like it was her idea."

"Not surprised. Great minds think alike." He slipped his hand over mine. "You two even sound like each other. And how do you find so much to talk about?"

"It's how we've always been. We meet, we jump right in."

> Happy New Year from your search committee!
>
> Ministers throughout the country have been reading our Congregational Record and many have indicated an interest in us.
>
> Curiosity at this stage is unavoidable. But the identities of the interested ministers must remain confidential for two reasons: 1. Confidentiality protects the ministers' relationships with their current congregations (who might not be so thrilled to know that their minister is looking elsewhere for work), and 2. Confidentiality allows our committee to function without interference and/or outside pressure.
>
> So: for the good of all, please respect the confidentiality of the process!

The first Thursday in January, Charlotte sent out a link to seventeen Ministerial Records.

> Jennie replied all: *17—IS THAT ALL?!!!!!!*

> Charlotte: *46 churches are seeking new ministers; 87 ministers are in search. 20 percent of those ministers are interested in the AUUCC—Impressive!*

Jennie: *100% SHOULD BE INTERESTED! LOL!*

Charlotte: *We are advised to move swiftly. Please read these records by Tuesday and be prepared to score each minister on a scale of one to five. Ideally, we'll swap packets with 8 to 10 ministers. Bear in mind that we're just beginning to know these ministers. Also: more records might come in. So don't set your heart on anyone—yet.*

The days were balmy for January. I pulled on sweatpants and a big holey old cashmere sweater and curled up with my laptop on the chaise longue under the oak tree outside my office. Squirrels gamboled through the branches overhead, sometimes gibbering angrily at me: *our oak tree, our yard, you—out!*

I wrote each minister's name on a legal pad before I read their record. The records were essentially long, enhanced résumés listing schools attended, degrees awarded, continuing education units. Also: publications, speeches, teaching, curricula developed, honors received. I had no idea that there were so many ministerial honors.

Jack brought me a hot cup of tea. "Anything interesting?" he asked.

"Gettin' there," I said.

The ministers who clicked on us allegedly had been vetted by the transitions team at headquarters, ostensibly to eliminate seminary students applying "just for practice," as well as those ministers attempting too ambitious a career leap.

Age, race, gender, and sexual orientation were nowhere stated, but often could be deduced from dates and personal statements.

The ministers described their management styles and a typical worship service; they expounded on the role of music in worship, the importance of religious education, their theology. The most idiosyncratic, revealing, and (to me) interesting entries were the narrative answers to various prompts: *Describe your call to ministry* and *Tell about a mistake you made in your job and what you did to repair it.* Curiously, the final free-for-all prompt, *Finish introducing yourself in any way you would like to,* yielded little, proving again that a tiny bit of structure—the smallest germ of an idea—is more generative than the deadly imperative, *Write about anything you want.*

One minister did write fifty-two pages "to finish introducing" herself, her prose degrading in a way that made me think a bottle—or two—of wine had accompanied the effort. No doubt this document was cathartic for her to produce; perhaps she was not so wise to hit SEND. Beside her name on my legal pad, I wrote *No.*

The *Tell about a mistake* prompt produced some classic humblebrags: "I worked too many hours." "I paid too many hospital visits." "I paid too much attention to hardworking lay leaders and too little to the big donors." "I pledged too much, which made some of our members feel bad about how little they gave."

Of course, the genuine mistakes we make (hurtful remarks, lies, outbursts of temper, vengeful gossip, financial missteps, sexual transgressions, getting drunk at the wrong time) are not the mistakes a minister lists when applying for a job.

Some of the call stories were particularly revealing. The same minister who had made too many hospital visits—a former actress—made ministry seem like another role she'd taken on:

I was cast as Agnes in a non-Equity production of *Agnes of God* and had to wear a nun's habit. It was itchy black wool and smelled like mothballs. When I saw myself in the mirror with the wimple, I suddenly got it why women like chadors and burkas; they take the ego out of how you look. Then, playing a nun woke up the selfless me, the me who yearns to do good, who believes in the God of Love that Catholics (on my mother's side) and Sikhs (like my paternal grandfather) believe in. It took me 3 years to get to seminary after Agnes (I had to get the acting bug out of my system), but the day I put on that habit I began moving toward ministry.

Rev Agnes of God was a young, new minister, having worked solely as a hired assistant minister on a three-year contract at a large urban East

Coast church. As she'd never held a senior position or served a church of her own, I wrote *No.*

No, no, and *no* I wrote beside the names of three accomplished ministers clearly deep in their sixties, bearing in mind Helen's warning about those seeking to pre-retire in sunny Southern California. Anyway, we wanted someone young enough to stay awhile, as Sparlo had.

Half a dozen women, some gay, some straight, seemed to be equally good managers, solid preachers, and skilled leaders; all were deeply committed to social justice and RE. *No* went to one whose writing was a mass of grammatical errors. The three most experienced, I dubbed "the Indistinguishables" because on paper they seemed so similar—in their forties, hardworking, energetic, efficient, if in no way sparkling.

The three also shared remarkably similar call stories: each said that someone suggested that she should be a minister and the idea hit home.

I ended up with a yes to nine Ministerial Records from ten ministers—one record came from a married couple hoping to share the job. Six women, four men. One woman stated that she was lesbian and two men mentioned that they were gay. All ten had been senior ministers for from four to twenty-four years. Six had only ever been ministers; the other four came to ministry after being a college professor, a lawyer, a schoolteacher, and a journalist.

Even this reduced pool seemed wide and deep.

17

The Interested

Of the youngest and least-experienced ministers, I was drawn to the couple looking to share the job and a young man in Detroit. All were midwestern and four to six years in, but already making a difference in their communities.

Judging from his education and work history, the Reverend Walt Harrison was in his late thirties. In six years at a small Detroit church, he'd grown a moribund, older, all-white congregation of 60 into a thriving, integrated church of 115 by going door to door and asking people what programs they needed. He'd then invite them to run these programs out of the church, programs that now included a food pantry, an afterschool tutoring program, an adult literacy program, and a tuba choir. A bread baker and beer brewer, Reverend Harrison also built an outdoor bread/pizza oven on the church's patio and invited the neighbors to pizza nights and bread bakes. (Here was a minister who understood the connection between spirituality and food!) On Saturday mornings, runners met at the church and together ran (or walked) a four-mile course, ending back at the church's "coffeehouse," where the high school group served them pastries (all proceeds to the summer camp fund). Walt Harrison was now eager to try his hand at a larger church where, with greater resources, he might accomplish even more.

His was an interesting call story. At least I thought so.

When I was in the Peace Corps in Sierra Leone, members of a small Christian sect came to talk to me about American customs. They were headed to the US as missionaries: the extreme materialism and consumerism there, they told me, required immediate intervention. The US had to reawaken to Christian values: feeding the poor, loving your neighbors, being stewards of the earth. These missionaries inspired me: there was so much work to do at home! When my two years in Sierra Leone ended, I went to seminary.

The couple who hoped to share the job, the Reverends Tammy and Rob Sanders, had met in seminary in Boston. Rob had grown up a Unitarian Universalist; Tammy's family was Methodist, but she'd "crossed over" shortly after they met. ("I never knew there was a whole denomination as full of questions as I was.") Both were trained singers, smart, and charmingly honest in their written responses. Both had won preaching awards in seminary. For four years, in a thrice-extended interim ministry, they'd served a 130-person congregation near Chicago, implementing a weekend arts and music program for neighborhood kids, after-school care, and a tree-planting club. The Sanderses had two young daughters and split the household/childcare tasks. Jennie, I thought, would adore them.

In Tammy's call story, she candidly articulated what I'd been ashamed to admit about my own foray into ministry:

> I had an idea that becoming a minister would make me an adult with a kind of mystical cachet! My seminary education and internships did make an adult out of me—by challenging and debunking almost all I thought and believed. Today I am far more humbled than exalted by my calling. Yet, if young, ego-driven, wrongheaded ambition brought me into this difficult, demanding, glorious profession, I can only be grateful to my misguided younger self.

Her husband, Rob's, call story also stood out:

> As a youth counselor at my UU summer camp, I slept in a dorm with five other male counselors. One morning the voice of God woke me up.

I knew it was God because His voice was loud and diffuse like thunder and He was only talking to me, because nobody else woke up. Who but God could do that—thunder to one person in a room of six? What God said was "Get thee to Meadville." I knew Meadville was the UU seminary, and I was probably just having a vivid dream. Still, those words spoke to my soul.

At breakfast, I told everyone the dream, and they were all, "Yes! Get thee to Meadville!" At my ordination, the minister of my home church began the service with "Well, Rob got his butt to Meadville, and we are here today to celebrate it."

I was drawn to Walt, Rob, and Tammy for their youthful energy—they were so hopeful and hardworking—even as I knew that ministers with more established credentials and experience were more likely to be our "pre-candidates."

I'd left my phone charging in the kitchen, but Jack brought it up to my office before he left for work in the morning. "She's called three times," he said.

Charlotte.

"I can't get them out!" she cried. "Tom agreed they should go, but the executive committee—including Adrian!—said it looked 'frankly racist' to kick off two people of color and wouldn't approve it. So that's that, I guess. We'll keep going as is."

I was both disappointed that we wouldn't have a smaller, fleeter committee and relieved that Jennie and Curtis wouldn't face a public demotion. "Jennie reminds me of this story about Gurdjieff," I told Charlotte. "You know who he is?"

"I saw a movie about him—a spiritual teacher—a guru type, right?"

"He had an estate south of Paris where his followers went to study with him," I said. "One group was having a marvelous time there—except that this one obnoxious, intrusive guy kept horning in on their meetings and conversations. Finally, someone went to Gurdjieff and suggested that the guy be sent away. 'Send him away?' Gurdjieff cried. 'Why, I pay him to stay!'"

"Hah!" said Charlotte. "Arne told us there was a spiritual component to the search, I just never dreamed it was Jennie."

Of the older, more experienced prospects, I was drawn to Elsa Neddicke, a former war correspondent who, in her twenties, had covered conflicts in Bosnia, Serbia, Pakistan, and Afghanistan. Now, in her midfifties (my age!), she was ready, she wrote, to start anew. ("The truth is, I love a smaller church where I can know everyone at least a little.") Her husband, a doctor from Syria, had just retired; their two daughters were "finally through college," so she could "downshift" to a smaller church. Her call story:

I was in Paris on assignment and went to the UNESCO building to interview an Afghan cultural attaché. In the garden near the entrance, a stone monument was inscribed in many different languages with this: "Since wars begin in the minds of men, it is in the minds of men that the defences of peace must be constructed."

This spoke to me. After five years of witnessing and reporting on wars, I wanted to construct the defenses of peace in human minds. But how? After much reflection and discussion with my family and minister—and writing a spate of frankly sermonic op-eds—I decided that ministry would best serve this goal.

Elsa Neddicke's "mistake" was apologizing in the pulpit for what she felt was a bad sermon. Afterward, the church president took her aside. Judging her own sermons was not acceptable, the president said; it interfered with the listeners' own experience of her words: "We make the judgment call," the president told her. "Not you."

I was also thrilled to see that Perry Fitzgerald had clicked on us. I had read his articles in *Tricycle*, a Buddhist magazine, and had bought and read (most of) his book on meditation. He was also, I now learned, a former college professor, an ordained Buddhist priest, and for the last six years, a UU minister. And gay. His ministry had not been without difficulty; his first church let him go with a "negotiated settlement," and he had served as an interim at three churches since. Here's his "mistake":

> For the two years I served as the assistant minister at TUUC, members complained about the announcement period during worship. It had gotten to the point where people wrote interminable doggerel or put on entire scripted skits to announce the rummage sale or the book club's monthly selection. My predecessor had issued many time limits and banned the theatricals to no avail.
>
> My first Sunday as TUUC's senior minister, I didn't include announcements in worship. That's when I found out how many people enjoyed them and felt that I'd acted precipitously, tyrannically in omitting them. I began, then, to understand that, as their inside candidate, I'd been hired to preserve the status quo. I learned, too, that change must come slowly, incrementally, thoughtfully, collaboratively.

I also liked the Reverend Mayeve Schindler, who served a church in Alabama and wrote this in her frank and high-humored bio:

> I should say outright that I have recently and amicably divorced my husband of twenty-one years and come out as the lesbian I have been in my heart of hearts since Pattiann Degler kissed me in the eighth grade. While I'm baring my soul here, let me add that I also identify as a pagan, a witch (Wiccan), and an environmental warrior. My totem animal is the black cat. . . ."

The AUUCC, I thought, might do well with a cheerful witch.

And then there were my three capable, hardworking "Indistinguishables"—Liz Dumenil, Phoebe Fetterman, and Anna Holbein—whose exhaustingly busy résumés at least qualified them for a closer look.

I also liked Roger Chang-Sumerson, who self-identified as a gay, Chinese American minister and had served seven years at a ninety-member church in a midwestern college town.

Tuesday morning—we were meeting that night—Charlotte sent us one more link. Russell Long was already known in the denomination for his slim, engaging book on UUism entitled *Who Needs God?* He'd also contributed two hymns to our supplemental hymnal, lyrics *and* music, and presently served a 350-member church in Ohio. He'd put out two CDs (possibly self-produced) of original songs. In the YouTube videos I found, he was a lanky, bearded, cowboy-handsome white male in his midforties. His goal, he wrote, was to grow the first UU megachurch—which made me wonder if his interest in us, a congregation significantly smaller than his present one, had less to do with who we were and more to do with our acres of languishing gardens.

18

We Vote for the First and Second Time

At this point in the search, we began meeting at Charlotte's house. She and Sheila lived on a block-long street of simple but elegant modernist homes. (It was in one of these homes, at a meeting of a local socialist society, that my parents first met sixty years ago—perhaps in this open kitchen/living room area with its polished concrete floor, jutting wood beams, and high clerestories.)

"We'll have a preliminary vote," Charlotte said, "and discuss the results over dinner. Then we'll vote again."

We gathered on cushioned bent-plywood sofas around the fireplace where gas-jet flames heated ceramic logs. Charlotte passed out half-page ballots. We were to put our names on them and be prepared to explain our votes. She reiterated the point system:

1. Does not match most of our needs
2. Matches some of our needs
3. Matches our needs
4. Matches our needs—and then some
5. Far exceeds our criteria

The most points any minister could receive was 40, the least was 8. We'd swap packets, Charlotte said, with everyone who scored 24 and above.

I'd come with my ratings done, but others on the committee started paging through the printouts and frowning at their phones. I'd given 5s to

Elsa, Perry, and Russell; 4s to the Sanderses, Walt, and Mayeve (the witch); Roger Chang-Sumerson and the three Indistinguishables all got 3s. Everyone else was a 1 or a 2.

Charlotte had us call out our numbers, so we could all tally them. Nine ministers crossed the threshold of 24 votes. The highest scorer was the former war correspondent Elsa Neddicke (37); Doris Gray, an older minister I had set aside for wanting to pre-retire in California, received the next highest vote (36)—only my "1" vote had kept her from a perfect score.

Perry Fitzgerald, the gay, former Asian religion and philosophy professor turned interim minister; Russell Long, the amiable singer-songwriter minister; and Roger Chang-Sumerson, the gay Chinese American minister were all tied at 35.

My three Indistinguishables and the witch, Mayeve Schindler, also made the cutoff, but none of my younger favorites did. Walt Harrison received 21 points. The Sanderses, 19. Alanna Kapoor, the actress (Rev Agnes O'God), who'd never served her own church, actually beat them with 23 points. Jennie, Riley, and Curtis, voting in a bloc, had each given Walt and the Sanderses 1 point and the actress 5 points.

Jennie said, "Oh but Alanna Kapoor is the minister I told you about, who gave that fantastic ritual workshop at General Assembly. She's super, super brilliant! I can't believe she even clicked on us. We're so lucky she'd even look at a church as small and poky as us. You guys are so wrong not to give her more points."

"Let's discuss it over dinner," Charlotte said.

We filled our plates at Charlotte's kitchen island with dry, take-out rotisserie chicken and plain steamed broccoli. Sam brought a bagged green salad and bottled ranch dressing. Thank god I'd made a big bowl of chunky guacamole and brought the thick, fresh tortilla chips prepared daily at my neighborhood market from their house-made tortillas.

People would have to up their game in the food department if I was going to get recipes from anyone other than Belinda and Jennie for my book.

At Charlotte's marble-topped dining table, I sat between Curtis and Adrian.

"Reverend Kapoor is undeniably talented and full of potential," Charlotte said, "but she's never served her own church. Or in any 'called' position."

I can never keep it straight myself, but *assistant* ministers are hired under contract for a specific time period and *associate* ministers are "called" by a congregation and can stay as long as they like.

"Alanna's been at a huge major church for three years," said Jennie. "More than a thousand members, with three assistant ministers, two associates, plus the senior. Only one new minister a year gets her assistant-ship and every UU graduating from seminary applies for it. Everyone who gets it winds up a big major minister. I'm sure we look like a little old starter church to her. We'd be as lucky to get her as getting Russell Long. It's amazing we have a chance with him, too—big fancy churches will snap 'em both up. We're probably just their ace in the holes, anyway. But we should at least get Alanna's packet so you can see how fantastic she is. If you ever met her, you'd just die."

"Then one rather hopes not to," said Belinda.

Jennie looked blank.

"Belinda's joking," Riley said.

"I'll give her another point," said Sam.

"Me too," said Curtis.

"You already gave her five, Curtis," said Charlotte.

Didn't anyone else like that Walt Harrison?" said Belinda. "And how he grew his church right from the neighborhood."

"Loved him," I said. "He's not afraid of footwork. Really effective, creative. A deep thinker. Yet so much fun—that pizza oven!"

Nobody said anything for a long uncomfortable moment.

"He doesn't have a lot of experience," said Sam.

"Six years, and look what he's done," said Belinda. "Doubled his congregation—*and* integrated it. Created quite the community and a blazing social justice agenda. Isn't that what we're looking for?"

"He just feels young," said Sam. "All that beer and bread making—who cares?"

"He has six years more experience being a senior minister than Reverend Kapoor," Belinda said. "To whom you just gave a qualifying point, Sam. If we look at her packet, why not see someone else's who is a lot more qualified?"

"I liked Walt," said Charlotte. "I'm happy to give him another point."

"Jennie?" I said. "You must have liked Walt?"

"Walt?" Jennie frowned at her pages. "Nah. He's a junior, grunge Tom Fox."

"Not as junior a Tom Fox as that Russell Long," I said. "Do you really prefer another tall, white, handsome middle-aged Southerner to someone your age who's done everything at his last church that we want done here?"

"But I know Russell. I met him at headquarters and he's way cooler than Tom Fox *and* like a zillion times cooler than that dorky Walt What's-his-name! I heard Russell preach at the Arlington Street church, everyone at headquarters went, and he was super funny and sooo smart! And he sang! He has this amazing voice. Your Detroit Walt is tiny potatoes next to him—and to Alanna, too. Russell and Alanna are two of the brightest UU stars! You don't realize what a big deal it is that they even clicked on us. So excuse me if I'm not impressed by some wussy bread baker with an all-face beard who wears black dress socks with his Birkenstocks."

"How do you know what he wears on his feet?" asked Charlotte.

"And his face?" I added.

"I know the wussy granola folk-singer type," said Jennie. "Major ick."

"I agree," Curtis said. "He doesn't seem strong. All that bread and beer stuff."

"Jesus made a big deal about bread and wine," I said to Curtis.

"Yeah, but he didn't make it."

"He let the women do it?"

"It was a miracle."

"So you have a problem with a man baking bread and making beer?"

"Not with a man. But a minister? What does that have to do with God?"

"I'm confused here," said Belinda. "Reverend Harrison pretty much doubled *and* integrated his congregation; he runs an impressive number of music and literacy programs for his community. He's obviously gifted. Why don't we like him?"

"He's a drip."

"Anyone other than Jennie?" said Belinda.

"Love the guy," I said.

"I'll give him four points," said Charlotte. "Riley? Is there a reason you gave him only one?"

Riley glanced at Jennie. "He didn't grab me."

"What about him didn't grab you?"

"I don't know. The whole pizza-bread gestalt."

"Did you read his record?"

Riley grabbed his hair. "Some of it."

"Maybe you could read all of it," Charlotte said lightly, "before you knock him out of the running."

"I think you'll like what you read, Ri," said Belinda.

"Can't we just agree to look at his packet?" I said. "I don't know what decided you young people to vote in a bloc against him—and I'm very curious how you know what kind of socks he wears, Jennie, and the kind of beard he has—but if you recall what the survey said were our priorities, Walt objectively meets and exceeds them, and that alone should give him *at least* twenty-four points. Remember, we are not just voting our own preferences, we're attending to what the church wants and needs. Which is why I gave those three women—Liz, Anna, and Phoebe—three points. Do I love them? No. But they objectively meet our needs. And so does Walt."

Into the pause came the muffled sound of a television some rooms off.

Charlotte said, "Moving right along, then. Anything else?"

"I actually don't think we should move right along," said Adrian, who'd been squinting at his phone. "Walt Harrison is the real deal. I didn't notice him till Dana and Belinda talked him up just now. But looking more closely at his record, I see a lot of skill and innovation. So you know what? I'm giving him four points, too." His voice thickened with emotion. "That's what it means to have an open mind: you get to change it when you've missed something. An open mind lets in new evidence. And it's not that I'm set on Walt being our next minister. It's acknowledging that his work deserves our serious consideration. We can't just dismiss him. So have another look at Walt's record, guys. Will you do that?"

Jennie harrumphed and turned her shoulder with the horse's head toward Adrian. "I can't help how I feel," she muttered.

"Riley? Curtis? Won't you give Walt a second look?"

"Sure," said Curtis.

"No problem," said Riley.

"Thank you," Adrian said gently.

My heart was full. "Bravo," I whispered to Adrian's neck.

He nudged my leg. Perhaps we were a cabal.

"Okay then," Charlotte said, "Anything else?"

People refilled their wine or water glasses. Papers were shuffled.

"I'm curious why everyone gave Doris Gray such a high score," I said. "She's impressive, but given when she got her BA, she has to be well into her sixties—didn't anybody else catch that? I thought we wanted someone who could be here a long time."

"Ageism!" Jennie sang out. "Better call Trish."

Charlotte said, "She'd give us seven to ten years, which is average these days."

"I thought she might be one of those ministers Helen warned us about—the ones looking to pre-retire to California. Or am I missing something?"

I was missing something.

"I'll overlook age," Charlotte said, "in the case of an incredibly impressive Black woman who's one of the more powerful and beloved preachers in our denomination."

"Oh." Admittedly, I had barely skimmed her record after deducing her age. "Where did it say she's Black?"

"I knew of her," said Charlotte, "but it's where she said her adoptive parents had her both bat mitzvahed in a reform temple *and* baptized in the AME church."

African Methodist Episcopalian. That's what I'd missed.

"I knew of her," said Adrian, "because I used her curriculum in the adult racial justice class I taught at the church last year. She's phenomenal."

"Her name was everywhere in Boston," said Jennie. "She's chair of the Black Ministers coalition. And I told them." She waved at Curtis and Riley.

"I'll reread her record," I said. "I also think the married couple, the Sanderses, deserve a closer look."

"I agree," said Belinda. "They're clearly gifted, committed, and creative."

"The husband-wife team?" Sam said. "We never discussed co-ministry as a possibility. I don't like the idea. You never know who to go to with an issue."

"They're very young and have no experience at this size church," Charlotte said.

"They're the same age as Kapoor," said Belinda. "And unlike her, they've served their own church for four years."

"Just as interims," said Sam.

"Long-term interims," said Belinda. "They keep getting renewed."

"I saw that they were into music," said Riley. "So I checked out YouTube videos of their worship services. They have good, trained voices, but their material was all very Christian. And I shouldn't say this, but they're both, um, overweight. By a lot."

"No fat-shaming!" Jennie called out, then more quietly added, "Speaking as someone still carrying twenty pounds of baby weight."

"You're not fat," said Riley. "Not like these guys. They're, like, clinically obese."

Charlotte said, "Weight is not something we discriminate against."

"It is kind of a turnoff, though," said Riley. "Hardly shows good self-care."

This from a scrawny man with dirty hair and bad bachelor housekeeping.

"I don't mind their being fat," said Jennie. "But can you spell b-o-r-i-n-g?"

"What troubles me about the Sanderses"—Charlotte raised her voice as if to elevate the level of discourse—"more than their inexperience or appearance, is that the man says he heard the voice of God. 'Get thee to Meadville!' That doesn't sit well with me."

"Yeah, that bugged me, too," said Riley. "Scary. I mean, like what's God going to tell him to do next? Start a war, like George Bush?"

"I checked out his theology," said Charlotte, paging through her printouts. "And he writes 'Mine is the theology of right relationship, in which we seek a loving connection with ourselves, with each other, with the earth, and with a loving God.' That's pretty theistic to me. And she was Methodist till a few years ago. They're obviously progressive, but maybe too Christian leaning for the AUUCC."

"They're too Christian for me," said Riley. "Especially their music."

"They're Christians?" Curtis paged through his papers. "I'd probably like them."

"So give them more points," Belinda said. "You only gave them one."

"Many UU ministers believe in an abstraction they call God, the divine, or the sacred," I said. "That's what makes it theology rather than philosophy or psychology."

"Yeah, but does that abstraction talk to thee?" said Riley. "I'm a scientist. When someone's God talks to them, I draw a line."

"I'm with you," said Charlotte.

Was something wrong with me? I had no such objections. "I can believe that some deep, good part of Reverend Sanders told him to go to seminary, and he experienced it as a disembodied voice in a waking dream," I said. "People have all sorts of ineffable psychic experiences, and some lead them to ministry and helping others."

"Yeah, right on their way to the nuthouse," said Riley.

"I'm with Riley there," said Sam.

Curtis, I noticed, kept very quiet. "What do you think?" I asked him.

"I didn't know God wasn't allowed to talk to us. I gave them a one because I didn't think that we wanted a couple. But I'll give them some more points."

"Curtis!" Jennie said in a sharp way that made everyone look at her.

"Curtis can vote any way he likes, Jennie," Charlotte said.

"I know," Jennie said. "But I don't have to agree with him."

"The other question is," Charlotte pushed on, "do we want a shared ministry?"

I said, "It is possible we'd get twice the minister for half the price."

"God, you know what would be really great?" Jennie sat forward. "If we got Russell and Alanna for a shared ministry. We'd have *the* superhero ministry of the whole country. Like, Sam, if you could find the money . . ."

"Let's not get carried away," Charlotte said. "One minister at a time. Let's vote."

With Sam's point, Alanna Kapoor made the cutoff. The Sanderses gained 2 points from Curtis, but Sam docked them 2: "I forgot about that talking to God nonsense." Walt Harrison went to 23, one short of the minimum: no young people had budged.

Stunned and furious that my personal young favorites were eliminated, I stood. "Okay, so the Sanderses are too Christian for you, fine. But Walt Harrison? Given his gifts and experience, shouldn't we at least swap packets with him?"

Everyone now studied the gray veins in the marble tabletop.

"You know," I said, "I have a real problem with you three young people voting in a bloc when it's clear that at least one of you didn't even read most of the records. And when Curtis said he'd vote differently, Jennie called him out—Jennie, you can't browbeat people into voting against someone because maybe you saw them at headquarters years ago and didn't like their facial hair. And, guys, if you haven't read a minister's record, recuse yourself, don't just let someone tell you how to vote. Because that's giving one person three votes. Which isn't fair to the rest of us."

"Hear, hear," said Belinda. Another leg nudge from Adrian. Nobody else spoke. Pink bloomed on Riley's face perhaps from embarrassment, perhaps anger.

"But, Dana," said Jennie, "it's not like we agreed to agree. We just agree."

I stayed back as the others left and stood by Charlotte as she loaded her dishwasher. "I can't believe you nixed the Sanderses because he said God spoke to him," I said. "Don't you have a higher power?" Charlotte, after all, was in AA.

"A higher self, maybe—I've never bought the religious side of the Twelve Steps. And I'm sorry, Dana, but to me two-way chats with the almighty are delusional."

"Yet we're swapping packets with a self-aggrandizing former actress with zero senior ministry experience whose call to ministry was putting on a nun costume!"

Charlotte settled a plate in its slot. "We could've squabbled all night down there among the low-point getters. The good news is that everyone agrees on the top contenders. We've got six or seven highly qualified ministers interested and that's the pool our candidate's in. But California alone has three larger, richer churches in search right now, so I'm far more concerned with how we can impress our front-runners than I am with what neophytes we'll trade packets with."

Walt and the Sanderses were hardly neophytes, and I said so.

"I can't see the Sanderses here," said Charlotte. "But Walt I'm sad about. And you were right to call out the kids for voting in a bloc. Jennie's exactly the problem I thought she'd be." Charlotte set a bouquet of rinsed forks in the dishwasher's silverware box. "Still, tonight relieved my anxiety. There's so much brilliance at the top, even the kids see it. Those junior ministers? They aren't really in the running."

For the first time it occurred to me that, despite the time I'd put in, despite my perfect attendance, it was possible that my voice and opinions could have no effect on the outcome.

19

Packets, Packets, Packets

After breakfast, on opening my computer, I found links to six packets in my in-box, with a note from Charlotte reminding us to maintain absolute confidentiality. And:

> While committee members are encouraged to communicate among themselves, and consult with district representatives (Trish Morningstar and Helen Harland), such exchanges should consist of ideas and opinions, *but in no way conspire to bring about a final result.*

Packets brought faces. Doris Gray was indeed an older Black woman, with wire-rimmed glasses and a short gray Afro. Perry Fitzgerald was white and stylish with his expensive-looking jacket worn over a black T-shirt, his hair and beard meticulously tended.

In other snapshots, our front-runner Elsa Neddicke looked small and intense, with short curly black hair, dark round eyes, and an olive complexion—her mother, she'd written, was Puerto Rican. Mayeve "the Witch" Schindler, with her wild curly mop of graying blond hair and flowing, pastel-colored clothes, looked more like a therapist than a practitioner of the dark arts or a minister. Liz Dumenil and Phoebe Fetterman, two of my three white Indistinguishables, wore dark blazers and emanated administrative capability.

Packets also brought us sermons—in text, audio, and video. Each minister included two or three of their best efforts (presumably), and we'd been advised to check their church websites for others. I downloaded audio files and listened in my car, and then through earbuds as I cooked, gardened, and walked the dog and donks. I had never read and heard so many sermons in my life, not even in my preaching class at seminary. Midweek, I sat on my favorite stone bench in the AUUCC's gardens and watched the low bubbler bubble while the donks weeded the flagstones and Perry Fitzgerald and Elsa Neddicke preached through my earbuds. Better than church.

A good sermon has the heft of a solid week's work (at least), yet wears its labor lightly. My homiletics professor said the rule was one hour of work per minute of sermon, say fifteen, sixteen hours on average, which always seemed scant to me. But I'm a slow writer. Then again, ministers don't usually write for publication and good delivery can finesse many an unpolished sentence and awkward transition.

Doris Gray and Elsa Neddicke stood out for going deep into their subjects and themselves. Both incorporated input from their congregants—stories, anecdotes, poems—which made their sermons collaborative, more of a dialogue.

Elsa, in an Easter sermon, listed the year's resurrections at her church: a moving litany of members who'd come back from illness, unemployment, grief, and other personal difficulties; she spoke, too, of deceased members, their memories resurrected in gifts to the church, in the trees planted, a new bench, a sculpture, a financial legacy.

She must have had a cache of stories of the saintlike, too: a six-year-old boy who collected money to buy a cow for a farmer in Zimbabwe; a man who cut and laid stone markers in city streets where people killed in the Holocaust had homes; a gay couple who rid their block of homophobia by befriending their neighbors, house by house. "*Making friends*: two beautiful words, pregnant with riches yet to be discovered."

Doris Gray had a more dynamic preaching delivery; she'd included in her packet a sermon cycle on world religions called "The Map of the World," which began: "A recent UN survey revealed that more than eighty percent of American adults cannot name the countries in blank maps of the continents. Nor can they say what languages are spoken or which religions are practiced in those countries. I, too, fail that test. So, with the help of our junior high and high school students, let's start this sermon series by filling in a map and learning about those who believe differently than we do—and let's see just what these countries and religions can teach us about love and community, worship and justice—and each other. Today, we look at Asia . . ."

Elsa was the more elegant stylist, but both she and Doris wrote in full chords, with emotional and spiritual intelligence, intellectual acuity, and a solid grasp of current events. The theologian Karl Barth famously said that a minister should preach with a Bible in one hand and a newspaper in the other; these two women replaced the Bible with texts of their choice. Elsa favored poetry; she often read a poem once as a reading and again, slowly, in the sermon so that listeners could fully enter into it. That she found good, contemporary, literary poems that gave over their meanings in so few readings showed an impressive working knowledge of the field. (Sparlo, to find accessible poems, had used a high school poetry textbook.)

Perry Fitzgerald's sermons were like dharma talks: he spoke as if casually following a train of thought, telling stories, recalling poems, and explicating spiritual and theological concepts as they occurred to him. On the page, however, the skillful construction of this conversational style was obvious.

I did the dishes one night to his sermon "Power." The most powerful person in any room, he said, is the one most fully present. Presence is the source of power. He mentioned a list of thirty-odd questions that could make people fall in love with each other; this worked, he said, because people had to sit alone together, face-to-face, and be present: a very powerful experience. Also, the final question on that list was actually an instruction: the would-be lovers were to look into each other's eyes for four minutes. "It's more potent than any love potion. Try it at home sometime," said Reverend Fitzgerald. "You just might fall in love!"

After I finished the dishes, I went into Jack's study where he was working on a brief that was due in a couple of days. I asked if he wanted to answer thirty-odd questions that made people fall in love. He said, "I thought we were in love."

"Well, why not really compound it?"

He swiveled side to side in his chair. "Can we not and say we did?"

"What if we just stare into each other's eyes for four minutes?"

He pointed at his screen. "I really have to finish this. Maybe try the dog."

I listened to sermons on my phone as I drove to the store, as I mucked out the donks' stalls, as I thinned my lettuce patch and drove across town to the *Times*. How do we live in—and change—a reality that includes climate change, mass shootings, and racism? How do we address income inequality, sexual predation, mass incarceration? By not turning away. By engaging. By cultivating kindness and compassion, by seeking justice, by loving the earth, and by tending the great interconnected web of which we are all a part. In such a deluge of spiritual thought, I felt charged, inspired to be better, more generous; I felt more dilated to beauty and suffering, and grateful for the slant of sunlight, the different greens of leaves, the sweetness of pets, the soft chuckling of our chickens, for my husband's amusing Albert Einstein hair.

I had Jack listen to Elsa's sermon on salvation as we drove to a Santa Monica restaurant ("Salvation occurs whenever a helping hand is extended, whenever truth is spoken to power . . .") and Doris's sermon on chastity on the way home ("To conflate the libido with the sexual drive is a categorical mistake. Libido is the *life* drive, and it's an entire symphony, not a single blaring note . . .").

"Does listening to all these sermons make you wish you'd been a minister?" Jack asked as we pulled into the carport.

"It makes me wish I could write sermons," I said.

"That's good. Because you'll have to," said Jack. Seeing my befuddlement, he added, "For the book. You can't just plagiarize these."

"Oh, jeez," I said. I hadn't thought of that. "But I can get permissions. Probably."

At three in the morning, I was wide awake, certain that this whole endeavor—the search and the book I'd get out of it—was a misstep, a mistake, a waste of time that could've gone into another book. But then I remembered permissions. Maybe I could write a couple of sermons and get permissions for the rest.

A nagging sameness clung to Liz and Phoebe. Their preaching voices seem *pushed* in the same way, as if both had been told to *speak up.*

At seminary, we'd been taught to preach to the stranger sitting in the back of the room whose very life might be hanging in the balance.

Neither Liz nor Phoebe, with their didactic, statistics-heavy sermons about health care and homelessness (Liz) and gun control and recycling (Phoebe) would have saved that life.

In her late forties, Mayeve Schindler, with that wild curly hair and the syrupy Southern accent of Biloxi roughnecks, filled my head with Lapland shamanism and the great fronds and mammoths of deep history. Her last year's Earth Day sermon, "The Stump and Us," began:

> In a forest in Ireland sits the eight-foot-wide stump of what was, fifty years ago, a mighty beech. This stump has no limbs or branches, which means it has no leaves to photosynthesize and feed itself. By all accounts, this stump should be dead and rotting. Yet sap still runs through its grain and oozes in any cut. The bark is yearly renewed. This stump lives on because the surrounding trees—and not just its sister beeches—supply life-giving nutrients through their roots. . . .

Two more packets trickled in over the week—Alanna Kapoor's, and, at the last, unexpectedly, Walt Harrison's (a bone for me!)—and that was it, for a total of eight. Walt's came because Roger Chang-Sumerson, Anna Holbein, and Russell Long never did send us their packets. We probably were their ace in the holes [*sic*]!

⌘

Walt wrote in lists of sentences; here's the opening to his Boston marathon bombing sermon:

In the tenth grade, I ran cross-country during last period.

As my classmates dozed at their desks, coach set us loose in the neighborhood.

I have never lost that sense of being set free to go wherever I wanted on my own two feet.

Every morning, leaving the house at six, I feel it again.

Freedom!

Running is my exercise, my meditation, my only solitude.

As I dodge cars and buses, pedestrians, dogs, and sidewalks buckled by the roots of our century-old trees,

my best ideas arrive.

I run alone—except on Saturday mornings when our running group hits the streets together.

Our destination, four miles off, is coffee cake and the smiling faces of our youth.

For many of us runners, a long training culminates in the city's marathon, when thousands become a river of beautiful human effort, a river that flows without impediment over the border of our neighboring land, where crowds line the streets to welcome us.

And some miles later, we flow back over to our side, where more crowds cheer us home . . .

Have you read your Walt Harrison's sermon on bread making?" Charlotte phoned at eight in the morning. "It's just wonderful. And I don't even eat bread."

I hadn't gotten to that one. "I've only read his marathon bombing one."

"He's surprisingly great," Charlotte said. "Of course he's a strong preacher, to double the size of his church. A good spot, Dana. What do you think of Liz Dumenil?"

An Indistinguishable. "Workaday," I said.

"I'd call her UU lite," said Charlotte. "You're right, she and Fetterman do seem interchangeable."

"Exactly! Except Dumenil has that super-annoying way of speaking—like a nursery-school teacher struggling to be heard."

"Really? I like her voice," said Charlotte. "So soothing, and you hear every word. If only the words were better. Both she and Fetterman do their research. All those facts and numbers. But they aren't very penetrating."

"They're a type," I said. "Administrators. Junior CEOs. Sweet, cheerful. Super-efficient. And so earnest, even when they joke!"

"They joke?" said Charlotte. "Not like Mayeve Schindler—now she's a hoot. Have you watched her video? No? Watch it and call me back."

In Mayeve's video, "Hello Search Committee!," she sat behind a book-cluttered desk in front of a window, so light haloed her heap of hair but put her face in shadow. "Hallo, Search Committee! Ah'm Mayeve," she said, pronouncing her name with a broad hinge. "Ah'm here in mah study at home. Theologically speaking, y'all'd call me a pagan. Ah believe in the old ways of loving the earth, treating it with respect and profound gratitude. And Ah'm a panentheist; that means Ah see God dancin' in ever' damn thing, living and inert. Now look. These here are mah instruments . . ." A wobbly swing of the camera showed a guitar, mandolin, dulcimer, fiddle, and banjo hanging on a wall. "Ah play 'em all!" she said. "Music is the breath of God. Oh and here's Conroy . . ." A black cat had leapt on the desk. "He's mah muse, aren't you, baby boy?"

It went on.

I called Charlotte back. "You liked the cat."

"I did like the cat," she said. "But don't you think she's wild? She could be just what the AUUCC needs: a funny, energetic, lesbian witch. That'd liven us up."

"I liked her deep history sermon," I said. "All her sermons are good, but they repeat. It's said that ministers always preach the same thing, and with her, it's the web, the web, the interconnected web," I said.

"True. But didn't you love the stump?"

"Loved the stump," I said.

"After reading three of her sermons," Charlotte went on, "I swear, I went outside and the trees seemed more alive, with actual personhood, and the whole world glowed. You'd agree, wouldn't you, that she and your Walt stand well above the Fetterman/Dumenil contingent?"

"God, yes. But Perry Fitzgerald's up there, too," I said. "He's got that easy chatting-with-the-sangha style. His insights sort of sneak up on you."

"But nobody's at the level of Elsa Neddicke and Doris Gray. They're a whole different order of magnitude. Doris's sermon on chastity—I couldn't believe it: a grandmother riffing on hookup culture and porn and the debasement of women, and I loved how she said that chastity isn't celibacy but holding oneself and one's body in tender esteem, and not sexualizing everything and everybody, but seeing their worth and dignity. Now that was a brave, take-no-prisoners, state-of-the-art UU sermon! I know she's oldish, but even if we got her for five years, she'd raise us up."

"I can see that," I said.

"So we're in great shape. What with Walt, Mayeve, Perry, and the two fabulous elder stateswomen, we can't go far wrong," Charlotte said.

"Elsa's not that elder," I said. (A year older than I was!) "But the quality's there. Let's hope at least one will take the job once they learn what houses cost around here."

"And let's hope," Charlotte said, "that we can reach a consensus with this group. It's not going to be easy. The kids have a thing for those boring young mothers."

"And Jennie won't let go of her Reverend Kapoor," I said. "Whose packet I haven't even opened yet—I'm afraid to."

"No danger! You'll see. She has presence—I mean, she's an actress through and through. You can't believe all the videos she posted. She must have taped every prayer, invocation, reading, and benediction she ever did. She's also awfully high church for us West Coasters, but her big city church puts on grand Sunday pageants. Weirdly, she only sent in the texts of two sermons. She's not stupid, but nobody could accuse her being a talented writer. The best acting couldn't bring those thunkers to life."

"Jennie might still hold out for her."

"It'd be good to know how the young ones are leaning before the meeting," said Charlotte. "I wonder if they're still conspiring after you and Adrian called them out."

"I thought Belinda had Riley in hand. But he voted Team Jennie all the way."

"Belinda's surprised, too. In fact, I had an idea. Not to impose on you professionally . . . if you could lure them to a restaurant . . ."

"You want me to take them to eat?"

"If you could. If it's too many for a review, I'll reimburse the cost."

"Let me check my eating schedule," I said. "See what I have coming up."

I didn't really have an eating schedule. I was more slapdash than that. I had a stack of press releases and some scribbled lists (somewhere) of possible restaurants to review. I dug around and found a good option, then sent an email inviting the four younger committee members (I couldn't resist adding Adrian) to lunch after church on Sunday at the renovated Rose Room Cafeteria. In minutes I had four RSVPs. Even Adrian!

When I finally opened Reverend Kapoor's packet, I was struck by her beauty and the professional quality of her website. Her homepage was a portrait from the waist up in three-quarters profile set against a moody gray background. She wore a pale violet tunic embroidered in darker thread. Her black hair tumbled down her back in glossy waves. God only knows why she didn't make it in Hollywood given those huge dark eyes, edificial cheekbones, and regal bearing. The webpage centered precisely on a small shiny silver chalice hanging from a fine chain around her neck. Subtle and lovely. The site menu, in white Helvetica caps, ran down the left side of the screen. The effect—subject and design—was lovely.

Under VIDEOS, I clicked on "Invocation 1" (of seven) to watch her open a service at her thousand-member church. In a glowing white robe and a stole featuring the planets, she stretched out her arms, palms upturned, as if offering a large, invisible tray. "You are welcome whoever you are, whatever you believe . . ." She looked like a sorceress. Her voice was throaty, incantatory, and inadvertently—one hoped—sexy. Each word was weighted. *Welcome. To. This. Beloved. Community.* I snorted. The performance was so stagy, so theatrical, it could have doubled as a comedy sketch.

As Charlotte had said, there were no videos of her sermons, only two pdfs: "Margaret Fuller, A Role Model for Our Time" and "Sikhism, My Grandfather's Gift." Both read like dry term papers, the prose flat, the facts piled on with no eye for the telling detail, no trace of humor. "My grandfather would take us kids to the Sikh temple, called a gurdwara" was as personal as either sermon got. In fact, her Sikhism sermon would have made a decent Wikipedia page if one very much like it wasn't already in place.

20

Cafeteria Free-for-all

For almost seventy years, the Rose Room Cafeteria had catered to the downtown office crowd at lunch, the fixed-income elderly at dinner, and the after-church crowd on Sunday. I had grown up eating there with my grandparents. Macaroni and cheese, confetti Jell-O, Parker House rolls, chicken potpie. The original owners, a family of tall, big-armed Nebraska transplants, had finally retired, and the new owner, a corporate restaurateur, had kept the menu but repapered the walls and hung glass-covered posters of lily ponds throughout the dining room. Easy listening pop tunes replaced the piped-in organ music of old.

We committee members gathered just inside the door. "Load up those trays," I said. "But everyone take something different, so watch what other people choose. We'll go back for dessert. And I have dibs on the boiled dinner."

We got in line, threading through roped-off switchbacks, to reach steam tables of meat and vegetables, then sneeze-guarded racks of salads and dessert. I went last and paid: under eighty dollars for five piled-on trays.

We claimed a long table among the elderly in their Sunday best. "It smells like the dining hall at my grandma's old age home," said Riley as we unloaded our trays.

The men had gone for meat: Curtis took the pork chops with applesauce and fried potatoes; Adrian picked a lamb shank the size of a caveman's club that came with corn and mashed potatoes; he'd added a side of mac and cheese; Riley had barbecued ribs on sauerkraut. "Nobody tell Eva and Sal," he said. "We've gone vegan at home."

Jennie tasted a quivering square of tomato aspic topped with half a boiled egg like a big yellow eye, then pushed it away. "Ew," she said. "Super-sweet!" She moved on to a wedge salad dressed with blue cheese, tomato, and bacon bits. A halibut steak, grilled to order (the most expensive menu item), was brought to her by a server.

We happily settled into our bounty. Riley's phone rang and he left the table to walk back and forth near the entrance.

"This halibut isn't bad," said Jennie. "The string beans are frozen. I sort of wish I'd gotten the fish and chips."

"Go get them!" I said.

"I'm trying to diet."

"You look fine, woman," Adrian said.

She lowered her face. Shy. Unaccustomed to compliments.

"So who's read which packets?" I said.

"I went through all of them," said Curtis.

"I've gone through the packets," said Adrian. "Now I'm into the sermons, which is the time-consuming part."

Jennie said, "Yeah, I still have a bunch of sermons to hear."

Riley walked up, slipping his phone into his pocket. "Sorry," he said.

Adrian said, "You know, Dana was right the other night—it does look suspicious when y'all vote the same way on everyone. It's not okay to stage a coup."

"Belinda met with the old people yesterday," Riley said.

"Hey! I wasn't invited," I said.

"'Cause you're not old," said Jennie.

"You're sweet. But I am. You four are the youngsters. I'm with the old."

"You're on the cusp," Riley said.

I felt like a cusp: an eye on both worlds.

"We're the middle-aged core," said Adrian. "Me and Dana."

How pleasing to be claimed by him!

"You both can be honorary young," said Jennie. "And Dana, you're way too fun and fashion forward for those old sticks. If not for you, we'd never have any fun on this committee. And"—her hand swept to indicate our food—"this is fun!"

"Yes, thank you, Dana, for inviting us," Riley said, with Jennie and Curtis chiming in: "Thank you, Dana . . ."

"Curtis," I said. "Any thoughts on the packets you read?"

"Let's see here." Curtis brought out a small notebook from his jacket pocket. "I listened to that Elsa woman's sermon about Trayvon. I liked it."

We all murmured in agreement. Powerful. Made us weep.

"Of course she's good," Jennie said. "She's famous for her preaching."

Jennie said this as if Elsa's fame somehow lessened her achievement. "Just because someone does something well doesn't mean it's easy for them," I said. "Elsa's sermons are researched and very carefully written. They are not first-draft productions. And the same goes for Doris's."

"I know, I know." Jennie scrunched up her face. "They're the great older women of color in the association: they've both preached the big important sermons at General Assembly. Everyone knows they're amazing."

"And that's a bad thing?"

"No. But there are also young people who have new and important ways of seeing and saying things. They maybe aren't as experienced as these great older women—and I know, it's unbelievable that big famous ministers like Elsa and Doris are even interested in us, but to me they're a little, I don't know, been there, done that. As you said, Dana, Doris probably sees us as the first step in her retirement plan and Elsa sees us as her next big Elsa Neddicke supersize-your-church production."

"That's a little cynical," I said, thinking it was very much so. "They have the experience and preaching chops we need. The preaching brings people in and the experience keeps the church running smoothly. Young ministers need to hone their chops at smaller churches—like Walt's done."

"I know. But it's already down to Elsa and Doris," said Jennie. "So why even look at anyone else?"

"First of all, that kind of prediction isn't helpful at this point," I said quietly. "We are just getting to know these people. And it's good not to get our hearts set on anybody. Doris and Elsa could be swapping packets with any number of churches."

"My heart's not set on anyone. I'm just saying that nobody else can stand up to those two. Even if they are kind of old hat."

"Harsh!" Adrian said. "That's like saying Beyoncé is old hat. Or Shakira."

"They are, kind of."

"Dana, if you think they won't choose us," Riley said, "maybe we should get behind some ministers we could actually get. Like the younger ones."

"Who might not retire in five years," said Jennie.

"Like who?" said Curtis.

"Oh my god. Alanna, of course. And I love that Phoebe Fetterman and, oh, love, love, *love* Liz Dumenil—those women are so on top of everything. They're like the opposite of worn-out old Tom. Who else? Riley? Help me out here."

"I haven't gotten to all the packets yet," said Riley. "It's a lot of reading."

"Have you liked anyone so far?" I said. "Have you taken a closer look at Walt?"

"I've had such a busy week," said Riley. "I guess, so far, I like Phoebe. And Alanna's videos are fantastic."

"Alanna is fantastic," said Jennie. "But right now? I'm leaning Liz!"

"Liz? Have you heard her preach? That voice!" I said.

"You don't like it? I think it's so-oh-oh soothing," said Jennie.

"Belinda and I heard Liz's Earth Day sermon when I drove her to church today," said Riley. "All about how we should compost and recycle—stuff that's been drummed into me since I was born. I don't go to church to improve my household habits."

Where could he go to improve his household habits?

"Mayeve's Earth Day sermon is a whole lot better," I said. "The one about deep history."

"Haven't got there yet," said Riley.

We grew quiet as we ate. The background music was a swelling Muzak arrangement of "Let It Be." My corned beef, a deep meaty magenta, was shaggy tender and served in a wide bowl with boiled cabbage, potatoes, carrots, and turnips.

"I like Perry," Curtis said tentatively.

"Me too," I said softly.

Adrian said, "I don't see either Phoebe or Liz becoming an Elsa or a Doris, who were already packing the pews with their preaching when they were forty."

"Aren't we afraid we'd be trading one tired-out old minister for another?" said Riley. "I mean, Tom's great, but it's obvious he can't wait to get the hell out."

"Not true!" I felt I should stand up for Tom. "He's preached his heart out this fall. And we are lucky to hear him."

"I'd feel luckier if we hadn't already heard everything he has to say ten thousand times," said Jennie. "I've only been back a year and I'm already sick of hearing about his four boys. And if I have to hear one more time about his blinding flash of light in the Sonoran Desert, I'll die . . . And, Riley, I liked Liz's environmental tips. It made me look up how to recycle those clamshell containers from Trader Joe's and what to do with dead batteries. I used to put everything in the trash, then feel guilty about it."

"I like Perry," Curtis said again.

"Yeah, but didn't he get fired from his only real church?" said Riley. "Belinda says that will have to be looked into. And he's only been an interim since."

"Of course. But he's still in good standing or headquarters wouldn't have sent us his record," I said. "And being an interim is being a real minister. In fact, it's more intense, like ministry on steroids."

"And Perry wasn't *fired*," said Jennie. "It was a negotiated settlement. That's when both the church and the minister agree things aren't working out."

"I like his preaching," I said. "It's like he's giving an off-the-cuff dharma talk at a meditation retreat. But when you see his sermons on the page, they're written and organized very carefully."

"I like that he's married to a man and has adopted two boys," said Curtis. "I never knew anybody could be like that and be a minister."

For some reason, tears sprang to my eyes.

Jennie said, "That's pretty much why I'm a UU, Curtis. Because our ministers can be gay, trans, Buddhist, atheist, any race, or same-sex adoptive parents with mixed-race families. You name it. That's the future. Everybody's in."

"Here's to the future," said Adrian.

We all lifted our water glasses in a toast.

I announced that I had to taste everyone's food. Plates were pushed toward me, and I took notes on my lap: *lamb shank, tender and salty; ribs falling-off-the-bone, sticky-sweet on haystack of sauerkraut; halibut firm and unfishy (tasteless?)* . . .

Adrian said, "And the verdict, Madame Critic?"

"It's all pretty good," I said, and jotted, *Home cooking, institutionalized.*

"Much better than the cafeteria at my grandma's old age place," said Riley.

"It's the salt," I said. "In that here they use it."

"Ima bring Jaz and Eric here," said Jennie. "Eric's from the Midwest, he grew up on this food. He'll go crazy."

"Again: I really liked Walt's packet," Adrian said. "Talk about young and innovative. And a truly decent human being."

"Ew, him again?" said Jennie. "Sorry, Aidy, but he's an icky Tom Fox clone to me. How come we even got his packet? He didn't get the votes for a packet swap."

"Because so many people we liked never sent in their packets," I said, "and he had the next most votes. And I don't know why you keep saying Walt's like Tom, Jennie. He's not like him in personality or looks or his style of ministry. Did you read that sermon on running and the marathon bombings? So emotional."

"His preaching creeps me out the same way Tom's does," said Jennie. "How he talks about himself like we're automatically interested in every little thing he does. Baking bread. Jogging. Making beer. And wasn't I right about that stupid all-face beard? Would it kill him to maybe give it some shape?"

"I know!" said Riley. "His beard makes me think of bristles on a pig."

"Your husband has a beard," Adrian said to Jennie. "Quite a substantial one."

"My husband's beard is very well maintained," Jennie said. "He takes time with it. Shapes it. Keeps it off his cheeks and neck."

"Perry has a beard, too," said Adrian.

"Yeah, but his is that super-tended, hip, four-day fuzz," said Jennie. "You actually need these special hundred-dollar clippers to get that look."

I said, "I can't believe we're talking about beards. Is that really our criteria?"

"It's not just Walt's beard," said Jennie. "It's the whole schlumpy package: the sincere, dorky white guy jogging and breathing home brew and preaching with a Bible in one hand and a loaf of bread in the other."

I couldn't help it. I laughed. "That's exactly what I like about him!"

"You really should reread his packet," said Adrian "The guy's cool."

"Or what older people think of as cool," said Riley. "No offense."

"We oldsters think you're cool, too," I said.

"But I don't come off as nebbishy as that dude. Do I?"

"Kind of," I said.

"Yup," said Adrian.

"Shit, man," said Riley.

"Joking!" In unison.

Jennie said, "What about that weirdie Mayeve?"

Curtis scanned the front and back sides of his notes. "I like her sermons!" he said, looking up brightly. "They're like biology lessons!"

Jennie said, "I liked the shaman one. But it's freaky she just came out. Do we want someone who's been in the closet for forty-five years? What do you think, Curtis?"

"I don't know. People come out when they come out," he said.

I said, "You guys! Who cares about their face hair or when they came out? It takes courage to apply for this job, to put so much of yourself on the line. We should respect them enough not to trash them."

"Amen," said Adrian.

Contrition silenced the table. Briefly.

Jennie said, "This isn't a real meeting. I thought we could talk off the record—you're not taking notes on what we're saying, are you, Dana?"

"Just on the food," I lied, and then, feeling bad, added, "Mostly."

We finished—or pushed away—our entrées, and to console ourselves after a scolding, we (the scolders and the scoldees) went back for dessert: Boston cream pie, brownie sundae, boysenberry pie à la mode, rice pudding.

Jennie said, "I like Liz and Phoebe because they're living my dream, being moms with careers who do tons of social justice work."

"They're a little too brisk and corporate for me," I said. "And neither is a good preacher. They fill the twelve-minute Sunday slot, but that's it."

Curtis thumbed through his notebook. "I watched Alanna's videos— she's good!" More thumbing. "And her sermons . . ." He frowned at his writing. "I liked them."

"Dana probably thinks she's too corporate, too," said Jennie.

"Too stagy," I said. "And her sermons are undercooked and pedantic."

"Alanna doesn't get to preach very often where she is now," said Jennie. "But I've seen her in the pulpit and she *owns* it. She's magical."

"She is definitely that." Riley gazed at a forkful of chocolate cake, then ate it.

"Hey, I'd better taste everyone's desserts," I said.

People shoved their partially demolished sweets toward me.

"This boysenberry pie filling is canned," Jennie said, prodding the dark purple bulge under a shiny, varnished crust. "You should put that in your review. 'Canned, cornstarchy filling—but not terrible à la mode.'"

21

Face-to-Face

W e began our Skype interviews in Belinda's dining room with Doris Gray, by asking how she preferred to be addressed.

"Reverend, or Pastor Gray for the present," she said.

I took a note: *Formal.*

Charlotte then asked for a five-minute summary of her career. Reverend Gray sat at her desk, self-possessed, in her wire-rimmed glasses, her back straight and shoulders squared. Soon we all were sitting up straighter, just from looking at her.

Starting out as one of only a handful of Black women ministers in the denomination, she said, she'd been given many privileged opportunities: She'd been invited on task forces and committees and panels that focused on diversity and race issues; she'd also been named to coveted leadership roles, some of them before she was sufficiently equipped with the necessary skill sets. "But I pride myself on coming up to speed and performing ably in every instance," she said. She'd risen high in the association; she'd preached and lectured all over the country, and in other countries as well. "Of course, many people assumed that I was placed into these positions to represent my race, and they were ready to make allowances should I fall short in my performance. I made sure not to fall short. But dealing with such condescension was a challenge. My first congregation had such low expectations of my abilities, they were astonished that I could do the job at all, let alone do it well."

She was sixty-four years old. The same age as Tom Fox!

In fact, she had gone to seminary with him. "We were study partners in New Testament," she said. "We did a joint report on the Gnostic Gospels. We had a lot of fun being tall and UU together. Folks called us The Terrible U's because we were both so progressive, so over Christianity, and so irreverent at that small Texas seminary."

Like Tom Fox, she said, she had "one more big career move" in her.

We'd each been assigned a line of questions for the candidates and she answered them as if it was her (somewhat wearisome) task to articulate answers long known (to her). She didn't smile once in the first fifteen minutes, and when she did (at Adrian saying, "And that chastity sermon, I mean, damn, woman!") it was such a relief, all we wanted was to make her smile again.

Imperious and intimidating, I wrote, *and v. compelling.*

My questions were theological: What was her theology, how did she come to it, and how would it fit in with the variety of beliefs among AUUCC members?

"I do have a theology," she said. "*Theo* meaning God and *-logy* meaning the study of. The study of God and the different beliefs in God."

She paused for a moment to let that sink in. Charlotte and Belinda glanced at me, acknowledging that I had said something very similar.

"My parents very carefully raised me in the liberal strains of two religious traditions, Judaism and Christianity. I went to synagogue and church. By the time I got to college, I was chafing at both, and if the Hare Krishnas had found me then, they might have bagged me. I was ripe for the picking. But before that could happen, a friend invited me to her UU church, and there among some exuberant secular humanists, I found a new religious home. In seminary and for maybe the first ten years of my ministry, I happily identified as an ardent secular humanist. Then something turned. The light dimmed. Where I had once woken up eager to meet the day's work, I found myself doing the bare minimum. Often, I sat at my desk and waited for each hour, each day, to pass. I had slid into an abyss. It was not even despair. It was a lack of feeling for anything. Even for my family. I took a leave of absence from my job, went on retreat, and worked with a spiritual counselor. I came to understand that I missed God's loving presence in my life. In my youthful enthusiasm for a deity-free religion, I had discarded too much too fast. Without hope, solely on my counselor's advice, I began to pray. I prayed to the Gods of my childhood. To Adonai and to Jesus. And slowly they drew me up, out of the abyss and into the world again.

"I still pray. Over the years, my conception of God has grown increasingly abstract and depersonalized, so that today, in prayer, I open myself to life itself, to the ongoing creation of which we are all a part.

"I would describe my present theology as constructive Black humanism seasoned with process, liberation, and eco-environmentalist thought."

I was trying to write this all down, which she must have noticed, because she paused until I looked up. She began speaking again, this time with mild thunder.

"My theology, since you asked, Dana, is all about life, and being alive— truly, deeply, vibrantly *fully* alive," she said. "I call it constructive because I have truly built *my own* theology, and that is an ongoing process. I'm a Black humanist in that I reject the supernatural in religion, but I find that not only the great books but the myths, the folktales, and the oral histories of my people call to the spirit in vital ways. I say I'm in process because I believe we're all in this ongoing creation that's as glorious as it is terrifying; I'm liberation and eco because, friends, we have got to pull out of this individualist, consumerist consciousness that's destroying the planet."

She paused again, then lowered her voice a notch.

"You ask, How can my theology serve differing beliefs and theologies at the Arroyo church? [She meant us, the AUUCC!] I would say, because my God is what you call life itself. And we must, all of us, wake up to life! To paraphrase the great theologian Howard Thurman, What the world needs is people who have come alive. So come alive, people! I say: Come alive!"

She began to thunder again. "It is not enough to witness. In the short time we have here, we must take action to heal what we can, to build up what we can, so that we—each and every one of us—leave the world more beautiful and more just than we found it. Nobody can do this alone—and, in fact, there is no life apart from our life together. So I would say to all of you at Arroyo, let us take our places in the community of the truly alive, the wide awake, the woke. We each have a life's worth of work to do. Soul work on the inside. The work of justice, compassion, and beauty out in the world. So let's work together. Let's get it *done!*"

Reverend Gray's words hung in the room, the way the closing chord of a Bach postlude hangs and slowly fades in church. I glanced around. Jennie's eyes had the fixed glow of the entranced. Riley's mouth was a small open O.

"All right," Adrian said. "Amen."

"So may it ever be," said Charlotte.

Having come forward and risen up a little from her chair, Reverend Gray resumed her straight-backed posture.

We rustled our papers, murmured, and took a little pause to calm down—then Sam asked what kind of salary she expected (large), and Belinda asked how she worked with her church boards and staff. ("I do need a staff, especially a strong administrator. I know my strengths," she said. "Fine print, numerical columns, spreadsheets, and technology are not among them.")

Adrian asked about how she took care of herself. (Prayer and meditation. "Old Lady yoga—no handstands or down dogs," and bird-watching). Adrian also posed the final question: Did she have any other skills or talents that we should know about?

She took off her glasses and pressed her eyes. "As a matter of fact, yes," she said, hooking her glasses back over her ears. "I'm an expert at extracting paper clips from between organ keys. And I can remove candlewax from every conceivable surface."

We all laughed—perhaps too loudly, for this was her first real joke. She looked pleased with herself and even, a little, with us. We said thanks so much and we'll be in touch, and when the screen went dark, there was a deep moment of silence before everyone started talking.

"She's epic!" cried Jennie.

"Epic!" said Curtis.

"That is the perfect word," said Belinda.

"I hope she will consider a pay cut," said Sam. "She wants thirty thousand more than Tom Fox makes now. Not sure we could match that."

"She'd be worth every cent," said Riley.

"Amen," said Adrian.

We got up and moved around.

This was the night that Belinda made her superb Ottolenghi chicken and the drifting aroma of caramelized onions, basmati rice, and warm spices made us hungry, so the thought of another whole interview before we could eat seemed onerous, even superfluous, after Doris. Riley queued us for the next call, then refreshed our drinks; he'd brought fresh grapefruit and tangerine juices, homemade grenadine, seltzer, and a bottle of arak—though we wouldn't add the alcohol till after the interview.

I followed Belinda into the kitchen to help her pick herbs for the garnish.

"She'd be different," Belinda said.

"She's a little intimidating," I said. "Like a strict teacher that you learn to adore."

"Exactly," said Belinda.

"Like you," I said. "Intimidating for years, and then beloved."

Belinda turned her enormous, clouding eyes on me. "Oh, Dana," she said. "You have such a way with words."

From the first moment she came into view—a plane of yellow forehead and two black-browed dark eyes—Elsa couldn't have been more different from Doris.

Doris had the persona of a magisterial, powerful minister. Elsa, as she wished us to call her, was only herself: small, with short black curly hair and intense, piercing eyes. Even on a computer in grainy light, she came off as sensitive and alert, as curious and responsive as a small wild animal. She took our questions in, far in, and then pulled her responses from that deep place.

Like Doris, she was known for her preaching and for how her churches grew. Her first church, she said, had 140 members when she arrived and 500 when she left. Her second had 200 to start and 700 when she left. She'd been in Colorado now for twelve years, and that membership had doubled to almost 1,000 members. "I prefer a church where I know everybody's name, and at least a little about them."

She was applying only to the AUUCC. "When I was a new minister, I knew next to nothing about church power structures and politics. As a journalist in war zones, I'd seen terrible conflict, but that in no way prepared me for the hot button issues in a church, such as who sponsors the book sale or who gets the seminar room on Tuesday nights. Loving tolerance, I discovered, only went so far. Luckily, I met Sparlo Plessant at a ministers' retreat and he agreed to mentor me. He taught me to be more pragmatic and strategic, to take disagreements less personally. And how to spot problems before they took hold.

"When Sparlo retired, he wanted me to succeed him at the AUUCC. But I'd just been a year at this church and I was committed to the congregation here, so I couldn't leave. Now this church has grown beyond my capacity to serve it well—at heart I'm not a large church minister—and I would love to come to the AUUCC."

To Riley's consternation, not one of her churches ever had a bell choir.

I asked, What was her theology, how did she come to it, and how would she address all the different beliefs at the AUUCC?

"My theology is rooted in the mystery, the unanswerable questions that arise from our deepest hopes and fears.

"In the nineties, I was in Israel when, not two hundred feet away from me, a suicide bomber activated his vest, and it was not like what you see on TV. It was so chaotic and horrifying, so unbearable and heartbreaking, my mind, my heart, my nerves have never been the same. Why do humans do such things?

"And as I sat there, stunned, with flames springing up, and cars on their sides, people ran past me, straight into the bomb zone, to help whomever they could . . .

"Why do humans do such things?

"And the men who carried out that attack—what horrors had driven them to it?

"What does it mean to be human? What are we doing here on this planet? What should we do with all the beauty and the horror? I spent a year as a hospice chaplain and what did I learn? That everyone wants to live. Even if just to gaze out a window at the sky. If life is so beloved, so precious, why as a species do we seem hell-bent on destroying our beautiful earthly home? How can we create a more just and peaceful world instead?

"When we take on these great questions, when we move away from the cant and the dogma that divides one group from another, when we engage with wonder and openness the great paradoxes of life; when we take them in and let them bloom within us, that is when we have truly entered the holy. . . ."

Elsa, too, relied on working hand in hand with a strong administrator. "I can barely keep my own schedule straight, let alone devise them for others. I am a preacher, a pastor, a community leader, and when I can be one, a writer. Although not a real writer like you, Dana," she said, startling—and, of course, charming—me, "the only book I've ever written is eighty pages with very large print and a lot of white space."

A meditation manual: she'd included its pdf in her packet.

Elsa remembered that Adrian was a therapist and founder of the racial justice task force; she asked Jennie and Curtis about their children and Belinda about her history projects. Before we said goodbye, Elsa told Sam that she'd loved meeting his wife on a retreat for church presidents and mollified Riley by admitting she'd "been intrigued" by the YouTube video of his "Ode to Joy" on handbells.

We were as hungry as hunters after a day of stalking prey. The word for Belinda's chicken, we agreed, was also *epic*, the meat deeply flavored, the rice flecked with tiny sour-sweet jewel-red barberries, and mined with woody spices you had to pluck out—cinnamon sticks, cloves, and black cardamom pods as big and wrinkled as prunes.

"This could be the best thing I have ever eaten," said Jennie.

"It's right up there," I said.

"The food writer agrees!" Jennie said. "Did you hear that, Belinda?"

"I just followed the recipe," said Belinda. "Anybody could make it."

Not true. Not everybody used quality organic chicken, high-grade extra-long basmati rice, hard-to-find black cardamom pods. The parsley and cilantro from Belinda's own garden were more flavorful than supermarket varieties. And Belinda had the great cook's touch; her onions were expertly caramelized, her chicken well browned, her rice cooked to the right tooth. . . . No, not everyone could make this.

"I'd have a difficult time picking between those two ministers," said Charlotte.

"And we have six more to go," said Adrian.

"I doubt anybody else will make the decision harder than it is right now."

"Yeah, these guys are shoo-ins," said Jennie. "But it's like they have more wisdom than any new, cutting-edge ideas."

"New ideas can come from older people, too," I said.

"Maybe," said Jennie. "But they'd be different new ideas than the ones from people who are up on the latest theory."

"I wouldn't assume these women are uninformed," said Charlotte.

"Who's more wide awake than Doris?" said Adrian.

"There is nothing old and outdated with either one," said Belinda.

"Well, maybe not to you," said Jennie. "No offense or anything . . ."

I laughed. I couldn't help it: Jennie was so Jennie.

Charlotte shot me the evil eye. "Jennie," she said sharply. "Just stop. You are being ageist and offensive. So enough."

"I'm just . . ."

"Stop. I suggest you reread the covenant and make sure you abide by what it says, or you could face dismissal from the committee."

"Why, what did I do? You can't . . ."

"I can and I will."

I had never seen the steely lawyer in Charlotte so clearly. Skinny, cold, straight, and sharp, she would terrify in a courtroom—or anywhere.

We hovered over our plates, not meeting one another's eyes. I took a long medicinal swig of wine; Adrian and Belinda did the same. I couldn't see Jennie—I was next to Adrian and she was on his far side—but we felt her seethe, and another outburst seemed imminent until Curtis said, "I like how Doris wants to be called pastor. That's what we called our ministers at First Cal. Once I called Tom Fox 'Pastor Tom' and he said to never ever *ever* call him that again."

"UU ministers rarely go by pastor," said Belinda. "I don't know why."

"In seminary there was a preaching/pastoral divide," I said. "You're intellectual and a preacher, or you're compassionate and caretaking and a pastor."

"I'd say that Pastor Gray has no problem with her preaching," said Adrian. "And coming up in the Black Baptist tradition, I always considered 'pastor' as reverential as 'reverend,' and maybe a little more personal and loving."

"Filipino churches, the same," said Curtis. "We love our pastors."

"Pastor Doris," Belinda said. "Pastor Anyone. That'd be a first around here."

22

Interims

We met again on Thursday evening, this time at Charlotte's with an even more taxing agenda: Skype interviews with three ministers: Phoebe Fetterman, Liz Dumenil, and Perry Fitzgerald.

Ignoring the no-red-meat rule, Charlotte had slow-cooked a brisket, so her house smelled like Passover dinner at my grandmother's on a cold spring night. Curtis brought hors d'oeuvres—olives, pita bread, and store-bought hummus (always a mistake). I was putting together a salad when Sam, who was supposed to bring a green vegetable, arrived out of breath. "Sorry, Gayle, I didn't bring the string beans," he said, but before I could say "You mean Dana," he turned to everyone in the living room and said, "Faithalma had a seizure. I came straight from the hospital. She's conscious, but her speech is very garbled. She's terrified, poor thing. So, guys, listen: before I get half that bad, you have to promise me something. Promise me you'll give me the pills or unplug me or put a pillow over my face. Promise?"

We burst out laughing.

"I'm serious," said Sam. "Dead serious. I'm asking for your help here."

Our amusement subsided into embarrassed silence.

"This is a conversation you need to have with Emma," Adrian said gently.

"I did. She said she can't and won't do it," Sam said.

"Then with Tom. Or our new minister, whoever it will be."

"But you all know me." Sam's voice grew husky with emotion. "Arne said that we'd get close. And I feel closer to you than to anyone else. That's why I'm asking."

How close can you be to someone whose name you can't remember? And had we become close as a group? I had a different idea of closeness. I certainly wasn't close enough to Sam to mercy kill him—what a thought! The others seemed as speechless, appalled, and embarrassed for him as I was.

"Oh, Sam," Charlotte said. "We get where you're coming from, but someone could go to prison for what you're asking us to do."

"There are ways . . ."

Belinda said, "Time for our call."

Riley had set up the monitor beside the fireplace and its heatless gas flames. We took our seats on the firm-cushioned bent-plywood furniture and met the two remaining Indistinguishables, one after the other. To interview them after Doris Gray and Elsa Neddicke was not fair; despite their six to eight years of experience, both women came off as pikers. Brisk "Reverend Phoebe" said absolutely nothing wrong and absolutely nothing of interest. "Just Liz" Dumenil was the quintessential young matron minister: easy-care short hair, unflattering horn-rimmed glasses, chalice pin on a dark blazer. Both women oversaw intense social-action programs; Phoebe's entire congregation had signed up for at least one of many "action groups": they built homes, tutored, fed the homeless, planted trees, sponsored refugees, marched, wrote letters, and lobbied.

Liz, who represented "a new intersectional model of UU ministry," had begun her present ministry with an uphill climb; the small, moribund congregation of ninety that called her, she said, "had devolved into a wine-and-cheese-tasting society. But I got them to take off their bibs and buckle on their tool belts! Five years in, we're up to one hundred and twenty members, with over two-thirds actively engaged in social justice projects."

Both ministers said their theology was "love." "Love is the doctrine of our church," said Liz. "Love is the thread of the interconnected web," said Phoebe.

Both ministers said they attended all committee meetings and most social justice activities. No wonder these women's sermons were so flat: when did they have the time to read and study, think deeply, and hammer out sentences?

"It's amazing how Liz turned her church around," Jennie said when the screen went dark.

"Thirty new members in six years is not amazing," said Belinda. "And, frankly, I'm exhausted just listening to them both. Since when is church all social action?"

Jennie said, "But didn't you love that 'take off their bibs and buckle on their tool belts' bit? Liz'd be great here because the AUUCC is such a wine-and-cheese-tasting society."

"I actually found that 'tool belt' business offensive," said Adrian. "It implies that anyone who doesn't volunteer is a baby who can't feed herself. But some people wear a tool belt all week, and they come to church worn out, in need of spiritual replenishment."

"To call any church 'a wine-and-cheese-tasting society' is degrading," said Charlotte. "For some single and older people, church *is* their social life—and that's a very important function churches serve."

"Both those gals are so self-confident!" said Sam.

"Without half a sense of humor between the two of them," said Belinda.

"You guys are all hardwired to like big, showy, egotistical white male ministers," said Jennie. "Which is exactly what Phoebe and Liz aren't. They don't just spew intellectual mishmash from the pulpit, then pass the plate for some hands-off charity of the month. They get people helping in person out in the community."

"It's not big personalities I want, Jennie, male or female," said Belinda. "It's brilliant preaching and experienced leadership. As is clear from the survey and cottage groups: inspiring preaching and sound leadership are our priorities. By their own admission, these two women do not put preaching first."

"I'm just sorry that the nonbinary minister I know isn't in search," said Jennie. "I'd pay anything to see the looks on everyone's faces when they stepped into our pulpit the first Sunday of candidating week."

Belinda said, "You underestimate this congregation. We love our ministers and trust our search committees. Anybody we present will be welcomed and respected."

"Maybe," said Jennie.

"Out of curiosity, Jennie," said Sam. "Why are you so anxious to have this non . . . nonbinary person as our next minister?"

"Because they're the gender-fluid future, where we aren't locked into old binary paradigms. They'd enlarge our understanding of how humans are." Jennie shrugged. "Though the learning curve might be too steep for some people."

"I hope you're not talking about me," Sam said. "I'm very open-minded."

"Oh, man, Sam," Jennie said. "You most of all!"

"Jennie," said Charlotte, "what did I say to you at our last meeting?"

Jennie gaped at Charlotte and almost looked contrite.

"Interview time," said Riley.

Perry, as he said to call him, had a studied, casual elegance: the T-shirt under the well-cut sport jacket, the short salt-and-pepper hair, the stubble. Sitting before an empty desktop, he'd lit himself well. Behind him, a dozen or more clay bowls were carefully spaced on shelves. All was spare, calm, and serene. His career history? Not so much. After getting a PhD in Eastern religious studies, he'd taught at a state university for six years until he was denied tenure. His books and articles, while highly regarded among Buddhist practitioners, were deemed not academic enough by his committee, too geared to a popular audience. Perry decided to leave academia then, thinking he'd write and teach meditation. He was lucky, around that time, he said, to have a brief meeting with the Zen master Thích Nhất Hạnh, whom he asked for guidance. "Thầy was completely unimpressed that I was a Buddhist monk and insisted that I should practice within my own Western religious tradition. I tried to explain that I personally had no religious tradition, but he wouldn't budge. I left our meeting feeling unheard and angry. But he'd planted a seed.

"Not long afterward, I was teaching a meditation course in a rented classroom at a UU church. The minister there sat in on a class and invited me to preach one Sunday. In that pulpit, I found the Western tradition I could work within."

Given his PhD, Perry completed the few course requirements and internships for ordination within a year. He was promptly hired on a three-year contract as an assistant minister at a 230-member church in the Midwest. After two years, the long-serving elderly senior minister retired due to illness, and Perry, as an inside candidate, became the new senior minister. He lasted two years and then left with "a negotiated settlement."

"I moved too fast. Even my small changes—replanting a flower bed with drought-resistant native plants—met with fierce resistance. When I tried to address real issues, like a too-large debt load and a lazy staff, the full tide turned against me. I realized that, as an insider, I'd been hired to keep things the way they were. To make matters worse, the beloved retired minister, who was dying, began coming to church on Sundays. I could hardly turn him away, but his being there further weakened my authority. I know now that the church should have brought in an interim to tear out the cobwebs, while a full search was conducted for a new senior minister. I had to leave for that to happen."

Perry then trained to be an interim minister and had since served one-year stints at two churches and was now in his third year of an extended interimship at another. "Our kids are almost school-age, so it's time I found a more permanent settlement."

Near the end of the interview, he had a question for us: "I'm curious why the AUUCC didn't wait till Tom Fox left to call an interim and conduct a search then."

Belinda and Charlotte, in a look, decided who would speak. "Since Tom gave a year's notice," Charlotte said, "he suggested that we could search then. Given that the last interim was so unpopular, the board approved it."

Perry, distracted, spun sideways in his chair. Affection softened his expression as he lifted a three-year-old boy onto his lap: one of the two brothers he and his husband, Harry, had adopted from Ethiopia. The boy, rubbing one eye, snuggled in his father's arms. "Zelly sweetie, meet my friends at the Arroyo church. Can you wave to them?"

The eye-rubbing hand fanned out.

That wave made Perry's chances.

It would be lovely to have a minister with a young family again," said Belinda.

"I thought Perry was a little dry," said Charlotte, "until the kid showed up."

"I had this instant fantasy that Perry would come here and Zelly and Jaz would grow up together and get married," said Jennie.

"Same here!" said Curtis. "Exactly! Only with Max."

The approbation Perry received as a parent irked: if Phoebe's or Liz's toddlers had interrupted their interviews, wouldn't we have seen the intrusion as less than professional—couldn't she keep her kid out of the way for one important interview?

"It could be expanding to have a minister grounded in Buddhism," said Adrian.

"Yah! Perry is about as far from a white hetero male minister as you can get while still being white and male and a minister," said Riley.

Perry was cool. Not self-possessed and commanding like Doris, and not present in the intensely relational way that Elsa was, he was present and detached, as if he saw us—and all our imperfections—clearly. I kept thinking of his sermon where he said that presence was power, and the person who was the most present in the room had the most power, and his presence did feel like a power trip. I wasn't sure I liked him.

Yet he would *never* make us repeat silly phrases to one another.

Again, we fell upon dinner with near savageness. Charlotte's brisket was fork-tender, with ample gravy for the mashed potatoes. I'd lightly dressed a salad made with tender garden lettuces.

"For some reason, red meat feels right tonight," Jennie said.

"That's 'cause we're nearing the kill," said Riley.

"We still have three more interviews on Saturday," said Charlotte.

"Oy," said Adrian.

This seems like a good place to disclose why we at the AUUCC were so averse to bringing in an interim minister.

When Sparlo retired, the AUUCC duly hired an interim to serve for the year that the search committee was conducting its search.

The interim who came to us was a tightly packed bald man of around fifty-five, with a wrestler's thick arms and short neck, and a meaty face with the high polish I usually associate with wealthy, frequently massaged men, men who care about their pores, like the successful TV writers and studio execs one sees around LA. This interim's wife, a beauty in her late forties, had thick honey-gold hair, a flawless jawline, and a sophisticated classic style; she telegraphed old money, old Newport money, in fact, which was the kind she had. While her husband served as an interim in churches all over the country, she remained in their Rhode Island home and worked as a therapist. She was in church on his first Sunday at the AUUCC and visited every six weeks after that.

I became friends with the interim the way I would become friends with Tom Fox: because Sparlo had recommended me to him. The interim also liked to eat out and aspired to write a book, so he sought me out. We went to lunch every month or so and talked about books and spiritual concepts. I had (and still have) a great hunger for the probing, metaphysical conversation I'd loved so much in seminary and had rarely enjoyed since. The interim had an interesting if musty mind; he identified as a Christian Unitarian, a dwindling, more conservative branch of the denomination rare in California. I enjoyed him, but nobody else at the AUUCC liked him very much. Or at all.

To hear him tell it, the churches that he'd previously served were all in dire shape when he arrived. He'd mopped up after "negotiated settlements" and all manner of ecclesiastical and clerical dysfunction. While I thought that Sparlo had made us into a strong, sane, healthy church with a board that functioned like an intelligent, reasonable brain and an endowment the envy of many, the interim, who was used to coming in and fixing things, found deep problems where we saw none. He found it ethically objectionable, for example, that a powerful lay leader was the church's salaried secretary. "That Belinda Bauer knows too much," he once told me over pho. "She thinks *she* runs the church."

He couldn't fire her. Sparlo had given her too much power. The church would descend into chaos if she left. "I wouldn't wonder if she blackmailed old Plessant about all sorts of things," the interim said.

(Sparlo, when I told him this, laughed loudly and slapped his knee.)

The interim yelled at the then-church president, our sweet-tempered Arne Greene, when Arne—still a working physicist at the time—had to miss a board meeting to use his allotted beam time on the synchrotron in Grenoble, France. In his absence, Charlotte—then a partner at DLA Piper—conducted the meeting, only to be scolded when it ran overtime. "Clearly, you know nothing of Robert's Rules," the interim famously said.

The interim was appalled, too, at the autonomy of our committees, and they, in turn, were appalled when he butted into every meeting.

The search committee back then flatly refused to let the interim attend their meetings, which enraged him. In spurning his expertise, he told me, the committee was unlikely to select the right person. The new minister, the interim said, needed specific skills and experience to deal with an overprivileged, overindulged, over-functioning congregation. He, the interim, would do his best to reacclimate the AUUCC to a minister who actually worked, one who didn't abandon the management of the church to a power-hungry secretary and a bloated church board. But he had only a year and our dysfunction was deep, he said. The new minister had his work cut out for him.

The congregation mostly ignored the interim. To us, he was a placeholder. He'd be gone come June. We knew we were healthy. Sparlo had always nipped trouble in the bud. Pledges had exceeded proposed budgets for five years in a row. Excellent turnouts continued on Sundays, even for the interim, whose warmed-over sermons couldn't hold a candle to Sparlo's spontaneous brilliance.

Perhaps the interim's greatest misstep was the communion service.

Rummaging in the church basement, he'd found the old brass communion dishes, which inspired him to reacquaint us with the Christian sacrament. We had flower communions and apple communions, but this would be the real version with wine and tasteless dissolve-in-the-mouth wafers he'd cadged from the minister at the Lutheran church down the street. He instructed the secretary—Belinda Bauer!—to polish the brass dishes. She preferred not to. He berated her so loudly that the lunch meeting of the Heritage Committee—five men who lobbied people to put the AUUCC in their wills—heard the yelling and intervened.

A janitor polished the brass.

For the ritual, the interim appeared downright papal in a gold-embroidered robe. "Come on up," he exhorted us hucksterishly. "Celebrate our community." He lifted the gleaming goblet and plate of wafers. "This is our blood, this is our body."

To be polite, I and many others—though none of the other Jewish-born members (including Arne Greene and Charlotte Beck)—approached the folding table where the wine and wafers awaited. Obediently, we stuck out our tongues for the tasteless morsel and sipped from the old brass cup. I personally did not gain any sense of community; in fact, I felt I'd betrayed my closest church friends.

The communion service was discussed afterward with near-universal dismay. Especially offended were those raised Jewish and those former Christians who had all come to the AUUCC to escape what they saw as empty and oppressive rituals. "I can't believe you have lunch with that tone-deaf martinet," Charlotte hissed one Sunday.

"I consider it spying," I said, not quite truthfully. I liked my talks with the interim. And to me he'd been charming: attentive, funny, and sharp.

After leaving the AUUCC in June, and before taking up his next year's appointment, the interim would lead his yearly interfaith tour of the Holy Land. I didn't consider going because (a) I couldn't afford it, (b) it didn't deeply interest me, and (c) I'm not a person who goes on group tours or can room with a stranger.

In late May, the interim asked if I'd like to tag along on the trip: a woman had dropped out due to a family crisis. Her fees were nonrefundable—and she'd paid the premium, too, for a single room. All I'd have to come up with was the airfare to Tel Aviv. "I think you'd enjoy it," the interim said. "I know I would enjoy it if you came." I could write about the food, he said. He knew the best places to eat in Jerusalem and Tel Aviv.

I pitched several magazines a Holy Land food article—and got some bites—but Jack, whom I'd just started seeing, wasn't keen on my going. He thought the interim had designs on me. I had seen the interim's beautiful, classy, old-moneyed wife and I didn't hold a candle to her in looks or net worth. Also, our ministers were exhaustively coached in what constitutes sexual misconduct and how it could end their careers. The interim, I assured Jack, would never risk his career and marriage that way, and even if he was inclined to, I wasn't at all romantically interested in *him*. Jack was not reassured.

When I turned down the interim's offer of free room and board in the Holy Land, he turned sulky and cold, then stopped speaking to me. Jack, I conceded, might have been right and the interim had envisioned a romantic escapade.

Even given the interim's sour personality, the congregation probably disliked him so ardently because he was not our beloved Sparlo. The interim took a lot of punishment for this. We were angry with him, at times gleefully so, and some of this was an anger we could never express to Sparlo, who had abandoned us, however justifiably. Bearing the brunt of our grief and anger was part of the interim's job, a kindness, even a martyrdom on his part, plus a huge favor to the next minister, who could then arrive like a conquering hero.

When the search committee named the Reverend Dr. Tom Fox as their candidate, and when the congregation heard him preach and unanimously voted him in—well, almost unanimously, as the usual half-dozen soreheads cast dissenting votes—spirits soared and there was much rejoicing, no small part of which was the enormous pleasure and relief of seeing the interim depart.

23

⁂

A Big Fertile Mess

I n the Arroyo House library, Riley set up the large monitor at one end of the long oak table. By nine, we were ready to go. Outside was a beautiful, clear February day, but you'd never know it once the heavy green velvet curtains were drawn.

Mayeve Schindler, too, was in a darkened room—in Alabama. A shaft of light caught her pile of curly hair, but a tea-colored shadow obscured her face. Having made enormous life changes by divorcing her husband and falling in love with a woman ("Can y'all just imagine?" she said), she was eager to start fresh at a new church.

"Ah've been here thirteen happy years," she said, and while her personality had an eccentric humorous cast, her approach to staffing, RE, and finances sounded well grounded, intelligent, and professional. She ran a tight ship.

Charlotte, Adrian, and I exchanged looks: *She'd do!*

"Ah became decisive and efficient," Mayeve said in her closing statement, "so that Ah could have time for what matters most, and in my ministry, that's worship, music, and the environment. We sing. We play a lot of music on the church's front porch. And we spend a lot of time outdoors, making conscious our connection to the earth. We might meet to bird-watch for an hour before church or plant trees afterward. The more intimate we are with where we live—the flora, the fauna, the cycles of life—the more at home we feel in the world. Our members know all the plant, bug, bird, and critter families on church property. We follow the weather, the stars, and the clouds. . . ."

Just before she signed off, she offered to sing us a song.

Plucking a dulcimer off the wall, she sat in an easy chair, positioned the instrument her lap, and started in on "Bridge over Troubled Water." Her hair fell over her face. Her voice was sweet, folksy, and in tune, reminding me of the country musicians recorded by archivists in the rural South. With the chorus, she began to keep time by slapping the dulcimer, and somehow each slap was a sharp, direct crack to our eardrums. Riley turned the volume way down and even then the cracks penetrated. Charlotte called out, but Mayeve, lost in the song, strummed and slapped her way through a long instrumental break. At the end, she looked up, smiled ecstatically, and waved. She said something, too, but the volume was so low we didn't hear it, and the screen went dark.

"There you have a case study in blowing an interview," said Charlotte.

"I wouldn't write her off completely," said Adrian.

"We'll have to write off someone sometime," said Belinda.

"Not my kind of music," said Riley.

"I didn't like how she hit her lute," said Sam.

"Dulcimer," several of us rang out.

"Her obliviousness was far more alarming than her singing," said Charlotte.

"I like that she's so unabashedly herself," I said. "She knows who she is, and her vision is strong. And I love her ideas for ministry—imagine people playing music outside the sanctuary or on our lawn. And how great if we knew every tree and plant and critter in our gardens!"

"I agree," said Adrian. "She's whole and strong and visionary."

If I ever did make Adrian my love interest in the book, I thought, this is when I'd kiss him.

Walt Harrison was sweeter and funnier than I expected. True, his eyes were small and squinty, his blond hair stringy, his beard red and, yes, untended and all-face. But so what? His laugh tumbled out with a sob in it.

As was our routine, we went around the circle and introduced ourselves.

Before Jennie could speak, he said, "Jennie Ross! I saw you were on the committee and that you have a little girl now. I'm so happy for you."

"Yes. Jasmine," Jennie said curtly and turned to Sam, who introduced himself.

"I have a Do Not Disturb sign on my door," Walt said. "But we're setting up our first art opening tonight—with pizza—so I apologize in advance if we get interrupted."

He was drawn to the AUUCC for its stability, beauty, and location—an older gay friend of his parents', an artist, lived in Altadena, and often bragged about how famously friendly the town was to interracial couples, homosexuals, artists, and spiritual seekers.

"Not to mention a wide assortment of cranks and soreheads," said Belinda.

"Well, then, I'd fit right in," said Walt.

His bookshelves were disorderly, the volumes shoved in all ways, with toys and religious figurines along the edges—a St. Sebastian bristled with arrows next to Sponge Bob and a pot-metal elephant-headed Ganesh: all of it a big, fertile mess.

Sam said, "You're thirty-five with six years of ministry under your belt. Don't you worry that you're too young and inexperienced to serve a church our size?"

"I'm not worried—though it sounds as if you might be. And I can only assure you that time will remedy both issues."

He was, he said, first and foremost a preacher. "But I can get carried away by outreach. My church administrator often sends me to my office to write. Of course, as Dana knows, it's easier to do almost anything else than write. But I preach three times a month, and my main theme is the breaking down of barriers. So one Sunday it might be the barrier between the self and the deeper self—how can we sit alone in a room? How do we listen for and embolden the still small voice within? How do we relate to those parts of ourselves we can't stand?

"The next Sunday, I might talk about the barrier between self and community: How do we find common ground with our different neighbors, or how can we reach and help those who suffer? The third Sunday I'll look at the barriers between ourselves and the world at large: how do we personally recognize and address global problems like climate change, world hunger, military interventions?"

Adrian said, "How does your identity affect your ministry?"

"As a white man with all the privilege that entails, part of my ministry is making those privileges conscious, to myself and to others. Where is life easier for me? When do I get a pass where others struggle? How can I be more awake to those who suffer from systemic injustice? How can I create more justice?"

"I have to ask," said Adrian. "How did you bring so many Black people to your church?"

"To begin with, I invite and welcome those who believe in a loving, personal God. But first I had to address the rampant God-hating in our denomination. Nearly eighty percent of all atheists are white, and nearly eighty percent of UUs are white. Atheism and even UUism, you might say, are white privileges. Comfort, education, and high self-regard have led some to believe that they make their own destinies, that they have no need of an interceding God. These humanists can be condescending to and intolerant of those who do turn to and love a personal God. It's time we recognize and call out the racism inherent in that intolerance."

Walt was preaching now, quietly, with force. "Who are we to demean a faith that sustained millions through centuries of institutionalized injustice? Who are we to deny a God that comforted the poor, the sick, the imprisoned, the orphans and widows who had nothing but faith to see them through? We UUs say, 'We welcome you, whoever you are, whatever you believe,' but we have work to do to live up to that. We do that work here at First UU when we worship together; when we have a community pizza night or a bread-baking class; when we run together, sing one another's songs; when we hold hands and say Dear God, Please Lord, God bless us, and amen.

"The other ways we welcome our neighbors into our church is to help them establish the services that they need. Tell me what you need and I'll pitch it to the congregation. When possible, the church will provide the resources to get you started. Maybe it's a room for a study group, a place to rehearse a jazz trio or start a school for African dance. But we never do anything for anybody that they can do for themselves."

Oh, god, enough with the loaf and pizza stuff," said Jennie. "And just what we don't need. A great white savior."

"I wonder why you call him that, Jennie," said Adrian.

"You of all people should see why."

"I see a caring, highly intelligent minister who helps people help themselves."

Jennie glowered. "It's his high-and-mighty vibe I hate."

Charlotte said, "It's time you tell us about your relationship with Walt, Jennie. Because if it was intimate, or he hurt you in some way, you should recuse yourself."

"It was never intimate. Never! Ask him. He'll tell you: one hundred per-cent nothing intimate."

We had no more time to talk before our final interview.

24

Agnes of God

"T here you are!" Alanna Kapoor said in a throaty voice, with what sounded like genuine pleasure. Her smile had a warmth and a sweetness not apparent in her photos or videos, where she'd seemed so ceremonial and (to me) false. Here she sat at an angle to the camera, with the same moody, cloudy-gray background seen on her home page— a photographer's scrim?—that set off her rose-pink tunic and her beauty: huge eyes and full lips, tumbling dark hair and classic facial structure.

Before we could introduce ourselves, she said, "I see Sam: hey there! Thanks for all the financial info. And Belinda! Thank you for arranging this interview. Your newsletter columns are so informative. You're such a compelling writer . . ."

Belinda, ever averse to flattery, gave a curt tuck of her chin.

"So I'm Riley Kincaid," Riley was saying.

"Of course! I watched your YouTube videos! I thought I'd watch one or two as interview prep and ended up watching all twelve! Such amazing performances!"

"And I'm . . ."

"Jennie Kanematsu-Ross!" Alanna cried. "I still think about that Asiatarian panel you did at GA—was it two years ago? Four? Gosh! Well, it sure stuck with me."

And so it went, around the room. She'd read two of my books and "as many of your articles I could find online—such compelling writing!" (Had she forgotten she'd just called Belinda's writing that?) She didn't cook, but a friend of hers had made my pomegranate chicken (". . . all those flavors went zinging around my mouth!").

Charlotte she recognized as the AUUCC president whose pledge drive raised twenty percent above budget. "Who does that? Every minister in the country would love to work with you." She'd heard about Adrian's work with the BIPOC task force, and she'd read an article he'd written in *American Behavioral Scientist.*

"That was ten or fifteen years ago."

"Yet there it was online," she said. And to Curtis: "I read the newsletter piece your husband wrote about losing your baby. I'm so sorry, and so moved that you're on such a hardworking committee when your heart must be aching. So generous of you."

"Thank you," he said softly. "I am heartbroken. But everyone here is so nice."

We heard again about her nun costume drawing her to ministry. And how, as an assistant minister at a large church in the South, she spent her first year in pastoral care, her second in social justice, and this year was in religious education, where she'd launched her Theater of the Body Dynamic. "We dramatize power dynamics, human suffering, and injustice through word and movement, and invite the audience to join in, which awakens their compassion and identification with the sufferers."

"Have you had any corporate-model administrative experience?" asked Sam.

"I managed a theater group in my twenties, which means I'm good with difficult people. And begging for money." She laughed and we did, too, for some reason. "And I took the required church management course in seminary, of course."

Her poise and humor, the alluring rasp in her voice, and her undeniable beauty were, as she would say, compelling. The men gaped.

"In your Ministerial Record, you rate preaching as a high interest but give yourself a low grade." Belinda was matter-of-fact. "And frankly, the two sermons included in your packet don't contradict that grade. Can you speak to this?"

Alanna dipped her head in modest assent. "Where I am now, I only preach twice a year, and I have used most of those opportunities to present alternative rituals, involving theater and visualizations. But because I'm seeking a preaching ministry now, improving my sermons is my highest priority. I have an incredible preacher mentoring me and I have six pulpits booked for practice over the summer. I promise there'll be improvement!"

Her theology? Love. What else?

She signed off with a dazzling smile.

We were all a little stunned.

"She's certainly self-possessed," said Charlotte. "And has a powerful presence."

"I'll say," said Sam. "She's just terrific."

"Don't be pathetic, Sam," said Belinda. "She's beautiful. And so inexperienced it's almost endearing. Like a kid playing minister."

"She's just starting out," said Adrian. "But what great energy and freshness."

"She's more down-to-earth than in her videos," I said. "But god save us from her worship services."

"In person, she's very tall," said Jennie. "And even more commanding."

This made me think of hardworking Amira, who feared herself too short and plump to be a star. I said, "Looks aren't everything."

"Who said they were?" said Jennie.

We went downstairs to the Arroyo House kitchen, where Charlotte unpacked a supermarket deli lunch of turkey sandwiches and corn chips. Adrian and I joined the kids outside on the front steps, and we ate, basking in the warm winter sunlight, the lawn spread before us like a wide lap. Down in the sanctuary, someone was practicing études on the organ. Riley said, "She really does look like a movie star," but nobody answered him. Adrian and I probably inhibited them.

Charlotte had us reconvene in the living room. She couldn't face another trip up the stairs; her hip and back were still giving her trouble. "Let's do a quick run-through in alphabetical order," she said.

Riley, Curtis, and Jennie supported Liz Dumenil. "She's young and so proactive . . . she'd attract the young families the AUUCC needs."

"The congregation has been very clear that they want a strong preacher," said Belinda, "and Liz is nowhere near that."

"I don't know," said Riley. "She's as good as anyone I've heard."

"I like her sermons," said Curtis.

Phoebe Fetterman got timid support from Riley; Sam said she sounded bossy and strict, and that the men in the congregation wouldn't like that.

"Sexism! Misogyny!" cried Jennie.

"Jennie's right," Adrian said, "but Reverend Fetterman is just not interesting."

Everyone liked Perry Fitzgerald—and little Zelly.

Adrian said, "He's one cool cat."

"Maybe too cool," I said. "But his sermons are sneaky good."

"Dana's right," said Charlotte. "Doris Gray?"

"What's there to say?" said Adrian. "Major league!"

"Couldn't stay with us long," said Jennie. "But I agree. Major!"

"Walt Harrison?"

"Crazy about him," said Belinda.

"Me too!" Charlotte, Adrian, and I said in unison.

Sam said, "He seems so disorganized."

"Plus, ew," said Jennie. "I can't help it. He creeps me out."

"Just how well did you know him, Jennie?" said Charlotte.

"I saw him around Boston, is all. Enough to see his sappy dweebiness close up."

"Still not getting your aversion to him, Jen," said Adrian.

"He's on a white male ego trip saving the poor Black people of Detroit, and now he wants to come here and save the poor Black people of Altadena. Can't you see it?"

"Not one bit," said Adrian. "I think he's a home run."

"Oh, brother," Jennie said. "Riley, Curtis, help me out here."

"Not crazy about a tuba choir," said Riley. "Or the hokey pizza and bread stuff."

"He's nice," said Curtis. "But, yeah, that cooking stuff's still weird to me."

Charlotte, weary, looked at her watch. "Reverend Kapoor?"

"So much better than how she comes off in her packet—I now understand how she got such glowing letters of support," said Adrian. "She's very appealing."

"Quite an accomplished young lady," said Sam.

Belinda viewed them with disgust. "She's a terrible flatterer. And you just lap it up."

"I'll take my flattery where and when I can get it," said Jennie. "Liz has more experience and I like that she has a family. But Alanna is just so . . . I don't know, *majestic?*"

"She's only thirty-five and hasn't had her own church," I said. "Her two sermons are poorly written, full of undigested research, way too long, and completely boring."

"The critic speaks," said Adrian.

"She's working on her preaching," said Jennie. "I bet she's already better than Tom."

"I like that she speaks Spanish," said Adrian.

"Elsa speaks English, Spanish, French, and Arabic," said Belinda.

"Good segue," said Charlotte. "What about Elsa Neddicke?"

"You mean our next minister?" said Jennie.

"Don't be preemptive, Jennie," said Charlotte. "We're just talking here."

"Who's preemptive?" Jennie said. "Everyone loves her. So she's as good as in, as far as I can see. Her or Doris. But Elsa gets points for being younger."

"And less expensive," said Sam.

"It feels a little regressive, her whole thing with Sparlo," said Riley. "I mean, if we choose the minister-before-last's protégée, isn't that kind of going backward?"

"Sparlo was one for the ages," said Belinda. "Nothing backward about him."

"Nothing backward about Elsa, either," said Charlotte.

I said, "For all you know, Kapoor's mentor could be some old white guy as well."

"I was just hoping we could skew younger," said Riley.

Charlotte looked at her watch. "I've got to leave for a doctor's appointment in five minutes. Thoughts on Mayeve Schindler?"

"Not workin' for me," said Sam.

"Thumbs down," said Riley.

"Way down," said Jennie.

"I like her," I said. "She's such a character. So unapologetically herself. A wonderful preacher and very sturdy on administration."

"Very sturdy," said Belinda.

"I like her, too," said Adrian. "A lot. She's eccentric, but in such a sunny way."

"Definitely a kook," said Charlotte. "The video in her packet was a hoot, but tonight's performance compounds my sense that she's too far out there for us."

"Too far out there for me," said Sam. "That's for sure."

"Not as far out there as the Theater of the Body Dynamic," I said. "And I'm not sure it's right to judge anyone by one Skype session."

"We have to judge them somehow," said Charlotte.

"It was weird how unreachable she was once she started singing," said Riley.

This from a man who often subjected us to ten (and once eighteen) minutes of amateur bell ringing—though aren't we all quick to condemn our own shortcomings in others?

"Mayeve's out!" sang Jennie. "Cross her off the list!"

"I agree," said Sam.

"Let's let it sink in," said Charlotte. "Go reread the packets, listen to a few more sermons, and we'll vote on Tuesday. So now let's stand, hold hands, and close this meeting."

25

A March Toward Disappointment

On Sunday, I played hooky from church. Jack and I took Bunchie and the donks up the Arroyo Seco, the canyon behind Jet Propulsion Laboratory. When we got home, I saw that Tom Fox had emailed me, *Lunch tomorrow?* and attached his sermon.

He was on his front porch waiting as I drove up. "Where shall we go?" he said.

I didn't have an urgent review option. "What about 101 Noodle Express?" This was a favorite dumpling place in Arcadia. Their dumplings were rustic and burly—leek and pork, pumpkin and pork, shrimp and bok choy—and their signature dish, a beef roll, was another life-shifting taste experience: long-stewed beef rolled in a crisp and chewy savory pancake with sweet hoisin sauce and a green chili relish.

We also chose two salads from the cold case—marinated cucumbers and soybeans with tofu, pickled mustard greens, and boiled peanuts.

"How's the search?" said Tom, unsheathing his chopsticks.

"Getting down to business," I said. "Finally meeting the contenders."

"Yes, I've been getting more phone calls. Which is good. They should be calling me. You guys face an embarrassment of riches. And a few, of course, to avoid."

"Is it kosher for us to talk about this?"

"I don't see why it wouldn't be."

I wasn't so sure. "I can say that narrowing it down to three or four will be tough," I said. "Who knows how we'll ever get to one."

Our pan-fried dumplings arrived, some trailing a dark lace where their juices had leaked onto the grill. We doused them with dark rice vinegar, chili oil, and soy sauce. "My old pal Doris could sing quite a swan song for y'all," said Tom. "And Elsa Neddicke is a real prize. She'd double the membership in no time. She can't help it."

"Those two do make everyone else seem like rank amateurs," I said. "But with Doris—do we want someone who's only going to be here five or six years?"

"Younger ministers—the ambitious ones—might not even stay that long."

"According to the survey, we want someone who'll stay forever. It's the lingering myth of Sparlo's twenty-eight-year run."

"Myth is right," said Tom. "Lifelong settlements are a thing of the past. These days, ministry's more a march toward mutual disappointment. You start off at a church with a few honeymoon years when everyone loves you. If you're at all decent and the congregation is sane, you then have a few stable years to get some good work done. At some point, though, the malcontents start their picking and poking and stirring up discontent. The trick is to get out before the discontent morphs into full-blown antipathy. I probably should've left two years ago. As it is, a whole contingent's only too glad to see me go."

"Maybe the Grangers, but they're hardly a contingent and they're never around anyway."

"Oh, I've disappointed my share—our pal Charlotte, for instance. I'll leave in good standing, but in the nick of time. The AUUCC has been a loving home for me and Pat and the boys, and I'll miss it. But wild horses couldn't keep me here."

"Wild horses!" I laughed. "But I'm glad to hear you'll miss us."

He chose a segment of beef roll and spooned on extra green chili sauce. "I will miss you, but I'm thrilled to never fill out another staff schedule. Or fire another RE director."

I doctored my beef roll and we gave ourselves over to the pliant, crispy pancake and sweet, stewed beef. "If someone's done well in a junior capacity at a big church," I said, "but never had their own church, do you think they could handle the AUUCC?"

"It depends on how much administrative experience they had at the big church. I'd especially look at how they've worked with their subordinates."

"Assuming they've had subordinates."

"Some talented young people are coming out of seminary these days," Tom said. "And there's a big trend in hiring them, they're so articulate and full of ideas. But a head full of theory is no substitute for experience."

"That's what I think," I said.

"When I started at my first church," Tom went on, "I was on fire with everything I wanted to do. I moved in, opened my office door, and one by one each staff person and maybe half the members came in and complained about everyone else. I called my mentor and said, 'I can't take it! I have ideas! I want to get to work, not be a wailing wall!' And he said, 'This is your work. Listening to people. Managing people.'

"But speaking of good managers . . ." He paused as more dumplings were delivered. "Let me put in a plug for Mayeve Schindler. She's super: a real pro, funny, and very smart. Theologically, she's a bit out there, but a little pagan tree worship in the Sunday mix won't hurt anyone. You could do far worse than Mayeve. Now she's gay to boot, which I assume is a selling point with your crew."

I couldn't—or at any rate didn't—tell him that Mayeve had already shot herself in the foot with her dulcimer-battering ballad. "I like her a lot," I said, which was true.

That night Charlotte phoned and said that she felt overburdened. Might I host the big vote on Tuesday—which also entailed making an entrée?

I checked with Jack, who agreed to spend the evening in my backyard office as long as I sent him food and one or two of Riley's famous cocktails.

I decided to make the seafood chowder I first ate twenty years ago in the English Market in Cork, Ireland—or at least my own version of that smoky, tomato-based soup with cod, scallops, clams, and shrimp; sometimes (in Ireland), it had periwinkles (sea snails) and enough smoked haddock to give it a wonderful campfire tang. Of course, I had to skip the periwinkles and for the smokiness I made do with frozen finnan haddie. I'd worked on the recipe over the years, cranking the flavors so that when I finally went back to the English Market a couple of years ago, their chowder was so bland and watery that Jack didn't believe it was the same soup I made at home. It was possible that the Irish cook was having a bad day, or someone was try-ing to stretch the last bit of a used-up batch, or they'd made the recipe from memory for so long, it had ceased being itself—a chef at a good restaurant here in Los Angeles once told me that vigilance is the key to consistency, and that if she or a trusted supervisor didn't keep an eye on the plates as they came out of the kitchen, a dish could become unrecognizable within hours.

Jennie, Riley, and Curtis arrived close on one another's heels, and a shared, jumpy energy made me think they'd all come, if not together, from the same place. A place, perhaps, that served alcohol.

Curtis brought the dense, one-layer, ganache-blanketed chocolate cake from Europane that I happened to know was depth-charged with finely ground espresso beans. Half a slice and I'd be awake till noon tomor-row.

Sam brought two bottles of French chardonnay. "I raided Faithalma's cellar, which could supply an army. Let's hope it's still okay. They're nine years old."

Riley shoved a thick glass bottle of orange-steeped vodka into my freezer and then set out that gin in a blue bottle and an array of syrups, bitters, and citrus juices. He had devised three new drinks for the occasion.

The Decision Maker: gin, cream, egg white, lime juice, blood orange syrup, lemon bitters
The Lively Discussion: orange vodka, tepache (a pineapple liqueur), navel orange juice, lime syrup, soda water, jalapeno bitters
The Slam Dunk: vodka, grapefruit juice, lemon bitters, preserved kumquat

Jack and I live in what was once an architecturally insignificant postwar wood-frame/stucco box. We had recently added on a whole new kitchen, and having employed architects, we now had architecture. I put candlesticks on the large farmhouse table and set eight places.

We gathered in the living room for cocktails and a preliminary vote, the results to be discussed over dinner. We were tense; you could see it in the nervous jollity of the three youngest members and in the grim demeanors of the oldest. I took my Decision Maker, a pungent Ramos Fizz, and retreated to the kitchen to finish the soup. Charlotte followed me. "Something's in the air," she said. "I don't like it."

"I think the kids went into a secret session," I said.

"That much is clear," she said. "But what are they up to?"

"Get Curtis in here," I said. "Tell him I want him to taste the soup."

Curtis came in, shadowed by Jennie. I asked Jennie to take a Lively Discussion to Jack in my outdoor office, then gave Curtis a taste of the broth.

"Very nice," he said.

"You don't think it needs some kick? A little sriracha?"

"That could be good," said Curtis.

I gave the soup a generous squirt and stirred. "So did you guys decide anything?" I said, and took a chance. "In your pre-meeting meeting."

"Jennie was going to invite you, but she remembered you were cooking," he said. "We just talked about who we liked."

"And who do you like?"

"Me? I like them all," he said. "But nobody as much as I like Tom Fox. I'm so sad he's leaving. I'm going to miss him so hard."

"But we do have some wonderful applicants."

"All of them," said Curtis. "I wish . . ." He stopped.

Jennie was back. "Time to vote," she said. "Come on, Curtis."

I sent the colander of scrubbed clams clattering into the soup and fol-lowed her into the living room, where Charlotte handed out ballots listing the contenders with a box beside each. *Check the box of each minister you'd like to learn more about. Check as many boxes as you like.*

I checked off Elsa, Doris, Walt, Mayeve, and Perry, put my ballot in the basket, and returned to the kitchen to add the mussels, then the shrimp and snapper to the chowder. Charlotte came in and lit the candles. "Riley and Adrian are counting," she murmured to my shoulder. "I didn't trust Riley alone."

I uncorked first one, then the other of the chardonnays Sam brought; both were off: sour and flat, undrinkable.

When the shrimp blushed pink, I yelled, *"À table!"* and began ladling out bowls, which Charlotte and Curtis served. Seated, we looked beautiful, al-most primeval in the candlelight, the steam rising off our soup. Spoons clacked against the shells. "Oh my god, this soup is God," said Jennie.

"Every dinner lately is my favorite so far," said Riley.

"Thank you for not adding mushrooms," said Adrian. "And here's the dope: Doris, 8; Elsa, 7; Perry, 8; Walt and Alanna have 6 each; Liz and Mayeve, 3; Phoebe, 1."

Jennie looked around the table furiously. "How did Walt get six votes?"

(Curtis, true to his word, had checked everyone's box.)

"I could say the same about Alanna," said Belinda. "How'd she get six?"

"Yes, we have a tie," said Charlotte lightly. "But as it stands now, Liz, Mayeve, and Phoebe are out of the running. Can we all agree with that?"

A murmur of assent was punctuated by Jennie's "I still like Liz, but okay."

"I'm seriously afraid we've misjudged Mayeve," I said.

Nobody said anything. Not even Adrian.

Charlotte pushed on. "So can we say we have three 'pre-candidates': Doris, Elsa, and Perry? Are we happy with that?"

"We are not," said Jennie. "At least one young minister should be on the list."

Charlotte let out an exhausted sigh. "We can vote again on just Walt and Alanna, and whoever has a simple majority can be our fourth precandidate."

"Can we talk about it a little first?" said Adrian.

"Of course," said Charlotte. "Riley, did you want to say something?"

"Yeah. The way I see it is, Alanna has never been a senior minister, but she's a brilliant, visionary pioneer in the new approaches to ministry. Obviously Walt has a couple years more experience at his small church, but he lacks personal appeal and, I don't know how to put this exactly, the *power* that Alanna has. To me, it's a toss-up. But everyone agrees it's time for a woman, so shouldn't we go with Alanna?"

"Alanna's potential, however promising, is not remotely comparable to Walt's solid six years of a successful, solo senior ministry," said Belinda.

"You talk as if Alanna is completely inexperienced," said Adrian. "Yet she's been awarded prestigious positions at two of our biggest, most important churches—her internship and then her assistant job are both highly coveted and selective gigs. And according to the letters in her packet, her work has been exceptional at both places."

"She is impressive," said Sam. "I like the young fellow, too, but he could look more professional."

"What are you saying, Sam?" said Charlotte. "That Alanna is prettier?"

"I'm saying that the impression our minister makes in the larger community is important and it wouldn't hurt to have someone well groomed and dignified."

Fury bucked through me. The soup, with its narrow black shells and pink shrimp, now looked inedible. "There is no equivalency between Alanna and Walt. He's had his own church for six years, while Alanna's big accomplishment is a Sunday school theater group that fakes suffering and invites the audience to writhe along."

"Harsh!" said Jennie. "Maybe Alanna's never had a dinky starter church like Walt's, but like Aidy says, she's gotten the positions at the big UU churches that every new minister dreams of. And a lot of the big UU muckymucks think she's pretty special."

"She does have a riveting presence, but her preaching opportunities and managerial responsibilities have been minimal," I said. "And the sermons she's shown us are not good. In fact, they're hands down the worst we've read."

"She's working on her preaching," said Riley. "And she had management experience running her theater company."

"Which had no assets and had a budget of zero," said Belinda.

Jennie said, "We might as well agree on Alanna because Walt won't ever be the candidate because that takes consensus and I could never vote for him."

I said, "Could we ever get consensus with you, Jennie, if it's not Alanna?"

The clinking of spoons came to a standstill.

"I haven't made up my mind about anyone yet."

"Except for Walt." I was trembling, hot and more than a little queasy.

Charlotte tapped her water glass to get everyone's attention. "Why don't we take a few minutes to enjoy Dana's beautiful food, and we'll vote again after dessert."

Sam was the first to resume eating. He ate noisily, clanking his spoon in the bowl and sometimes slurping. Adrian took a slice of bread and tore it in two, then set both pieces down. "We all have to be open-minded here," he said. "We know very little about any of these applicants. We'll get to know them more when we meet face-to-face."

"I know, I know," Jennie said. "I just get so excited at the thought of a woman. Isn't that what we all want? Wouldn't it be great for AUUCC women to see themselves represented in the pulpit for once?"

"Doris and Elsa are both women."

"I can't help preferring someone more my generation," said Jennie. "No offense."

When we voted for Alanna and Walt, one vote each, it came out in a tie. Four to four. We voted again. Then three more times. On vote number six:

Alanna 5, Walt 3. Belinda had defected. Belinda! "I thought you loved Walt. I thought you were his champion," I said.

"I do like him. But somebody has to bend. And given the qualifications of our three other pre-candidates, this fourth choice seems largely symbolic."

We traded soup bowls—many unfinished—for salad plates. As Curtis cleared, I ferried some soup and another Lively Discussion to Jack in my office. "Don't ask," I said to him.

Back at the table, Adrian said, "I have to say, I'm thrilled we've chosen two women of color."

"Who other than Doris is of color?" said Riley.

"Elsa!" said Adrian. "She's half Puerto Rican."

"And Alanna identifies as mixed race," said Jennie. "So that's all three, actually."

"How's that?" said Sam.

"Oh, Sam," said Jennie. "Didn't you read her sermon? Her grandfather's Sikh."

"Ahh." Sam went back to his lettuce.

I'm sorry, Dana," Belinda said, picking up her cheeseboard in the kitchen. "Better to throw the kids a bone early on, so they'll see we old folk aren't so inflexible."

"But why does that bone always have to be Alanna?"

"It's going to be fine," she said. "We have great options."

Charlotte came in next, as I dumped expensive seafood into the garbage disposal. "Thanks for hosting," she said.

"That was shocking," I said. "What I can't figure out is how Alanna got six votes in the very first round."

"That was me, obviously," said Charlotte. "I wanted to load the vote against Liz. And I didn't want the old folks voting in a bloc like the youngsters. I should have known that the men had Alanna covered. Even you have to admit she's prettier than Walt."

"Not to me," I said.

Adrian was the last to say goodbye. He stood in the kitchen doorway. "You okay?"

"Not really. You?"

"I prefer Walt, but Alanna's not so bad, and at least the kids will feel they've had some say in the process."

"I can't see beyond the fact that Walt is more skilled and qualified in every way except maybe personal grooming," I said. "But all this strategizing and second-guessing and placating the kids, it's . . ." —I actually made sputtering noises— ". . . it's so screwed up!"

Adrian gave a shout of laughter. "Oh, Dana P. There you go again. Caring."

Hey!" Jack was dozing on the sofa in my study with Bunchie beside him. He opened his eyes and slowly sat up. "That last, uh, Lively Discussion was lethal." He looked at me groggily. "How'd it go?"

"My favorite young guy's out of the running."

We walked down toward the house, pausing in the lower yard to let Bunchie do her business. The night was cold and clear. "You know," I burst out, "I would've made a lousy minister. And don't ever let me be church president, either. I'm not sporting enough. It's not a game to me. I lack the nerve for it."

Jack put his arms around me. He runs hot—I like to say he's a human furnace—and as Bunchie snorted around in the bushes, he warmed me up.

Still, I couldn't sleep. The search was veering off course and nothing I said had made a difference. Capable, funny Mayeve was out because of a weird Skype transmission issue; Walt was out because of his beard and bread making; the Sanderses were out because God spoke in Rob's gently humorous call story. And Alanna was in because . . . she looked like a movie star? Even Adrian gave Alanna too much credit. (If I were to make him the love interest in my book, I thought, this would be when doubts set in.) To this day, when I think of whom we rejected and why, the old fury jolts through me, bringing a tide of achy, flu-ish regret.

Charlotte phoned our four pre-candidates by noon the next day and Belinda arranged for them to visit on successive weekends, starting in sixteen days, with Elsa.

26

Thank You for Sharing

Your search committee recently conducted Skype interviews with eight ministers interested in serving as our next senior minister. The depth and range of talent was impressive and inspiring.

The Skype interviews were followed by intense discussions over several remarkable dinners—the quality of cooking and Riley Kincaid's mixology has risen in direct proportion to the gravity of our decisions—and now we have chosen four pre-candidates. Over the next month, we will spend a weekend with each one of them in turn. We'll interview them, eat five meals with them, show them the sights, and hear them preach at a "neutral pulpit."

It is natural to be curious at this stage of the search, but confidentiality is crucial. Some of our pre-candidates might continue serving their present churches, where the congregants might not be pleased to learn that their minister has been looking elsewhere.

I was in my office grinding out the week's restaurant review when a call came in from an unfamiliar area code. Curious—and willing to be distracted—I picked up.

"Dana? Is this my old friend Dana Potowski?" said a faintly familiar male voice. "Bert Share here! How the heck are you?"

I'd forgotten what a smooth, good voice he had, and despite what I knew about him—his irritating self-confidence and the things Helen had told me—I was pleased that he remembered me: after all, I had abandoned ministry twenty years ago, and he'd barely noticed me back then. "Bert!" I said. "Wow. How are *you*?"

"Great. So glad you picked up." Bert was never the scruffy, milk-hued, sock-and-sandaled UU male ministers Jennie so abhorred. He'd grown up on a pear farm near Redding, California, but by seminary, he was already the handsome, spiritual cowboy—stylistically akin to Russell Long, the singer-songwriting minister who never sent us his packet. "You know," Bert went on, "a friend of mine is pre-candidating at Arroyo, and when she said you were on the search committee, I couldn't believe it. I just had to call and say hello."

"You know I never went into ministry."

"Of course. I've bought both your novels. Congratulations, by the way."

They were *memoirs*, and there were three of them, and he said "bought" not "read," but never mind. "Hey, thanks! Where are you these days?"

He was still in Philly, he said, president of his district's ministers association and "busy a thousand ways from Sunday." He'd divorced and married again. "I'm now the old gray-haired papa to two little girls, Pina and Julietta."

So his coffee-brown hair was now gray; still, he'd nabbed a young wife. I recalled Helen's story, of seeing him with a student late at night—and wondered.

If he'd read my books, he already knew about my romantic history and later-in-life marriage. At any rate, he didn't ask about that. "So who's your friend?" I said.

"Alanna Kapoor? She was my intern four years ago," he said. "I've mentored her since. It's a bit like mentoring Mozart—but I do my best."

"She makes quite an impression." I picked up a pencil and pulled over a legal pad in case he said something I should remember.

"Most impressive young minister in the denomination today. Wait till you meet her. If I were on your committee, I'd be concerned about her age and inexperience. But I'll tell you. She's a lightning-fast learner and institutionally she's very savvy. She'll go far in the denomination. We've been working on her sermons and I've never seen such dramatic improvement. The AUUCC could do far worse. She's the real deal."

So he was the great preacher mentoring her. He'd been a clever, forceful writer back in seminary, winning the preaching award the year he graduated. Of course, he'd already served a pulpit for two years by then and had a lot of practice. A thoughtful sermon of his (about UU prison work) was published in the UU magazine a few years ago, and when I'd read it, I had felt a rush of pride to have known him.

"Hey!" he barked. "How's my old pal Tom Fox? Happy to be leaving ministry?"

"I didn't know you two knew each other," I said.

"We were in the same district for years. We used to get hammered at district retreats and grouse about our congregants. He gave the Sermon of the Living Tradition one year—a big honor. I'd given it the year before and can't remember what I said, but I'll never forget Tom's about his live-in nanny—such a powerful personal story of race and privilege and the price some mothers pay to feed their kids."

"Huh," I said. Of course I'd heard all about Tom's nanny, Delora, in sermons and private conversations. He'd crawled into her bed at night when he was scared; he accompanied her to her ecstatic, gospel-singing church; he ate with her and never with his folks. Then, when he was twelve, she vanished, no goodbye, no explanation: the first enduring loss in his life.

"How's the church taking his retirement?"

"Okay. But he's not actually retiring."

"He is from ministry. But I imagine he'll leave the AUUCC in good shape."

"Oh yes," I said.

"And how's the search going?"

"It's time-consuming."

"They always are. But between us, Dana, Alanna is every bit as remarkable, as talented as you think. Of all the churches she's considering, I think the AUUCC's her best match: not too big, not too small, just a good solid, little chugger of a church. Your congo will love her, I promise."

"Okay," I said. On my legal pad, I wrote *chugger* and *congo*.

"Great talking to you, Dana. I'd love to keep in touch as this plays out. Whoever's talking to Alanna's references will be talking to me. But if you have any questions, give a shout anytime."

"Will do," I said.

"Oh—and want to hear something funny?" he said. "Ten, eleven years ago, Tom and I were pre-candidates at both my church here and there at the AUUCC. I got offers from both places, and when I decided to come here, Tom got the AUUCC."

"That is funny," I said. "Good to talk to you, Bert. Glad you're doing well."

"And you. Again, congrats on your books."

I hung up. Bunchie was asleep on my rug. "That was weird," I said to her. Tom Fox had been our second choice. Wow.

Bert Share never should have told me that. The jerk. This was one conversation I'd keep entirely to myself.

The AUUCC had lucked out, though. Seriously. I, for one, might not have lasted through a BS ministry.

W̲e have four excellent pre-candidates," Charlotte said, after lighting the chalice. "We should be proud to have reached this benchmark."

But Walt was out! And Alanna in!

We were once more at Charlotte's, this time for a special Thursday night session—no food, 8:00 p.m. start—to plan the pre-candidates's visits. I was still aching with anger over Walt's exclusion. My aversion to Jennie was such that I couldn't stand to see her face. Nor could I look calmly at Sam or Riley. Even sweet, beautiful Curtis repelled me. Adrian sat next to me on the sofa and I shrank away from him as far as I could.

Witty Wat sauntered into the living room area, his tail high, and rubbed against my legs. I scooped him up and set him on my legal pad. He let me burrow my face in his soft buff-colored fur, then walked over to Adrian's lap.

Charlotte said, "I've thought a lot about what Arne said at the very beginning of the search: how this is a sacred task that will grow us spiritually. I think we've lost track of the spiritual aspect of this work. And I've been asking myself how we can treat this search as less of a political fight and more of a sacred process of discernment. I have ideas. One: Let's cultivate a kinder, more grateful and respectful attitude toward the ministers who have put themselves on the line for our judgment. Two: Let's remember to pause to defuse anger and resentment before our discussions overheat. Three: Some of us are disappointed; those who are jubilant, please be tender with them. Four: Remember, all of you, that this is a spiritual journey—and it's getting rocky—so let's move ahead with more reverence, love, and faith."

I scribbled minutes to recede. As one of the disappointed, I wasn't yet on any spiritual plane.

Charlotte suggested that we clear the air. "Let's go around the room and say where we are. No cross talk. Let's hear everyone out calmly, without reacting. Be honest—and respectful of others who might not agree with you."

Nobody spoke up. From Adrian's lap, Witty gazed at me with clear amber eyes.

"Okay. I'll start," said Belinda. "Here's where I'm stuck. Some of us have no idea what it takes for a church this size to function. They have no knowledge of policy governance, the bylaws, or the institution's history. This cohort treats the search like it's a beauty pageant or an awards show, where the prize goes to the contestant with the most star power rather than to the person most qualified for the job. We have been entrusted by the congregation to find a superior preacher with a demonstrated ability to run a complex organization that has a robust financial portfolio. If we fail to meet these requirements, we have failed in our task and done damage to the church."

Another tense silence.

"I'm truly sick at heart about Walt. In fact, I'm deeply offended that he's not a pre-candidate and Alanna is." Apparently I was speaking. "I know—neither she nor Walt is likely to be called. Still. And I'm sick of how so much of what is said in our meetings is in reaction to one provocateur. She says something outrageous, and we breathlessly try to reason with her. Which is far from the thoughtful, adult discussion I'd imagined for this search."

"I guess I have to go next," Jennie said, "because that's just wrong. I know, Dana, you were all extra about Walt. I felt like that about Liz. But we have to move on. And I'm sorry if you think I say stuff just to provoke people. I say what I think. And I know that Walt's not a good match for us, because the other young adults at this church would never like his kale-eating, bread-making, running with the Lord shtick, and I'm here to represent them. I love you, Dana . . ." She turned to me, her plump hands gripping her plump knees. "You're the most fun person on this committee, but I know in my heart, we've picked the right pre-cans."

"And, Belinda . . ." Jennie swiveled around. "I grew up in this church, so you can't say I don't know it. Arne picked us young people for reasons just as important as why he chose you long-timers. We haven't been here forty years, but we hope we'll be. We want a church we want to go to, with a minister we can relate to. My folks had Sparlo, who was kind of their age and had kids around my age, and I always heard how much fun the adults had, the kids running around, the parents drinking wine. Well, we want a minister to raise our kids with. Yeah, and maybe not just another straight white guy."

Riley chimed in next: "I'm sad about Liz, too." He scratched his head with both hands. "I've had a hectic few months and maybe I haven't read as many sermons as people who don't have to work full-time. But I feel good about our decisions."

Adrian said the barbed comments were making him sad. "Remember, friends, like our chairperson says, this is a sacred task," he said. "A spiritual undertaking. So let's be kind to one another. We have a good roster, with a lot of range. So—onward!"

I was a little abashed then, and maybe others were, too, because another minute passed and the only input was Witty's loud purr.

Curtis, his voice wobbly with emotion, said, "I'm just so blown away that you'd all consider a married gay man to be the minister of your church."

"Of course," said Charlotte. "And it's your church, too, Curtis."

"We have four terrific pre-candidates," said Sam. "And I feel so close to everyone in this room. When I asked you for help with my end-of-life business, it's all because of how much I've come to trust and care for all of you."

I made wide stare-y eyes at Charlotte so we could share a little smirk, but she was looking at her notes. "Okay," she said with a big sigh. "I'm also sad that Walt isn't a pre-candidate. But I'm determined to keep an open mind until we meet everyone. Next, let's see . . ." She gazed for a long unsteady moment at a trembling piece of paper. "Oh. Right. I've sent our list to headquarters, so they'll send us a summary of our pre-cans' files. Jennie, where are we on references?"

Jennie passed around a handwritten sign-up sheet so we could choose a reference to talk to. By the time the sheet got to me, only Perry's references hadn't been chosen, so I took one and Adrian took the other.

Belinda passed out a schedule for Elsa's visit and a sign-up sheet for who would drive her where—which gave everyone time to be alone with her between her arrival Friday night and her departure Sunday evening.

Conveniently, Belinda had put Elsa and Perry in my neighbor's Airbnb (my old friend from high school was a "super host" with a beautiful small apartment—I'd recommended it). Doris and Alanna would be in a different Airbnb on Charlotte's street.

Charlotte said, "The lunches after they preach are said to be especially revealing because pre-cans tend to relax then and let their guards down. Now, Dana." She turned to me. "Would you find us restaurants for all the lunches?"

Charlotte had one last announcement. "Apparently I need surgery on my back. The operation is scheduled for Friday, March 20. We'll be done with pre-candidating by March 15. I suggest we choose our candidate on Tuesday, March 17. Does this sound doable?"

Adrian checked the handbook. "We can't make an official offer till April 4."

"Official, yes, but we can pretty much nail it down before then."

I knew she was thinking of Elsa, who would not be waiting for any other offers.

"If we get all the references checked and we've followed up on any concerns, I don't see any difficulty," said Belinda. "The sooner, the better."

Everyone murmured in agreement, so we stood and held hands while Charlotte blew out the chalice.

27

Elsa in Santa Paula

Charlotte and Riley were scheduled to pick up Elsa from the airport, but that morning Charlotte called to say she couldn't move, let alone drive—would I go instead?

I parked outside of Riley's apartment and texted him. I wasn't in a hurry, but after five minutes I texted again. He texted back: **2 minutes, please.** I contemplated the great bay fig tree and its ropy roots until a sheriff came out of the sheriff's station and sat on a low wall by the tree. A squirrel leapt up beside him and snatched nuts—or what I took to be nuts—from his hand.

"Sorry." Riley's hair was wet and he had on a long-sleeved plaid shirt and khaki long pants—who knew he owned long anything? "As you once said, our arrangement takes a lot of talking," he said. "I feel like I've been talking for five years."

I pulled away from the curb. "Everything okay?"

"I want Eva to move out with me, so everyone's mad at me. Fine, but then they want to process endlessly. The other day I was helping Belinda and forgot my phone, and when I got home, I had fifty-two text messages. Speak of the devil." He pulled out his phone, grimaced, turned it off.

"What were you doing for Belinda?"

"She was finally getting rid of her husband's clothes and all the stuff her sons left behind. I bagged it and hauled it to Goodwill. She's thinking of renting out a room to have someone else in the house."

"You're very nice to help her."

"I like Belinda." He lowered his voice. "And she feeds me. The other night she made me these white sausages with a crisp potato thing and a green salad," he said. "And a seriously good Alsatian wine. So simple. But. Oh. My. God."

"So you guys get along though you don't agree on the search?"

"We don't? We both like Elsa and Doris. And Perry. She liked Walt more than I did and I like Alanna more than she does. No biggie."

No biggie! No biggie! How lightly he regarded that which caused me such anguish! And could it be for Belinda too that voting for Alanna over Walt was also *no biggie*?

If so, why was I still so worked up over the least likely contenders?

Elsa Neddicke was child-sized. Barely five feet. She stood at the curb in a charcoal pantsuit, crisp white shirt, and sensible low-heeled pumps.

Riley loaded her roller bag in the back of my Subaru and insisted that she sit up front. Reading glasses hung on a chain around her neck.

"Charlotte couldn't make it, so I came—"

"Yes! Dana!" "Her eyes were bright, intelligent, piercing. "I just finished *Yard to Table* on the plane. How fun to meet you in person!"

"Likewise," I said. "After reading and hearing your marvelous sermons."

She buckled her seat belt and turned to Riley. "And Riley! How are the bells?"

As Elsa was staying at my neighbor's Airbnb, I dropped off Riley, then took her to my house, where I walked her through the shared backyard gate to her accommodations. She wanted to get out of her airplane clothes, she said, and have a little lie-down.

"Dinner isn't for another hour, so wander over when you're ready," I told her, "and I'll drive us to Charlotte's."

I'd signed up to bring crudités, so I picked some carrots and washed them, then I, too, had a ten-minute lie-down.

I was up and washing celery by the kitchen window when I spotted Elsa at the donks' corral. Grabbing a few carrots, I went out to join her. Bunchie, overexcited to see a new person, jumped on her leg. "Get down, you ill-mannered beast," I said, walking up.

"Aren't you adorable." Elsa crouched down to scratch Bunchie's ears and accept a few licks.

We fed carrots to the donks—and the dog—then I showed her the chickens, the vegetable garden, the two bathtub ponds, the beehives. She said, "I just read about your little farm and here I am—it's as if I've walked right into your book."

Indeed she had, I thought. In more ways than one.

In the kitchen, she peeled carrots while I cut them into sticks, and we found a subject in Sparlo, both of us pausing to recall his narrow face, his red Harvard robes, the beauty of his concentration. "The last time I saw him," said Elsa, "was at a ministers' retreat. A speaker had talked about power dynamics in churches and quoted a survey that said that eighty-five percent of churchgoing women reported having sexual fantasies about their male ministers. Sparlo said he was so glad he heard this after he'd retired; had he known that was going on while he preached, he never could've concentrated on his sermons."

I'd never had sexual fantasies about any minister. "Eighty-five percent ... Really?"

Elsa carried her carrot peels to the compost bucket. "Which maybe helps to explain why it took so long for women to be accepted in the pulpit."

Tonight's was an informal meet and greet, no agenda, and only picnic fare—turkey sandwiches and chips—for dinner. We committee members were excited, self-conscious, and shy, as if we'd conjured this small, bright-eyed, alert woman and weren't exactly sure what to do with her. Everyone asked about her plane ride. She was happy, she said, to be out of the snow.

"I'd forgotten how green it is here in February. And all the flowers! Of course," she went on, "the first place I went was Dana's. Her garden! Those pretty chickens—and tiny donkeys! She has rainbow chard the size of canoe paddles!"

As I'd had time alone with her, I stood back and watched her engage the others.

She loved the names of Riley's drinks—though she'd accept only a virgin Slam Dunk—and asked how he preserved his kumquats (he boiled them in honey) and what made bitters bitter (gentian root).

Jennie came in late and flustered. She apologized to Elsa. "But I went back for my keys and caught Eric giving Jaz a pacifier. And I'm trying so hard to get her off them." Elsa sat down with her, knee to knee, near to me. "I'm the one who's read all the child-rearing books," Jennie continued. "I mean, I blog about all this. But he never listens to me." Elsa talked to her quietly, and for longer than I ever would have, right up until Charlotte called us to dinner.

We took our plates to the red sofas and ate off our laps. Elsa sat between Charlotte and Curtis and spoke to them in turn; when people got up for more food, she did, too, then placed herself between Adrian and Sam. Several times, Adrian's glorious laugh filled the room. Elsa approached each of us with frank, penetrating interest. You don't realize how thirsty you are for such full attention until it comes to you. One by one, we bloomed under her gaze.

Over ice cream, we made plans for the following day. First came the three-hour interview, of course, and lunch, then free time in the afternoon. Elsa asked to see Owen Brown's grave. "I read Belinda's pieces about it in your packet."

"Who is Owen Brown?" said Curtis.

"Owen's the son of John Brown. The Great Liberator?"

Curtis shook his beautiful head.

"John Brown was an abolitionist visionary who understood that only violence could end slavery," said Elsa. "To arm slaves for a revolt, he planned a raid on a US armory in Harpers Ferry, Virginia. His own military adviser told him that he needed forty-five hundred men for the mission, but Brown went in with twenty-one, three of whom were his sons! Two of his sons were killed in the raid and Brown himself was caught and hanged for treason. The only son who escaped was Owen—and he hid on an island in Lake Erie for twenty years before coming out here to join his sister and another brother in Altadena." Elsa touched Curtis's arm. "Here he was hailed as a hero. He was known to attend your church and grew very close to the minister."

"He was also a good friend of Lemuel Rourke's," said Belinda. "Sam's great-great-grandfather-in-law, who founded the AUUCC."

"I had no idea," said Sam. "Why don't I—we—know about this?"

"Because nobody reads my newsletter columns," said Belinda.

"Because nobody reads the newsletter, period," said Charlotte.

"When Owen Brown died," Elsa said, "more than three thousand people—many of them Black, some of them freed slaves—walked up in a column from Pasadena to his grave in the hills. That grave just got landmark status, and the Heritage Society is putting up a stone. Which I find so moving. When so many cities are pulling down Confederate monuments, Altadena's erecting one to an abolitionist."

"Do I hear a sermon in the making, Reverend Neddicke?" Adrian said.

"Workin' on it, Mr. Jones," said Elsa.

In the morning, we met at the church. To prevent chance encounters with stray congregants, Charlotte locked the gates (who knew those old iron gates could close, let alone lock?) and we took Elsa through the gardens, the sanctuary, the Rourke Chapel. We moved slowly in deference to Charlotte's hip and back, but also because Elsa asked such careful and interested questions. What happened to the fruit in the citrus orchards? (It went to two food pantries.) Was there an irrigation system? (Not a functional one.) Who tended the gardens? (A weekly landscape crew. And volunteers.) Was the amphitheater ever used? (Not often.) What parts of the campus did the private school use? (The classrooms, kitchens, chapel, and lawn.) Did they pay for their own janitors? (No.)

We ended up at Arroyo House, where, carrying cups of coffee and Jennie's superb cinnamon rolls, we climbed to the library and grilled Elsa for three solid hours.

Her confident, thoughtful, intelligent answers came from a deep well of experience. It soon became obvious that as much as we thought we knew about the AUUCC and churches in general, she was the true professional in the room.

Belinda asked how she'd grown her churches.

"My first church was a very old but depleted congregation whose average age was sixty-six. Yet almost every Sunday, a visitor or two slipped in. If they signed the visitor's log, I called on them that week. I was always treated warmly, and most of the time I was invited in. I asked why they'd come to church, and for every one of them the impulse was attached to a deep loss or fear or change and a longing for connection and community. Someone's brother died in a bad car accident and she now had trouble seeing the world as safe; parents were looking for a Sunday school after their preschooler came home terrified about hell. A gay couple wanted a minister to officiate at their wedding. A woman who'd won a MacArthur genius grant said she'd come in gratitude hoping to find a way to give back; a man received a terrifying diagnosis and came for solace, and to not feel so isolated by his illness. I invited them to help me bring the church back to life—by being an usher or singing in the choir; by teaching Sunday school or tutoring kids or starting an environmental impact committee—and gradually, the church filled up on Sundays and grew lively and then we had to build a new sanctuary to accommodate everyone. . . ."

She couldn't be as hands-on at her second, larger church, but her membership committee was; they did the visiting, and that church grew, as had the one she served now, to more than a thousand members.

Charlotte asked what, according to the search handbook, was the "key" question: "What do you feel you can do for our congregation?"

She would keep the AUUCC healthy and prosperous, and help it grow. She'd "try mightily," too, to continue the tradition of distinguished preaching. (This was modesty, as everyone knew that Elsa's preaching was what drew people and kept them coming to her church.)

"I sense a deep vein of creativity in this congregation," she said. "So many writers and artists and musicians; so many teachers, scientists, and good cooks. I'd call on this creative energy to nourish and enrich church life. More art on the walls! Music in the air—and maybe in that charming amphitheater! Flowers in the garden! Delicious meals cooked in those big kitchens and eaten together! Let's get people reading the newsletter again— even if it means mailing it out on that famous yellow paper—yes, Sparlo sent them to me for years. And let's start an AUUCC arts and literary magazine with contributions by members. Let's hold poster-painting parties before each protest, so we'll wield clever, eye-catching signs that speak truth to power! Together, let's inspire one another to radically reimagine how to responsibly inhabit—and save—this precious, endangered world for our children and theirs."

Adrian asked about her work/life balance. On her day off, she said, she put her church phone in a drawer. On her three writing days, she didn't answer emails until 3:00 p.m. "Nor is my husband allowed to speak to me before noon."

I made note of that.

After lunch at a pretty café on Lincoln Avenue, Belinda, Jennie, and Riley took Elsa on the short hike to Owen Brown's gravesite. Charlotte and I watched them drive off. "She's prepping for her candidating sermon," Charlotte said. "Smart choice, to preach about a local hero with UU ties."

I would've liked to have gone to Owen Brown's grave, too, but I was behind in my eating. So I went home and dragged Jack out to a late second lunch at a new Lebanese-Armenian place in Glendale.

Dinner that night was one of our best. Belinda had marinated and then grilled salmon steaks. I brought a salad of my fresh escarole and fava beans with mint, and pecorino; Curtis had his mother bake another buko pie.

Riley devised a drink in Elsa's honor: the Owen Brown, with oat milk, sweet plum brandy, and gunpowder green tea.

We left the AUUCC at 8:00 a.m. sharp, our destination the UU church in Santa Paula, ninety minutes northwest of Altadena. Adrian drove us in a large rental van up Interstate 5, then west on a two-lane blacktop through a beautiful valley of citrus and avocado groves to the small, old-fashioned agricultural town.

Built in the 1880s, Santa Paula's UU sanctuary had white plastered walls, high redwood beams, old wooden theater-style seats, and a Shaker-like simplicity. Stained glass sent light in red and yellow shafts through the room. Fifty-odd people filed in, filling half the seats. At ten, a woman at the piano nimbly played two Goldberg Variations. Calmly, Elsa read two poems, then led a prayer. Her sermon was called "Listen":

The world calls on us to listen. Listen, says my daughter, who is writing a paper on Emily Dickinson. Listen, says my son, tucking an earbud in my ear so I can hear the angry rap song that he *loves*. Listen, says a friend, I have to tell somebody what just happened. . . .

Among mammals, our hearing isn't even very good. Bats, elephants, dogs, cats, owls, horses, dolphins, and rats all hear far better than we humans do . . .

And yet those of us in the hearing world take even our unremarkable ability for granted; we tune out, we often listen and think at the same time, we half listen as we plan what we'll say when it's our turn to talk. There's so much going on—the rumble of traffic, voices, birdsong, dogs barking, the whoosh of our own breath—that we filter out most of it, too often including what is really being said to us. What needs attending.

Listening, true deep listening—when someone takes your words in deep—that kind of listening is rare and healing, and when you go to buy some, it's expensive. The going rate for therapy is $190 an hour. And up.

But some listening is free or has a put-a-dollar-in-the-basket fee. So far, the best treatment for alcoholism we know of is a room full of drunks listening to one another, listening without offering advice or argument— cross talk is forbidden—so that whoever speaks is truly heard.

Laughter fills these meetings. The great, knowing, soul-gusting laughter of shared experience . . .

The best listening, Elsa said, was silence dilated by love and attention.

Some years ago, I drove home from a peace march with a good friend whose marriage was in trouble. I was exhausted and sore; I didn't know it at the time, but I was coming down with a bad flu. My friend told me her troubles and my heart ached for her, but all I could manage in reply was the occasional *uh-huh, uh-huh* to show I was listening. A few days later, she wrote me this email:

> Dear Elsa,
>
> I must thank you for all the wisdom you shared with me as we drove home last weekend. Once more your advice was perfect.

It is no wonder that many mental-health practitioners have renamed "the talking cure" "the listening cure . . ."

Deftly, Elsa moved on to the racial tensions in our denomination and how white defensiveness so often interrupted the conversation. Instead of turning the conversation back to our own discomfort, she said, *keep listening.* Hidden in the etymology of *listen,* she said, was the old English root word *hystan,* which meant "to obey." In deep listening, she claimed, there is a humility, a willingness to affirm another's reality.

A young minister I know has gone door to door in his largely Black neighborhood and listened when people spoke to him about what they needed. His church now provides Twelve Step meeting rooms, a rehearsal space for dancers and musicians, adult literacy tutoring, and a class on simple home repairs. In an area where half the churches are shuttered, his congregation is growing. Sunday service now includes a children's African dance troupe and a tuba choir . . . Because he listened.

In my seminary years, I had found preaching strangely exhausting; afterward, ringing from the effort and the exposure, I'd feel hollowed out and awash in self-loathing, certain that every flaw in my thinking and delivery had been duly noted.

Elsa had been preaching for twenty-odd years; surely she had long ago made peace with her performing self and slipped in and out of it like a swimmer with water. As we walked to our lunch spot—a Mexican café— she did not seem at all depleted. Wasn't the pianist marvelous! she said. Such a pretty little church; she loved the intimacy of the space. And yes, that was Walt Harrison, she said. Did we know him? A gifted young minister, her former intern, doing such remarkable things in Detroit.

I glared at Jennie, who pretended interest in the local stores we passed, which might have dated from the 1950s: a ladies' dress shop, a jeweler's, a work-boot store.

At the restaurant, Elsa ordered a lot for such a tiny person: a chile relleno with rice and beans, two carne asada tacos. "I'm always starving after I preach," she said.

Perhaps she felt depleted after all.

"I found your lesson so inspiring," Curtis said as we sat at picnic tables on the patio, "But I'm wondering, Rev Elsa—do you think God works in our lives?"

"That's a good question. What do you think, Curtis?"

"I think so, but nobody else here does. But I just changed from a Christian Evangelical, and I'm still not sure what I'm supposed to believe as a UU."

Charlotte and I exchanged mortified glances.

Elsa said, "Do you feel you're supposed to believe anything in particular?"

"I know I'm not supposed to think that there's a God who talks to us."

"Does your God talk to you, Curtis?"

I had grown fond of Curtis, but I wondered what Elsa thought of him—and of a church that put someone so clearly unschooled in our faith on their search committee.

"I think God *listens* when I pray," Curtis said. "I think He listens in the way you said is the best kind of listening. He takes it in deep."

"And how does that make you feel?"

"Like He hears what I'm saying and understands."

"That can be very powerful," Elsa said. "And I imagine very helpful."

"Very helpful," said Curtis.

Back at the AUUCC, the others said goodbye to Elsa and I drove her back to my house. Someone else would take her to the airport. We parted at the back gate. "That was a wonderful day," I said. "Thanks again for coming out and ministering to us."

"Thank you. You all made it so lovely." She stilled, and the full, bright force of her attention fell on me. "You know, Dana, in my experience, the people who join search committees are often seeking a change for themselves—the internal self is conducting its own search alongside the church's."

This set off an internal clamor of thoughts. Of course I was on a parallel search. But what for? "I suppose," I said weakly. "I'm definitely learning things about myself."

"What have you learned, may I ask?"

"How much I care," I said. "About the church. And doing the right thing. And also that what I think and how much I care might not matter much to anyone else."

She smiled. "You sound like me," she said, and a look flashed between us then, as if she'd caught yet another meaning, one sent inadvertently: that no matter how much I cared, no matter how much I might want her to be our senior minister, she could not get the job.

28

Perry in Montclair

I could definitely see Elsa as our minister," Adrian said. It was Tuesday night, and because Charlotte's back was out again, we were once more at Belinda's and eating crazy-good chicken with preserved lemon, rice, and my green salad. "In fact," Adrian continued, "she slid right into the role. She's quiet, but how easily she connected with each of us, how mindful and warm she is. It's as if we've known her forever."

"She's definitely the best of the old guard," said Jennie. "But kind of bug-eyed the way she looks so hard at you."

"I really liked her," said Curtis.

"A real pro," said Belinda, and everyone murmured, "Amen."

"I thought she handled the racial stuff in her sermon so well—like how to talk about it," said Sam.

"Like, don't even talk, just listen," said Jennie.

"Yeah," said Riley. "She nailed listening."

"She's great, really great," said Jennie, "but why, when I think of her as our next minister, do I feel, um, a little letdown?"

"Because now that we're seeing people in person," Adrian said, "they'll all fall a little short of the ideal ministers in our minds."

"It's always a little letdown when the endless field of possibility narrows down to a few actual choices," I said.

"In fact, this whole process feels more like dating than I care to admit," said Adrian. "You know, when you're single, you think, I can date anyone in the world. But when you go to find someone, there are the geographically possible, and of them, the age-appropriate. Then there's compatibility—religion, taste in movies, politics, not to mention chemistry—and before you know it, you're down to two or three possibilities and each one has drawbacks."

"Elsa's so ministerial we drank it up and pretty much forgot to court her," I said. "She could always change her mind about the AUCC. I mean, what have we offered her besides a big cut in pay?"

"She is fifty-six and winding down," said Riley. "She said she has at most nine years of ministry left. Don't we want someone on the rise, not the decline?"

"In her decline, as you call it, she could still double our size," said Adrian.

"Maybe," said Jennie.

"Anyway, seven years is the median term for ministries now," I said. "Which means that half don't even last that long."

"I'm nervous of hiring someone who focuses so much on preaching," said Riley. "She admits she relegates the rest of the service planning to a worship committee."

Elsa had told us that she preached three times a month, the associate preached once, and on fifth Sundays, the worship committee put lay members in the pulpit. I said, "The church's website has videos of all their Sunday services. I saw one where three people did 'This I Believe' statements and another one when three people did 'My Favorite Things' statements. You know me—I hate that kind of thing—but these were all smart and thoughtful and moving. Clearly they'd been edited and rehearsed."

"I agree," said Adrian. "Those videos were great. So I'm curious, Riley: Have you seen any of them—or any of her preaching—and if so, what rubbed you wrong?"

"I'm not as sermon fixated as you guys," said Riley. "But lay-led services give me the heebie-jeebies."

This, from Mr. Amateurs-Playing-Handbells-Ad-Infinitum.

Jennie said, "Face it, Riley. Your perfect Sunday is your bell choir and the sermon and even then the sermon's optional."

"What's wrong with that?" he said. Then: "Joking!"

Charlotte, who'd so far been quiet, leaned forward. "Riley," she said, "perhaps you could look at a couple of Elsa's worship videos so we can have an informed discussion about them. In the meantime, folks, we have Perry Fitzgerald coming in three days."

"God, what if we like him as much as we like Elsa?" said Jennie. "And then we like Doris and Alanna that much, too. What then?"

"Then we have the meeting called 'a long day's journey into night,'" said Adrian.

"Then we can't lose," said Charlotte. "But unlike Elsa, the next three pre-cans are probably swapping packets with other search committees. As Dana suggests, we do need to court them and not just let them minister to us like we did with Elsa. Or our decisions will be made for us."

Which wouldn't be a bad thing, I thought, if we ended up with Elsa.

Adrian had heard that Perry's Airbnb was next door to me, but he hadn't bothered to get the exact address, which is why the two of them had walked into my living room on Friday afternoon. I wasn't expecting visitors; the parrot was out on her perch, my long hair was down, and I was in my loose, long Indian-block-print nightie-dress so that I looked like the aging hippie I am. Mortified, I'd ushered them in.

As was her way, Bunchie ran to both men, leaping joyously. Adrian the behaviorist stopped her short with a voice and hand command. Abashed for a moment, she then leapt at Perry. At twelve pounds and short-legged, fully extended she barely reached his knees. He shook her off once, and as she bounded at him again, he pushed her aside with his foot. Firmly. Even forcefully.

Adrian and I looked at each other—did Perry just kick Bunchie?—while Bunchie, insulted, stood back and barked her sharp terrier bark.

"Sorry," I said, scooping her up. I expected ameliorating murmurs—*No, no, that's all right*—but none came. I locked her in our bedroom with her favorite toy, taking the time to twist my hair into a knot before joining the two men in the kitchen. They'd found the parrot on her wheeled perch that

I take from room to room with me—parrots, like the five-year-old humans they mentally resemble, enjoy company and require supervision. "Be careful, she bites," I said, but I didn't say it soon enough, because Perry's index finger now bore a triangular cut, oozing blood.

I apologized again, profusely.

"It's my fault," Perry said. "I stuck my big old finger right in her face."

I gave him a clean paper towel to press on the bite until the bleeding stopped. Then I applied antibiotic ointment and a Band-Aid. "Some welcome," I said.

He was simply, expensively dressed in chinos and a tobacco-brown crewneck sweater (cashmere: I grazed it while bandaging his finger) that exactly matched his eyes. "But I feel very well doctored," he said, smiling. "Thank you, Dana."

He had a cool exterior, but it could crack into warmth.

Still, I was unsure about anyone who didn't like Bunchie.

He didn't like cats, either. Charlotte again hosted the Friday-night casual dinner at her house. This time, she'd bought a dozen of a famous local sandwich known as "the Sandwich" from the Italian grocery on Lake Avenue. A crusty white roll was split, moistened with olive oil, then layered with three deli meats (mortadella, salami, and capicola) and a slice of provolone cheese: simple, but brilliant. Charlotte served them with potato chips and stubby machine-rolled baby carrots.

We'd settled into the living room, again with plates on our laps and Charlotte's hygienic gas fire licking its ceramic logs, when Witty padded in and made a beeline for Perry, who flicked his napkin and hissed. "Allergic," he said.

We went around the room to reintroduce ourselves, and Perry, glancing at notes, had a question for each of us. What had brought Jennie back to the AUUCC as an adult? ("I grew up at the AUUCC and want my daughter to, too.") What inspired Adrian's work in bringing more diversity into the church? ("So many people like me, with the Baptist bends, could find a religious home here—but not if they're the only dark person in the room.")

"Ah. So, Dana." Perry turned to me. "You asked about my theology in the Skype interview—and I see that you yourself were a seminarian. What's your theology?"

I said, "I'm a nontheistic Process Buddhi-Jewnitarian."

He repeated that slowly, then looked up. "Me too!"

"With a name like Fitzgerald? Jewish?"

"My mother's Jewish," he said, "which makes me Jewish by birth."

"Me too," I said. "Jewish by birth. But not raised in any religion."

"Exactly," he said. "Which is, of course, the lack that made us religious."

The next morning, we duly subjected Perry to three hours of questions, with breaks for coffee and tea and Jennie's inventive, fruit-dense take on the morning glory muffin. Perry said, "Can these muffins be written into the salary package?"

We again heard about the life-changing encounter with Thích Nhất Hạnh. "I've come to agree with him. The Bible is an essential, important religious document and if we don't read and interpret it according to our own faith and values," he said, "then the fundamentalists will own it."

To the so-called showstopper question—What would you do for the AUUCC?—he said, "People come to church to seek more meaning in their lives and more connection—to themselves, to others, and to something greater than themselves. A minister gets an hour—really more like half an hour—a week to help them along. At the AUUCC, I would increase programming to help all ages develop personal spiritual practices. Drumming, chanting, yoga, meditation, Build Your Own Theology classes. Maybe memoir writing and intuition training. And I'd begin worship with three minutes of silence." (Three minutes! Sparlo told me that thirty seconds in, people began to peek and rustle.)

Perry would also introduce sacred music from other traditions. This year he'd had masters of the guzheng, the koto, and the sitar play at his church. And no—this in answer to Riley—none of the churches he'd served had a handbell choir.

Perry had a question for us. "Do you know of any issues, any rivalries or long-held grudges, among your top lay leaders?"

"No," Charlotte said. "But we're in a good place financially, with no polarizing controversies. Knock wood."

"As a retired minister once told me," Perry said, "'if you think your church is going along just fine, you don't know everything that's going on in your church.'"

"You remind me of another interim minister," Belinda said, "who was determined to find the worm in the apple whether it was there or not."

"That's the interim's nature, I'm afraid," Perry said, and smiled.

He could seem so diffident and detached, as if observing us dispassionately. But when he smiled, as now, his eyes grew bright and merry and it was as if the sun had broken through the clouds.

Because Perry had requested Chinese food in the San Gabriel Valley, we ate chunks of cumin-spiced lamb on toothpicks and hot pots of fish boiled with mouth-numbing Sichuan peppercorns at a Chengdu-style restaurant in Alhambra. "Not my cup of tea," Charlotte whispered, "and this chair is murdering my back." She took a pill with her ice water. She'd signed up to take Perry to see the Asian art collection at the Norton Simon Museum after lunch, but before we finished, she asked in a whisper if I would take him instead.

I do find it perplexing that the AUUCC didn't wait to hire an interim," he said as we drove. "A good interim could have helped your committee form a clearer picture of what direction the church wants to take."

Guilt panged—again—for the bad job I'd done on the ministerial profile. "Are other churches really so much clearer in what they want?"

"Sure. They want an expert fundraiser. Or someone to tackle an ambitious project, like buying a new church property. They want a stronger voice in local politics. Your requirements are so general: strong preaching and more social justice. What kind of preaching, what kind of social justice? An interim could've helped refine that."

"Maybe. But we had such an unpleasant experience with our last interim."

"As to that, I have a funny story, which I'll tell you, Dana, but on the QT."

I've never been sure what *on the QT* means, but I assumed it meant *in secret*, and you know me: I like a secret. "My lips are sealed," I said.

"During my interim training, one trainer told us how he came to interim work. After being ordained, he said, he was called to a small, conservative church—exactly what he wanted."

This sounded like our interim!

"Three years later," Perry went on, "he was let go. He blamed the church for being small-minded and stuck in the past. He reentered search and was called to another small church, where he lasted four years before they asked him to leave. It's this screwed-up denomination, he thought. So he went to the Methodists, who sent him to one of their churches. Three years in, that church kicked him out. Finally, he had a long soul search, which ended in one question: 'What kind of work *can* an asshole do in this profession?'"

"And that was our interim?" (As if I had to ask!)

Perry hummed an affirmative.

"And you?" I said. "Are you an asshole?"

"One hopes not," he said. "But I don't please everyone."

Sparlo hadn't pleased everyone, either. But he'd held true to himself, which, he told me, was what people need most in a leader. Someone who holds fast and steady to what they believe and who they are.

Perry and I took the museum's circular staircase down to the Asian art galleries. Perry wanted to see the South Indian bronzes, the dancing Shivas and the big-bellied, elephant-headed Ganeshas with their consorts and transports. "Do you know about darshan?" Perry asked, then explained the profound visual exchange between a believer and a sacred image. We stood before a fifteenth-century Shiva and his pert-breasted consort, Meenakshi. "Meenakshi means fish eyes," Perry whispered. "Because, like a fish, her eyes never close. If she blinks, the whole universe, all of existence, is obliterated."

We spent most of an hour in that room practicing darshan on the ancient bronzes. Never in my life have I been so aware of blinking.

He had me drop him off at Tom Fox's house. (Elsa, too, had met with Tom.)

Did I like Perry enough to want him as our new minister? When the sun came out. And then, nowhere near as much as I wanted Elsa.

The San Gabriel Mountains were a cool violet that clear chilly Sunday morning as we drove east along their foothills. With few cars on the road, we reached the small, unassuming Montclair church half an hour early. The doors were still locked. When I was in seminary just a few miles away, I'd preached here twice. Then, the cinder-block building had sat alone in the scrubby flats, but the town had since lapped up to it: next door was a mini-mall with a dentist and a nail salon; across the street, a dialysis center.

Perry's sermon was "Generosity." He began as if just talking, barely using notes.

I collect antique Japanese tea bowls, simple vessels used in the ancient tea ceremony ritual. The bowls I like are hand-formed, somewhat crude, imperfect—their very nicks and cracks are treasured as signs of change and impermanence. I have about twenty bowls that I've gathered over as many years.

Not long ago, I was invited to the wedding of very old, dear friends, two men who had been together for thirty years. Now, finally, they could marry under the law. Because they had always admired my bowls, I wanted to give them one. When I went to choose it, well, let's say I felt the powerful pull of material attachment. Here I was, a Buddhist teacher—and I wanted to keep ALL of them . . . My strongest pang came from the rough replica of a famous kind of tea bowl, an Ido, which is prized for its rustic, handmade beauty. The original Idos were made in the sixteenth century of a very porous clay and dipped in a glaze the pale orange of loquats. My Ido was a copy, probably made in the early nineteenth century, so maybe only two hundred years old. I'd found it behind some mustard jars on a back shelf in a dusty antique shop in Seoul, South Korea, and while I did not pay anything near what it was really worth, it was not, um, inexpensive. This Ido was a favorite bowl. I did not want to give it away.

I also knew, because it meant so much to me, that it was the perfect bowl for my friends, who meant so much to me, on the sacred occasion of their marriage.

There is a saying that gifts should be things that you yourself want.

To say that I wanted to keep this bowl is an understatement.

I took it off the shelf. I wrapped it in tissue, set it into a box, and wrapped the box. I felt sick to my stomach with resentment and greed. At the reception, I placed it on the gift table beside the Instant Pot and the electric kettle—and the strangest thing happened. When the bowl left my hands, I had a glimpse of something bigger, something infinite.

I felt free.

I had let go of something I was sure would be painful to live without. Instead, a space opened up in me—more space to breathe, to think, to have my being.

Everything we hold on to takes up mental energy. Our minds are knotted with the strings of our attachments. We can feel bound to things—to objects, ideas, people—as if by steel cables.

I have not rearranged the bowls on my shelves, so that the empty space where the Ido once sat can remind me what it means to let go. It means freedom.

There is a famous Japanese declutterer who says, If it doesn't give you joy, get rid of it. I would add, if it does give you joy, give it away. You'll see.

In this way, generosity teaches us freedom.

He went on to talk first about emotional generosity (erring on the side of love), then philanthropy and the questionable generosity of tainted money. The poor were the most generous, he said, and ended with the story of his Thai teacher's funeral, where the local villagers fed (for free!) all fourteen thousand mourners who came to pay their respects.

Adrian was sitting next to me. His verdict? "Better than Tom."

We ate lunch at a patio restaurant in downtown Claremont. Perry, too, seemed more at ease after preaching, and was looser and warmer than he'd been all weekend—and not as ravenous as Elsa. The kids commandeered him down at their end of the table where phones displaying baby pictures were passed around.

That afternoon, I called Perry's reference. She'd been on his ministerial relations committee at his first church, the one he'd left with a negotiated settlement. "We did wrong by him," she said. "People expected him to be a clone of our last minister, and when Perry did things his own way, they felt betrayed. He was actually an energetic, dedicated, creative minister. Oh, he made some rookie mistakes, but his critics were unforgiving."

I thanked the reference, then hauled Jack out for Sunday dinner at the expensive new restaurant in a high-end Hollywood hotel.

29

✤

A Lot Happens

Walking into the Milkfarm cheese store and café at lunchtime, I was greeted by the pungent funk of melting aged Gruyère. Helen Harland was in town for a seminar and I was meeting her for lunch. I found her studying the sandwich case. "Gosh," she said. "I don't know what half these things are: Speck? Guanciale? Taleggio? Just pick one for me, please. Nothing too strong or spicy."

I ordered her a grilled cheese made with Irish cheddar and French ham on pain au levain, and for myself, speck and young pecorino on a baguette. I grabbed a couple of bags of chips, and we sat in a corner by the plateglass window.

"Dare I ask how the search is going?" she said. "I've been getting calls from some very interested ministers. You happy with your pre-cans?"

"Some."

This brought the therapist's forward lean, the sharpened focus. "But not all?"

I tore open a bag of truffle chips—really truffle-flavored potato chips—that cost $3.95: a novelty I'd never buy on my own. I shook them onto a small plate and the scent of truffles, at once earthy and faintly metallic, filled the air. That scent always triggers a free-floating longing in me, the ache of a bittersweet memory, but with no specific memory attached. (Did such poignancy make the chips worth twice as much as the Lay's?)

I said, "I liked this fantastic guy in Detroit, but the kids banded against him."

"Walt Harrison? Yeah. He called me. I thought he'd have a good chance with your group, but I guess he had history with we-know-who. At first he wasn't sure if that history would help him or hurt him."

"Hurt," I said. "Did he tell you what it was? A romance gone wrong?"

A server brought us iced green tea; we waited till she moved out of earshot.

"Not even. He met her at some denominational event when he was in seminary and she was interning at headquarters. He liked talking to her, but he had a girlfriend and made that clear right away. But Jennie started showing up at his church and asking him to do stuff with her. He kept saying he was attached—to the woman he later married—but Jennie kept calling and emailing him and walking by his apartment and showing up at the Starbucks where he studied. He said it was almost like stalking."

"Sounds exactly like stalking to me," I said.

"Eventually he had to block her calls and texts. But all that was five or six years ago and they've both married and had kids since, so when he saw she was on the AUUCC's search committee, he thought she might have advocated for him."

"The opposite, in fact," I said.

"She should've recused herself," said Helen.

"No kidding," I said. "Instead, she said she'd never reach consensus on him and convinced the other kids to vote against him. And Charlotte let it go."

"Yeah—what's up with Charlotte? The last time we spoke she sounded, I don't know, a little blurry."

"Her back's bugging her. And she not only let Jennie squash Walt, she let her push this failed actress on us who's never even served her own church. And Walt's been a senior minister for six years!" I was getting worked up.

"Which reminds me," said Helen. "This is what I wanted to tell you! You'll never guess who called me."

"Bert Share? Yeah. He called me, too."

We squinched our faces at each other. "Poor old BS," Helen said. "I tried to talk him down. No way the AUUCC's going to hire his ingenue."

"Knock wood." I tapped a nearby shelf, probably painted MDF.

"But you've got some great people. The astonishing Doris Gray—she'd wake you guys up. And Elsa Neddicke's the best." Helen took a large bite of her sandwich.

"And we just pre-canned this guy who's a Buddhist monk, Perry Fitzgerald?"

Helen held up her hand—wait!—and finished chewing. "Yeah. You guys might want to develop your references on him."

"Really? I talked to one reference already, who adored him."

"Yeah? Well, call that person back and ask for a neutral reference," Helen said. "This is Perry's third year in search; he pre-cans everywhere and never gets called."

"It could be his intermittently unpleasant personality, which I kind of like," I said. "Except he kicked my dog—I mean, he pushed her firmly away with his shoe."

"He's obviously not winning the popularity contests."

"That's depressing," I said, and unsure if I'd crossed some confidentiality line, added, "I wish you'd tell Charlotte about Jennie and Walt, and Perry. It will sound more impartial coming from you."

Helen agreed, and we ate silently for a few minutes. I watched two women behind the counter cut up a resin-colored wheel of cheese the size of a small car tire.

"I've made you glum," said Helen.

"I thought the search would be more fun," I said. "Some of it's ego—nobody cares what I say or think. I wouldn't mind except that Jennie has so much clout. She just persists until she gets her way. And I feel so bad for Walt—he should have been a pre-candidate instead of Bert's movie-star intern."

"Don't worry about Walt. He'll do great."

"I feel like we missed the boat with him."

"I doubt he would have pursued the job, not with Jennie still so reactive."

Helen and I parted outside the cheese store with my promise that Jack and I would visit her soon. In a gift shop next door, I browsed among the scented candles and trivets with silly sayings (PUT YOUR HOT BOTTOM HERE), then bought a birthday card for Jack. Walking back to my car, I got a text from Charlotte. **Call me ASAP.**

"I have some not good news," she said. "So prepare yourself. Okay?"

I stopped on the sidewalk, took a breath. "Tell me."

"Belinda had a stroke. She's expected to live, but she's paralyzed on her right side and she can't talk. Maybe she'll recover some movement and speech, maybe not."

Luckily, Belinda's cleaning lady had been there when it happened, and called the ambulance in time for Belinda to get immediate treatment. Luckily, too, Belinda had it on her health-care directive to notify the church in case of emergency. The secretary, Vera, had called Charlotte.

"What can I do?" I asked.

"If you'll bring the entrée for tomorrow night's meeting that will save me a lot of trouble. Adrian's agreed to host on Saturday. Is there any chance you can host Doris the next Saturday? I'd be eternally grateful . . ."

How could I say no?

For the Tuesday-night entrée, I made a dish I'd learned in Jordan called chicken freekeh, freekeh being green wheat that's roasted on its stalk in a fire, then threshed on the ground; part of the prep is picking out the little stones before cooking. I boiled the smoky grain in broth, roasted the chicken and the caramelized onions separately, then put them together in one pan with a lashing of good olive oil, a scattering of pine nuts, and a generous dusting of sumac; twenty minutes before serving, I'd stick it in Charlotte's oven to toast the pine nuts and marry the flavors.

Charlotte was putting out her supply of soda, mostly the big bottles of half-flat diet colas we hadn't finished. Riley, who'd signed up to bring drinks, was at the hospital. "He says Belinda's alert," she said. "She can't get a word out, but her eyes are bright. He doesn't want to leave till she's asleep."

At the table, Charlotte lit the chalice and asked for a moment of silence for Belinda—odd, I felt, given how much Belinda disliked moments of silence in church. Check-in was quick and unanimous: we were all worried about Belinda and already overwhelmed by pre-candidates. "I can't believe Alanna will be here in three days!" said Jennie. "And Doris after that."

Adrian said, "They are a-coming thick and fast!"

Charlotte said, "So what do we think about Perry?"

"Very different from Elsa," I said. "And not as easy to like."

"I think he's a lamb chop," said Curtis. "I like him a lot."

"He's actually adorable," said Jennie. "I'd love a minister with a mixed-race family. And it's so cool that he's Buddhist."

"Why is that cool?" said Sam. "I ask because I know nothing about Buddhism."

"Because he's not Christian. Sparlo and Tom Fox supposedly weren't either, but they were all 'Bible this, Bible that.'"

"Perry says it's important to preach from the Bible," I said. "For us to keep hold of it in our own religious tradition."

"Yes, but he'd also make everyone meditate in church!"

"My skin crawls at the thought," said Charlotte. "Though I do find Perry compelling. He can seem so controlled and remote; but when he smiles, it's like a blessing."

"Like the sun coming out," I said.

"Exactly," said Charlotte. "And his institutional knowledge is very impressive. He'd keep us in good shape."

"I felt as if he was observing us," I said. "And wasn't so impressed."

"He felt judgy to me, too, at first," said Jennie. "But he loosened up."

"He might just be shy," Adrian said. "A lot of shy people seem aloof and standoffish till you get to know them."

"When I drove him to the airport," said Jennie, "Jaz was in the back seat and Perry and I sang along to the radio—he knew all the words to 'The Lazy Song'—and he did this funny hand-dancing thing with her. You can tell he has kids."

"We do like him," said Curtis. "Don't we?"

"He has good ideas for deepening spiritual practice," I said.

"I'd like to believe him—and Elsa, too, for that matter—that a deeper spiritual practice naturally leads to social action," said Adrian. "But I've also seen meditation encourage self-involvement and exacerbate narcissism. I'm not ruling Perry out. He's not as gregarious as Tom, but not as sloppy, either. I spoke to one of his references." He pulled out his phone and peered into the screen. "She's the board president at the church he's serving now. She called him a miracle worker and let's see . . ." He scrolled down. "'Best preacher ever,' 'well liked,' 'very organized,' 'we'd like to keep him.'"

"Excellent," Charlotte said. "Who else talked to a reference?"

"Me," I said. "Also glowing. Mine was from the church he was forced to leave; she said he'd been drummed out for what she said were 'rookie mistakes.'"

"Can you two call those references back and ask them for names of some neutral references? People who aren't champions of Perry's, but not his enemies, either."

Helen, obviously, had spoken to Charlotte.

"And remember to clear the names with Perry before you call anyone. We can't talk to a reference he doesn't sanction."

"Why? Is there a problem?" said Adrian.

"I've heard he's been passed over by a number of other churches and it would be good to find out if it's more than coincidence."

"Hey!" Jennie waved her arm. "I thought I was in charge of references," she said. "So I think I should decide who calls the neutral people. Like I'd like to talk to one. Dana, do you mind if I follow up with the person you talked to?"

I checked with Charlotte, who shrugged.

"Fine," I said, glad to offload a task.

I far preferred Elsa—and probably Doris—but barring some damning revelation, I could see Perry at the AUUCC. He'd change the tone of the place, especially after Tom's warm'n'fuzzy crusade. In Sparlo's time, the AUUCC had been famously reserved. When I first attended, some months went by before anybody talked to me—but I'd liked that, mostly. I liked drifting unknown at the edge of things and entering church life at my own speed. I appreciated that nobody forced a name tag on me or demanded my contact information or knocked on my door unannounced at dinnertime; or I might have felt pressured and fled. I did have some self-conscious moments on the patio after worship, when I would have liked to chat with someone. (I'd since made it a practice to greet the loners and strangers adrift in the coffee hour.) Of course now, thanks to Tom Fox's decade-long warm-up-the-AUUCC campaign, a squad of membership committee members descended on strangers, issued name tags, and hounded visitors to inscribe their contact information in the membership book.

I probably preferred Perry's self-containment to Tom's needy extroversion. I wished that I was more self-contained and that my shyness came off as aloof and mysterious rather than inept, rude, or self-conscious. Sparlo, too, had been shy and socially awkward, but when he was uncomfortable in social situations, he talked nonstop. He and Tom had that in common. Those two—one an introvert, the other a flagrant extrovert—could dominate the hell out of any conversation.

"Does anyone know what Riley thinks of Perry?" said Charlotte.

"Perry's taste in music scares him," said Jennie.

We were subdued. Belinda's illness had cast a pall. And now a cloud hung over Perry, too.

"I can't believe we have a whole nother pre-candidating weekend already," said Jennie. "But this one will be fun!"

After the kids left, I joined Charlotte at her sink. "I guess you heard about Jennie's history with Walt," she said.

"Yes. We should make her recuse herself and pre-candidate him."

"It's too late for that, Dana. I have surgery in less than three weeks."

"But we still have six weeks before the offers go out," I said. "We can squeeze him in. I'll handle the logistics."

"Oh, Dana." She squeezed a sponge and started wiping the counter. "We don't have the budget or the patience for another pre-can. And the other kids would do what Jennie wants whether she recused herself or not."

"Dana P? You coming?" Adrian, it turned out, had been waiting to drive me home.

"Okay, fine," I said, and left with him.

30

Alanna in Desert Country

T hat Friday evening, one of the donks got out of the corral and made a game of evading capture. Springtime made him frisky. I couldn't leave him out—he'd decimate the garden—and by the time I got him locked in and fed, I was late to the Friday dinner at Charlotte's. Everyone was in the living room clustered around Alanna, whose face was more beautiful—more radiant, more striking—in person. She wore a long embroidered lavender tunic of coarsely woven silk and darker leggings. Some of her lush black hair was pulled up in a bun at the back of her head and the rest rippled down her back. "Oh good, here's Dana," she said warmly, her voice low and raspy. Her lush clothing, her stature, and—how else to say it—her physical *thrum* were all riveting. Among us drab mortals she shone like a mythic creature, a mermaid or Hera herself. Sam stared openmouthed.

Adrian brought her a drink, a scorching Michael Servetus.

Like Elsa, she knew all of our names, our roles at the church, our interests. She raised her glass and said, "To Belinda, may she recover fully and rejoin you soon!" After a sip, she said, "Riley, you might have to quit that day job of yours and make these drinks for a living!" Her laugh was a deep chortle. She demanded to see photos of Curtis's Max and Jennie's Jaz. At dinner, she called to me from across the table, "You know, Dana, I love ministry as I love life itself, but if I ever had to choose another line of work, it would be yours—though I could never write as cleverly as you do. I read in an interview how you see each restaurant as a manifestation of the human spirit. I just loved that."

I had said, as a *peculiar* manifestation of the human spirit, but never mind.

Alanna had grown up in Fresno; her father was an internist, her mother a sociology professor at Fresno State. One brother—"the rich one," she said—was "a hedge fund guy" in San Francisco while her other brother was "a starving poet" still in Fresno. "Of course I'd love to be near to them again," she said. "And I do love LA." She'd gone to Occidental College and spent eight years after that knocking around Hollywood.

She praised the quiche, and when told it was takeout, said, "Oh, I never cook, either! But I do love to eat!"

Me: "Really—you don't cook? Ever?"

"My Catholic grandmother—who had seven kids—told me never to learn how or I'd get stuck cooking instead of doing what I really wanted to do."

Had I gotten stuck cooking instead of doing what I really wanted to do? What had I ever really wanted to do except write books, books with recipes?

I helped Charlotte load the dishwasher while everyone else adjourned again to the living room area. Alanna took the one armchair, and all gathered around her on the sofas.

"She is charismatic," Charlotte whispered. "Jennie had that right."

"Almost too much for this small space," I whispered back. "Don't tell me you're falling for her."

"She does have something. Look. Even Adrian's gaga."

For her interview in the morning, Alanna dressed the part: black suit, deep pink silk blouse, a relaxed bow at the neck over which a small silver chalice dangled on a fine chain. Her hair was rolled into a bulging French twist, and she wore glasses, their heavy black frames manly and stylish. Only as she sat down beside me did I register how large she was: six feet and one-eighty, easy. Which might be why Hollywood spit her out. And partly why she had such presence: sheer mass.

If Elsa had answered our questions from a deep well of experience and Perry from acquired expertise, Alanna answered theoretically. She had a lot of ideas.

"I call my ministry model 'Raquel,' spelled R-A-C-L, which stands for ritual, activism, community, and learning." (This was not an original concept, but a jumbling of the standard LARC model they teach in seminary.)

She'd seen in our packet that preaching and worship were among our top priorities—and they were top priorities for her as well! Her master's thesis had been on worship, though the term she preferred was "ritual craft," which signaled "the recent revolution in liturgical theory."

She explained: "Protestants, in recoiling from Rome's excesses, embraced austerity; for them, worship was limited to sermons, hymns, and prayers. Today, if churches are going to survive, that model has to change. So many of us have grown up with an endless stream of images: rollicking, sexy, free-associative music videos; immersive and suspenseful video games; multisensory experiments in art and theater. No wonder young people don't come to church: their phones and other screens have far more stimulating content."

Her goal, Alanna said, was to create new rituals that touched all the senses. Instead of a few colorful banners collecting dust in the sanctuary, why not use projected images, films, more dramatic lighting? Instead of dribbling a little water on an infant's brow during our naming ceremonies, why not meet at a beautiful stream or lake or ocean, wade in, and give the new little creatures a good dunk—and then have a picnic after! How about a bread communion featuring the different breads of the world, from Chinese pancakes and Swedish flatbread to matzoh, pita, baguettes, and African fritters? (The bread communion, too, was a seminary standby.) And why not provide olfactory stimulation: a drift of incense, or the passing of spice boxes as in Havdalah services at the end of Shabbat? Why must Protestant austerity dominate? Why not borrow from ecstatic traditions:

call-and-response is "so invigorating!"—and add theater, mime, chanting. "Why shouldn't we dance in the aisles?"

When Adrian asked about her greatest successes, she enlarged on her Theater of the Body Dynamic. "Participants start by writing scripts together on the themes and then they act them out, drawing on sacred dance, yoga, tai chi, and other movement traditions. In performances, audience members move among the actors and they, too, experience the postures of suffering and redemptive joy."

Here, I thought, was yet another way to torture introverts like me.

Community, too, was "a top priority!" "We UUs have to eat together more. Why not have lunch after church every Sunday? I'm sure Dana knows what I mean!"

I did. And I agreed: there should be more food around the AUUCC. My husband's synagogue held onegs after Shabbat services; they hewed to the maxim: "Whenever three or more are gathered, food is served."

Sam said, "I'm still concerned that you've had no experience running a church on your own."

"Not a church, no, but I do have a solid business background," Alanna said. "I minored in business, undergrad. And at my theater company, I kept the books. I hired and fired people, I coordinated productions. And where I work now, I've observed from the inside how a very large church is run."

Love, she reiterated, was her theology.

I asked her to elaborate.

"Love unites all beliefs," she said. "Love is the oxygen of the great web, the fuel fueling all creation . . ."

As for her home and family life? There had been a partner—male—and a recent breakup. "Which is why I can look far afield for a job . . . And why I'm drawn to California, to be closer to my family."

I had signed up to drive Alanna to lunch. As she too had wanted to eat Chinese food in the San Gabriel Valley, we headed to a Szechuan noodle restaurant in San Gabriel—noodles, I hoped, would not be such a challenge for Charlotte. Alanna filled my Subaru with the jangling of silver bangles, scents of musk and coconut shampoo and, as she lifted her arms to re-pin her bun, a whiff of nervous, oniony sweat. I took Altadena Drive with its dramatic glimpses of our steep foothills, now fuzzed with green. Puffball clouds drifted overhead. "I forget how beautiful it is here," she said.

I asked where she'd lived in LA (Echo Park, West Hollywood) and she asked me the usual questions about restaurant reviewing: Did I announce myself? (No.) Did I ever wear disguises? (No.) Was I ever recognized? (Sometimes.) How many times did I visit a place? (As many as it took.) How did I know which restaurants to review—did I find them, were they assigned, or did restaurants invite me? (All of the above.)

I didn't hate her. I didn't dislike her. We simply didn't connect. She was a big, showy bustle of a person of a type unfamiliar and not congenial to me. I couldn't get anywhere with her. And where did I want to get? To some human moment. A shared laugh. An exchanged look of mutual understanding. That click of recognition. We were people who otherwise would never get to know each other. Of course, life and even the AUUCC were filled with people like that. But did I want one as my minister?

I'd be fine with a minister who wasn't a friend so long as I could connect in meaningful ways—to their intellect, their theology, or their spiritual depth.

At the restaurant, we colonized a large round table; I sat across from Alanna, but the place was so clattery and loud and the table so wide, I couldn't hear anything she said. I watched her preside. Her poise, her beauty, the ceremonial way she passed dishes, the way she poured out the tea like a generous hostess: All of it seemed enacted. Yet the others leaned toward her. She formed the center. She starred.

I sat between Sam, who slurped his noodles, and Charlotte, who pushed hers around. "This food is still too far out for me," she murmured. "A fried egg in soup?"

"And what about our visitor?" I asked.

"Quite a production. I quite like her. I didn't expect to, but I do. She's no Elsa or even a Perry. But she's got real magnetism and personal power— which is good in a minister, so long as they don't exploit it. I think she's sincere. She'll definitely go far."

I wasn't convinced. Personal power, I've found, is too often a product of self-mythologizing. But then I'm a critic, suspicious by nature.

Jennie and Curtis were taking Alanna to the Huntington Gardens after lunch, so I drove Adrian and Sam back to the church.

"She's just terrific, that girl," said Sam.

"She's even more impressive in person than she is on Skype," Adrian said from the back seat. "A highly competent, talented young woman."

"Too theatrical for me," I said. "Like she's an actor playing a minister."

Silence. Then Adrian grabbed the back of my seat and pulled himself close. "Hey," he said, "Jill's very nervous about cooking for you. She's making her best dish. She'll probably leave before everyone comes, but if you do see her, be kind."

"Of course," I said. People are often nervous cooking for a food critic, but the truth is, this critic prefers good home cooking to most restaurant fare—not the least because far fewer cooks have had their fingers in the food.

I'd been curious to see where Adrian lived, but when the time came to pick lettuces and change clothes for the dinner, a strange drag overtook my limbs, and my mood soured. Alanna didn't interest me and I resented that I had to spend an evening pretending otherwise, when I could spend the Saturday night at home with Jack and the animals. We weren't going to hire Alanna—why go through the pantomime?

I might have called in sick—I had yet to miss a single meeting—but there was Jill's best dish, which might be a good one for the book.

Grouchy and late, I followed GPS instructions to a low-slung ranch house on a cul-de-sac in the foothills. A side entrance brought me inside a long, open living space: grand piano, sunken living room, dining area, and, at the far end, a large, bright kitchen. Most of the room's south wall was glass, revealing the vast grid of lights from here to the Palos Verdes hills. My colleagues were settled with drinks on two huge button-and-tuck leather sofas in front of the fireplace. Alanna sat on the hearth and raised her glass. "Here she is! Dana P!" I lifted my sack of lettuces in response, and in that moment really saw the fireplace, a massive sprawl of bad rockwork:

shaggy, sharp slabs of dark, glittering granite grouted sloppily with concrete. In its huge black maw a small pyre of Presto logs burned wanly. Who could live with such an eyesore, much less cluster sofas and chairs toward it and not the view? Alanna, wrapped and vaguely Madonna-like in a dark shawl, said, "I was just saying, Dana, that after the Huntington, Jennie took me to Owen Brown's grave and told me all the history . . ." I barely heard her; my mind was busy with remedies for the fireplace: they could paint the rocks white. Or gray. Or sledgehammer the whole thing away.

Riley got up to make me a Decision Maker, and I took my lettuces to the kitchen area, where Adrian was setting out silverware on a long, marble-topped island. "Hey," I said. "Spectacular view! How long have you guys lived here?"

"Twelve years," he said.

With that fireplace? He could never, I now knew, be the love interest in my book.

I took my drink and sat next to Charlotte. I missed Belinda; without her, we lacked a center, a gravity. Alanna was recounting her adventures in Hollywood; she'd had a nonspeaking role in a film starring Pierce Brosnan, who sang her name whenever he saw her on set. "Ah-Lon-Ahh, Ah-lon-ahh, I just met a girl named Alanna!" she sang in her husky voice. And once, she said, she'd run into Nicole Kidman at her physical therapist's. "So pale and fragile-looking! I guess her back is just a tragedy."

Tom Fox had loved pre-candidating, he told me, because it was all about him. Elsa had deflected such a focus by meeting our interest in her with her interest in us. Perry, with his self-possession and steel boundaries, seemed indifferent to and untouched by our attention. But Alanna basked in it, soaked it up, and beamed in return.

I went to dress my lettuces just as Adrian set out a bubbling pan of green-sauced enchiladas. Briefly, he and I stood side by side, observing the others. Everyone was tilted toward Alanna, who, in that shawl, face aglow, looked like a saint in a painting.

"Tell me that's not an actor hamming it up," I muttered to Adrian. "And not a very good one, either. Another Hollywood reject who's found her captive audience."

"I like her." Adrian pulled off his oven mitts. "But then I like, admire, and respect actors. My wife is an actor." He turned away from me. "Everyone! Come eat!"

Stung, I joined the others at the buffet. We ate in front of the fireplace. Everyone else praised Jill Jones's green chicken enchiladas, which were smothered in jack cheese and sour cream; rich, bland, gloppy, and seriously fattening, they were a definite no for the book. Claiming a headache, I left before the pie.

The Desert Country Unitarian Universalist Fellowship met in the recreation room of a senior center in a strip mall. As we entered, a male volunteer wheeled a pulpit to the center of a small stage in front of a snow-white movie screen. A female volunteer placed an order of service on every other folding chair in a field of sixty. Dusty UU banners—such as Alanna disparaged in her interview yesterday—sagged forlornly on the side walls. (LOVE MOTHER EARTH! WE BELIEVE IN THE WORTH AND DIGNITY OF ALL.) Alanna and a male volunteer struggled to connect her computer to the AV system; Adrian and Curtis went to help them while the rest of us found seats. I sat two rows back, as ever, on the right, with nobody in front of me.

The order of service gave the sermon title as "The Octopus and the Pizza Toss."

Congregants drifted in: a small group from a retirement community arrived by shuttle bus, some pushing walkers. More people around my age, and a few young families with children, scattered themselves among the folding chairs. All together there were thirty-one of us. A morning chant—I knew it from yoga classes—played on the sound system, then faded away.

Alanna came onstage in a purple robe with a colorful stole featuring the symbols of major world religions. Her hair was piled on her head. She looked grand and imposing, a high sorceress. "Good morning, Desert Country!" she rang out.

A murmured response. To my surprise—I was sure he hated me after my snideness last night—Adrian slid in beside me.

"Oh, now, we can do better than that!" Alanna said. "Let's try it again. Good morning, Desert Country!"

A slightly more effortful reply (not from me) resulted. She smiled her dazzling smile as if we'd roared, then welcomed us "whoever you are, whatever you believe."

A small adolescent girl played a quavering Bach gavotte on a very large viola.

A bearded man with wild gray hair accompanied the first hymn, "Hail the Glorious Golden City," on his guitar. The lights went down. A series of images flashed on the screen: people sunbathing on a crowded beach; Michelangelo's muscular marble David; two plump old ladies walking arm in arm. Alanna, who had stepped into the wings, now came to center stage and, washed in the colors of this slide, she paused. The image disappeared and a rosy-gold klieg light shone on her. Her expression was beatific: her eyes shone, her beautiful face shone. She lifted her arms as if offering a hug. "Before coming here to Desert Country," she said,

> I read a little about your fellowship and learned that it includes Buddhists, Jewish people, humanists, pagans, Taoists, atheists, Sufis, Christians, and others!

As she named the religions, she pointed to its symbol on her stole: the Jewish star, the Tao's yin-and-yang commas, the Islamic crescent moon, the Christian cross . . .

> Such glorious diversity under one roof, in one community, reminds us: whatever our differences, we . . . are . . . all . . . one!

I looked around, embarrassed that we were inflicting such theatrics on this small, raffish congregation. But the audience was rapt. She lowered her arms.

And one thing that we have in common is . . . we all have bodies! Our bodies are as unique and distinct as our beliefs, but young and old, all colors and sizes, we are all living, breathing *embodied* beings. And today I want us to pay our bodies extra attention. So—hello you torsos, arms, and legs, you fingers and toes [she wiggled her fingers at some kids near the front]; hello all you stomachs and kidneys, you hairs and necks, spines and hearts. So glad we're together today!

She waved. Many, including Adrian, waved back.

"You're loving this, aren't you," I whispered.

Today, Alanna said, she was going to talk about the wisdom and intelligence of the body. To this end, she said, "Let us consider the octopus." The image of an enormous, speckled octopus, arms aswirl, filled the screen, washing over Alanna.

The octopus is so unique that some scientists think that the seed cells from which it evolved arrived on a meteor or asteroid that crashed into Earth. True or not, this tells us how unusual these beings are. The octopus is also among the most intelligent of creatures and—get this—it has no centralized brain! No brain! Its intelligence and thought processes are all over its body; the octopus thinks with its arms, its tentacles, its suckers. I mention this marvelous cephalopod because I want us to think about intelligence in a new way—as not just in the brain, but throughout our entire bodies. . . .

Reverting to form (the form of the two sermons we'd read of hers), she recited a brief, dry Wikipedian history of dualism and the mind-body split from Plato to Descartes.

We see ourselves as minds that inhabit bodies. The mind is the thinking part of us, the self, who we are. The body, well, that's the animal whose instincts must be tamed. This kind of thinking dates back to pre-enlightenment times—really, to Plato—when we lacked the science to understand how the body works and humans were seen as pillars of flesh with a brain on top.

The Protestant religions, embracing this model, have privileged the mind, the intellect, reason. To this day, in church, we are meant to sit quietly without moving and apply our *minds* to the lesson.

(A slide of a church, with the male minister in a raised pulpit)

But cognitive scientists now say things don't separate out so neatly. The brain, though an amazing processor in itself, does not run the whole show. For starters, the body is a series of at least ten different systems— can we name them?

She cupped her ear. People called out: "Circulatory . . . Respiratory . . . Lymphatic!"

Don't forget the reproductive system! And the integumentary system! What's that? Skin and hair! All of these systems work independently *and* with the brain *and* with each other. Intelligence, it seems, is a shared, ongoing, full body process!

There's even a kind of secondary brain in our guts—yes, science has verified it: you can trust your gut!

This new understanding of intelligence came to us, she said, through robotics:

When scientists first designed robots, they gave them a central, brain-like computer—and guess what happened? When told to walk, the robots fell over! Movement, it turns out, involves far more than a centralized calcula-tor. It involves an intricate web of sensors and learning storage apart from the brain, a body-wide intelligence scientists call "embodied cognition."

She pointed out the body intelligence of break-dancers, cheerleaders, great athletes; she spoke of "embodied cognition" in the hands of mechanics, surgeons, seamstresses, and cooks. Ducking behind the pulpit for a moment, she came forward on the stage, hefting a pale, beige blob in her palms.

My first job in high school was waitressing in a pizza joint. There, a team of teenage boys stretched the dough into large perfect rounds. They handled it so confidently and sent it flying into the air with so much style, I envied them.

(A slide showed a couple of young men in toques tossing pizza dough in the air.)

I had never cooked a thing in my life, but I wanted to do that! Whenever business was slow, I'd try. They showed me how to stretch it over the back of my hand,

(Here she stretched the dough over the back of her hand.)

and how to send it into the air, and how to catch it and rotate it.

(The small disk flew up a foot or so. She caught it.)

I soon had all the verbal instructions memorized, but my hands still had to learn. Every day, I practiced.

(She kept stretching and tossing the dough.)

And after a couple of months my hands knew. They'd learned how. I can't fry an egg and I can barely boil water, but my hands have this beautiful knowledge.

She flung the dough high, where it spun and flapped; she caught it and flung it again and again, and finally held it out draped over her forearm like a sacred cloth.

People clapped. Including Adrian.

She folded it up and stuck it back under the podium.

Let us be ever more aware of the miracle of the body and the intelligence in our brains, our guts, our hands, our feet. Science tells us that the mind is more varied and elegant, more fully embodied, than we imagined. This is religious knowledge, for to see ourselves as fully embodied beings is to be awestruck, humbled and grateful before life's intricate beauty.

Alanna stepped back. The bearded guitarist sang the first verse of "This Little Light of Mine." Then all the verses—five of them!—appeared on the screen. The audience stood, sang, and clapped along—Adrian singing and clapping with the best of them. Mortified (of course), I stood up so as not to stick out, though I could not clap. I gripped the chair in front of me. Like one of Riley's bell choir performances, the song went on and on. Alanna called for "the first verse again!" Here, she came to the edge of the stage, singing and pointing to the children in the audience and clapping to them, like a country music star.

As the last chord faded, she stood center stage and stretched out those arms.

Slides of each body system—blowups of medical illustrations—washed over her.

And as Walt Whitman says, "O I say these are not the parts and poems of the body only, but of the soul,/O I say now these are the soul!"

Bless all of you, all you beautiful soulful bodies. Forever and ever. Amen.

She strode down the center aisle, robes billowing.

Adrian turned to me. "Wow. Just wow."

The only restaurant I'd found nearby was a Panera in a shopping center. Again, we sat outside on a patio, this time under a cloth awning with a view of the enormous parking lot. The warm, late-morning desert air was soft and dry and breezy.

"That went extremely well," Adrian said to Alanna. "The slides were wonderful. And I loved how you welcomed the body parts."

"You made us so aware of our physical selves," said Jennie, "and being alive!"

"Oh, good," said Alanna. "I want us to bring more than our brains to church."

"I found it all very stimulating," said Riley. "Of course, no serious scientist believes octopuses come from outer space."

"I don't know," said Alanna. "Some were biologists from MIT."

"Definitely not serious then," said Riley.

"I loved your lesson," Curtis said. "How the body is divine and all."

Alanna's face went blank, then formed a gorgeous smile. "Thank you, Curtis."

I found it hard to believe that Bert Share encouraged her to put on such a show—did he know about the pizza dough? "Do all your sermons have visuals?" I said.

"I try to work some A/V and physical movement into all my worship time. Like today, I knew there'd be kids. So I thought they'd like the flying pizza."

"Would you ever put on a more contemplative or traditional service?"

"Oh god yes, many. Contemplation especially is a top priority. I'm famous for doing guided meditations in place of a sermon—which is why I had so few sermons in my packet. I've been developing new visualization journeys since seminary."

"And what about good old-fashioned sermons?" said Charlotte.

"Also very high on my priority list," said Alanna. "I like a mix of everything."

"And that's exactly what we need," said Jennie.

Jack and I were on our way out to eat that evening when my cell phone lit up the media screen in the Subaru. I recognized the area code. "Bert," I said. "What's up?"

"How'd she do?"

"She makes quite an impression." Praise, I've found, disarms, and often leads to more information.

"I thought she had a bang-up sermon. Smart, fresh, contemporary subject."

"It was definitely livelier than the two in her packet."

"Right? Well, she did weeks of research, then we worked like the devil on it."

"It showed," I said. "Now, Bert, I'd love to talk more, but I'm in the car with a hungry husband who's listening in on all of this."

"Go! I just wanted to check in, see how she did."

"She did well."

"Thanks, Dana. Hopefully, we'll talk more soon."

"Bye, Bert." The screen went dark.

Jack said, "You really don't like him."

"How could you tell?"

"You wouldn't tell him the truth."

IOUs

During check-in on Tuesday night, Riley said that Belinda was "about the same": alert, but unable to speak or move the right side of her body. "She can squeeze with her good hand: we agreed that one squeeze means yes, two means no."

Charlotte reminded us that her surgery was in ten days, a week from Friday. "Which means if we can't decide on the Tuesday after Doris comes, we'll have to meet again that Thursday."

Sam shared that Faithalma was "almost certainly on her way out." "The doctors say she's got a week at most, but I'm not sure the old gal actually has it in her to die."

Witty rubbed against my legs. I picked him up: a full-grown, well-fed cat.

"We hold Belinda and Faithalma in our hearts," Charlotte said. "And now, before we discuss Alanna, can we have the report on Perry's neutral references?"

Jennie went first. "First I talked to Florence, the reference Dana spoke to. She was at the church that Perry left with a negotiated settlement. She was on his ministerial relations committee and loved him. I asked her for a couple of neutral references. Perry said I could call the one named Eliot. Eliot said that he, too, had been on Perry's ministerial relations committee at that church—not the committee that Florence was on, but an earlier one, the one where they all quit in protest because Perry was behaving so badly.

"Eliot said Perry was financially irresponsible. Like, he used the church credit card to buy stuff for himself. When he got caught, he reimbursed the church, but then he kept using the card for personal stuff. And when the treasurer went to take the cash collection to the bank on Monday mornings, she'd sometimes find IOUs from Perry. He paid everything back, the credit card and IOUs, but then another time," Jennie went on, reading from her notes, "he gave receipts for the same meal to two different staffers for reimbursement. I mean, nobody would go to jail for what he did, but some people at the church really didn't like it and told him so. Perry wouldn't admit he'd done anything wrong or that he had any issues around money. That's when his whole ministerial relations committee quit in frustration. A new committee was formed—the committee that Florence was on. But all the money stuff on top of the other things we know about like not allowing announcements and getting people mad at him finally convinced the board to ask him to leave."

"That was five or six years ago," said Charlotte. "Maybe he learned his lesson."

Adrian raised a sheaf of papers. "My neutral reference, Cindy Truong, from his next-to-last church also said Perry was weird around money. She told me some similar stories, like after a church carnival, the organizer went to get the cash out of the church safe and found an IOU for more than six hundred dollars. The check Perry wrote to cover it bounced—though the next one didn't. Then Perry bought a suit for a church function with the ministerial discretionary fund. And not a cheap suit. A Hugo Boss. The credit card bill came to the treasurer, who alerted the board, who voted it was an inappropriate use of the fund. Perry paid that back, too, but in installments. Then he turned around and spent almost the whole discretionary fund on a sofa for his office. In Perry's defense, Cindy Truong said, the fund is meant for expenses and things that the minister might need, and a lot of money had accumulated over the years. But some board members believed that the discretionary fund was intended to help members in an emergency and, on occasion, to take a guest speaker out for lunch. Of course, when Perry moved to his next interim job, he left the sofa."

"I don't like any of this," said Charlotte.

Sam said, "Me neither. You don't want a minister helping themselves to the offerings or any other kitty, ever."

(Sparlo always told me that ministers should never get anywhere near the money—they should never touch the collection plate, and all draws over fifty dollars from the ministerial discretionary fund should go through the finance committee and church treasurer.)

"Cindy Truong said—I wrote it down—'Perry likes to spend money, his own and other people's,'" said Adrian. "The sofa was around five thousand dollars. From Design Within Reach."

"Not within reach of any church budget I know," Charlotte said. "There's a sense of entitlement I really don't like. What minister goes and buys a five-thousand-dollar sofa with the discretionary fund? Or an expensive suit?"

Riley said, "I don't know. He paid everything back. And maybe he did accidentally submit those expenses to two places. I don't know what sofas cost, but maybe he wanted one that would last."

"I have to send in my expenses for eating out," I said. "And if I use a credit card, I can have two receipts for the same meal. But not once in twenty years have I submitted both. Then again, I'm terrified of making a mistake. A food stylist at the *Times* once used a company credit card for personal stuff. He apologized and paid it back. The second time he did it, they fired him on the spot, no further discussion."

"It's as if Perry's testing the limits, seeing what he can get away with," Charlotte said.

"And he won't admit he did anything wrong," said Adrian. "That's a flashing sign of narcissistic arrogance. Cindy said her church board censured Perry and reported him to headquarters. But so far there's been no formal rebuke. He still got his next interim gig. Though there might be a letter in his file."

"I got a summary of his file that said he was in good standing," Charlotte said. "What kills me is that Perry's good. Easily one of the better preachers we've seen. I suppose we could set things up in a way that he couldn't get his hands on any money—but having to do that is reason enough not to hire him. Can you imagine telling the executive committee, 'By the way, the new senior minister can't be trusted with the discretionary fund'? Or the collection plate? Or the church credit card?"

"Maybe it's not as bad as we think," said Riley. "What if we called him and said 'We like you, but we have this concern,' and see what he has to say for himself?"

"I don't know what we'd get out of that," said Adrian. "Unless he promised to get counseling. But first he'd have to admit he did anything wrong."

"He's had every opportunity to come clean," said Charlotte. "In his Ministerial Record, his packet, the Skype interview, his pre-candidating weekend—how many times was he asked about mistakes, regrets, what he's learned about himself in ministry? And he never mentioned a single thing to do with money. What was his mistake? Oh, right: getting rid of the announcement period at church. And creating a native plant garden."

"I don't want a minister who steals," said Curtis.

We all turned to him.

"And I really liked Perry," he went on. "And those sweet little boys! Oh, this is making me so sad."

Sam, who was sitting next to Curtis, put an arm around him.

"At least we know why he's a perpetual interim," said Adrian. "Word leaks out, and nobody will hire him."

"It does feel characterological," said Charlotte. "A real tragic flaw."

"It's so odd, too—for a Buddhist monk to be so improvident," I said. "And he seems so in control. Maybe too controlled. I guess it has to come out somewhere."

"What has to come out?" said Jennie.

"The stuff he doesn't like about himself. That he pushes down, disowns. Won't face. His venal nature."

"Maybe he thought being a pastor would make him be good," said Curtis.

Again, we all turned to Curtis.

"Maybe so," said Adrian.

"It still doesn't sound so bad to me," said Riley. "I think he's trying to address it. Look at his sermon—it was all about generosity and giving up what he loves."

"And how does that address looting the collection plate and overspending on a sofa?" Charlotte said.

Her question hung in the air.

"Okay, let's take a little break," she said. "We'll talk about Alanna over dinner. Right now, I think we could all use a blood-sugar boost."

Riley said, "I have a new drink using the apricot eau-de-vie I started last June. Raspberries muddled in sugar, eau-de-vie, tangerine juice, and club soda. Garnish of preserved kumquats."

"And what do you call it?" I asked.

"The Looming Decision."

They were beautiful drinks, the rosy red at the bottom slowly bleeding into dense orangeness, with a cap of pale froth crisscrossed with thin strips of kumquat.

I'd made a tomato, onion, and cheese quiche with Gruyère from the fancy cheese store, and if I say so myself, it quite improved upon the supermarket quiche Charlotte had fed Alanna last Friday. (Was that only four nights ago?) Sam supplied an airy supermarket baguette and Adrian a bag of romaine hearts and bottled ranch dressing.

We ate on our laps before the gas-jet fire. "Who wants to start in about Alanna?" Charlotte said.

"Me." Jennie put her drink down on the floor. "First of all, I can't believe Belinda gave her such a shitty place to preach."

Charlotte held up a hand. "Now, Jen—"

"Sorry. It wasn't even a church. I guess I could've said I can't believe Belinda gave her such an ugly, depressing, shabby, old rec room with cheapo plastic chairs, bad acoustics, and lousy lighting, but I shortened all that to 'shitty.' Sorry, but it really was."

"I'm with you, girl," said Adrian.

Jennie accorded him a deep nod. "I mean, I've been to the church where Belinda has Doris preaching this Sunday and it's a real church with a high ceiling, a choir, comfy upholstered chairs, and a high-end sound system. But Alanna she sent to an old-age rec center in a low-rent mini-mall out in the middle of the desert? With only a pervy old folk-singer type for music? Oh, and a preteen playing from book four of the Suzuki method? It's so unfair I'd scream except that Alanna still blew us away. In spite of everything Belinda did to sabotage her."

"Well, now, I wouldn't . . ." Charlotte said.

"I agree with Jennie. It was an insulting, demoralizing venue," said Adrian. "And Alanna made the best of it. Gloriously. She was a very good sport."

"A good sport, yes." Charlotte sat back in her chair and closed her eyes. "Sam?" she said. "Any thoughts?"

"The young lady puts on quite a show," said Sam.

"Is that a good thing?" I asked.

"I admire her spunk. She's very lively, very fresh."

"That sermon was a quantum leap from the two in her packet," said Adrian. "Much more clever and inspired and so different from Elsa's and Perry's. I agree with Sam—very fresh. Very bright and new."

Curtis said, "I liked the way she related to the kids. And all the slides."

"What about that pizza stunt?" I said, thinking of how Curtis disapproved of Walt's bread making. "How'd you like that, Curtis?"

"Loved it. She really tossed it up there," said Curtis. "And the kids loved it too!"

"The whole service was thrilling," said Riley. "Like, guess what? Sermons don't have to be about books nobody else has read. Church doesn't have to put you to sleep!"

"And she pulled it off even in that depressing rec room with only a hairy Pete Seeger wannabe for a choir," said Jennie.

"Alanna's performance—and that's what it was—was not boring," Charlotte said. "Her delivery was effective; her theater training very much on display. She's obviously used to a larger, less personal venue; her gestures are so grand and stylized—she'd have to tone them down for our smaller, more intimate church setting. The slides were entertaining, though she flicked through them too quickly. You young people don't mind that fast pileup of images, but I find it anxiety-making. I agree with Adrian: her improvement deserves an A, but the actual sermon, which was more Science Guy than spiritually nourishing, is a B, or B minus. Especially next to the others we've heard."

"Harsh!"

"And she had a lot of help with that sermon," I said. "She's been working with a minister I went to seminary with. He brags about how much he helps her. I'm sure a lot of the improvement is thanks to him."

"Getting help is a positive," said Adrian. "Some people can't take criticism, let alone make use of it. If she's improved this much so fast, she'll go far."

"Her preaching tutor might not help her with every sermon." Me.

"She might not need him to, she's such a fast learner." Adrian.

"Says who?" Me. "But I agree, it was a better sermon, but where was she in it? Where was her soul; where were her considered reflections—in the pizza toss? And what about the person who's slipped in the back of the church, whose life might be hanging by a thread: what did that sermon give to them? Elsa made us more attentive and compassionate, and Perry stirred up our own generosity. What did Alanna do?"

"She made me think in new ways about intelligence and the body," said Jennie.

"Me too," said Curtis. "And how exciting and fun church can be."

We went on in this way. Jennie, Curtis, and Riley extolled Alanna's gifts; Adrian echoed their praise; Charlotte and I tried to formulate criticism in ways that they might hear: "Yes, she's talented . . . but she's never had her own church"; "Very charismatic . . . but with only one acceptable but trying-too-hard sermon under her belt"; "Yes, she's highly attractive . . . if perhaps too theatrical"; "Would love to see her in six or seven years . . . when Elsa or Doris retires."

The kids were unmoved, and we gave up. "So I'll write to Perry and tell him we're passing on him," Charlotte said. "Oy. And this Friday, Doris comes. Or rather, Reverend Gray."

A sign-up sheet was passed around. Since I was cooking dinner on Saturday, I volunteered to drive her to the airport on Sunday.

I found Belinda sitting up but strapped to her hospital bed around noon on Wednesday. How tiny, how pale she was, her hair just see-through fluff. Her enormous eyes brightened as I walked in. She waved her left hand over her mouth—indicating that she couldn't speak—then reached it out to me. I moved to her side and took hold. "I'm so sorry you're here," I said, sitting down. She gave me a friendly squeeze. "I know one squeeze means yes, and two, no," I said, and she squeezed once. I asked if she'd heard about the meeting, and how we'd dropped Perry, and how much the young 'uns liked Alanna.

One squeeze.

Had she seen the video of Alanna's service?

One squeeze.

Had she liked it?

Squeeze, squeeze.

Squeeze, squeeze.

Squeeze, squeeze.

Home from the hospital, I unloaded the groceries and the dishwasher, and when I turned on my computer, I found an email from Charlotte with the subject line in caps: CHANGE OF PLANS.

> *Searchers All*, Charlotte wrote. *The next pre-candidating weekend has been canceled. See the email below.*

> My Dear Friends,
>   As I have been deeply honored to be your pre-candidate, it is with sadness and regret that I write to you today. I was very much looking forward to meeting all of you this weekend. Serving the

AUUCC was a dream that, if realized, truly would have been the golden capstone of my life's work.

Friends, I had thought I had one more career move in me, one more settlement, one more church to serve and to love. Yet, when faced with even the preliminary exertions to make such a move, it became clear to me that I lack the life force, the nerve, and the mettle to take on a new ministry. With a heavy but certain heart, I have decided to continue in my present position and retire within the next few years.

I know that all of you worked hard to arrange this weekend; I apologize for the inconvenience and (if I may) any disappointment I may have caused.

I remain deeply honored, and grateful to all.

Blessed Be,

Reverend Doris Gray

Charlotte added:

Luckily, we have trip insurance. And Amira has agreed to preach for her, as we are responsible for covering her pulpit time at the Valley church.

Jennie Replied All: *Shall we all go hear Amira?*

Charlotte: *I already canceled the rental van. Of course, you are free to go hear Amira, and to take whomever you like, so long as you do not connect your outing with the search in any way. CONFIDEN-TIALITY remains imperative at this time. Personally, I'm taking the weekend off.*

Curtis: *Disappointed. I really liked Doris. I'll go with you, Jennie, to hear Amira.*

Adrian: *Major disappointment. Will take the weekend off to sulk.*

Me: *I'll stay put and sulk in solidarity with Adrian.*

Sam and Riley did not weigh in. When the volley of emails ceased, I phoned Charlotte. "Why don't we see if we can bring Walt out as our fourth pre-candidate? He might even come this weekend."

"Oh god, Dana. I feel like Doris. I'm exhausted. I don't have the bandwidth for another pre-candidate. And why go to all that trouble when, even without her, Team Jennie would never vote him in?"

32

The Intractable One

O
n Tuesday, we met in Tom's office in Arroyo House to select our candidate.

Charlotte lit Tom Fox's Anasazi chalice and pointed to the chair behind Tom's desk. "Tonight we decide who will sit there next September. For nine months, we have talked and eaten and drunk together; we've read eighteen Ministerial Records, Skype-interviewed eight ministers, and driven all over Southern California to hear our three pre-candidates preach. We are sadly diminished in our committee and in our choices. But we are left with two very talented, very different pre-candidates and tonight we must decide between them. Yes, Dana?"

"I've been thinking about the timing. Since we can't make an official offer till early April, couldn't we wait a few weeks to vote? Let everything cook? Your surgery doesn't have to be the deadline. We have more than three weeks—you'll be on the mend and Belinda might be well enough to vote by then. We could even pre-candidate someone else."

"Nooooo!" said Adrian. "No more pre-cans!"

The others echoed him in a group howl.

"Tell it to the hand, Dana P," Jennie said, her palm a stop sign.

"Shall we wait a few weeks?" said Charlotte. "All in favor?"

Sam and I were the only yeas.

"Moving on," said Charlotte, "let me say that consensus is not just everybody agreeing. It's more as if we're an orchestra: everybody plays a part and everyone's contribution is essential. When all of us have been heard, we will hit a final chord together that incorporates everyone's hard work and discernment."

Indeed, I thought. And where did this wishful hokum come from?

"What if we can't hit that final chord?" said Riley. "Or it's too discordant?"

"Then the search has failed," said Charlotte. "This committee is dissolved, the church is out around twenty-five thousand bucks, the congregation is demoralized if not traumatized, an interim is brought in, and a new search committee starts over."

"Nobody wants that," said Adrian.

"I'll say," said Sam.

Charlotte then proposed two separate votes "just to see where we are."

Vote #1: Who could see Elsa being our senior minister? (Charlotte, Sam, Adrian, Curtis, and I could. Jennie and Riley could not.)

Vote #2: Who could see Alanna as our new senior minister? (Riley, Curtis, Jennie, and Adrian could. Sam, Charlotte, and I could not.)

"So let's talk," said Charlotte. "Jennie? Why not Elsa all of a sudden?"

Jennie sat up straight and set her shoulders. "Because in Alanna I have seen something better than a great old-style minister. I have seen a spectacular new talent who will take us into the future. If we ever want to be more than an all-white, bleeding-heart liberal church full of upper-middle-class old folk, we need someone energetic and forward-facing like Alanna."

Curtis clapped and looked around, encouraging us to join in. We did not. Charlotte said, "And I feel a responsibility to steer the church in a tried-and-true direction. I like Alanna more than I thought I would. If her preaching continues to improve, she'll be a force to reckon with down the line. But why take a chance on someone so unproven when we can have Elsa? Let's grow the AUUCC and then hire Alanna—whose present lack of management experience frankly scares me. Our finances are complex; we're the property manager to a private school and two private homes. The grounds and buildings need constant attention. We have nine employees. A more-than-million-dollar budget. Can Alanna manage all that?"

Adrian said, "Most of what you describe is handled by staff."

"Can Alanna manage staff?" said Charlotte. "We don't know. Does she know how to grow a church? Can she get people to raise their pledges? Can she keep the major donors happy? These are skills acquired over years of ministry. My point is, the AUUCC is a lot for anybody *who has* experience."

I said, "I really wish Belinda was here."

"Belinda likes Elsa," Riley said simply. "Though she gets that younger people need someone like Alanna to relate to."

"Anyway, she isn't here and can't vote," said Jennie.

"Harsh!" I said.

Jennie laughed. "I can't believe you just said that, Dana!"

Curtis said, "I like Alanna for how she related to the kids in the service."

"And Elsa?" I prompted.

"She was very nice, too. She believed God listened to me."

"Yes, but Curtis, you also have to think of the whole church when evaluating these ministers," Charlotte said. "Which minister has the skills to run this church? Who is the better preacher? Who has the greater vision? Elsa's vision for us is of creativity and growth; Alanna's is . . . uh, I don't know . . . more theatrical, more performative?"

"I feel I've been listening more consciously since Elsa's sermon," I said.

"I listen for a living," said Adrian, "but since Elsa I've also been listening more proactively and deeply. I loved her idea that listening has an element of obeying, of submitting to another's point of view—and in that humility lies healing."

"Then you should submit to what I want," said Jennie. "It'll really heal ya."

We laughed for what would be the last time that night.

Sam said, "Elsa is a great minister. Yes, she might retire in eight or nine years, but she'd double the size of this church in the meantime. Imagine! We might finally build a new big, beautiful sanctuary!"

"And you can run the capital campaign," said Charlotte.

Sam bowed to her. "With pleasure, Madame President Ex Officio."

"Elsa could double our size," said Riley, "but who with? A whole bunch more aging boomers? We're at a big turning point here when we can choose our future. Elsa is the status quo. She tells us to listen exactly when we need a louder, younger, more audacious voice reimagining religion in whole new ways. And who says Alanna won't triple or quadruple the size of the church?"

"Growing a church is not easy," said Charlotte. "It's more than novelty preaching and programming, it's setting a tone that brings people back, plus a well-oiled membership apparatus that integrates newcomers into church life. Elsa's growth rate is highly unusual for our denomination."

"I believe in my bones that the AUUCC needs Elsa," I said. "Let Alanna build up her chops elsewhere and come to us when Elsa leaves."

"And we believe, in our bones"—Jennie made a horizontal gesture that included Riley and Curtis—"that the AUUCC needs Alanna right now."

Sam said, "At least we have two great possibilities. We can't go wrong."

I felt we could go very wrong and glanced at Charlotte for confirmation. But she shrugged, if not to agree, at least to concede. Was I the only person left who *knew* that this was not a choice between equals but a classic false equivalency?

"It concerns me," I said, "that Alanna is the only pre-candidate who has not talked to Tom about the job. Even Doris had several long conversations with him."

"Alanna asked me about that," said Jennie. "If she should talk to him. But I told her, I said, what can an old white guy tell you that you haven't heard a thousand times?"

Which was more alarming, I thought, that Alanna had asked Jennie for advice or that Alanna had taken it? "Tom could tell her how this church operates, with all the different factions, who's an ally, who's a troublemaker. What the upcoming issues might be with the buildings and grounds, with the staff, with everything."

"Alanna's smart," Riley said, "She'll figure it out."

⸙

On and on we went, taking votes every half an hour or so, with nobody budging until Adrian crossed over around ten. "I've got to say, I'll love seeing a vibrant young person in the pulpit."

"Elsa is not *that* old!" I cried.

"But not that young," said Jennie. "Or vibrant."

The arguments repeated; after eleven, Sam cast a vote for Alanna. "Look," he said. "Young people are the future of this church. I've had two ministers I could call friends, Sparlo and Tom. Young people should have a chance to be friends with their minister. Elsa's my first choice, but Alanna impressed the heck out of me. I reread both of their packets, and in Alanna's, I was impressed when her senior minister wrote in his letter how Alanna was scheduled to preach one Sunday, but then their minister emeritus died that week. At first the senior minister thought he should be the one to eulogize the old emeritus. But he was so sure that Alanna would do a good job, he let her keep the pulpit that Sunday. And she did great. That her boss trusted her to lead such an important service, and liked how she did it . . . Well, to me that is quite an endorsement."

I thought that the senior minister was probably relieved when, on his week off, he didn't have to write a sermon for the dead emeritus; and how convenient that such a pesky, last-minute responsibility could not only be passed on to an assistant minister, but would also be perceived by her as an honor—which made it a win all around except maybe for the poor dead emeritus, who probably deserved to be eulogized by a peer.

Around eleven forty-five, we took a vote, and Charlotte went over.

"Charlotte!" I cried. "What are you doing?"

"Charlotte can vote for whoever she wants, Dana," said Jennie.

Charlotte looked at me, glassy-eyed, exhausted. "We're outnumbered, Dana. It's either this or fail the search. Is that what you want?"

That left me and, in absentia, Belinda, for whom I felt I owed a fight.

"This is why consensus is problematic," I said. "Because the intractable activist faction wears everyone else down. Jennie hasn't changed her mind since this whole search began. She wanted Alanna before anyone else had even heard of her, before the survey and the cottage meetings, before we saw a single packet. She maneuvered Alanna into a pre-candidacy she didn't deserve by casting aspersions on someone with far superior credentials. Jennie can and will outwait us all to get what she wants. The two of you"— I pointed to Curtis and Riley—"rather than think independently or do your own work, you let Jennie tell you what to do. You, Riley, tell me the subject of one sermon of Elsa's other than the 'Listening' sermon that we all heard. Can you?"

A long pause. Riley rolled his eyes, as if I was being unreasonable.

"Right. And we took a whole Saturday to be warned not to think in categories, but to think in terms of the skills that our church needs. The survey told us that we want a wonderful preacher—not a beginning preacher with promise, but a skilled, gifted, mid-career preacher in their prime, such as we've always had. The survey also said we want an experienced manager. Alanna has no experience running a church. How do we know she'll be any good? Because she took a class?

"You young people think that she's going to bring in other young people. But what if she alienates the present congregation with her weak sermons and silly theatrics? What if the older members leave in droves, taking their big fat pledge checks with them? Do you know where the money comes from in this church? Not from you and your ten dollars a week in the collection plate. Let Alanna make her rookie mistakes elsewhere, at a real starter church. We have the incredible chance to hire a brilliant, tried-and-true church-growing minister whose pre-candidating sermon—if you remember—left us all gobsmacked. Alanna's better than I thought she'd be, but she isn't half as accomplished and wise as Elsa. I just can't believe you'd all pass on Elsa in favor of a failed actress with a half-baked theology who'll subject us to frenetic slide shows and the writings of the body dynamic. I don't come to church to watch a stage show. I come to have my soul cared for, my values refreshed, my heart opened."

I stopped. Everyone was looking at me.

"So?" said Charlotte. "You'll fail the search?"

"It already failed. A long time ago. This committee was not even se-lected according to our own bylaws or denominational guidelines, which stipulate that only members with a depth of church experience should serve on it. I love all of you, but Curtis is not even an actual member. Riley has been here three years and his one involvement—and his only interest—has been his bell choir. I know, Jennie, that you were here as a kid and you worked at headquarters for a summer, but you have also been gone for a decade and haven't been involved in anything but the nursery and this com-mittee since you've been back. And you wouldn't even be on this committee if your parents didn't have so much influence . . ." I couldn't bring myself to blurt out the whole truth, *the twenty-thousand-dollar inducement.* "Can you tell me, Jennie, who ran the capital campaign to get the new chapel built? And you, Curtis, do you even know the name of the minister who was here before Tom Fox? And, Riley, who was the church president the year you first came to church? And who is the present events coordinator—Curtis, Riley? Do either of you know the secretary's last name?"

Nobody spoke.

"We covenanted to keep an open mind, to be willing to reach a consen-sus, not to be strong-armed into submission. Alanna should never have made it even to pre-candidating except that somehow we kept voting until she was, after her champion here set all her friends against a guy who hurt her feelings six or seven years ago"—again, I couldn't say the truth: *because he wouldn't date her*—"who is a far more experienced, remarkable young candidate than the woman we're considering now. I for one did not cove-nant to do Jennie's will, as powerful as it is.

"To my mind," I kept going—nobody had tried to stop me yet—"this committee has no business picking the next minister. With Belinda inca-pacitated, it is even less capable of speaking for the whole church. So, yes, despite all the time and effort we've put in, I am willing to let the search fail. In fact, I see it as my sacred duty. I now believe we need an interim minister—one who would make sure that a slightly senile sweet old man doesn't disregard the bylaws in picking the next search committee. A good

interim could help the whole church determine more explicitly what direction we should take and what kind of a minister might take us there. Maybe
we'll even get Perry as an interim, if we're lucky—even if he pilfers from
the collection plate, at least he knows how to run a church. I think Alanna
is a talented young minister, but she's not for us. If we pick her, the search
committee will have failed in its charge to choose responsibly."

Jennie turned sideways in her chair. Riley smirked.

Charlotte drew herself up. "You exaggerate, Dana," she said softly. "I
know, from the start, you've had an antipathy to Alanna."

"I don't have an antipathy toward her, I just don't think she has the
chops to serve the AUUCC. And Elsa does."

"Alanna is not my first choice, either," said Charlotte. "But she comes
with impressive references. I reread her whole packet in the last two days,
and it is striking the level of support and enthusiasm she's garnered—from
the president of her seminary, the illustrious minister who employs her
now, the highly respected ministers where she did her internships. All of
them insist that she's a gifted, hardworking colleague, that we'd be nabbing
a strong talent on her way up. Elsa is the more conventional choice, but I'm
willing to stick my neck out to get this done."

"I'm not," I said. "I care about this church and the people who come
every Sunday to hear good preaching and write their pledge checks confident that the minister can keep the place in running order."

"You have absolutely no proof that Alanna's a bad manager," said Jennie.
"You're awfulizing her inexperience. She is super smart, super creative, and
everyone but you thinks she's amazing. I wonder what she did that got you
all angsty about her.

"Of course you're right, Dana," Jennie went on, with a downshift in tone,
"I don't have much adult time in at the AUUCC. But I'd never do anything
to hurt this church. Alanna is not some newbie fresh out of seminary. She's
worked full-time as a minister for four years. And it's not like she'll put on
nonstop slide shows. Remember when you said you liked quieter worship
and she said 'Oh, there'll be plenty of that.'"

Yes—guided meditations in place of a sermon. Oy.

Riley raised his hand. "Besides feeling personally attacked," he said, "I can't take anything Dana says that seriously. We're a legitimate committee—in nine months, not a single other person has had any concerns about our qualifications. Sort of strange to hear some now. To me, the survey clearly expressed that we wanted high-quality preaching and worship services, a good manager, and change. Alanna's a genius at worship and it's not like there's evidence she's a bad manager—or a thief like Perry, who you really liked, Dana. Experience isn't everything. We've seen some pretty experienced ministers who are real duds charisma-wise—I mean, what about that dulcimer-hitting witch? And Alanna won't be inexperienced forever. I don't see either candidate as that much better than the other. But according to Dana, I'm not qualified to have an opinion. I shouldn't have spent the last nine months coming to meetings, mixing you drinks at my own expense, and giving Belinda rides."

Which was all he had done—though again, I said nothing.

"Curtis?" said Charlotte. "Did you want to say something?"

"I didn't know I'm not supposed to be on this committee or I would have taken myself off. But I've learned so much, and I love everyone here—you too, Dana."

"I feel I am also speaking for Belinda," I said.

"Hey," said Riley. "Belinda never held it against me if I didn't agree with her. I think I speak for her, too, and she'd be fine with a young minister if that's how we vote. Alanna might not be her first choice, but she wouldn't fail the whole search because she alone wanted someone else. And remember, she voted for her over Walt, too."

"That's because Belinda understands consensus," said Jennie.

I ignored the hot roiling in my chest and held my voice steady. "So all of you think that Alanna is sufficiently skilled and experienced to be our next minister, and I'm the only one who doesn't think so?"

A murmur of assent.

"Charlotte?"

"What?" She turned her exhausted, glassy gaze on me. "I'll go with the flow."

"And you think that if I cause the search to fail, even if I believe in my heart it's the absolute right thing to do, that I would be wrong?"

A murmur. Well . . . yes . . .

"Even though we are not really reaching consensus, but in reality caving into the intractable will of one person?"

"You go too far," Adrian said coldly.

"You're the intractable one," said Jennie.

"Let's take a breather," Charlotte said. "Ten minutes."

33

⌒

We Choose

I t was twelve fifty-five in the morning.

I walked down the grand staircase and across the checkerboard marble foyer. I heaved open the heavy door and stepped outside, where it was cold—for California: the mid-forties. A fine drizzle glinted in the porch light. For all my self-righteousness, I thought, I was no more legitimately on the search committee than Jennie, Curtis, or Riley. Who was I to fail the search, who began it with one foot out the door and a secret agenda to write a book?

But I did care—it surprised me how vehemently, how profoundly——about our next minister. And I believed, as deeply as I believed anything, that Elsa was the better choice. I would go to her church. And not to Alanna's.

A weight amassed in my chest. Grief.

In terms of the book, Alanna would provide a more unexpected and dramatic ending—especially if she actually did well.

Yet how gladly would I sacrifice such an ending to have Elsa!

But Elsa was no longer on the table. My choice was now to junk the search or to join the consensus for an inexperienced charismatic young woman whose style I found stagy and hollow, who could never be "my" minister or friend. In going for consensus, I might well be voting myself out of a church.

Sparlo was the minister of my life, and I'd had more of him than most congregants ever get from a minister: his attention, his wisdom, many hours of his time. And I'd had a warm, decade-long friendship with Tom Fox, too. And I'd probably had more quality time with the unpleasant interim than anybody else at the AUUCC. If we had one minister I didn't befriend, was that so bad?

Not if she did a good job.

Besides, ministers came and went . . . and how long would this one last?

The AUUCC was just a "little chugger" of a church in a small unincorporated suburb of LA. Alanna had bigger fish to fry. She'd move on, and we'd still be here, three acres of raffish gardens, an ugly sanctuary, a deliquescing Italianate mansion, a jewel-box chapel used mostly for yoga classes.

How much damage could Alanna really do?

Tom would leave the AUUCC in good enough shape that it could run itself while any new minister learned the ropes. Our church administrator was highly capable; she and the board would steer the ship. The congregation had always loved the young interns and assistant ministers who passed through and helped nurture them into fine professionals. They would surely do that for Alanna as well.

Sunday worship services might be painful—but only if I attended them.

Charlotte and her cane came tapping up to me, and together we regarded the dark sweep of lawn to the sanctuary, the black fringe of trees, the steady drizzle glinting amber in the argon light. "I'm not crazy about Alanna," she said. "And it kills me to give up Elsa. But I can't fail the search. Alanna's a little young, but she's probably the real deal, and if she takes the job, we can mold her into what we need. Besides, if you and I fail the search, who's to say the next search committee won't make this one seem enlightened?"

"I can't bear to think of Alanna doing Belinda's memorial service."

"Oh Dana, Alanna's not a monster. She's just young and full of big ideas. She'll simmer down. They all do. What was it that your Walt said? Something like, Time alone can solve the problems of youth and inexperience."

"She's an actress and a flatterer and I'm not sure I trust her."

"Some of the top people in the denomination have written her support letters. And some theatricality is good in a minister. Look at your Indistinguishables. Their messages were fine, but their delivery?"

"You can't think that we'd be as well off with Alanna as with Elsa?"

"I don't. But the others do. And now it's up to us to show the youngsters how consensus is done."

"I doubt that'll be their takeaway. We've been bullied into submission— that's what they'll learn. Push till you get your way."

Charlotte rested her hand on my arm. "Two things," she said. "If you fail the search, we lose any chance of Elsa. Remember, Dana" —she lowered her voice to a near-whisper—"Alanna could choose another church. If she does, we can still get Elsa—if we make that a stipulation for our votes. And there's candidating week. If the congregation doesn't support Alanna, she's done. Let the church decide."

"But congregants trust us and this process, as I've badgered them to do in every newsletter. We promised to deliver the best candidate and most people will vote for whomever we pick, even against their own inclinations, because they trust us. And we're not trustworthy, not if we've ditched an exceptional, proven candidate for a lousy actress who puts on garish slide shows."

"You've got to stop holding her acting career against her, Dana. The world is full of repurposed actresses, some of them quite remarkable in their second careers."

"Maybe," I said.

"Anyway, who knows if we're her first choice?"

"I'm pretty sure we are," I said.

"So let's say she doesn't get her ninety percent—and she might not. I think I could talk the board into candidating Elsa in the fall. Searches are expensive. If we have a sturdy backup candidate, they'd probably go with her rather than paying for a whole new search."

"I thought we got only one candidate, up or down."

"We can do what we want. If we want a second candidate, who's to stop us?"

"That could never happen," I said. "Besides, what if Alanna gets her ninety percent?"

"She might. And it's not the end of the world if she does, Dana."

"It feels like it to me," I said. "And I can't believe that you of all people would give this church that we both love to such a weak applicant."

"So, fail the damn search—if you can." Charlotte's anger rose, sharp and mean, a long skinny knife. "Technically, if you're the only one objecting, we can overrule you in two rounds of votes. And then it would be too late to make them promise Elsa as our backup."

"You'd do that, Charlotte? You'd overrule me?"

"I've got surgery in two days, and one way or the other this will get done."

I might have said, again, that her surgery was an artificially imposed deadline, but Charlotte's tone shocked and frightened me. "Give me a minute," I said.

Charlotte went back inside and I stood on the porch listening to the soft hiss of the light rain. I have never been strategic about anything in my life. When my friends were settling down and having families with disappointingly regular guys, I wasted my reproductive years searching for one great love among self-obsessed artist types. In negotiations with management at work, I was always too quickly strident and emotional, too much of a blurter to make my case. Nor were my present impulses tactical: I had an overweening, vengeful desire to fail the search partly because Alanna was a bad choice, but also because my opinions and ideas were being so flagrantly disregarded and dismissed.

I was the intractable one.

Riley stuck his head out the door. Softly: "Can I make you a drink, Dana?"

"A Decision Maker," I said. "Thank you."

Okay, guys. Jennie, you're a holy terror. Riley, you might be right that Belinda is more open-minded and conciliatory than I am. And, Curtis, you have been a beautiful presence at each meeting, and I'm glad to know you and I love you, too. That said, I fear for the AUUCC under Alanna. Her preaching is underdeveloped and her ideas for worship will alienate a lot of people. I'm not convinced that she can run the office and manage all the weird stuff that comes up at a church. But none of you are worried and why should I care more than you do? So I'll go along with you under one condition: that Elsa's officially our backup candidate. I want it in writing." I held up my legal pad. "If Alanna doesn't accept our offer, Elsa's our candidate. No further discussion."

All eyes, even mine, looked to Jennie, who lifted and dropped one shoulder. "Sure, why not?" she said.

"I'm putting it in the minutes. Elsa is our official backup candidate."

"Fine," said our shadow leader. "For what it's worth."

"And if Alanna is voted down and Charlotte can somehow convince the board to candidate Elsa without another search, you guys will agree to it."

"That could never happen," said Sam.

"I agree," I said. "But Charlotte thinks she can swing it."

"I could swing it," Charlotte said.

Jennie: "Fine, but it's not going to happen because Alanna's going to get in, and with 99.9 percent support, because only Dana will vote against her."

I put it in writing that Elsa was our backup candidate, and possibly our second candidate, and they all signed the yellow legal pad. Then Charlotte called for a vote. Once around the room, with a chorus of yeas, Alanna became the candidate.

The young people—including Adrian—stood and clapped and hugged one another. Sam said, "What about me?" and got a hug from Curtis.

"We did it!" Jennie cried, her arms around Riley and Curtis. "We got her in!"

Charlotte said she'd call Alanna in the morning and reminded us that the outcome must remain secret until the first Monday in April, when candidates nationwide received their offers. "Alanna might be waiting to hear from other churches," she said. "And maybe she'll choose one over us. And maybe she'll choose us but won't commit to it till then."

It was one thirty in the morning.

I pulled my jacket off the back of the chair, feeling numb and unsure. The meeting, however, was not over. Charlotte had us all sit down again. "Belinda and I will be out of commission," she said, "so you'll have to meet on your own after this."

"We keep meeting?" said Curtis. "I thought this was it."

"There's still candidating week to organize. Riley? You're chair now, so it's on you. Jennie, you can be cochair from here on out. You have to arrange flights and lodging for Alanna—or Elsa, if Alanna turns us down. Belinda worked up a preliminary schedule back in January listing all the committees and staff you'll need to arrange for the candidate to meet with, and all the meals you need to plan. Book meeting rooms as soon as you confirm dates with Alanna. And don't forget the meet and greets with members. And the picnic after her first Sunday in the pulpit needs to be catered . . ."

Incomprehension replaced triumph on the younger faces.

"And there's the cocktail party for big donors. Very, very important. Sam, see if we have enough in the budget to cater that. Maybe Adrian can host."

"Dana's house is cool," said Curtis.

"No way," I said.

"I'll send you what Belinda's done, Riley," Charlotte said. "It's not much, but it'll get you started."

In the cold darkness lit by dim yellow streetlights, I walked west on Stanislaus Street in a deep silence, everyone else in bed and worlds away in their dreams. How had we all caved into the enthusiasms and undisciplined reasoning of youth?

Adrian rolled up alongside me, window down. "Let me take you home."

"Ima walk, thanks," I said. He kept driving even with me. Irritated, I flapped my hands at him. "Go! I mean it. I have nothing more to say to any of you."

Charlotte in her Prius was next. She slowed and called across the empty street, "It's late, Dana. I'll drop you off."

"Ima walk, thanks," I said and turned away. At Marengo Avenue, I stopped to let a skunk and her four kits cross the street ahead of me. They shuffled like little moving mops and nosed out of sight under a leafless pomegranate hedge. At the next intersection, I saw two coyotes lounging in the middle of the side street. They watched but did not move as I walked past.

34

The Candidate

After nine months of meetings, your search committee asks for your patience for a few more weeks. All will be revealed the first week of April.

On Sunday, after worship, I stopped by Trader Joe's and bought two bunches of tightly closed white peonies (one bunch seemed too skimpy) and took them to Huntington Hospital, where the person at the information desk could not find Charlotte Beck listed anywhere. Had I gotten the hospital wrong? I texted Charlotte. No reply.

I tried to visit Belinda instead, but the nurse said she was doing so well that she'd been moved to a convalescent home—but she was not sure which one.

Our Tuesday-night meeting was called for 7:30 p.m. in the church library. "No food," Riley had declared. Jennie, perhaps as a peace offering, brought the whole wheat chocolate chip cookies I loved. I didn't touch a single one.

I had the idea, too, to boycott all the rest of the meetings, and I might have out of sulky bad sportsmanship if it weren't for the book. I had to see the search through to its end for the book. As it was, only five of us showed up that night.

Riley lit the chalice and thanked us for coming. "Some announcements," he said. "Faithalma Rourke passed away today, so Sam is with his wife and family tonight.

"I talked to Charlotte before she went in for surgery," he said. "She'd spoken with Alanna, who assured her that we are her first choice and was ready to talk about the salary package. So, looking good. And when I talked to Sam this afternoon, he said that the negotiating committee has started talking to Alanna, and so far she's refusing to take less than what Tom makes."

"Which is only right," said Jennie.

"How so?" I said. "Tom has thirty more years of experience."

"She'll be doing the same job. Why shouldn't she make the same salary?"

"Amira, who actually has more experience than Alanna, will want a big raise."

"And she should get it," said Jennie.

The meeting lasted forty minutes. Riley said he was working on a spreadsheet for candidating week, but it wasn't ready yet.

All the way to Golden Deli, Tom Fox monologued about his most recent trip to Texas, where he and Pat had purchased a thirty-two-hundred-square-foot two-story house on a golf course; the house had a pool, a pool house, a Jacuzzi, and a three-car garage, all for half the price of their small cottage in Altadena. After we'd parked and put in our name at the restaurant, he turned to me. "So what the hell happened with the search?"

I had taken the one empty chair out on the sidewalk where people waited to be called inside. Tom stood in front of me, blocking the sun so I could look up at him.

"Cone of silence," I said.

"I know you've chosen someone because I heard that the negotiating committee is negotiating. It's not Doris or Perry, because they both called me to tell me they were out of the running. And it's not Elsa because I was on the phone with her an hour ago, and she hasn't heard anything yet. So that leaves the one."

"And you don't approve?"

"Amira'd be a better choice. At least she knows the place."

"But can Amira look like a sorceress in a Harry Potter movie?"

A group of men, summoned to their table, filed between us. "If I didn't already know better," Tom said, once they passed, "I'd never believe Charlotte could let this happen. She should have stepped down."

"Charlotte, step down?" I squinted up at him. "Why? And do you know where she is? She's not at Huntington. No answer at home. Did she have her surgery?"

"Charlotte's in rehab," he said.

"What?" There are times when I *know* that we are all woven in a great sentient web, and this was one of them because the news about Charlotte yanked all my fine nerves in one sharp, exquisite shock. Charlotte, thirty-plus years sober, in rehab! And twenty-five years of knowing her and caring about her—the steady church kind of caring—was so ingrained in me, I twanged *hard* in sympathy and fear. "Did she drink?"

"Opioids. Her surgery was delayed for a few hours and she went into withdrawal in the hospital. They sent her to Las Encinas—without operating."

Charlotte! Strict-with-herself, starchy, perfect-on-the-outside Charlotte! Of all people! "I knew she was in pain and taking pain meds, but . . ."

A young man called us into the restaurant. Dazed by shock, I followed him to a small table against the wall.

"I hear candidating week is a big mess." Tom settled in across from me. "Jennie Ross was in yelling at Vera yesterday. Like who would yell at Vera, the sweetest person in the world? And Riley called to get a list of big donors, then asked if I'd host a cocktail hour for your gal. I told him to ask Arne or one of the Rourkes. It's not for me to give her a party—especially since she's the only pre-candidate who's never contacted me. No, I take that back. When I heard she was interested, I sent her an email saying she could call me anytime, but all I got back was 'Thanks for your note.'"

"You'd think she'd at least want to pick your brain."

"You'd think. But I'm just an old white guy, so what could I offer her?"

We ordered our usual: cha gio (the egg rolls with lettuce and herbs), then bun (vermicelli rice noodles) with grilled pork and shrimp, and sweet iced coffee.

I was still trying to process: Charlotte in rehab!

Tom took a lettuce leaf. "Oh, and you heard Faithalma died, of course."

"I did. So now Sam and Emma can move home," I said, just to say something.

"Yes, and the AUUCC will be around four million dollars richer."

"No, really?"

"Her yearly pledge was the interest on one fund, which paid my salary and then some. The AUUCC is the fund's sole beneficiary. So now the four mil comes to us."

"So maybe Amira can get her big raise!" I wrapped my eggroll. "Hey! Too bad Perry Fitzgerald isn't our candidate. He'd have ideas for spending that money."

"I've heard he has a free hand with a discretionary fund," said Tom. "Good preacher, though. And it would have been nice to have a young family at the church."

"Stop. You're making me sad all over again."

"I'll tell you what's sad—what's truly tragic—is passing up Elsa Neddicke. Boy, did you-all miss the boat on that."

"Maybe not," I said. "Charlotte promised that if this one doesn't get voted in, she'll talk the board into candidating Elsa in the fall."

"Can't and won't ever happen," Tom said. "For a thousand different reasons." White curls bounced as he shook his head. "Dana, Dana, that's exactly the baseless claptrap people on search committees will say under duress to get their way!"

Your search committee has chosen Reverend Alanna Kapoor as the candidate for our next senior minister. With a Master of Divinity from Harvard Divinity School, Reverend Kapoor, 36, is presently finishing a three-year assistant ministry at —– UU. There will be various opportunities to meet her during candidating week. The week's schedule will be in the next newsletter.

⟡

Adrian emailed me:

Could you have been less enthusiastic?

Alanna stepped forward in a floor-length oyster-gray gown and a purple, lavender, and pink stole. Her hair was piled atop her head. She paused, majestic and commanding. She spread out her arms. "Good morning, Arroyo!"

Silence. We were not used to being called Arroyo, so it took us a moment to remember that that's what the A in AUUCC stood for.

A faint, scattered greeting was returned.

"Oh now, we can do better than that," she said, exercising her wide, beautiful smile. "Let's try it again. Good morning, Arroyo!"

Some—not I—returned a more rousing response, including Jack, whose presence I had formally requested: I wanted his opinion of the candidate.

Sparlo never said "good morning" from the pulpit—out of respect, he told me, for those present who were not having good mornings.

I was not having a good morning. I was mortified that people would think I'd endorsed this sideshow. I itched to rip off my blue search committee badge.

Her sermon title, as printed in the order of service, was "Love Is the Answer."

She was "ambushed by gratitude" to be our candidate, she said, and today we would begin to get to know one another. She would start by telling us about herself.

The movie screen was pulled down behind her, the podium set to one side. On the screen slid a black-and-white image of a dark-eyed boy beside an old, bearded man in a turban. Both were in dhotis—the long loincloths men wear in India and Pakistan.

My grandfather Vachan Kapoor was born in 1926 in Punjab. That's him with his grandfather. He and his parents came to Fresno in 1940. They're Sikhs.

Another slide, of a dark man in a suit with a blond woman in a wedding gown.

My grandfather met my grandmother in medical school. She was Anne Platt, from Nebraska. My father, Nirmal Kapoor, was born in 1952.

Another wedding photo: two dark-haired beautiful people, the man in a tuxedo, the woman in a lace wedding gown.

My father, Nirmal, met my mother, Maria O'Brien, at UC Davis. She was half Irish American, half Italian American, and all Catholic. This makes me one-quarter each Sikh, Italian American Catholic, WASP, and Irish American Catholic. Clearly, I was destined to be a Unitarian Universalist.

The next slide showed the young family. At six or seven, Alanna, winsome in a white dress and long braids, clutched a large orange cat clearly struggling to escape.

Here I am with Oscar our cat—as usual, taking on a little more than I can handle!

Laughter in the sanctuary! But not from me.
I was a dramatic child," she said. "I loved plays and home movies and putting on shows." A short video clip played then, showing Alanna as a girl, her hair braided with flowers, spinning in a long skirt with her arms outstretched.

Some things never change . . . Another thing that has never changed is my fundamental theology. Growing up, we kids sometimes went to the Sikh gurdwara and sometimes to a Catholic church. My parents tell the story about my coming out of Sunday school one day with a lollipop. "Where did you get that?" my parents demanded. I said, "The Sunday school teacher asked a question and if you gave the right answer, you got a lollipop." I'd given the right answer. "So what was the question?" my mother asked. I couldn't remember. I could only remember my answer, which was . . . *love.*

The audience, including Jack, gave a communal *Aww.* I elbowed him.

At Occidental College, I majored in theater and minored in business. Which, it turns out, is ideal training for ministry; you could say it's the minister's equivalent of premed.

More soft, appreciative laughter from the audience. But it wasn't funny. Or true!

I acted in many Equity-waiver theater productions and a few TV shows. Walt Whitman says that we contain multitudes. Here is a sampling of what I've contained (a quick flurry of slides began): I have played several cops, one secretary, several murder victims, and two best friends to a lead. I have played Juliet, Ophelia, and a raging Lady Macbeth. I have played an assassin and a nurse . . . In commercials, I've been a housewife, an expert on floor cleaners, a vitamin salesperson, a shoe model. This might sound like a lot, but the jobs were actually few and far between. I kept hearing the same thing: you are too tall, you are, um, too wide! And then this happened.

A slide of Alanna, years younger, in a full nun costume; she beamed beatifically, her face exquisite. A murmur of admiration rippled through the room.

Hiding my hair, hiding my body, I felt the great relief of invisibility. And with that came a desire to do something good, something selfless. I believe acting and all the arts are a form of generosity, but I yearned to do more. To serve others.

It didn't happen all at once. I still had work to do.

Another barrage of slides: Alanna as a dog walker, a waitress, a businesswoman with a briefcase, a clown at a children's party.

One morning, I woke up to someone speaking softly in my ear: a calm, soothing, loving voice. "You must worship, Alanna. You must worship." I opened my eyes, and there was nobody in the room. A dream? An angel? God herself? That voice was so insistent, so sweetly loving, I had to obey. I went first to the Episcopalians, then to the United Church of Christ, and then to the UU church in Studio City, and that was it. Because in this church I heard the same sweet love and concern for others that had stirred inside me . . .

Her tone rose to exaltation. Around me, people were rapt, including Jack. I was prickling with fury: God spoke to her!—the very thing that had disqualified Rob Sanders.

"In seminary," Alanna went on, "I discovered ritual."

Rituals are road maps through life's transitions. They are stylized reenactments of our sacred stories. . . . Love is the lifeblood of every ritual. Nothing focuses love like a new baby: hence baptism! Nothing celebrates love more than a wedding! Nothing is more loving and comforting for the bereaved than memorializing a life.

Love called me to ministry. Whether it is writing the staff schedule, counseling a couple engaged to be married, laboring over a sermon, love is the engine. Love has called me here today.

My love for ministry is not untested. In my first semester at seminary, I finally, finally, finally was offered a role in a movie. Not a starring role, but a good supporting role—in a Brian De Palma film! Isn't that always the way? Just when you give up on something, it comes to you. All my life I had dreamed of such an offer, and here I was, in seminary, done with acting.

Arroyo, I didn't know what to do. I meditated. I prayed for a sign. And then a seminary friend said to me: "Alanna, it comes down to love. Where is your love? Do what you love."

I had loved acting, but frankly, acting had been like a bad boyfriend to me, luring me in, then rejecting me, again and again. Were twenty lines in a thriller enough to draw me back into that world?

All this was going on in my head when, walking to my Multifaith Theology class, I missed a step and fell on the sidewalk. I went down hard and it knocked the breath out of me." [On the screen, a GIF of a man falling flat played multiple times, then stopped with him facedown.] "Half a dozen people ran up and asked if I was okay. 'Catch your breath,' they said. They sat me up, and made me rest for a few minutes. Everyone stayed until they saw I was fine. The concern. The good humor. This was care. This was loving kindness. People are kind everywhere, but they are especially so in seminary. So if you have to take a bad fall, let me recommend the path between Andover Hall and the library.

When I rose from that sidewalk, I knew what love was asking me to do. Dusty, sore, and late, I went to my Multifaith Theology class with a full heart.

As it turns out, the Brian De Palma film [stills of a blonde and a brunette in tight dresses, a bloody knife] was a box-office disaster.

I ask you, here, today, to take a moment and think of a time in your own life when love has asked something of you. When has love asked you to step outside of yourself and help a stranger, or march for justice, plant a tree, or change your whole life around to do something more meaningful . . .

My husband nudged my arm. I gave a tight shake of my head: *Don't even.* I knew what he was thinking. He was thinking that Alanna's story was so like my story. Perhaps too much like it. Twenty-odd years ago, when I was struggling to decide between journalism and ministry, hadn't someone said

something to me very much like "Where is your love? Do what you love."?
And wasn't that someone Bert Share?

Riley and his handbells then played that old earworm "Ode to Joy,"
proving once again that five minutes can indeed last a month.

Alanna asked us to stand and then sang to us, unaccompanied, in a
lovely contralto, Sparlo's favorite hymn—of all things:

And I'll bring you hope, when hope is hard to find.
And I'll bring a song of love, and a rose in the wintertime.

She opened her arms. "I call on all of you, now, tomorrow, and forever
and ever: Let love lead the way!"

People clapped, and kept clapping as she swept down the aisle.

Some, I saw, wept.

And what of that person in the back row, who stumbled into church this
Sunday, their life possibly hanging in the balance—what would they have
made of such flagrant self-promotion?

Adrian was in front of us in the coffee line. "Happy?" I said to him.

"Relieved. I wasn't entirely sure she could pull it off," he said.

Had she? "Hmmm," I said.

"I know she wasn't your first choice . . ."

"Or my fiftieth. I voted for her exactly once, at one thirty in the morning, when I'd been beaten to a bloody pulp."

"I know," Adrian said. "But she'll be a good change for this place."

"She'll be something," I said. "Look. I don't want to be a prune-faced old
spoilsport. But this was so not my cup of tea."

Adrian started to respond, but Jennie ran up, grabbing our arms and
yanking on them like bell ropes. "I told you, I told you. She blew it away!
Oh my god! Can you believe it! Fan-fucking-tastic!"

My phone buzzed: a text message from BS himself. **How'd it go? Pls call
when u can.** "I have to do this," I said and, abandoning Jack to the coffee
line, I slipped into the gardens to the courtyard with the wide round fountain. I had to find out: Had Bert given Alanna my story? Or had she really

faced a decision so like mine? Sitting on the cold stone bench, I pressed Bert's number.

"How was she?" he said.

Praise, as I knew, would encourage disclosure. "Magnificent."

"That's my girl," he said. "Only don't say I called her that. She'd rip my head off! How was the sermon?"

"A showstopper," I said. "Even stronger than her pre-candidating one. The interweaving of story and exposition was very smooth."

"Bravo," he said. "I worked long and hard on that."

"She got a standing ovation. I mean, we were already standing, but people burst into applause."

"They clapped?"

"Nobody's ever been able to stop the clappers."

"Nobody," he said. "So the sermon went over well?"

He wanted more. Okay. Ministers (like writers) are never sufficiently praised. "Absolutely," I said. "Terrific illustrations, some laugh-out-loud lines—and all of it perfectly delivered."

"You don't say. Well. That's immensely gratifying. I really appreciate the report, Dana. I knew you'd give me an objective opinion."

"Now, about that story when she decides between acting and seminary . . ."

"I thought you'd like that," said Bert.

"It seemed awfully familiar . . ."

"I know, huh? She's gotten pushback from another search committee that ministry was a fallback and not her genuine calling. I thought we should address it directly with you guys, make it clear she'd made a real choice between acting and the church. I remembered how you got that job offer in seminary—god, how you agonized with our little group over what to do! So I worked in a little of that, with you in mind!"

"I'm flattered." In fact, I was horrified, but there was more I wanted to know. "And did De Palma really offer her a role?"

"He's my favorite director," Bert said, chuckling. "She'd never heard of him. But everything else—her falling down, the students sitting with her—that was all hers."

"Ahhh," I said.

"Next Sunday's sermon should be even better," said Bert. "Oh, but did you like the lollipop?"

The lollipop. The lollipop. Ah—yes, the lollipop awarded to little Alanna for giving the correct answer: love. "Yes. Very sweet."

"That just happened with my daughter Pina. Four years old, and 'love' was her answer. Pretty cute, right?"

"Very cute," I said.

Back on the patio, my husband was browsing the book cart, all the volumes by UU authors, including yours truly. He handed me my cardboard cup of cooled coffee and together we wandered to the picnic buffet and got in the line for food. Because of my blue search committee badge, people kept coming up to me to comment on the search. I jotted down the things they said:

"Now that was different."

"Utterly superficial."

"She's a real talent. Congratulations."

"I guess I just have to trust the search process."

"Is there another candidate next week?"

"I liked her. But I can do without all the special effects . . ."

"Love love love love love love love."

"Is she technically a giant? I mean, genetically?"

Elsa would never have provoked this zigzag of equivocation. She would have stirred excitement for the future. And brought us a quiet, deep sense of joy.

35

The Church Chooses

At the Golden Age Convalescent Hospital, Belinda occupied a bright, ugly room with high-gloss off-white walls and yellowing canvas curtains. Riley had brought a Stickley dresser and chair from her house and some potted succulents and family photos, which did little to subdue the hard-used institutional vibe. Belinda was working with a speech therapist, but I couldn't understand more than her *Eh* for yes and *Uoo* for no. Still, we managed. Was Riley going to be her proxy? (No.) Was I? (Yes.) Even if I voted against the candidate? (Yes.) Because I was going to vote against the candidate—should I do the same for her? (Yes.) I handed her the long thin proxy ballot. Her signature looked like that of a first grader using her nondominant hand.

From the Golden Age, I drove across town to Las Amigas, the halfway house, where Charlotte met me in the visitors' lounge. By now, I was deeply angry with her—for her false promises about Elsa, for pushing a decision to fit her schedule, for checking out when the AUUCC most needed her—but she'd asked me to cast her proxy vote and I'd come to get her signature. The lounge had soothing pale green walls and heavy armchairs arranged in pairs and small clusters. We sat by the piano and I set my large red bag on a walnut coffee table. Charlotte looked as she always had: perfect in a pastel polo shirt, creased slacks, preternaturally smooth pageboy. I pulled a proxy ballot from my bag. She signed her name and handed it back to me. "Vote how you vote."

"You know, and I know, we'll never get Elsa now."

Charlotte acknowledged this. "I'm sorry. I should have kept a tighter hold on Sam and Adrian; I never should've given Jennie an inch. I was using. The shame of that, and the pain . . . I didn't have the bandwidth."

"What's done is done."

"I don't blame you for being angry."

"I'll get over it someday," I said.

"I'm very sorry," she said.

"And as long as we're telling the truth here, I actually am writing a book about the search." I blurted this out like an angry teenager. "It's not a joke. I wanted to help pick the next minister, but I planned all along to get a book out of it."

"You were an excellent committee member, whatever your motive," Charlotte said. "You, Curtis, and Adrian were the only ones who never missed a meeting and did everything you said you'd do." She glanced up at the heavy ceiling beams. "And you cared, Dana. Don't deny it. In the end, you cared more than I did."

With candidating week in full swing, I kept to the sidelines. I wasn't invited to Monday's dinner with the board; only board members—Sam and Adrian—went. On Tuesday, Alanna met with three committees, then attended a potluck dinner in the chapel. I gave that a miss, too.

On Wednesday morning, I walked the donks and we ended up at the AUUCC, where I let them graze and gambol on the lawn as the sun tried to burn through the marine layer. Vera, the tall, pale, red-haired secretary who was only ever gracious, emerged from Arroyo House with a bag of baby carrots, followed by Alanna, who called out, "Dana! Hey! I haven't seen you since Sunday!" In high wedge sandals, she was awkward on the grass.

Ralph, Caspar, and Bunchie trotted up to Vera, who fed the donks from a flat hand and made Bunchie sit for hers.

Alanna gave them a wide berth. "I've been hoping to see you," she said and twisted away from Bunchie, who'd left wet paw prints on her pink leggings. "It's been so hectic," she said again, "and so disorganized. Though I had almost twenty people come to walk the labyrinth this morning, so that was a success."

Vera waved her empty carrot sack and went back to work. The donks ambled over our way. Alanna grabbed my arm and stepped behind me. "Sorry. I'm such a city girl, those ponies kind of scare me."

"They won't bother you," I said and, as if on cue, the boys stopped to eat grass.

"The thing is"—Alanna squeezed my arm—"nobody's planned lunch for me today or tomorrow. Yesterday, I ate with membership and Friday's the RE luncheon, but today and tomorrow? Nothing. I have meetings back to back and I'm already starving. No dinners, either, tonight or tomorrow. I don't mean to complain, Dana"—again, her grip tightened—"but this is the most unplanned candidating week. At my church, even a candidate for RE director gets better treatment."

"Yes. But our arranger had a stroke and our chair's in the hospital."

"I know," she said. "But it's not exactly rocket science to plan a few meals."

"Has Tom had you over?"

She looked blank.

"Tom Fox?"

Still no flicker of recognition.

"Our minister? Who's leaving. Shouldn't you have dinner with him?"

"Oh, right. Tom Fox." She shook my arm. "What I really need, Dana, is something to eat in an hour. I just had a banana for breakfast, and I've got Social Justice all afternoon. Can you maybe get me a grain bowl sort of thing?"

"I have to get those guys home." I pointed to the animals. "But I'll figure it out."

"Something delicious, please. I know you can manage that. If I'm in my meeting, just leave it with Vera." Releasing me and giving the donks another wide berth, she picked her way back to Arroyo House.

As much as I felt that Alanna was a mistake, I still felt responsible for her candidating week. I used a food delivery app to have a vegetarian Indian thali delivered to the church and emailed the search committee, *Alanna needs lunch tomorrow, and dinner tonight and Thursday*. Then I called Tom Fox.

"Might you invite Alanna for dinner tonight?"

"I did," he said. "I offered any night this week. She said her schedule was full."

"She just told me she has no meals planned for two days."

"Too bad she's avoiding me," said Tom. "I could tell her some things."

"Such as?"

"We'll talk," he said. "I'm on the golf course now. Lunch on Monday? When the die is cast?"

Riley and Adrian, I heard, took Alanna out to dinner that night, and got the Quilters for Justice to hold a home potluck on Thursday.

The first hymn was "John Brown's Body (Lies A-Moldering in the Grave)"; the second, "The Battle Hymn of the Republic," was the same song, with the words rewritten "for palatability" by Julia Ward Howe, a Unitarian. "Julia made the imagery less morbid," said Alanna, "but she did not shy away from a mighty, warlike stance against slavery."

The preaching protocol for ministerial candidates is no secret: the first Sunday, you introduce yourself, the second Sunday, you say why you're a good match with the church. Alanna had indeed told us all about herself the first Sunday. Her second sermon, however, deviated from the norm in that she told us, um, all about us. Her sermon was called "Change," though it might have been called "You Are a Church That" because this was the mnemonic phrase she used exhaustively throughout. (Because the text was published online, I was able to determine through the "find" function that in a four-page single-spaced sermon she'd used the phrase twenty-seven times.)

You are a church that has a lot of treasures hidden under bushels. In the packet your search committee sent was a link to Belinda Bauer's history columns. In them I discovered *that you are a church that*, like the early Christians, started in a home. A household of faith. In Lemuel Rourke's living room, the Arroyo Unitarian Fellowship began . . . and today, Lemuel and Sarah Rourke's descendants are still among you. For *you are a church that* has staying power. *You are a church that* values, and cares for, and so keeps its members for generations!

We were also a church, she went on, that had befriended a great abolitionist—and now honored him with a monument.

When I was here pre-candidating, Jennie Ross took me to the gravesite of Owen Brown and told me how, out of all the churches in the area, this son of the Great Liberator, John Brown, had come to Arroyo [she persisted in calling us that] because you are a church that from the start embraced progressive ideals.

Jennie had given Elsa's idea for a candidating sermon to Alanna! Where was Charlotte when I desperately needed to elbow someone?

You are the church whose minister provided conversation and companionship to Owen Brown in the last years of his life, and today, at a time when monuments to the Confederacy are being toppled, you are a church that's erecting a monument to that great abolitionist!

A murmur went through the sanctuary as congregants checked with one another. Vera, who sat one empty seat away from me, leaned over it and murmured, "Do you know anything about this?"

"Kind of," I said. "I'll tell you later."

Had Alanna read Belinda's columns more carefully (and perhaps relied less on Jennie as a source), she might have known that the Altadena Heritage Society (of which Belinda was a member) and not the AUUCC was responsible for Owen Brown's gravestone and plaque. Alanna should have checked her facts.

Alanna plunged on: The changes that Owen Brown fought for, she said, changes that ended centuries of injustice, were not easy ones.

And today you are a church looking at a different kind of change. For a hundred and thirty years, since Lemuel and Samantha Rourke invited like-minded friends into their home for Sunday worship, no woman has been your senior minister. I am deeply honored as a candidate to be proposed as the first woman, and the youngest senior minister Arroyo has ever called. Also—the first Sikhitarian!

She paused, and what started as a smattering built to full-blown applause.

The man behind me scooched forward and spoke in my ear: "I don't care if she's young or female or Sikh-whatever: does she have what it takes?"

Soon enough, as the postlude was being played, people snaked through the sanctuary to shake Alanna's hand. In fifteen minutes, we'd be summoned back inside for a congregational meeting to vote on whether to call Alanna Kapoor as our next senior minister.

Riley hustled Alanna to Arroyo House to wait out the vote. Members clustered in small groups on the patio; voices rose in volume and intensity. As cochair, Jennie called the search committee—now just Adrian, Curtis, Sam, and me—into the sanctuary before the meeting began. "First comes a Q and A period," Jennie said. "So remember, we covenanted to present a unified front." She was looking at me.

Members trickled back into the sanctuary, each one pausing at a desk to have their membership confirmed before receiving a narrow white ballot. The ballots read: *I herein agree to call Reverend Alanna Kapoor as the AUUCC's next senior minister.* Yes_____ No_____ .

The current church president, a middle-aged NASA engineer named Sandra Easley, hit the pulpit with a gavel and called the meeting to order. She asked the search committee to stand and face the congregation. I felt like a petty criminal in a lineup.

One of the Quilters for Justice raised her hand. "I'm very impressed by Alanna, but also concerned by how young and inexperienced she is."

"I'll take this." Jennie stepped forward. She wore a short, sleeveless pink shift that put her ink on display: the hummingbird, the horse's head, the indecipherable words snaking down her inner arm, the yellow petals on her sunflowered thigh. "In fact, after her internship, Alanna was acting senior minister while her boss took a leave of absence, so technically, she had her own church then . . ." So scantily dressed in front of two hundred people, Jennie appeared smaller, plainer, younger, and not very articulate. De-fanged. "And where she works now," she went on, "is, like, five times bigger than we are. She does stuff there we only dream of here. She runs a huge RE program. And a whole theater group she started herself."

How had this person pushed us around?

A businessman in his fifties said, "I did some research and most ministers at churches our size are in their midforties and older. Alanna's a decade younger. Are you confident that she has enough experience for us? Please, someone else answer?"

Sam stepped forward. "This young lady comes highly recommended by prominent leaders in our denomination," he said. "She is a strong institutionalist and will keep us well connected with the mother organization."

"And you're certain she can manage this institution?"

Adrian said, "Any minister coming in will have to learn the ropes—and the one thing everyone has said about Alanna is, she's a fast learner."

Mary Packer, a fiftyish nurse practitioner, said, "Just a comment. I find Reverend Kapoor very attractive and charismatic as a person, but to me both of her worship services seemed"—she grimaced—"amateurish . . ." Heads nodded. "She reminds me of that intern we had who preached wearing all those different hats. A good sermon doesn't need props."

Adrian said, "In fact, Alanna has had only limited opportunities for preaching in her present position, but in just the few months we've known her, her sermons have become more inventive and inspiring. I can promise you, she'll soon be up there with the best."

"I'm with Mary." This from a female board member. "Reverend Kapoor seems awfully green. Could we really not attract a minister who's more fully formed?"

"We asked ourselves all these questions," said Adrian. "The survey revealed that we wanted a younger minister. Recall that for the last twenty years, our ministers have been fifty-five and older. Any young candidate will seem—and be—less experienced."

Jennie took a step forward. "Yeah. We've had old white male ministers forever—and the survey said we wanted change. Alanna is that change. That doesn't mean she's less than. She went to Harvard. She got prestigious internships and her first real job—the three-year assistantship she's finishing now—is the one that every UU seminary grad applies for and only one gets each year. And everyone who gets it goes on to have a major church, more major than us. We're lucky she even wants to come here."

"Was she really the most qualified female minister you guys could find?"

Curtis said, "We met wonderful ministers, but Alanna was the most exciting!"

"My question is for Dana," said a financial planner I'd had in one of my Soul Circles, "whose opinion I trust. Is Reverend Kapoor the change you think we need?"

My face went hot. I hugged my arms. Two hundred people looked at me. I could not say yes. And I felt too much constraint to break with the committee and say no. How to present a unified front and not lie? Even this accumulating silence was treacherous. I should have failed the search!

I said, "Alanna was the minister we reached consensus on. And yes, she is young, and very different from Tom and Sparlo. But we at the AUUCC have always loved and nurtured our young ministers—the interns, the assistants and associates, the directors of religious education. Our love and support has helped so many of them to excel in their ministries. If Alanna is inexperienced in some areas, I'm sure we will love her and nurture her and grow her up."

Some people couldn't hear me. "What did she say?" hissed through the room.

I raised my voice. "And yes, Alanna will be a big change. She's female, obviously, and she's very charismatic—not in the Evangelical Christian sense, but how powerfully she draws people to her. Those of us who remember Sparlo recall that he, too, was charismatic, so we know that it's a good thing in a minister, as long as it's not misused. Alanna's worship style is more performative than what we're used to here, but I'm told it will bring more young people to the church. And god knows, every church in America is looking for ways to attract more young people. Alanna also has very strong support from all the ministers she's worked with." The financial planner's chin tucked then, as if I'd answered his question. "So we've made our decision, now it's up to you to make yours."

"But, Dana . . ." In fact, the financial planner was not done with me. "Are you genuinely excited about her? Is she your personal choice?"

I made big *help me* eyes at Adrian. He looked annoyed.

"My personal level of enthusiasm doesn't matter. Alanna is our consensus candidate," I said.

In the murmuring and rustling that followed, Adrian whispered to me, "I can't believe you," then he stepped forward.

"Going off what Dana just said," he called over the voices, "yes. Alanna is young and not as experienced as some ministers we met during the search. But she is by far the most talented, the most riveting, the most innovative and promising minister we considered. I believe that Alanna is not only the change the AUUCC wants and needs, she's more talented, intelligent, and innovative than we imagined possible. She is young and will need to learn the ropes here, but I can promise, as your incoming church president, that the board and I will work closely with her as she settles in."

The room still pulsed in time with my frightened heart. More questions came and were answered: What happens if she doesn't get voted in? (Interim, new search.) When would she officially start? (Labor Day weekend, but she'd be in the office by mid-August.) Who would be in charge over the summer? (Amira, in contact with Alanna.) When would we get to meet the next candidate? (How about never?)

Finally, the questions stopped and straw baskets were passed. I folded and dropped in my ballot along with Belinda's and Charlotte's proxies. The

baskets were emptied into a cardboard box, which the church president carried to Arroyo House, where the executive committee members would
count them. The rest of us went outside to await the results. Though the
sky was still gray with fog, the air was heating up. Hans Alpenfield, a radi-
ology technician who'd been a member for four or five years, said to me, "I
liked her, but I voted no because I'm curious to see who else is up for the job."

Riley came down from Arroyo House about twenty minutes later and
motioned to us to meet him around the side of the sanctuary, out of sight of
the milling congregants. "Eighty-six percent," he said.

"So she's in!" said Jennie.

"I doubt she'll take it," Sam said.

"Eighty-five percent is the cutoff," said Jennie.

"It's her decision," said Adrian. "What did she say, Riley? Could you tell
how she's leaning?"

"She's thinking," he said. "And making some phone calls."

"I sure hope she says yes," said Curtis.

I sure hoped she'd say no, but I kept quiet. In fact, silence, I vowed,
would be my new m.o.

I walked away from them then. I walked along the row of citrus trees
screening the parking lot. I took the path through the pomegranate
hedges—their slim, brand-new leaves a bright yellow-green—into the
courtyard by the round fountain, where I sat on the old stone bench.
The bubbler barely rippled the reflected blue sky. I prayed. I prayed to
chance, to the universe, to the ongoing churn of creation. "Let her realize
she's not ready. That it's too much for her. That she doesn't have enough
support. Please let her bow out . . ." Sunlight twinkled on the water and
baked through my sweater and shirt.

A peripheral flickering was Curtis, beckoning me. "We're going in," he
called.

We took our seats at the front as the rows behind us filled. The room
simmered with expectation. A minute passed, then another. Alanna entered

through a side door and stepped into the pulpit. Still wearing her robe, she seized the edges of the pulpit with both hands and gazed at us for a long seesawing moment.

The woman knew how to hold a room.

Slowly that dazzling film-star smile bloomed. "Thank you, Arroyo!" she called, low and throaty. "I am honored to accept your call and serve as your new senior minister."

A pause. Others—many—were as shocked as I was.

And then the clapping came. And some stamping of feet. Jennie sprang to her feet to lead the ovation. And yes, everyone stood. "Thank you, thank you," Alanna kept saying, letting it go on for a while, before asking us to please be seated.

"I want to thank the search committee for their faith in me and all of you for your support. I look forward to getting to know every one of you. I will work hard to honor your sacred trust. I promise to stand with you through good times and bad; to love and comfort you; to join with you and lead you in your march for justice and world peace. And I think we'll have a lot of fun along the way. Thank you."

People rose again and clapped some more. And yes, some wept.

I was washing dishes after dinner—it must have been near midnight where he was—when Bert Share called. "Bit of a squeaker," he said thickly. "But we got her in."

"Yes," I said. "A squeaker."

"Yah, but she'll win 'em over. To know her is to love her."

"So you say."

"I'm just glad to get her in somewhere." Into the pause came the sloshy clinks of ice cubes. He was drunk! "T'wasn't easy."

"You were so generous to be such a hardworking advocate."

"I owed her. I mean, she's a good girl. She saw me through the worst of my divorce—when I was out of my head and did some pretty stupid stuff. She kept her cool!" More sloshing with ice. "Rewriting—or hell, *writing* a couple of sermons is the least I could do. She could've had my head on a platter! Though don't blame this last mash-up on me. I told her, I said, 'You've got to put in more heart in it, babe, more soul; the more personal, the more universal.' But she fought me. She liked all that Owen Brown business. I'm sure it cost her support. Eighty-fucking-six percent. Squeak squeak! Still"—another pause, with ice cubes—"all's well that ends well. I just hope she can handle it."

"You and me both," I said.

"At least she's in. She might pull it off. She's a good girl. A big girl. A handful. Not as smart as she thinks she is, but she'll do for Tom Fox's little sinecure . . ." His voice faded as if he'd set down the phone and walked away. Then he was back: "I just called to say thank you, Dana, for your help in getting her in. I hope you and I can keep in touch. Now that my girl's got her place in the world, we can talk about other things, like what you're up to and if you've got another novel in the works."

"Sounds good," I said. "But now I've got to go. The dog wants out. Goodbye, Bert."

36

Goodbye and Hello

I ditched church two Sundays to take the paperback of *Yard to Table* on a short book tour, but I was back in time to hear Tom's last two vale-dictory sermons and attend his going-away bash. Three days before he left for Texas, I took him out on a review lunch to a hip new Chinese place in Alhambra.

The bright café was the new style of eating establishment where you wait in line to order from beautiful young people at a counter, then take a number, sit at a table, and wait—and wait—for your food. We ordered and chose a table by the front window. "I'm glad to be leaving," Tom said. "My time here is up. But I'm worried. I hope your young star is a top-notch fundraiser."

"We'll see," I said. "Why?"

He checked the room for eavesdroppers. "Don't tell anyone," he mur-mured. "Nobody else knows yet. But Faithalma's big bequest? The four mil? The Huntington Library got it. Not us. For which she'll get her name on a room in a gallery."

"Wow," I said. "She left the AUUCC nothing?"

"Half a million."

"So the fund whose interest paid your salary?"

"It's now a wall plaque. Won't affect me, thank god. But losing it makes a significant dent in the old budget."

"I thought the AUUCC was rich."

"Not rich enough to absorb that blow. There'll have to be some major belt tightening."

"Poor Amira won't get her raise."

"Especially since Kapoor will make more than I did. Quite the negotiator, I hear."

Our entrées arrived before the appetizers. The house specialty, beef noodle soup, was bland and overconstructed: the noodles, made in house from organic, locally ground red wheat, were too thick and gluey. The pork fried rice bowl contained two ingredients: grease-soaked rice and a ridiculously generous heap of rubbery cubed pork belly. "Sorry," I said. "I thought the food would be better."

"The price is right," said Tom. Meaning the *Times* was paying.

"Does Alanna know about Faithalma's money?"

"Sam thought he'd wait till she got here to tell her. Or she might not come."

"Someone should tell her now," I said. "Maybe you. It's only fair."

"She has no interest in talking to me. Which is too bad. Because I could have told her a lot of other things, too. Instead, she's got some surprises in store."

"What else would you have told her?"

"The accountant's given notice. Both the sanctuary and Arroyo House need new roofs. The prep school's hunting for a bigger campus; they haven't signed next year's contract, so they could leave anytime. That would be another major loss of income"

"If you tell her all that," I said, "maybe she won't come."

"Oh, she'll come. I heard she pre-candidated all over the place, but only the AUUCC made her a candidate. I still don't understand how. Sam said the kids liked her, but there were only three of them. So what happened? You can tell me, I'm out of here."

So I told him how Doris bailed and Perry was eliminated, and we were left with a generational choice between Elsa and Alanna. "The kids wouldn't budge," I said. "So it was go with Alanna or fail the search. I was the last person standing, and they could've overridden me, but on the off chance that Alanna turned us down, I got the kids to agree that Elsa would be our candidate."

"Alanna shouldn't have said yes with her level of support," said Tom. "No minister I know would've. Most would think long and hard about anything under ninety-five percent."

"The rule of seventeen," I said.

"Around two hundred of our members voted, so that means at least twenty-eight voted no. I wouldn't want to walk into a church where that many people were against me."

"Maybe they'll grow to like her."

Our appetizers arrived: three small pork dumplings in a pool of chili oil and a tiny dish of smashed cucumbers. We each popped a dumpling: lukewarm and bland.

"I could've eased her transition," said Tom, "the way Sparlo did mine. He gave me the lay of the land, said who was who, the Rourkes and the Rosses, the big donors, the busybodies, the troublemakers. He said you were a good listener and a real ally—and I've really valued and enjoyed our friendship. I hope we stay in touch."

"Of course we will." I had been taking Tom's departure in stride, but now my eyes welled up.

So did Tom's.

We picked at the cucumbers with chopsticks. "You'll have to tell me how Kapoor does," he said. "Vera says she's a cold fish who turns the charm on and off."

"She's an actress."

"May I?" Tom snagged the third dumpling, then held it midair. "At least I probably got my wish," he said.

"What wish is that?"

I had to wait for him to finish chewing.

"That whoever comes after me will make me look good."

· ℘ ·

Summer began, with its welter of stone fruit, warm weather produce, and new seasonal menus. Jack was working twelve and more hours a day on his refinery case. One Sunday afternoon, we went to see it, driving north through the Tehachapis into the hot, hazy Central Valley. North of Bakersfield, we turned west off the interstate onto a two-lane blacktop, and after miles of dry scrubland, a steampunk postapocalyptic vision rose from the desert floor: a tangle of windowless buildings, unidentifiable silos, chutes, tubing, and catwalks festively strung with lights that were on in broad daylight—never mind that the refinery had been inoperable for four years. We walked the perimeter of the high hurricane fence, peering through wadded litter that had collected against it. Hazard signs were everywhere. "Systems that hazardous shouldn't be so complicated," said Jack. "If there are too many things that can go wrong, several can and probably will go wrong at once and create a scenario that nobody could anticipate."

Back in Bakersfield we had roast lamb and inky red wine in unlabeled bottles at a family-style Basque restaurant. "Here's to your book and my lawsuit." Jack raised his glass. "May they actually someday, somehow, get done!"

It was some weeks after that, on a morning when the marine layer was thick and cool, that I walked the donks and Bunchie to the AUUCC, where the leathery red blossoms on the pomegranate hedges were swelling into small fruits. I went to my usual courtyard, dropped the donks' leads, and was drowsily contemplating the low bubbling, algae-dark water when someone said, "Hello, Dana."

I grabbed Bunchie before she could jump on Alanna's long, gauzy pink skirt. "I didn't know you were in town," I said weakly.

"I came out to go house hunting and just last night made an offer on a condo in Silver Lake." She drew a dark pink shawl tight over her shoulders. "Chilly," she said.

"Silver Lake?" I said. That was ten, twelve miles from Altadena—and sometimes an hour away with traffic. "Isn't that kind of far?" Both Sparlo and Tom had lived within a ten-minute walk of the AUUCC.

"I have friends there and in Echo Park. May I?" She pointed to the bench.

I slid over. I'd forgotten how imposing she was—like a larger-than-life statue—as I inhaled her gingery, coconut aura. "I hear you and Bert Share are old friends," she said.

"We were in seminary together. I really didn't know him very well. But he sure thinks the world of you."

"He should." She opened and closed the shawl like a bird flexing and folding its wings. "My internship with him was a real trial by fire. He's better now, but back then . . ."

"He told me you saw him through a rough spot."

"He was a mess. His wife had left him and he was living on Pop-Tarts and vodka. And here I come, right out of seminary, so excited to work at this iconic church with its famous preacher. Who was completely checked out. The whole office was covering for him and expected me to, too. The secretary was bringing him a sandwich every day so he'd have something decent to eat. He wasn't even toasting the Pop-Tarts, just eating them out of the box. The poor associate was already overworked, but she and I did all the staff schedules and worship planning; we put together the orders of service. She made me do most of the weddings—including premarital counseling—and all the memorial services. Bert sobered up enough to give off-the-cuff sermons three Sundays a month, so the congregation didn't know what we were going through."

So she did have experience running a large church! "All that'll end up being good practice for the AUUCC," I said. "Still, bad on Bert."

"It was really tough, Dana. I was so overworked and so disappointed. Bert was going through a hard time, but he did some things . . . I still haven't really gotten over . . . So disappointing . . . I, uh . . ." She kicked her heel into the hard-packed ground.

Seeing her falter, I felt a lunge of sympathy. "I'm sorry," I said.

She straightened up and rewrapped her shawl. "Then, when he went to rehab, the associate and I had to hold down the fort for ninety days entirely on our own."

Bert had been drinking—drunk!—the last time I'd talked to him, but what good would it do to mention it now? Alanna and I sat, side by side, and took deep breaths. Wild parrots squabbled in the deodars. A helicopter thwacked by overhead, probably on its way to rescue a hiker in the hills. The piano tuner plinked over in the sanctuary.

"Say." Alanna shifted to face me. "Did you know about the Rourke money going away?"

"I heard something."

"When?"

"Gosh, I don't know. A few weeks ago?" It had been over a month.

"Nobody told me till I got here last week. Which I'm trying not to think of as a dirty trick."

"Tom Fox told me," I said. "Maybe you should've talked to him before he left."

"Anyway, the board legally can't lower my salary. The contract is signed."

"Has anyone tried to touch your salary?" I said.

"The whole executive committee yesterday. Even Adrian and Sam." She stared at the fountain, then hissed: "They asked me to take a fifteen percent cut. I said, *No way!*"

"You should still call Tom. He might tell you some things. Save you from other surprises," I said, thinking of the school pulling out, the leaky roofs . . .

She tightened her shawl again. "I don't want an earful from Tom Fox. Tom Fox, Bert Share, they're exactly what's wrong with this religion, the whole entrenched white heteropatriarchy: they're what we have to put behind us." She leaned in close, as if to tell me a secret. "I saw what Bert got away with. And I've heard how lax Tom Fox got in his last years here. But the system protected them; paid them in full, with no consequences. And then I'm supposed to give up a chunk of my salary?"

Tom's phoning it in hardly seemed the same as what Bert did, but I saw no need to argue the point. The donks' resonant chomping and the shrill cheeps of birds filled the silence. How long would Alanna sit there?

"Oh, but I can tell you my good news, Dana," Alanna burst out. "As one creative to another"—here came the dazzling smile—"I have two auditions! I told my agent I'd be in town, and she set them up right away. I guess large, dark women are hot now, in the push for diversity."

"Gosh," I said. "Will you have time for that? Won't the AUUCC keep you busy?"

"I always had a full-time job when acting—and usually a couple of part-time gigs as well." She leaned closer to me. "The great thing about ministry is, you can make your own hours. And you get the summers off."

I didn't know what to say, so I let the birds and a breeze in the treetops reply.

"Now, Dana, on a different note, as long as we're chatting: I'm asking everyone—Are there any changes you'd like to see happen at the AUUCC?"

Elsa was the change I'd wanted: an introspective, brilliant woman close to my own age who would go deep rather than broad, and develop our spiritual lives through her existential questions, her dialogical preaching, her encouragement of the arts.

I didn't say this, of course. I said, "I'll have to think about that."

Alanna smiled at her lap. "I know I wasn't your first choice, Dana."

"We have different styles," I said, again weakly.

One donk—Caspar—wandered close, and abruptly, Alanna stood and moved off. "All I ask, Dana, is that you give me a chance."

Postlude

This Tuesday afternoon in March is almost three years to the day that Alanna Kapoor became our candidate for senior minister. I am again in the AUUCC's gardens, writing on my lap on the stone bench in the courtyard by the round, dark, bubbling fountain. Caspar and Ralph are assiduously demolishing the weeds that have again sprouted between the paving stones. Bunchie is in the shrubbery hunting lizards. The year has been wet; the lawns and hedges and trees are lush and shaggy, in dire need of trimming. Due to budget cuts, all of the AUUCC's gardening is now done by volunteers, and it shows.

Alanna is closing in on her third year here. I did give her a chance and attended often enough—once or twice a month—during her first year, and was duly subjected to videos, flurries of slides, and the occasional contortions of the body dynamic; also, a flower communion, a water communion, an apple communion, a breads-of-the-world communion, endless visualizations, plus solstice and equinox celebrations involving rain sticks, maracas, tambourines, and much bowing to the four directions.

Except for memorial services, I haven't set foot in the sanctuary since.

I might have missed it more but that the writing and rewriting of this book essentially took me to church every day for months on end. I have not entirely given up on the AUUCC—although, once this book is published, the AUUCC might well give up on me. I still pledge, if just half of what I once did, but enough to keep my membership and to feel I have a right to sit where I'm sitting.

I am not the only face missing on Sundays.

Curtis and Mark moved over to St. Joe's shortly after Alanna came; Curtis is happier there because, while the Episcopalians are as socially progressive as the UUs, their clergy still speak of God and Jesus and preach from the Bible.

Jennie and her small family—a baby boy arrived last year—now live in Oakland while she attends the Starr King School for the Ministry and works part-time at an artisanal bakery in Emeryville.

Charlotte went to rehab two more times before kicking oxy, and she, too, has stopped going to church. We have lunch every few months, often with Belinda, who keeps us up-to-date with what's going on at the AUUCC.

Belinda's speech is a little slurred, but she is as sharp as ever. After the search, Riley left his *ménage à quatre* and moved into one of the spare rooms in Belinda's Craftsman that he'd helped her to empty. He drives her places, does the grocery shopping, and has also taught her how to use Lyft and to text. She's teaching him how to cook.

The bells, Belinda says, play often now because the music budget has been cut and the new music director doesn't hire professional singers or audition volunteers: it's all amateur hour now.

The loss of the Rourke income was compounded first when the high school abruptly abandoned the AUUCC's classrooms and again when the organ sustained extensive damage from the sanctuary's leaking roof—and then there was the reroofing. For now, a tiny, very conservative Christian school rents part of the campus. Pledges are way down, says Belinda, as is attendance, and membership is dropping. Alanna, in her newsletter column, attributes this decline to a national trend of dwindling church attendance.

Sparlo always said that that lowered pledges are the main way that members can signal their unhappiness with a minister.

"I really wish you two would come back," Belinda tells Charlotte and me. "Ignore Alanna. We're the church."

"Not there yet," I say.

"I'm done," says Charlotte.

❧

Last month, I was walking up from the parking lot to Arne Greene's memorial service when I heard "Hey there! It's Dana P!" Adrian, appealing as ever in black slacks and a bright white dress shirt, bounded up laughing. "Damn! Where have you been? I've missed you! How are those donkeys?" He gave me such a good, long hug that the old hope—for a friendship that would never be—flared for a good five minutes.

Afterward, on the patio, I saw Sam Rourke-Jolley. Sam was eighty-two now; he had lost weight and, sadly, acuity. Exactly what he feared would happen was happening. He doddered behind Emma, saying, "Yup, yup, hiya, yup," to everyone he met. I went over and said, "Hi, Sam, how are you?" He looked right at me and in his raspy old man's voice said, "Dana, how nice to see you. How've you been?" I was so surprised and touched he remembered my name that for the next few days, I gave serious thought to killing him.

I often bring the donks here on a Tuesday—Alanna's day off. When she and I do run into each other—mostly at memorial services—we're civil, and move on.

As I write this, my pockets bulge with apples, which is how I'll catch Caspar and Ralph if they get frisky. No more carrots come from Arroyo House. Alanna fired Vera a month after they began working together. Amira, too, is gone; she's now the senior minister at the Valley UU church, where she'd preached when Doris withdrew from our consideration. Amira's sermon must have been a knockout, because when the Valley's senior minister retired, their search committee asked Amira to apply for the job. As she'd never received a raise, and seeing that her new boss, who made twice her salary, had either appropriated or eliminated her pet projects— the radio show, the mosque, the lobbying work—Amira sent in her packet. The AUUCC now can't afford to replace her.

. ↝ .

Helen Harland and I talk often, and close to the old way we talked in seminary, discussing our days, our mates, what we've read and studied with a familiar intensity. Ours is truly a friendship restored. She still consults part-time for headquarters on searches and personnel issues, and recently told me that under new guidelines for reporting sexual misconduct, four women have filed complaints against Bert Share. Alanna is one of them.

He must have stopped writing her sermons.

Tom Fox is happy! He loves teaching his one class, but sometimes complains in emails that he doesn't have enough "mental" work to do. This is from a recent message:

> With all my free time, I had great ambitions to write either a memoir or a novel, depending on how truthful I dared to be. I have been amazed at how difficult it is to sit down to work without a Sunday morning deadline. And how difficult writing still is, even to produce my tepid results. The question hovers: Why would anyone take on such punishment when a golf course beckons out the back door?

My paltry pledge still nets me the denomination's quarterly magazine, in which I check the lists of ministers who have been ordained, moved, retired, quit, or died. The year Alanna came to us, I saw that the young couple I'd liked, the Sanderses, landed at a 450-member church in a Seattle suburb, while Walt Harrison was called to a 600-member church in the Chicago area. I sometimes read Walt's sermons on that church's website; they are gaining the density, imagination, and music of his mentor.

• ⌘ •

That mentor, Elsa Neddicke, still serves the same church, which, contrary to supposed trends, now has 1,100 members and is still growing. I wrote to her after we called Alanna, setting off such a vigorous correspondence that we have become close friends. Twice, at her suggestion, we've met at a weeklong meditation retreat outside of Sedona, Arizona. Last summer, she and her husband joined Jack and me on a trip to southern India: Tamil Nadu, Karnataka, Kerala. (I sent a postcard of the Meenakshi Amman temple in Madurai to Perry Fitzgerald, who is three years into a five-year contract as a "consulting" minister in Wisconsin.)

Elsa read this manuscript in various iterations. Each step of the way, she urged me to go deeper, take more risks, put more of myself onto the page until transposing that difficult year into words became its own spiritual journey, harrowing and revelatory until finally it coalesced into a book, an object apart from myself, soon to have a life of its own out in the world.

I am not worried about a post-publication emotional plummet this time, for my writing life won't revert to listicles and reporting pie contests. When the paper offered me a buyout last fall, I took it. No more restaurant reviews: it was high time to hand that baton to a younger person, someone who can eat pork belly without thinking of artery blockage and drink a glass of red wine without losing the next day to cotton brain.

Our Best Year, my second book, about my senior year in high school when I took over the kitchen from my mother, was picked up by Netflix for a series. (It was pitched as a cross between *Mom*, *Freaks and Geeks*, and *The Great British Baking Show*.) I was brought on as a writer-consultant. I'm already taking notes for my next book: *A Year in the Room: A Memoir of Writing Episodic TV, with Recipes*.

Search Recipes

Amira's Grandmother's Lamb Nihari

Nihari is a Pakistani meat stew with an incredible depth of flavor. The most time-consuming part of this recipe is gathering all of the spices together!

Nihari can be at once so spicy-hot and so delicious that you are weeping and howling even as you can't stop eating it. Since I don't enjoy weeping and howling, I use about half the amount of chili powders and dried chili suggested below, though Jack prefers it with the heat full throttle.

Some cooks use the packet of nihari masala mix available at most Indian markets—and are so attached to its distinctive flavor that they add some even to their homemade versions. (See option below.) If you are missing some of the spices or can't find the specific chili powders, don't worry. Nihari has been adapted by countless home cooks to fit their own taste and pantry.

Tasting the nihari as it cooks, you'll notice that different spices come to the fore at various stages. At one point recently I thought the stew tasted strongly of cloves; later, of cardamom. By the time the nihari sits overnight, is reheated and has thickened, a stunning balance is achieved.

The next great revelation is squeezing the fresh lemon on your nihari!

If you are missing some of the spices or can't find the specific chili powders, don't worry. Nihari has been adapted by countless home cooks to fit their own taste and pantry.

Atta flour is made from an Indian wheat and is very fine and powdery. You'll have to buy a whole bag of it, so you might as well make fresh roti to serve with your nihari (follow the directions on the atta package); it's the easiest flatbread to make and goes perfectly with this stew. If you can't find atta, you can substitute regular all-purpose flour or rice flour to thicken your nihari.

Finally, Amira's grandmother and I both prefer to use a pressure cooker, but a slow stovetop (or even a slow cooker) works just as well: the nihari is done when the meat is easily broken apart with a fork.

Serves 6 to 8

For the Meat Preparation

2 tablespoons ghee ·

1 large onion, chopped to ½-inch dice

1 tablespoon salt

5 teaspoons grated ginger (25 grams)

5 teaspoons grated garlic (25 grams)

1 tablespoon ground coriander

1 tablespoon Aleppo chili powder

1 tablespoon Kashmiri chili powder

½ teaspoon ground turmeric

4 to 5 bone-in lamb shanks (about 10 pounds)

For the Nihari Masala Preparation

1½ tablespoons coriander seeds

1½ tablespoons fennel seeds

1½ teaspoons caraway seeds

1½ teaspoons black peppercorns

1 teaspoon whole cloves

1½ teaspoons cumin seeds

2 bay leaves

½ teaspoon grated nutmeg

1 3-inch cinnamon stick, broken in two

1 piece star anise

½ teaspoon ground mace

½ teaspoon ground ginger

5 black cardamoms, seeds only

5 green cardamoms, seeds only

1 teaspoon nigella seeds

1 tablespoon red chili flakes

1 tablespoon commercial nihari powder or to taste (optional)

6 cups water

For the Thickener

⅓ cup atta flour (white flour or rice flour can be substituted)

1 cup water

Rice (preferably basmati)

Lemon wedges

Julienned ginger

Fresh cilantro

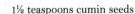

TO PREPARE THE MEAT: In a large, heavy pan, melt the ghee over medium-high heat and sauté the onion until golden, about 7 minutes. Remove the onion, squeezing out the ghee. Save the onion for later.

In the same pan, with the ghee, add the salt, ginger, garlic, coriander, chili powders, and turmeric. Stir for half a minute over medium heat, then add the meat and stir to coat with the spices, then cook over medium to medium-high heat until the meat is browned and the spices are cooked, about 5 minutes.

TO ASSEMBLE THE NIHARI MASALA: Heat a dry frying pan over medium-high heat, then toast all of the spices together until fragrant, about 30 seconds. Then using a spice mill or a mortar and pestle, grind the spices into powder.

Place the meat and the masala mixture in a stew pot or pressure cooker. Add 6 cups of water and stir.

STOVETOP: Bring to a boil and simmer, covered and undisturbed, for 4 to 5 hours until the meat is very tender.

PRESSURE COOKER: Cover and cook at high pressure for 25 minutes. Let the pressure release naturally. If the meat is not falling-apart tender, return to high pressure for 3 to 5 more minutes, this time doing a quick release.

Skim off any scum that has surfaced. Add the reserved fried onion and bring the nihari to a boil, then turn it off. Let it sit until cool. Refrigerate overnight. Before reheating, remove the fat that has risen to the top. The nihari probably will have "set" thanks to the gelatin from the bones. Reheat over medium heat until fully liquefied. Remove the bones, and be sure to extract any marrow from them and add it back into the pot.

Whisk the atta flour slowly into the water, making sure there are no lumps. Add to the nihari and cook for another 10 to 15 minutes until thickened and the flour is cooked. Taste and add more salt and chili powder if desired.

Serve over or alongside the rice, with the lemon wedges, ginger, and cilantro (diners can pluck the leaves off the stems themselves!).

The Pledge Drive's Chicken Fiesta

Chicken Fiesta is the potluck go-to at the AUUCC. Pretty, flavorful, and easily made in larger quantities, this is the sheet-pan version. You can use any kind of freshly cooked rice you like.

Serves 3 to 4

For the Chicken and Rice

2½ pounds bone-in, skin-on chicken, cut up

Salt and pepper

1 teaspoon ground cumin

1 teaspoon chili powder

½ teaspoon onion powder

1 tablespoon olive oil

Juice from ½ lime (about 1 scant tablespoon)

For the Fiesta

1 tablespoon olive oil

½ red onion, cut into ¼-inch dice (about ¾ cup)

½ red pepper or a mixture of red and orange peppers, cut into ¼-inch dice (about ¾ cup)

1 cup yellow corn (fresh or frozen)

Salt and pepper

Dash of chili powder

3 cups of freshly cooked rice (1 cup of dry rice)

¼ cup white wine + ¼ cup chicken broth, or ½ cup chicken broth

¼ cup cilantro leaves, chopped coarsely

1 lime, quartered

Preheat the oven to 375 degrees.

TO MAKE THE CHICKEN AND RICE: Place the chicken in a large mixing bowl and season with salt and pepper, then add the cumin, chili powder, onion powder, olive oil, and lime juice. Use your hands to distribute the spices evenly. You can let the chicken marinate in the fridge for several hours or use it right away. Place the chicken on a sheet pan. Bake for 35 to 40 minutes until brown and the juices run clear.

TO MAKE THE FIESTA: While the chicken is cooking, heat the olive oil in a large skillet over medium-high heat. Sauté the onion for one minute, then add the pepper and sauté for another minute. Add the corn, salt, pepper, and a dash of chili powder, and stir until the corn is bright yellow and cooked, about 1 more minute.

Spread the warm rice in a shallow, oven-proof baking dish you are not ashamed to put on the table for serving.

Press the baked chicken parts into the rice. After removing most of the fat from the sheet pan (this is very important; otherwise your rice will be greasy), deglaze the sheet pan with half the wine and broth mixture (or just the broth), being sure to get all the tasty baked-on bits, adding more wine-broth to make about a third of a cup. Drizzle the deglazed liquid over the chicken and rice.

Distribute the fiesta mix over the chicken. Cover loosely with a sheet of aluminum foil. Return to the oven to "marry" the flavors until warmed through, 12 to 15 minutes. Remove from the oven, garnish with the chopped cilantro, and serve with the lime wedges.

Ottolenghi's Chicken with Caramelized Onion and Cardamom Rice

from Jerusalem: A Cookbook *by Yotam Ottolenghi and Sami Tamimi*

When Belinda makes this dish, she prefers to use black cardamom pods, but the green ones will also work beautifully. She varies the herbs, sometimes using mint instead of dill and other times using only two of the three listed.

In making this dish, I have found that it's important the rice be cooked before covering the dish with the tea towel and letting it sit. If your rice is still too chalky or al dente, add a few more tablespoons of water and cook for a little more time (5 to 8 minutes), then cover with the tea towel and let sit for 10 minutes, which steams the rice off the bottom of the pan, making it easier to serve and giving access to all the bottom-of-the-pot richness of the dish.

Serves 4

> 3 tablespoons sugar (40 grams)
>
> Scant 3 tablespoons (40 ml) water
>
> 2½ tablespoons barberries, or use currants (25 grams)
>
> 4 tablespoons olive oil
>
> 2 medium onions, thinly sliced (2 cups, or 250 grams)
>
> 2¼ pounds skin-on, bone-in chicken thighs (1 kilogram), or 1 whole chicken, quartered
>
> Salt and freshly ground black pepper
>
> 10 cardamom pods
>
> Rounded ¼ teaspoon whole cloves
>
> 2 long cinnamon sticks, broken in two

1⅔ cups basmati rice (300 grams)

2½ cups boiling water (600 milliliters)

1½ tablespoons flat-leaf parsley leaves (5 grams), chopped

½ cup dill leaves (5 grams), chopped

¼ cup cilantro leaves (5 grams), chopped

⅓ cup Greek yogurt (100 grams), mixed with 2 tablespoons olive oil (optional)

Put the sugar and water in a small saucepan and heat until the sugar dissolves. Remove from the heat, add the barberries, and set aside to soak. If using currants, you do not need to soak them in this way.

Meanwhile, heat half the olive oil in a large sauté pan for which you have a lid over medium heat, add the onion, and cook for 10 to 15 minutes, stirring occasionally, until the onion has turned a deep golden brown. Transfer the onion to a small bowl and wipe the pan clean.

Place the chicken in a large mixing bowl and season with 1½ teaspoons each salt and black pepper. Add the remaining olive oil, cardamom, cloves, and cinnamon and use your hands to mix everything together well. Heat the frying pan again and place the chicken and spices in it. Sear for 5 minutes on each side and remove from the pan (this is important, as it partly cooks the chicken). The spices can stay in the pan, but don't worry if they stick to the chicken. Remove most of the remaining oil as well, leaving just a thin film at the bottom. Add the rice, caramelized onion, 1 teaspoon salt, and plenty of black pepper. Drain the barberries and add them as well. Stir well and return the seared chicken to the pan, pushing it into the rice.

Pour the boiling water over the rice and chicken, cover the pan, and cook over very low heat for 30 minutes. Take the pan off the heat, remove the lid, quickly place a clean tea towel over the pan, and seal again with the lid. Leave the dish undisturbed for another 10 minutes. Finally, add the herbs and use a fork to stir them in and fluff up the rice. Taste and add more salt and pepper if needed. Serve hot or warm with yogurt if you like.

Belinda's Preserved Lemon Chicken

I f you have preserved lemons, this is the easiest chicken recipe ever—
you basically dice the lemon peels, scatter them over the chicken,
and pop it in the oven. You can use any form of cut-up chicken: thighs,
legs, breasts, the whole bird cut into in parts. (Belinda prefers bone-in
thighs with skin.) If you use boneless, skinless thighs or breasts, you
will want to drizzle the pieces with olive oil before baking.

You can easily adjust this recipe, using 1 preserved lemon for every
3 pounds of bone-in chicken.

Serve with basmati rice or boiled or roasted baby potatoes and a
fresh green salad.

Serves 4

> 3 pounds of cut-up, bone-in chicken or 2½ pounds boneless,
> skinless breasts or thighs
>
> 1 whole preserved lemon, with juice
>
> Smoked paprika (optional)
>
> Thyme sprigs or fresh or dried thyme leaves (optional)
>
> Olive oil
>
> Water or white wine or chicken broth

Preheat the oven to 375 degrees.

Arrange the chicken in a roasting pan with enough room so that the
pieces don't touch.

Remove the pulp from the preserved lemon and set aside. Chop the
lemon peel into ¼-inch dice. Chop the pulp. Drizzle 1 tablespoon of

the lemon juice over the chicken. Then take the chopped pulp and smear it lightly over the chicken pieces, top and bottom; try to get a little under the skin as well.

Reposition the chicken in the pan, skin side up. Place a small clump of chopped peel on each piece, then sprinkle a little paprika over for color. Position the thyme sprigs on the chicken, or sprinkle with a few thyme leaves, if using. If you are using skinless chicken, drizzle a little olive oil over each piece.

Put the pan in the oven and bake, checking at intervals, until the chicken is nicely browned and the juices run clear when pricked, about 35 minutes. If the pan drippings are cooking too quickly, add a few ounces of water or white wine to the bottom of the pan.

Remove the chicken to a serving dish, then deglaze the pan with a few tablespoons of water, white wine, or broth, or a mix of them; scrape up the baked bits. This is your sauce.

Serve with basmati rice or boiled or roasted baby potatoes and a fresh green salad.

Belinda's Salmon Steaks

The basis of this recipe is a marinade that works equally well with chicken, shrimp, other fish, and pork.

Serves 4

2 tablespoons fish sauce

2 tablespoons lime juice (about 1 lime)

1 tablespoon soy sauce

1 teaspoon sesame oil

1 tablespoon brown sugar

½-inch piece fresh ginger, grated or finely minced

2 garlic cloves, grated or finely minced

1½-pound salmon steak, skinned and cut into 4 pieces

Lime wedges

Combine the fish sauce, lime juice, soy sauce, sesame oil, sugar, ginger, and garlic. If you have a small food processor, you can combine all these ingredients in its bowl (no need to grate or mince the ginger and garlic beforehand) and process until the solids are reduced to tiny particles.

Place the salmon steaks and the marinade in a plastic bag large enough so the steaks can lie flat. Marinate for 15 minutes to 2 hours, turning occasionally to uniformly distribute the marinade.

Preheat the grill.

Cook the steaks on a hot grill, approximately 4 minutes on each side for medium done. Adjust the cooking time based on the thickness of the steaks and how you like them cooked.

Serve with rice and the lime wedges.

Charlotte's Wet Brisket

This is a two-day brisket, with most of the work done on day one, so your dinner on day two goes together quickly. This is especially helpful when serving a large party.

Serves up to 12

> 1 7- to 9-pound beef brisket, trimmed
>
> 1 teaspoon salt, plus more for seasoning
>
> 1 teaspoon ground pepper, plus more for seasoning
>
> 4 tablespoons neutral oil
>
> 4 pounds onions (about 5 cups)
>
> 5 garlic cloves, minced or grated
>
> 1½ teaspoons sweet paprika
>
> Water

Preheat the oven to 375 degrees.

Season the brisket with salt and pepper.

In a large heavy skillet, heat 2 tablespoons of the oil over medium-high heat, then brown the brisket for 5 minutes on each side. Remove to a roasting pan and place in the hot oven, uncovered, while you prepare the onions.

Wipe out the skillet. Heat the remaining 2 tablespoons of oil over medium-high heat, then cook the onions, stirring, until soft and lightly golden, about 6 minutes. Reduce the heat and keep cooking, stirring occasionally, until they are a deep golden brown, about

20 minutes. Add the garlic, paprika, salt, and pepper and sauté for 1 minute. Add 3½ cups of water and bring to a boil.

Distribute the onion mixture over the brisket and return it to the oven, lightly covered with aluminum foil. Cook for 3½ to 4 hours, checking at least every hour and adding more water, if necessary, until the meat is fork tender. Remove from oven and let cool for an hour.

Scrape the onions off the brisket into the roasting pan, then wrap the brisket in foil and refrigerate overnight. Put the onion mixture and all the pan drippings into a bowl or jar, cover, and refrigerate overnight.

When ready to serve:

Preheat the oven to 350 degrees.

Unwrap the meat and slice it thick or thin, however you prefer.

Remove and discard the fat from onions/pan drippings, then pour into a blender, adding enough water to make around 4 cups. Blend until smooth. This is your gravy. Heat the gravy in a roasting pan on the stovetop until just warm and liquid. Taste for seasoning, adding salt and pepper as desired. Arrange brisket slices in the gravy, spooning some gravy over the top of the meat. Cover the pan loosely with foil and heat in a 350 degree oven until the slices are warmed through, about 20 minutes.

Dana's Seafood Chowder

This is a very easy, fast, and luxurious soup. It also takes well to improvisation. You don't have to add all of the different seafood—clams, shrimp, and cod make a perfectly respectable chowder; just be sure to adjust the amounts.

You can prepare the chowder base a day in advance, so that on the day you serve the chowder, all you have to do is add and cook the seafood.

Serves 6 to 8

For the Chowder Base

3 tablespoons olive oil

1 large onion, chopped into ½-inch dice

2 stalks celery, chopped into ½-inch dice

2 carrots, peeled and cut into ½-inch dice

1 bay leaf

2 to 3 cloves garlic, minced

2 medium potatoes (about 1 pound), preferably red or Yukon Gold, peeled and cut into ½-inch dice

½ teaspoon smoked paprika

¼ cup good white wine (optional)

6 cups vegetable or chicken broth

1 28-ounce can tomatoes, chopped with juices, or 2 pounds fresh tomatoes, peeled, seeded, and chopped

1 tablespoon chili sauce or to taste

Salt and pepper

For the Seafood

¼ pound finnan haddie or other smoked fish, cut into ½-inch cubes

1 pound clams in shell

1 pound mussels in shell

1 pound raw large shrimp, peeled and deveined

1 pound bay scallops

¾ pound firm, filleted white fish (cod or snapper), cut into 1-inch cubes

½ pound squid, cleaned and cut into rings and bite-sized pieces (optional)

Small bunch of parsley, leaves only, coarsely chopped

Lemon wedges

6 to 8 sea scallops (optional)

1 tablespoon butter (optional)

TO MAKE THE CHOWDER BASE: Heat the olive oil over medium-high heat. Add the onion and sauté for one minute, then add the celery and carrots. Lower the heat and sauté until the onion is soft and turning gold and the carrots are mostly cooked, about 7 minutes. Add the bay leaf and garlic and sauté for another minute, then add the potatoes and smoked paprika. Stir to combine and let cook together for another minute or so. Deglaze the pan with the white wine, if using, or ¼ cup of the broth.

Add the tomatoes with their juices and the remaining broth. Bring to a boil, then turn down the heat, add the chili sauce, and simmer until the potatoes are done, about 10 minutes. Taste for seasoning, adding more smoked paprika, chili sauce, salt, and pepper as desired.

TO COOK THE SEAFOOD: Add the seafood in the order given, with a 2-minute gap after the mussels. Simmer until the shrimp are pink and opaque, the shellfish have opened, and the filleted fish is cooked through, about 3 minutes.

Garnish each bowl with parsley and a lemon wedge on the side. Serve with crusty bread, butter, and a leafy green salad.

Optional garnish: Top each bowl with one large sea scallop sautéed in butter.

Dana's Escarole Salad with Favas, Mint, and Pecorino

Fava beans need to be double-peeled—but they are worth the effort, especially for this bright, juicy spring salad.
If you want to gild the lily, add an avocado.

Serves 4 to 6 as a side salad

For the Salad

1 pound fresh fava beans in their pods

1 head escarole, chopped into 1–inch sections

1 small bunch fresh mint leaves (5 teaspoons), chopped, plus more to taste

1 avocado, cubed (optional)

For the Dressing

2 tablespoons fresh lemon juice

1 clove garlic, finely grated

½ teaspoon salt, or to taste

Freshly ground black pepper to taste

2 ounces (6 tablespoons) olive oil

½ tablespoon warm water

¼ cup grated Pecorino Romano cheese, plus more to taste

TO MAKE THE SALAD: Prepare the fava beans. Set a small pot of water on the stove and bring to a boil. Remove the beans from their pods. You can do this by running a razor blade down the length of the pod, just deep enough to nick each of the beans within. (This nick will prove useful later.) Parboil the shucked beans for 1 to 2 minutes in the boiling water. Strain and let cool until you can handle them. Squeeze each bean from its pod through the nick you made with the razor, or if the bean has no nick, either make one now with your thumbnail or use a razor. A small nick is all that's needed for the bean to exit.

Place the escarole, favas, mint, and avocado, if using, in a salad bowl.

TO MAKE THE DRESSING: Combine the lemon juice, garlic, salt, and pepper, then stir in the olive oil and the water.

Pour about half the dressing on the salad and toss. Add the Pecorino and toss again. Taste and add more dressing as desired. The salad should be juicy!

Dana's Daily Salad Dressing

This dressing has a sharp citric tang, which can be controlled with salt and/or more oil. Sometimes I add anchovies; sometimes I leave out the mustard. Sometimes I put everything into the mini food processor and make a thicker, almost homogenized dressing. To me, it's all about the lemon/salt balance. When you get that exactly to your own taste, your dressing is perfect.

Makes enough for 3 to 4 salads, 4 servings for each

1 shallot, finely chopped

½ teaspoon salt, plus more to taste

2 tablespoons lemon juice (from 1 lemon)

1 teaspoon Spanish sherry vinegar

5 ounces olive oil

1 tablespoon warm water

A few grinds of black pepper

1 teaspoon Dijon mustard (optional)

2 anchovy fillets, chopped into pulp (optional)

Combine all of the ingredients in an 8-ounce container. Shake vigorously. Taste. If it is too acidic (sour), add more salt. If it is too salty, add more lemon. Before dressing a salad, mix vigorously. Then spoon it on, reaching for the shallot, which tends to sink.

Jennie's Whole Wheat Chocolate Chip Cookies

from *Good to the Grain* by Kim Boyce

Kim Boyce's cookbook, *Good to the Grain*, published in 2010, proved that whole grains are a delicious and desirable alternative to refined flours. A former pastry chef at Spago and Campanile, Kim has her own bakery, Bakeshop, in Portland, Oregon.

These are big, burly cookies, thick with a "toast-like" crunch, moist centers, and good-sized chocolate chunks. Be sure to use a high-quality bittersweet chocolate for your chunks, because the better the chocolate you use, the better it stands up to the whole wheat flavor.

I have cut the sugar to almost half (of what the original recipe, below, asks for) and enjoyed the results, which means you can adjust the sugar to your own taste.

I have made these cookies with a hand mixer and they come out perfectly.

I actually weigh out each cookie on a small kitchen scale; 45 to 50 grams seems ideal.

Although nothing beats eating these cookies when they're still warm, they do freeze well.

Makes about 20 cookies

Parchment paper for the baking sheets

Dry Mix

3 cups whole wheat flour

1½ teaspoons baking powder

1 teaspoon baking soda

1½ teaspoons kosher salt

Wet Mix

8 ounces (2 sticks) cold unsalted butter, cut into ½-inch pieces

1 cup dark brown sugar, preferably muscovado

1 cup granulated sugar

2 eggs

2 teaspoons pure vanilla extract

8 ounces bittersweet chocolate, roughly chopped into ¼- and ½-inch pieces

Place two racks in the upper and lower thirds of the oven and preheat to 350 degrees. Line two baking sheets with parchment. Although you can butter the sheets instead, parchment is better for these cookies because the large chunks of chocolate can stick to the pan.

Sift the dry ingredients into a large bowl, pouring back into the bowl any bits of grain or other ingredients that may remain in the sifter.

Add the butter and the sugars to the bowl of a standing mixer fitted with a paddle·attachment. With the mixer on low speed, mix just until the butter and sugars are blended, about 2 minutes. Use a spatula to scrape down the sides of the bowl. Add the eggs one at a time, mixing until each is combined. Mix in the vanilla. Add the flour mixture to the bowl and blend on low speed until the flour is barely combined, about 30 seconds. Scrape down the sides and bottom of the bowl.

Add the chocolate all at once to the batter. Mix on low speed until the chocolate is evenly combined. Use a spatula to scrape down the sides and bottom of the bowl, then scrape the batter out onto a work surface, and use your hands to fully incorporate all the ingredients.

Scoop mounds of dough about 3 tablespoons in size onto the baking sheet, leaving three inches between them, or about 6 to a sheet.

Bake the cookies for 16 to 20 minutes, rotating the sheets halfway through, until the cookies are evenly dark brown. Transfer the cookies, still on the parchment, to the counter to cool, and repeat with the remaining dough.

These cookies are best eaten warm from the oven or later that same day. They'll keep in an airtight container for up to 3 days.

Jennie's Midmorning Glory Muffins

Jennie said she wanted to make morning glory muffins that contained enough fruits, vegetables, and eggs to serve as a nourishing stand-alone breakfast food. Because these take some time to assemble, bake, and cool, it's midmorning before they're ready to eat.

Those who prefer a less sweet muffin can cut the brown sugar down to ⅓ cup (100 grams).

Makes 12 muffins

½ cup raisins, preferably golden (100 grams)

½ cup dried cranberries OR dried cherries (100 grams)

½ cup grated apple (100 grams)

½ cup grated carrot (60 grams)

½ cup grated zucchini (60 grams)

½ cup fresh blueberries (100 grams)

¾ cup pecan halves

Dry Mix

1 cup almond flour (100 grams)

½ cup whole wheat flour (85 grams)

1 cup flax meal (110 grams)

1 teaspoon baking powder

½ teaspoon baking soda

1 teaspoon kosher salt

1 teaspoon cinnamon

¼ teaspoon each ground ginger and allspice

⅛ teaspoon ground cloves

Wet Mix

1 cup orange juice

2 eggs

¼ cup olive oil

½ cup dark brown sugar, packed (125 grams)

1 tablespoon dark molasses or date molasses

Preheat the oven to 350 degrees.

Soak the raisins and cranberries (or cherries) in hot tap water until ready to use.

Grate the apple, carrot, and zucchini

Combine the dry ingredients in a medium-size bowl.

Toast the pecans in the 350 degree oven for 4 minutes. Set aside twelve pecan halves, then chop the remaining nuts fine.

Drain the raisins and cranberries (or cherries) thoroughly.

In a large bowl, combine the wet ingredients, whisking until the egg is thoroughly combined and the brown sugar is dissolved.

Add the grated carrot, apple, and zucchini and stir to loosen the clumps. Add the raisins, cranberries (or cherries), blueberries, and chopped pecans.

Add the dry ingredients and stir until just combined. Allow the mixture to rest for at least 5 minutes to let the flax meal absorb some of the liquid.

While the mixture is resting, either oil or insert paper muffin liners in a muffin tin.

Fill the muffin cups full. Bake for 35 to 40 minutes until a toothpick inserted comes out clean.

Gently remove the muffins from the tin and allow them to cool before eating.

Jennie's Violet Bakery Cinnamon Rolls

Jennie used this recipe from the marvelous *Violet Bakery Cookbook* by Claire Ptak to make some irresistible, easy, non-yeasted cinnamon rolls.

I make this with a handheld mixer, which works just fine.

Makes 12 rolls

Butter, for greasing the pan

For the Filling

⅓ cup unsalted butter (75 grams)

1 cup plus 2 tablespoons light brown sugar (250 grams)

1 tablespoon ground cinnamon

For the Cinnamon Rolls

1½ cups all-purpose flour, plus more for dusting (560 grams)

2 tablespoons baking powder

2 teaspoons kosher salt

2 teaspoons ground cardamom

1 cup plus 1 tablespoon cold unsalted butter, cut into small cubes (240 grams)

1¼ cups cold milk (300 grams)

Sugar, for dipping

Preheat the oven to 390 degrees (355 degrees convection oven).

Butter a deep 12-cup muffin pan.

TO PREPARE THE FILLING: Melt the butter and leave in a warm place so that it remains liquid. Mix together the light brown sugar and cinnamon until no lumps remain, then set aside.

TO MAKE THE DOUGH: In the bowl of a stand mixer with a paddle attachment, combine all the dry ingredients with the cubes of butter and mix until you have a coarse meal. Slowly pour in the cold milk while the mixer is running, until the dough forms into a ball and comes away from the bowl. Turn the dough out onto a lightly floured surface and leave to rest for a few minutes. Fold the dough gently over itself once or twice to pull it all together. Let the dough rest a second time, for 10 minutes.

Clear a large surface, dust lightly with more flour, and roll out the dough into a large rectangle until about 5mm (⅛ inch) thick. Brush the surface of the dough with the melted butter and, before the butter hardens, sprinkle the cinnamon sugar onto the butter. You want a good, slightly thick layer.

Now roll the dough up, starting at the long side, keeping it neat and tight. Gently tug the dough toward you to get a taut roll while rolling away from you into a spiral. Once it's all rolled up, gently squeeze the roll to ensure it's the same thickness throughout. Use a sharp knife to cut the roll crosswise into 12 even slices. Take a slice of the cinnamon roll, peel back about 5 cm (2 inches) of the loose end of the pastry and fold it back under the roll to loosely cover the bottom of the roll. Place in the muffin pan, flap side down. Repeat with the remaining slices.

Bake the buns for 25 minutes. As soon as they're out of the oven, flip them over onto a wire cooling rack so that they don't stick to the tray. Dip each cinnamon bun into a bowl of sugar and serve straightaway.

Curtis's Mom's Buko Pie

This pie is not a traditional buko pie. Rather, it is a coconut custard pie that uses fresh young coconut—buko—and coconut cream for its flavor.

Coconut cream is as different from coconut milk as cream is from whole milk. You can find coconut cream in most grocery stores, as it is often used to make piña coladas. Buy an unsweetened brand.

The labor-intensive part of this recipe is extracting the fresh coconut meat from two coconuts. Using a large knife, you can (eventually) hack an opening in the top, pour off and reserve the coconut water for drinking, then carve off the meat with a sturdy tablespoon. Sometimes, I use a power drill to make two large holes, drain the coconut water, then use a hammer to break the coconut apart (keep at it—it will crack . . . eventually!). You can also crack the coconut by hurling it down onto a concrete surface, which is somehow quite satisfying. Then it's marginally easier to scoop out the meat with a spoon. This all becomes less daunting with practice! Six coconuts in, you'll know what you're doing!

The good part about quarrying your own coconut meat is that you are now intimately acquainted with the young coconut. And you have delicious cold fresh coconut water to sip while the pie is cooking.

Ideally you want the very young, tender coconut meat for this pie. Slightly older coconut (also sold as young) is crunchier. You can still use it, but if you have any patience or time left, shave it into thinner, flat slivers. Or not. Even crunchy fresh coconut makes a good pie.

You can make the pie gluten free by using a standard almond-flour piecrust recipe and substituting almond flour for wheat flour in the streusel.

Piecrust for 9-inch Shell

1½ cups flour (200 grams)

1 tablespoon sugar (20 grams)

½ teaspoon kosher salt

1 stick cold unsalted butter (125 grams)

3 to 5 tablespoons ice-cold water

½ teaspoon apple cider vinegar

Combine the flour, sugar, and salt. Using a pastry cutter, knives, or a mini food processor, cut the butter into the flour mixture until it is in small crumbs.

Combine the water and vinegar. Add the water mixture to the flour and butter mixture 1 tablespoon at a time, working quickly and lightly with a fork to distribute it. When all is very lightly moistened (it will still seem dry, but when you pinch it, it sticks together), pour it out onto a flat piece of plastic wrap and, gathering the edges of the plastic wrap, pull the dough together and form it into a ball. Wrap the ball tightly so that no air gets in and put it in the refrigerator for at least half an hour, or up to 3 days.

Preheat the oven to 350 degrees. Remove the dough from the fridge and unwrap it onto a sheet of parchment paper. Press it into a flattened disk and, lightly flouring a rolling pin, roll it out to a 12-inch circle.

Gently place the dough on its parchment paper, dough side down, over a 9-inch pie pan and carefully remove the parchment paper. Very gently press the dough into the pie pan, trimming the excess, then crimping the edges.

Coconut Custard Filling

5 ounces fresh young coconut meat (see the headnote for how
to remove meat from the coconut)

4 eggs or 6 yolks

1 cup milk

1 cup coconut cream, unsweetened

⅓ cup sugar

½ teaspoon salt

¼ teaspoon vanilla extract

Cut the coconut meat into 1-inch pieces. Set aside.

Place the eggs, milk, coconut cream, sugar, salt, and vanilla in a
blender and blend until fully combined.

Place the coconut in the bottom of the pie shell. Pull out an oven
rack and place the pie shell on it. Fill the pie shell with the egg-milk
mixture and very carefully slide the rack in (try to avoid sloshing!);
bake until the custard is firm, if still a little soft, about 45 minutes.

While the pie is baking, make the streusel topping.

Coconut Streusel Topping

1 tablespoon butter, melted

A few drops vanilla extract

3 tablespoons all-purpose flour

½ tablespoon granulated sugar

½ tablespoon light brown sugar

Pinch of salt

Dash of cinnamon

1 tablespoon unsweetened shredded coconut

※

Combine the butter and vanilla and set aside. Mix the flour, sugars, salt, cinnamon, and coconut. Add the melted butter-vanilla mixture bit by bit to the flour mixture until all is moistened, then, using your hands, crumble into small irregularly sized crumbs.

Place the crumbs in a pie pan or on a small tray and toast, stirring every few minutes until golden brown, about 15 minutes. Cool.

Right after you have removed the pie from the oven, sprinkle the streusel topping evenly over the top. Cool the pie thoroughly before serving.

Acknowledgments

This book owes much to Mona Simpson, whose conversation and literary friendship is so sustaining, inspiring, and endlessly interesting.

I am deeply grateful to Lily Tuck, for decades of friendship and some truly excellent advice.

When I was deep in the wilds of a first draft, the John Simon Guggenheim Foundation gave me a timely, generous boost: thank you.

Many ministers and church members spoke to me frankly about their search experiences, material that I then remixed and repurposed for my own fictional use: The Reverend Dr. James Nelson, the Reverends James Ishmael Ford, Anne Hines, Anne Cohen, Sara LaWall, Hannah Petrie, Jake Morrill, Daniel Hotchkiss, and Keith Kron; also Roger Patterson, Christine Bender, Irene Burkner, and Judith Lovely. Any inaccuracies, distortions, or errors are mine alone.

Early readers provided invaluable suggestions and enthusiasm. Thank you, Michele Zack, Sara Zarr, Victoria Patterson, Laurie Winer, and Kyle McCarthy.

I am so grateful to Scott Moyers for bringing me to Ginny Smith, whose excellent edits were not only thoughtful, apt, and intelligent, but also fun to implement—and made *Search* a stronger book.

Thank you, too, to the whole team at Penguin: Caroline Sydney, Darren Haggar, Jon Gray, Cassandra Garruzzo, and Gail Brussel.

Brettne Bloom, I appreciate your taking me on with such enthusiasm and so many enlivening ideas.

Thank you, Astrid Preston, for letting us use your marvelous *Mountain Path* on the cover.

This book was written in loving memory of Brandy Lovely, Irene Burkner, Carol Blake, and Jonathan Gold.

Jim Potter, husband, close reader, videographer, bread maker, and laughing companion, has carried me through the writing of another novel and proved, yet again, that love is the answer.